OCCASION FOR LOVING

NADINE GORDIMER

With a New Introduction
by Paul Bailey

Virago

Published by VIRAGO PRESS Limited 1983
41 William IV Street, London WC2N 4DB

First published in Great Britain by Victor Gollancz Ltd 1963

British Library Cataloguing in Publication Data

Gordimer, Nadine
  Occasion for Loving.
  1. Title
  823[F]   PR9369.3.G6
  ISBN 0-86068-312-5

Printed in Finland by Werner Söderström Oy,
a member of Finnprint

NADINE GORDIMER

was born in a small mining town in South Africa in 1923, and educated at a Convent School. Her first novel, *The Lying Days*, was published in 1953, followed by *A World of Strangers* (1958), *Occasion For Loving* (1963), *The Late Bourgeois World* (1966), *A Guest of Honour* (1970), *The Conservationist* (1974), *Burger's Daughter* (1979), and *July's People* (1981). She has also published six volumes of short stories: *The Soft Voice of The Serpent* (1952), *Six Feet of the Country* (1956), *Friday's Footprint* (1960), *Not For Publication* (1965), *Livingstone's Companions* (1972), and *A Soldier's Embrace*, (1980). Selections from five of these volumes are published in her *Selected Stories* (1975) and *Some Monday For Sure* (1976)

Nadine Gordimer left Africa for the first time at the age of thirty. Since then she has travelled widely in Africa as well as Europe and the USA, but continues to live in her native country, and in Johannesburg. One of the greatest contemporary writers in the English language, Nadine Gordimer has created with insight and subtlety a fictional world that is powerful in its personal and political conflict. She has received the W.H. Smith Award (1961), the James Tait Black Memorial Prize (1971), the Booker McConnell Prize (1974), the Grand Aigle d'Or (1975), the CNA Prize (three times), and the Modern Language Association International Award (1981). Her work has been translated into sixteen languages.

"We have all become people according to the measure in which we have loved people and have had occasion for loving."

BORIS PASTERNAK

"In our time the destiny of man presents its meaning in political terms."

THOMAS MANN

". . . servitude, falsehood and terror . . . these three afflictions are the cause of silence between men, obscure them from one another and prevent them from rediscovering themselves in the only value which can save them from nihilism—the long complicity between men at grips with their destiny."

ALBERT CAMUS

INTRODUCTION

As its title suggests, Nadine Gordimer's third novel is about love. It is also very much about politics. *Occasion for Loving* is concerned with the terrible authority of "a line in a statute book" — a line that proscribes and forbids; that decrees who shall love whom, in South Africa now.

Most lovers in contemporary fiction are either blissfully or miserably unaware of the outside world. Think of Iris Murdoch's tireless band of serenaders and serenaded, for ever panting and for ever expectant; of Jean Rhys's doomed girls, blind to almost everything but their own feelings; of innumerable men and women, in innumerable books, waiting for phones to ring and letters to arrive, their minds incapable of concentrating on anything else. These people are real, their condition recognisable — as Nadine Gordimer often acknowledges. Genuine passions are fulfilled in isolation, whether in Tokyo or Grimsby, Paris or Johannesburg — except that, in the latter, their fulfilment can, and does, have dangerous consequences.

In *Occasion for Loving*, Jessie Stilwell senses this isolation whenever she is in the company of Ann Davis and Gideon Shibalo. Their obvious absorption in each other irritates and dismays her. Apart from the usual irritation lovers cause to those who are not themselves demonstrably in love, which Jessie naturally experiences, there is in the couple's behaviour a certain unwarranted complacency which she finds upsetting. For Ann is already married, to a gentle Jew called Boaz Davis. Boaz is a dedicated scholar, who has travelled all over the country in search of African music and the extraordinarily varied instruments that give it expression. Jessie realises instantly what Ann and Gideon appear to have overlooked — that Boaz is no common cuckold. Gideon Shibalo is black, and a black must not make love to a white, according to that "line in a statute book".

It is in the nature of Boaz's goodness, Jessie understands, that he should deny himself the justified anger of one who is cuckolded. Were Gideon white, Boaz could have the appropriate scene with him. But Boaz is on the side of the struggling South African black, and Gideon — a talented painter — is of that number. Or is it as simple as that? The liberal Mrs Stilwell, playing reluctant hostess to the law-breaking lovers in a house by the sea once owned by her chilly stepfather, Bruno Fuecht, is forced by circumstance, and her own worrying character, into weighing up the impossible situation. She muses:

> How impossible, how unfair for Boaz that the time should come in a situation like this when the *one thing that matters* — the reality — gets flung aside by something external and irrelevant. A line in a statute book has more authority than the claims of one man's love or another's. All claims of natural feeling are over-ridden alike by a line in a statute book that takes no account of humanness, that recognises neither love nor respect nor jealousy nor rivalry nor compassion nor hate — nor any human attitude where there are black and white together. What Boaz felt towards Ann; what Gideon felt towards Ann; what Ann felt about Boaz; what she felt for Gideon — all this that was real and rooted in life was void before the clumsy words that reduced the delicacy and towering complexity of living to a race theory . . .

I have quoted at length from Jessie Stilwell's troubled reflections because they seem to me to contain valuable clues to the precise quality of Nadine Gordimer's considerable art. She is a novelist who unceasingly takes account of humanness. The pleasure I get from her books is in following her through the labyrinth of human emotions, and in trusting her not to come out of it with some conveniently life-enhancing banality. Hers is, essentially, a tragic vision, and would have been so, I should hesitantly suggest, had she not been born in a country hell-bent on pursuing a tragic course. And since no respectable tragedy can function without irony, her view of the ways of this world is also keenly ironic.

Nadine Gordimer has been aware from the very outset of her career of the "delicacy and towering complexity of living". A writer can deal delicately with complex matters, and that is the manner of her dealing. She can be alarmingly delicate at times, with a sudden, perfectly placed phrase that, scalpel-like, reveals the specific nature of a relationship — what's causing it to flourish or decay. There are dozens of such phrases in *Occasion for Loving*. They flash out little points of brilliant light from the darkness of the labyrinth.

Jessie Stilwell describes South Africa's cruel racial laws as "external and irrelevant". The description is in accord with Nadine Gordimer's purpose in book after book. It's an ironic purpose and a humane one, for it concerns itself — first and foremost — with the business of living. Her abiding awareness of the irrelevance of her country's political doctrines prevents her from writing stuff that is calculated to warm the hearts of liberals everywhere. The idiocy, the simple-mindedness of the notion of white supremacy is so transparently obvious that she relegates it to the background of her fiction: it's always *there*, a fact of South African life. She refuses to thump that conveniently positioned tub. Her novels contain no noble blacks, no especially evil whites.

Because Nadine Gordimer is a writer "rooted in life", her books may strike some readers — particularly younger ones — as being in some ways old-fashioned. Fantasy and fable are all the rage these days, and irony is less in vogue than surrealist farce. Yet, just as she resists the necessary simplicities of polemic and the short-cuts of satire, she has refused to become a fantasist or fabulist. Her most recent novel, *July's People*, is set in an entirely credible future, too ghastly to be fantasised. I think of her, principally, as a latterday George Eliot, worrying away at the problems that will always beset men and women. And she is mature, too, in her unshaken belief — a belief that sustained her great predecessor — that relationships are important; that they reverberate beyond the merely private; that there are periods in human history when the irrelevant assumes an appalling importance. *Occasion for Loving* gives moving evidence of that maturity.

Gordimer's characters are responsibly presented, as Eliot's are, from a variety of angles, through the eyes of more than one person. Your idea of Ann changes as the story progresses, for example. Questions are raised: Is Boaz really so good? Is Gideon really so attractive — isn't he, in fact, rather unscrupulous? And just as you are thinking that Tom's and Jessie's marriage is of an unparalleled dullness, Gordimer deftly breaks up their believable routine and shows them, however briefly, as true lovers. What makes *Occasion for Loving* so impressive is the subtle way in which it summons up other occasions — of loving and not-loving. There is Jessie's strangely possessive mother, enduring a loveless second marriage; there is Jessie's dead first husband, the father of her only son, who might not have remained her husband had he lived; there is Morgan, that only son, on the verge of sexual discovery, visiting suspect dance halls; there is Gideon, with several affairs, and a marriage, behind him; there is Ann, who takes whatever she wants whenever she can, playing — or is she? — with two men's emotions; and there is Tom, diligent, hard-working, devoted to his three daughters and to Jessie, who sometimes wonders if she loves anyone at all.

"Jessie remembered that she had once thought, of Tom and herself, how you had to stop the ordinary business of living in order to love properly": you stop, and then you go on. Our ordinary lives require extraordinary interludes. Yet what *Occasion for Loving* finally demonstrates is that love has to function — and can indeed do so — ordinarily, in ordinary circumstances. After the fulfilment, the endless promise. At least Ann and Gideon know a fulfilment of sorts. *Occasion for Loving* was written more than twenty years ago. The laws have been tightened since then. That irrelevant "line in a statute book" is more insidious than ever. Nadine Gordimer is reminding us that its clumsy words have a temporary power to reduce "the delicate and towering complexity of living to a race theory" in novels that contain other reminders. It's because of those other reminders that they transcend local problems and speak to all — as the best fiction must, in any age.

Paul Bailey, London, 1983

x

PART ONE

ONE

JESSIE STILWELL HAD purposefully lost her way home, but sometimes she found herself there, innocent of the fact that she had taken to her heels long ago and was still running. Still running and the breathlessness and the drumming of her feet created an illusion of silence and motionlessness—the stillness we can feel while the earth turns—in which she had never left her mother's house. It happened now, while she walked slackly from out of the shade of the verandah into the dry, hot wind of September that battered and mis-shaped the garden. It blew her dress in behind her knees; she was alone and did not trouble to straighten her back. The tap turned in her palm with a dry squeak; the spray from the hose sounded like a shower of gravel on the parched leaves. While the wind pushed and shoved at her, and every now and then the water came back in her face, she was conscious in exactly the way she had been at the age of eight, bent double in her mother's garden. There was the inner hum of a wordless empathy with the plants sluicing and drinking, the shrubs with their glossy leaves obscured like dirty mirrors, the flower-petals curled at the edges at the flame of the sun, the grey weeds growing where they could, on stems of old string. It was an empathy gentle, sensuous and satisfactory. There was nothing peripheral to it; she had never been out of the garden, or challenged the flaming angels at the gates.

Suddenly this level of consciousness dislodged, was borne away in the stream of the present; instead, she remembered, now in words, that other garden. "What's the water-bill going to be this month, I'd like to know!" her mother accused the plants. Nothing grew well in the baked red surface that was given a lick of water twice a week. A few coarse, bright blooms—a single iris, a yellow daisy—stuck up like hat-pins.

The garden of this house, where the Stilwells lived, did not have many flowers but it was dark and green. Veils of water

9

from Jessie Stilwell's hose swayed over shrubs cumulus-shaped and trailing, palms glinting their knives, great woody old fuchsias dangling cerise tassels; the water tore through dust-thick spider-webs and beat on the glistening pine-needles bedded under creaking trees. By the time Tom Stilwell came home, the water had released the smell of spring into the air. It made him smile but he did not recognise it; it came to him like the smell of baking bread or a bottle of spilled scent—spring has no smell in Africa. He waved a roll of papers at Jessie but went straight into the house. Presently she turned off the tap and followed him, stamping her feet, as she went up the steps, to rid her sandals of their rim of mud and pine-needles. The house was old, full of decently obscure corners where various homeless objects could lie; in one of these corners there was a wash-basin, where she put her hands under the tap, and dried them on her wide skirt. She wandered into the living-room and out again, she looked into the kitchen and passed some remark to the servant, shelling peas there. She hated to call out, she hated to make the house restless in the few pauses of peace that fell upon it. She found him upstairs, on the old wooden balcony closed in with modern windows, where he worked.

"She's arriving on the sixteenth," said Tom. He had dumped down his pile of books and was sorting his students' papers, laying them on a mess of newly-opened letters, catalogues, and accounts.

"Well, that's all right." They were still at an easy distance from each other; always at the end of the day that took them away, each into his own activity, it was a little while before they could drift into the private harbour of their relationship again. They had married to share life; but, of course, there was no getting out of it, even by marriage : each must live his life for himself. Jessie sometimes thought, without blame or a sense of having been deluded, of the year they weren't married, when, she now understood, they had splendidly stopped living; that was what it amounted to—to celebrate love, you must do no work, see no friends, ignore obligations.

Two boats, rocking gently on the same evening water; she went over and ran her finger down the side of his face. It was waxy from the day, he had not washed yet, so she did not kiss him. "How do you feel about it?" he said. "No, it's all right."

But the silence after she had spoken seemed to echo doubt. "We don't have to do it if we don't want to," he said firmly. The evening before, they had discussed whether they ought to offer to have a musicologist friend of Tom's, who had been away for several years in England, to live with them when his young wife joined him in South Africa.

Tom began to say over again the things that he had said the night before. "A boarding-house is out of the question, with all his stuff; and I don't like the idea of them in a nice, compact Hillbrow flat."

"Heavens, no."

"I just thought it would help them out. And really make very little difference to us." He felt himself struggling against a heaviness in her response.

"It's quite all right so long as Morgan's not home," she said, wanting to say something perfectly willing and reasonable. Her son, who had the big attic room with a wash-basin, was away at school.

"Well, Morgan's gone out on to this porch before now; or they could, if it came to that."

And the matter was left there. There was the noise of some shrill, roaring quarrel, suddenly, in the house beneath them—it seemed to have been blown in and, as swiftly, blown out again—and then the approach of slow, sulking, plodding steps, coming up the stairs with exaggerated stamps; Jessie pushed the door closed with her foot. Tom stirred restlessly, patiently, over something preposterous that he had come across in a student's paper. The heavy breathing outside the door went away; Jessie experienced a moment of what she thought of to herself as childish triumph—she had escaped the child.

He put the paper away and turned to her, with his fair, crimpy beard, and his deeply-indented, kind frown—his was a fading, undergraduate shagginess that would miss out the assurance of middle life and one day suddenly be the shabby distinction of an old don. "You're not wildly enthusiastic," he said.

All at once, she spoke up out of herself. "I don't want any observers."

"Observers? Observe what?"

She felt ashamed, weakly happy, relieved. She went to him

and put her hand for shelter between his arm and his chest. "I want to live in secret," she said, half-joking.

"We do, don't we?" he said.

"*We* do. But only between us. So far as our life is for each other. The rest of our lives is all set out open for anyone to see. Then it actually hardens into that which anyone can see, so that it stays set, fixed, accepted. But if one wants to change? How is it to change while everyone's looking, being curious, and making comment? And if it's not to change, then it will get to the point when it has no truth in it. Won't it? Like a dance that acts out some great ceremony whose meaning the dancers have forgotten."

There was no one upstairs now, but the life of the house, coming into its power, was beating on the door : the servant's loud argument with a child in the kitchen, the clatter and bang of pots and doors, the nasal rise and fall of a voice on the radio, children's voices, the telephone persisting with its nagging double ring. He made the effort to keep it shut out, away from her, but it gave a sense of scamping haste to the necessity to understand what she was getting at before the chance was lost. He found it difficult to relate their life to what she had said, and she looked at him with the intensity of helpless deceit, for, of course, she was really talking about herself. The urgency overcame him and he gave up, saying, "Jessie, for God's sake, don't let's have them if it's going to be a nuisance to you."

She scrambled back to the level of half-truths on which daily life is conducted. "No, there's no earthly reason why they should be a nuisance. Of course it's all right. You'd think we'd never had anyone before." "Not much chance of that," he said with a good-natured ironic emphasis; he yawned sympathetically, a yawn that ended in a smile. They had never really lived alone; right from the beginning there had always been her son, Morgan, and ever since, kindness towards periodically homeless friends (of whom they seemed to have a number) or the need of money had made it necessary for them to share their house.

"Let's go down and get a drink," said Jessie.

"I'm coming."

She left him and went through the big, old-fashioned landing and down the stairs. All the house was always full of litter eloquent of interrupted activity; she passed a shoe-box on which

12

a doll's bath stood, half-filled with scummy water, an empty cornflakes box which was being used as a garage for some small lead cars, and two chairs linked to the dirty brass knob of the bathroom door by a web of hairy red wool. Gestures that ended in mid-air, interrupted sentences—a house full of growth, the careless and terrifying waste of nature, that propagates in millions, and lets millions die. What did children care about "finishing what is begun"? They lived out of the abundance of things untried; their untidiness was the appalling untidiness of life itself, that had flung away a thousand thousand sperms to bring about the single birth of each of them. She railed against them, threatened and preached, saying, as she had been told in her turn, that she *would* teach them to be tidy; but the instinct that drove her was not housewifely or even motherly—she was aware that she was frightened, in a way, that she struggled in the hands of an elemental force.

At the elbow of the stairs she met her daughter Elisabeth, trailing up. Snail-trails of tears on her cheeks showed that her anger and sorrow had ended before the tears had had time to fall. "I've got a lady-bird," said Elisabeth. "Clem's going to give me a box and I'm going to put some nice leaves for him to eat. He's going to be my pet lady-bird for ever." She went on up the stairs. Yes, for ever and ever, and tomorrow the beetle will be thrown away dead in the cigarette box.

Jessie passed through the smell of cooking in the hall and went into the living-room. They had papered it themselves, and though it was attractive nothing in it was of good quality. Sometimes when she walked into the room she heard her voice saying, as if she had released a trip-wire, "We don't see why we should ape Europe . . ." as she so often did when someone remarked on the curtains made of mammy-cloth from West Africa, or fingered a wooden bowl from Swaziland, or a clay pot. Like all statements of a stand, reiteration tended to make it smug and rhetorical; she must stop saying it. She took a half-full bottle of gin out of a home-made cupboard, and rummaged for a bottle of tonic water. When she went into the kitchen to fetch some ice, her middle daughter, Madge, attached herself to her. In the living-room, while Jessie poured the fizzling water on to the heavy-looking substance of the gin, the six-year-old girl clasped her round the hips. "Hi, I'll spill." She writhed free and sat down. Madge came and stood in front of her; vaguely feeling something was expected of her, Jessie blew up her one cheek in a comic invitation for a kiss. The child kissed the cheek, and then flung her arms round her mother's neck and embraced her passionately. She stood again, her eyes on a level with her mother's, and, meeting the child's eyes, Jessie saw them fixed on her, blurred, impassioned, sick with love that would fasten on and suck the life out of her.

Two or three nights later, Tom brought Boaz Davis home to dinner. Jessie had met him once before, briefly, at some convocation cocktail party, but that was all. He was about thirty, eight or nine years younger than the Stilwells, a slender young Jew; his face had the special pallor of mutton-fat jade rather than the hardened shaven monotone of an adult male. There was upon him, curiously at variance with the rest of his manner, the unmistakable mark of mother's indulgence that touches so many Jewish boys for life. A firm and attractive fruit, Jessie thought, but suddenly your thumb might go right through a soft spot.

He drew the three of them into a quiet huddle over talk of his work, which lasted through dinner and well on towards midnight. When he had left South Africa ten years before, he had gone because he couldn't get what he wanted then—a training that would equip him to be a composer; his ambitions had changed during the intervening years and now he was returning because Africa could give him what Europe couldn't—a first-hand study of primitive music and primitive instruments. The confidence of his European studies filled him with an excited, almost proud approach to the field of study he had grown up in, all unknowing. Every now and then, the talk arrived at a point where his knowledge and Tom Stilwell's met—Tom was a lecturer in history, and there was a record of unrecorded history in the tracing of the introduction, from one tribe to another, of various types of musical instruments. "We might do a paper on it together," said Tom. "At any rate, I could help you—or you could help me." He laughed. He had been at work for two years, collecting notes for a history he hoped to write—a history of the African subcontinent that would present the Africans as peoples invaded by the white West, rather than as another kind of fauna dealt with by the white man in his exploration of the world.

14

"You know Tom's going to do a history of Africa from the black point of view?" Jessie told Davis.

"Not the black point of view! For God's sake! The historical point of view!"

"Ah well, you know what I mean," said Jessie.

"Hell, I couldn't agree with you more," said Davis to Tom. Jessie had the feeling that he was relaxed in a special way in their company; he spoke, it seemed with a curious, luxurious pleasure, in the emotional, slangy, drawn-out South African way that so often appears to leave the speaker defeated, even dazed; as if *all* speech were like a foreign language to him, in which the use of a few lame phrases helped out with repetition and over-emphasis must serve to carry an impossible load of self-expression. He fell into this manner of speech as a man may fall into dialect.

"A-ah, you don't get me into *that* trap," Tom assured. "I'm not getting busy cooking up a glorious past for the blacks in opposition to the glorious past of the whites."

"It's like hope-of-heaven, in reverse," Jessie said. "Don't you think?"

"How d'you mean?" They did not yet know each other well enough to talk all at once.

"You can assure yourself of glory in the future, in a heaven, but if that seems too nebulous for you—and the Africans are sick of waiting for things—you can assure yourself of glory in the past. It will have exactly the same sort of effect on you, in the present. You'll feel yourself, in spite of everything, worthy of either your future or your past."

Jessie hunched her arms together as if to say, I can make it all clear when I choose.

"I'm dead off politics," Boaz said to them both.

"That's right," said Tom.

"Oh yes," said Jessie, "but they blow in under the door."

"I mean, you get together with a bunch of South Africans in London, and you begin to wonder how you would ever draw a breath here again without it meaning something political. I wouldn't have come back for that."

"You've come to do your job." Tom stated it for him.

"I'm not going to worry about anything else," he said firmly. And then he added: "But I'm glad it brought me back here."

They laughed. "Well, naturally. I've come back free, in a way. I can go about among these people, and not—at least, without—" he was feeling for the right definition.

"Without hurting them," said Jessie dreamily, nodding her head as if she had suddenly read aloud from a phrase in her mind.

"He doesn't mean that," Tom said.

"Without being hurt by them."

"No, no." Yet the real identification of what had not been expressed lay suspended somewhere between the two phrases. Tom and Jessie went on trying, forgetful of Boaz Davis himself. "Without responsibility?" said Jessie.

"No, *with* responsibility, that's just it; not irresponsibly, but with responsibility to his work, which is impartial, by its very nature, disinterested."

"And all that's left is for him to feel partial or impartial, as he pleases, as a man?"

"Exactly!" "Yes, that's it!" The two men came down where she had hit upon it, loudly, laughing.

"I'm not so sure that it's as easy as that." Jessie spoke soberly, though her mouth was twitching with pleasure. She looked up to Davis. "Anyway I suppose Tom knows what you feel as a man." It was her first reference to the fact that Davis was about to find a place in the Stilwell house.

The young man grinned. "He knows all about me."

"You'll pass, you'll pass," said Tom, with a gesture of acceptance that waved him towards the brandy bottle.

"I don't think I want another one?" he said, smiling.

"Yes you do," said Tom, and, turning practical, added, "By the way, the usual system—I mean the one we've found works best, before—is that you pay your set whack for board-and-lodge, but then we split the liquor bill between us, each month. You'll probably find you lose, in the end, as we're bound to drink more than you do." There was the usual exchange of laughing protests. But when the young man excused himself, a little while later, he said simply when he came back into the room: "I think we're very lucky. I like this house. What's there about it?"

"We've convinced it that it doesn't have to feel it's a disgrace to be an old house, after all." Tom made a precious face.

"It'll be a surprise to Ann. After my descriptions of Johannesburg, she'll be ready for yellow brick or split-level with picture
windows."

"Can't be done, I'm afraid. Can't afford it."

"Ann's English, is she?" said Jessie, rousing herself to make
some show of interest.

"Well, she was born in Rhodesia, actually. But she's grown up
in England and never been back."

"And how long ago was that—this being born in Rhodesia,
I mean?"

"Darling, what elaborate circumlocutions!"

Davis smiled. "Not very long. She's twenty-two."

"A-ah! The pretty little dear! You'll have to watch the old
man, Jessie, I'm telling you!" said Tom in a cracked cackle,
leering.

The heat drew each day a little tighter than the last. Jessie
fought sleep, after lunch, and went about the house stunned with
the battle. She walked bare-foot and her only point of consciousness was the contact of the soles of her feet with the cool wooden
floors. The children stood the sun like hardy flowers, taking it
in, and exuding it in colour and energy; their legs and arms
flashed in the yard. Jessie continued to water the harsh foliage
of the stonily silent garden. But the heat broke the day the girl
came. Jessie raced about town in the early afternoon under a
great fist of contused cloud. The faces of people in the streets
took on the alarmed look that comes to the faces of animals at
the sense of some elemental disturbance. "It's going to come
down," said a liftman, and Jessie heard his voice small against
an electrical vacuum in her ears. From the seventh-floor corridor of a flat building where she called in to see a friend on the
way home, she saw the enormous height of the sky, a sulphurous,
flickering distention behind which a turmoil of disintegrating
worlds seemed to be taking place, a pacing and turning of
elements. Below, the ghastly outlines of the city were beginning
to disappear in weird dissolving light.

She had scarcely thought of the fact of the Davises coming
until then. It was not so much conscious avoidance as apathy.
The couple were about to come upon her unrealised; so it was
that she sometimes met the face of some child who was a school-

friend of her eldest daughter, Clem, encountered in the house on
the very day that Clem had told her mother, weeks before, she
would be bringing a friend to lunch. "But Mummy, it's
Kathleen." "Yes, of course, I know. How are you, Kathleen?"

Yet she responded now, as to a sudden recollection, to the
urgency of practical things that must be done. She dropped her
trappings in the living-room. "What's the rush?" Tom followed
her to the kitchen. "No dinner. Agatha's off. I meant to be home
by four." "You know Boaz is coming?" "Of course, idiot.
Where's Clem? Please tell her to put on the bath. She must see
that Madge baths and she must do Elisabeth." She slammed
through the kitchen, bringing it to rocking life. Her face as she
worked took on the grim, hot openness of the manual worker;
Tom thought, she might be firing an engine in the hissing cab
of a locomotive. She came thrusting into the living-room, where
he sat deep in the clamorous dissonance of the music he loved.
"Where's that parcel?" She tore the paper and shook towels
free of the string. She resented spending any money on the
impersonal needs of the household, and she made off with the
cheap bright towels with distaste. "We're in rags. They wouldn't
have had anything but holes to dry their faces on." He gave a
little comforting signal of approval, but she was gone. He remained, skimmed by, juxtaposed with, over-towered by blocks
and spires and egg-smooth eclipses of shifting sound. He felt them
shaping all round him, himself among them, sounds that were
not at all like the voices of fire or wind or sea, or the cries of
living creatures; not like anything. He had his freedom of them;
and then they toppled, and were razed down to a hiss and
scratch as the record finished and the faulty mechanism kept
the needle going round an empty groove. He became aware of
the measured, emphasised knocking—spelling out syllable by
syllable the request to be let in—of the kind that has gone on
unheard for some minutes. He jumped up and rushed to the
door, and Boaz Davis and his wife stood there in the cold pause
of the breath drawn before rain. As they bundled in under
Tom's happy cries, a gasp of chill wind, smelling of rain, running
before rain, swept in round their cases, their card-board boxes,
their strangely-shaped objects in newspaper leaning against each
other like a family of freaks huddled on the doorstep. The door
slammed behind them in furious force. As they were helped by

18

Tom, rearranging the baggage against the wall, arguing in unfinished sentences whether they should drag everything upstairs at once or leave it till later, hindered by the presence of the children, who had immediately appeared and established themselves underfoot—rain fell upon the house.

The two women met in the deafening roar of it. They might have been standing behind the curve of a waterfall. Jessie appeared straight from some mirror; she had found time to push up the wisps of hair that hung from the twist she piled up once a day; over-laying the sheen of effort, haste, the efflorescence of the kitchen, all the self-forgetful attrition of the day, was another face. It superimposed the textureless surface of powder, the painted lips of the woman whose first concern is the presentation of her beauty; it was the sign, if worn any-old-how, that she still belonged to the height of life, the competitive sexual world. The girl saw an untidy, preoccupied woman whose face was beginning to take on the shape of the thoughts and emotions she had lived through, in place of the likeness of heredity with which it had been born.

Ann Davis was a nearly-beautiful girl, saved from prettiness and brought to the brink of beauty by one or two oddities—her eyebrows were thick, for a fairish girl, and she had one small pointed tooth that changed the regularity of her smile. Jessie saw her, so young that her share in the commonest kind of beauty was all the distinction she needed; she even wore with distinction clothes distinguished only by a better cut and material from those of the little gum-chewing girls who hung around the coffee bars. Her neck, flecked with small dark moles, shone living white in the turned-up collar of her black blouse. They exchanged shouted greetings against the excitement of the storm, and the girl's introduction to the house was brought about at once, because everyone was pressed into service to go dashing from room to room to close windows. Then they settled into the living-room and drank sherry, to keep off the chill that the rain had brought.

"To Ann, who came in like a lion," proposed Tom.

"But I promise I shall behave like a lamb," she said.

The three children stood around as if at the scene of an accident. "Don't mind them," Jessie explained. "They'll follow you round gaping for a day or two, and then it'll be all right.

Just don't think you have to be polite and strike up a conversation, that's all. Then they'll never leave you alone." Boaz Davis was a little embarrassed at such a dispassionate view of children; he remembered them, perhaps, in some sentimental context of the centre of the household. He tried to talk to them, to jolly them along, but they turned away and sought shelter from his attention. His wife chattered easily, but he himself seemed different from the young man who had come to the house without her. He appeared slightly strung-up, and inclined to show off, in his eagerness to fabricate a ready-made intimacy between the four of them. "Annie, you don't have to eat apricots just because it's your first night here. You can tell them right away that you loathe apricots." "I don't *loathe* them, they bring me out in bumps." "She's not always such a polite little thing, she's on her best behaviour for you." And he buttered a roll and put a wedge of cheese on it for her—"Here." Jessie and Tom accepted the little display calmly; they knew from previous experience of living together with couples that with real familiarity, real intimacy—if it were to come—would come more reticence and a comfortable front that would exclude the nature of the couple's private relationship, except in moments of crisis.

After dinner Jessie took the girl upstairs. "I've got rid of all traces of Morgan in here," Jessie said, and added, for truthfulness, "There wasn't much anyway." She had been surprised to find how little of her son there was in the room; how tenuous his hold on this house was. Part of a cupboard had been enough to take the stained, half-out-grown schoolboy's suit, the two or three holey pullovers, the cricket bat and the broken bagatelle board that made up his possessions.

Jessie was anxious to make her guest comfortable. "Here—look—there's at least another shelf going begging. You could put things you don't need every day in here. And on top of the wall-cupboard in Clem's room—you can put your empty cases up there." Ann came running to see. "How marvellous! There's bags of room. Thanks so much."

"It's dreadful not to be able to have order," said Jessie, her hands dropping to her sides in the manner of a woman between one task and the next. "I long for order."

"Oh yes!" With careless, social enthusiasm, the girl suggested that she did, too; but she did not even know what chaos was, yet.

She lugged her things cheerfully up and down the room, while Jessie sat on the bed and talked to her. Her ankles, fine as a race-horse's, took any weight steadily although she wore such high-heeled shoes; she was really very gay and pretty. She gave a thump with her long-fingered hand on a drum that was part of Boaz's collection of African instruments, and disentangled the belt of a dress from a pair of sandals.

"Do you know anything about all this?" Jessie leaned over to pick up a gourd decorated with an incised design and mounted on a reed. "Look, I can play that!" said the girl. She dropped an armful of dresses back into the suitcase. She took the contraption and blew into it, laughing and struggling with it. She produced a few low, blurred notes, surprisingly sweet. "It's a *chigufe*, a special end-blown flute." Jessie tried it, but nothing came. "I can usually get something out of these things," said the girl, smiling. "Do you work with Boaz—I never asked him what you did," said Jessie. "Nothing much." She was hanging up dresses again. "What sort of work do you do, I mean? What are you going to do while you're here?" "Oh, I don't know. I'll wander about with Boaz quite a bit, I suppose. And I'll want to get to know what's going on in Johannesburg. When I go somewhere I haven't been, I like to get into it up to the neck, don't you?"

The two women got on pleasantly enough in the feminine preoccupation of making ready a place to live, but each was conscious of reservations about the other. Ann Davis, in her innocent self-absorption, busy making herself comfortable, would never have remarked on this, but when they were alone in their room Boaz said anxiously, "Wonderful pair. I told you." "Did she really want us to come, I wonder?" said Ann, curious. "I mean, she couldn't have been kinder, but I had the feeling she wasn't interested in me."

"She doesn't seem to work," said Jessie to Tom.
"I don't know what she did in England."
"Nothing. She has no work of her own."
"That may be." Jessie's feeling of the extraordinariness of the fact did not strike him.

"It seems so odd."

He gave a sensible laugh. "Why odd?"

"Everyone works," she said stubbornly.

"Now and then there could be someone who didn't feel the need."

Work was an article of faith by which they—Tom, she herself, their friends—lived. How could it become, by the casual word, the mere presence of the girl, a dead letter? Yet it was, it could be. And what was the good of an article of faith that would deny it? There was life beyond life as she had conceived of it for herself; there were freedoms beyond the freedom she understood. She added another word or two to the near incoherent consciousness that had been in the process of coming to birth in her for a year or more, and that perhaps would only be completed at the end of her life, or not at all. How many of the other articles of faith by which she lived were undiscovered dead letters? Is one living, while they remain undiscovered? She felt tired, solitary, and dogged.

She opened the window and hung out. The rain, like a quarrel, was over. The earth breathed warm and damp in its sleep. Clumsy drops fell from the old trees. Suddenly she saw her life as a bird let into a series of cages, each one larger than the last; and each one, because of its comparative freedom, seeming, for a while, to be without limit, without bars. It's time to get out again; she knew, but told no one. She stared down at the dark and forgot herself. Under the plastered, hammered earth there was a fecund stirring in the old garden. Under stones, out of decay, sticky wings, moving jaws, feeble millipede wavings— they were all coming back to hunger and reproduction, to crawl and swarm and eat their way through the feast.

TWO

THE UNEASE THAT Jessie Stilwell had felt at the idea of the presence of two observers in the house was forgotten. Their presence belonged to the static on the surface of daily living; another voice or two interrogating, another laugh in the garden, another set of footsteps on the stairs. The girl was easily amused, and amused herself; she quickly became friendly with the Stilwells' friends as well as Boaz's, and she was in and out of the house, with a word and a telegraphic smile, between one diversion and another. Boaz was in a daze of work, and, if he was in the house, was not seen for hours at a time. Tom was busy and absorbed, a little grimly and reluctantly, sometimes, in his lectures and the life of the university. Jessie, whose current job was that of secretary to an association of African musicians and entertainers, worked every morning at the town office of the Agency, and sometimes in the afternoon or evening as well, and cared for the house and children and the demands of friends in those fits and starts of activity that served quite well to keep them going. In this immediate present—the continuing present of life going on—the Davis couple took a place unobtrusively; on any other level, she was hardly aware of them at all. She remained intact, alone.

Like many people, Jessie had known a number of different, clearly defined, immediate presents, and as each of these phases of her life had closed by being replaced with another, it had lost reality for her; she no longer had it with her. The ribbon of her identity was always that which was being played out between her fingers; there was no coil of it continuing from the past. I was; I am : these were not two different tenses, but two different people.

The latest, and present phase—her association with Tom Stilwell, their way of life, their children—she accepted without question as the definitive one (by this, for whatever it turned out to be worth, would her life be known). For the best part of eight years she had lived it honestly, wholly, and even passionately. But for some time now, she had been aware that though this was the way she had chosen to live, and by that fact deserving of all the fervour and singlemindedness and loyalty that she had it in her to put into it, it was not the sum total of her being. Not all the spit and polish of effort, the grace of love could make it so. She was feeling towards the discovery that there is no sum total of being; it flows from what has been, through what is, and so on to what is becoming. She had created herself anew, in eight years, as she had done several times before that; but this self was the creation of man; it did not belong to the stream of creation. From the fullness of life, she had, at last, time to ask herself why she lived, and although she had scarcely begun to know how to formulate the question, let alone grope for the possible answers, she had suddenly come to know, in her bones, that there is no possibility of question or answers, outside that stream.

So far as the past was concerned, Jessie believed that she had torn the grandmother's clothes off the wolf long ago. She had looked him in his terrible eye with the help of someone who loved her before she met Tom, and though as an adult she openly marvelled that she had survived her childhood, she refused to make it an excuse for her inadequacies. She was bored and irritated by the cliché of the unhappy child who makes a mess of his life when he grows up. "In any case," she once told Tom, "I don't think I qualify. I was not unhappy at all. I was only unhappy when I grew up and discovered what had been done to me. I am only wild and unhappy now, when I think of it."

She was the daughter of a petty official on a gold-mine; her father had been manager of the reduction works or something of that sort—she did not remember him. He died when she was eighteen months old and by the time she was three her mother had married again, this time a Swiss chemical engineer on the same mine, an intimate friend of the family, Bruno Fuecht. The Fuechts had no children and Jessica Tibbett remained a cherished only child. She was her mother's constant companion, and this intimacy between mother and daughter became even closer when the child developed some heart ailment at the age of ten or eleven and was kept out of school. She was taught at home by a friend of her mother's, and when she grew up, during the war, she left her mother's house only to marry. A son was born of the war-time marriage, and her young husband was killed. She lived on her own—with the baby, of course—for the first time in her life, and worked and travelled for a few years before she met, and finally married, Tom Stilwell.

Those were the facts, with their apparently easy graph of formative events; there were all the obvious peaks, labelled. But the true graph of her experience lay elsewhere, and ran counter to the high and low of the facts. Horror and sorrow were contained in the cherishing, for example, and the death, off-stage and unrealised, was no more than losing touch with a summer's companion who would, anyway, have been outgrown. Jessie knew the truth—coming to know it had been the biggest experience of all, in her life so far—and for some time she had thought that, knowing and accepting it, she had done with it. She had pulled out the sting; but all the rest of the past had been thrown away along with it. There were signs that it was all still there; it lay in a smashed heap of rubble from which a fragment was often turned up. Her daily, definite life was built on the heap, but had no succession from it, like a city built on the site of a series of ruined cities of whose history the current citizens know nothing.

Before she had begun to take any account of them at all, the Davis couple had been part of that daily life for three months. Morgan, child of the war-time marriage, came home from school; he was put into the closed-in verandah that was Tom's work-place, and Tom moved his desk into the bedroom. The house was full, and at night charged with sleeping presences. Jessie, roused, one night, by a child's whimpering that ceased before she got to the child, felt furtive, standing in the passage with the sleepers all round her, hibernating in dreams. Yet how alive they were, simply breathing; the mysterious tide of breath reached out to her and retreated, reached out and retreated, in the dark. The house smelled of them, too; the warm smell of urine and cheap sweets in the little girls' room, the peppermint-and-wet-towel smell from the bathroom, the smell of crumbs and leatherette from the suitcases lying under dust in the boxroom, the smell—exuding from the closed door as if from a cedarwood box—of nail varnish, dried gourds and cigarettes, coming from the Davises room.

Jessie rustled quietly back to bed, by feel. She was asleep again almost at once, but just before she joined the others, she experienced—exactly like the silent flash of sheet-lightning that lifts the dark—another wakening in another night. She stood behind her bedroom door at home on Helgasdrift Mine and listened, above the pounding stroke of her heart, to small clinking noises in the bathroom. The gathering beat of her heart had woken her like a fist beating at her consciousness; she knew, before she was awake, why she was at that door. A tap turned on and off—the hot tap, that squeaked. More slight clinks, as of things picked up and put down. Silence. Then the sound of the bathroom door opening, the tsk! of the light turned off. She opened the bedroom door and confronted her mother. She put out her hand and turned on the passage light so that her mother should be spared nothing. There the woman was, the grease of the cream she put on her face before she went to bed shining like sweat, the celanese nightgown showing her drooping, middle-aged breasts, the triangular shadow of her sex.

"What's the matter?" the girl rasped out.

The woman was caught; light found out her face in a moment of private disgust, weariness, the secret shame of unwanted lust. "Go to bed; go on."

They stood staring at each other, afraid of each other. The girl was not a child, but nineteen years old; her body could have been risen from the act of love. But she knew it only in books; she knew it only through the distaste her mother expressed for men; the things her mother did not say; the grouping of her mother and herself as opposed to the exclusion of her stepfather. The girl's feelings were violent : was she trembling with pity and shame, for the outrage of her mother? There was a struggling animus, horrible, in her—did she want, as well, to shame her mother, to expose her, to force her to admit that she was outraged?

"What's wrong? Are you ill? I heard you in the bathroom." She would not let her off.

"Nothing. Go to bed." The woman's voice was hysterical, stern, almost on the point of foolishness, with embarrassment.

26

"But why were you in the bathroom so long?" the girl said cruelly, pitiful. She had caught her. She had shamed her. She had forced the unspoken into tangible existence.

"*Nothing*. Go back to bed." Her mother gave in and appealed to her nakedly, as a woman.

Bruno Fuecht. He had no name. A creature lying on the other side of a door, in bed as in a lair. Love. Her mother, Bruno Fuecht, and—. A conclusion reached only once, in the middle of the night. Left unfinished, for ever, in her daytime self. Love. Mrs. Fuecht is so close to her daughter. "My daughter is my life."

At last, she slept beside Tom Stilwell.

The next day there was a letter for Jessie from Mrs. Fuecht. Jessie ladled out macaroni cheese at lunch, and opened her post in between times. "That's odd—I dreamt about them last night," she said, picking up her mother's letter. But it was not true that she had dreamt. She shook her head as she read : "The old man's in a nursing home again. What a queer woman she is; she writes with a real air of triumph about it." "Relieved to have him off her hands, I suppose," said Tom; the Fuechts had retired to the coast just after he married Jessie : he had not met old Fuecht more than three times in his life, though Mrs. Fuecht had come up for a few awkward days each time a child had been born. He was satisfied that they had no part of Jessie, and he merely concurred with her token interest in them. Since Fuecht had got old, he had become ill, eccentric and difficult. "He's been giving her a hell of a time. She says he threw his diet food out of the window and then got dressed and slipped out of the house to a restaurant in town."

Ann Davis, who had been driving around all morning with a photographer friend who took pictures of rich people's houses and gardens, was questioning Boaz about some arrangements he had promised to make for Sunday.

"Ann wants to see the mine dancing—do you know if it's on every Sunday?" Boaz asked. Tom shook his head enquiringly. "Shouldn't think so. Not every week. Eh, Jessie?"

"Definitely not." Jessie ate slowly, reading booksellers' catalogues, circular letters and advertisement pamphlets, though she chivvied the children for their slowness at table, and banished them if they brought toys with them.

"How can we find out?"

"Phone the Chamber of Mines."

Morgan was at just that age at which, the moment a grown-up noticed him, he was asked to do something; for the rest of the time, he was not taken into account at all. "Morgan can ring up for you," said Tom. "Bring the phone book, old chap. Chamber of Mines. Publicity department—something like that."

Morgan was a smallish boy, for nearly fifteen; only his hands, big-knuckled and long, had shot ahead of him, and were nearly a man's hands. He went readily; whenever Jessie felt people's eyes upon him, she was impelled to make some remark to break their attention—it was an unconscious reaction. For the first few days at home, for some reason or other he continued to wear his school clothes—a clean, ink-freckled white shirt and clumsy grey flannel pants that reached to the knee and were held up by a belt made of striped webbing in the school colours. Jessie, before the fact of the institutional cast of his figure, at once created a diversion, like a bitch running senselessly back and forth before the humans who have come to look at her litter. Her remark drew attention to him, but deftly turned it off focus. "What a tramp he looks! Tom, you must take him to town next week and get him some decent things." But the child wore the uniform as though he had been born in it.

"There's no answer," said Morgan, coming back into the dining-room.

"Of course not," Tom remembered. "There's no one there after lunch on a Saturday."

Challenged, they began telephoning everyone they could think of who might be able to give them the information they sought, and the lunch table broke up, except for Jessie, and the three little girls, who were eating custard. Ann stood about in the alert way of someone having her way. Morgan stood about ready for orders.

"Leeuwvlei Deep, half past nine tomorrow," Tom came in and announced.

"There, are you happy now?" said Boaz to Ann.

"Goody!" said Ann, and the little girls took it up, Goody, Goody! "We'll all go," she said to Jessie. "Shall we?"

"Well, the little girls've been. I'm not keen to go again, are you, Tom?" She looked at the boy, Morgan, who said nothing. She went on quickly, "But I suppose Morgan would like to go.

Yes, I don't think he's ever been—have you, once when you were small, d'you remember?"

Ann took the coffee tray from the servant Agatha and carried it out on to the verandah. "I'll pour."

"Give me mine first, please, Ann; I must fly." The Agency was running a jazz band contest that afternoon, and Jessie was to be cashier at the hall. As soon as Ann heard this, she turned : "Oh, could I come along? Could I?"

"If you want to, of course. It'll be awfully hot and noisy. I don't know how you feel about jazz bands in the afternoon. Wild horses wouldn't drag me, if I didn't have to."

But the girl was off upstairs. Changing in her own room. Jessie couldn't help warming towards her; everything attracted the girl, she expected interest instead of shrinking from the risk of boredom. Was that youth? Jessie had forgotten. She only knew that she herself became more and more aware of the need to protect herself from what she thought of as waste. Down in the garden, Clem and Madge and Elisabeth burst out of the house with their hands before them, in pursuit of dragonflies. Jessie and Ann went off together, looking, in their thin, bright dresses and sandals, curiously alike, for once, like acolytes who have both, at one time or another, served the same gods.

Ann was talking about the tribal dancing they were to see next day. "I remember someone—must have been our servant— kicking and jumping around with a shield made of a skin with brown and white fur. I suppose he was drunk. It was connected with some sort of a row in the house, I'm sure."

"But I thought you'd left Rhodesia when you were a baby?" said Jessie. That was what Boaz had said.

"No ... no," the girl said tranquilly, smoking. "I remember that boy, his name was Justin. He was yelling, too, some sort of song."

She remembered more of Africa than she told Boaz; she told Boaz, perhaps, only what she wanted to. She was unembarrassed by the lie, and made no attempt to disclaim it. For the first time, Jessie felt some curiosity about her; yet she sensed that the curiosity would be brought up short : Ann might rush into things with her hands out before her, like the little girls after dragonflies, but it would probably follow that, like the little girls, she would not be aware of her own motives.

She was helpful at the hall, and did not give way to any of those signs of bossiness that usually exhibit themselves in those who volunteer in situations of disorganisation. The afternoon session of the bands contest was for people of various shades of colour only, and a large, amiable and lagging crowd, mostly Africans, wandered in and out. A row of seats that had been shown on the booking plan did not exist in the hall, and this, added to the fact that nobody seemed to stay in his allotted seat for long anyway, confused Jessie's box-office. Someone who had promised to be there to help her failed to turn up, and so Ann cheerfully did what she was told in his place. By the interval, Jessie had lost Ann entirely; walking up and down the aisles, she came upon her, sitting three rows from the front between two African girls who had been programme sellers, and drinking a green lemonade from the bottle. Jessie had with her, by this time, the young man who should have been there earlier to assist as the row emptied. "Here's the culprit—Len Mafolo—Ann Davis." The young man, with the sleepy, veiled look that many town Africans have, murmured some excuse, and sat quietly, letting the smoke curl out of his mouth before his face. Ann had already formed the fervent championing loyalties that take hold of spectators at any sort of contest. "Well if the third lot don't win, I'll eat my hat. I mean, there's no comparison, no one else in the same class . . ." ". . . like a lot of tired grasshoppers—don't you agree?"

"I came too late; I didn't hear them," said the young man.

A crowd of young bloods in the front row were whistling piercingly and throwing paper darts at the girls in the aisles; most of them wore teddy-boy clothes, inhabiting them with abandon, hilarity and vulgarity instead of the dead coldness, like lead, with which their white counterparts filled the get-up. Blasts of disgust from a trumpeter warming up off-stage were followed by a long, tootling sigh from a saxophone.

"D'you think I could go now, Len?" said Jessie, asking a favour.

"Yes, why not. I'll do the returns. It'll be quite all right, Jessie. I'm sorry"—he indicated an apology for being late.

"Good. Thanks so much, then—Ann, if you want to hear bands, we can fix it any time. You'll get lots of chances."

"Of course, if you want to go." Ann did not demur, though she was enjoying herself. She edged smiling along the row; she had taken stimulus and excitement from the crowd, as some people can. She enjoyed the feeling of being among these good-natured strangers. As she passed before Jessie's friend, who had stood up, loosely, to let them go by, she said in her dazed glow, "I'm going to see the mine dancers tomorrow."

"Oh you are," he said coldly; and then, confused by his snub, seemed to forget they were there. "Len, goodbye," Jessie called from the aisle, and he recovered himself, half-rose again, and waved to them.

Tom Stilwell met Ann on the stairs when she and Jessie got back. He had been working all afternoon and was coming down to the sound of Jessie's voice mingled with the voices of the children, in the garden. "Eardrums still intact?"

Ann checked her light flight up the stairs. "Oh yes!" she called, and added, in her English way, "It was splendid. Simply splendid." He flinched a little, as if he had come too quickly from the gloom of his desk into the sun.

Jessie, as so often, had been waylaid by some need of the garden, and had not got as far as the house. She had kicked off her sandals in order not to muddy them, and was picking her way about gingerly between the leaning apricot tree and the bunch of palms. The palms were of a kind that had nothing of the tropical beauty that the word suggests; they opened out like a pen-knife with a bristling array of blades; once a year a tall stem rose out of the middle and bore a head of cream-coloured bells that usually proved too heavy for the plant : it keeled over, as it had done now. Jessie was trying to right it. The little girls gathered a pile of early windfall apricots, wasp-stung and smelling richly of perfume and rot. Tom lay on the coarse grass and watched these various forms of activity. Presently he called out, "That pepper tree ought to come down. And that bit of the hedge." Jessie did not answer, obstinately propping one arm of the palm behind another that sagged less. He got up and strolled over to her. "Ought to come down." He knocked at the crusty trunk of the old tree with his fist. Every few months he would come into the garden, "like Fate," as Jessie said, and make pronouncements of this kind. They were true; necessary; sensible. He showed her the garden, in a word, as it

31

was; she saw the broken macrocarpa hedge, the stooping pepper trees, the tangle of woody growth bald on its lower level and reaching towards the light. "Oh no," she said. "Trimming a bit, perhaps." She withdrew quietly, driftingly, immediately from the garden as he presented it; she picked up her sandals and disappeared inside the house.

The Davises had gone out again, and the emptiness of the house was emphasised by the buzzing of a few sleepy flies; suddenly she remembered that it was not empty—Morgan must be somewhere about. She went to her room and forgot him, for ten minutes, occupied in putting away the clean shirts and socks that Agatha had laid out on the bed. Then, on her way downstairs again, she looked in on his room. She did not think he would be there and so she did not knock, but simply opened the door. He smiled up at her, from the bed. He was lying on his back, with the little bedside radio playing on the window-sill beside him. The curtains of the converted verandah were drawn against the afternoon sun. "Hullo. Is that where you are." He moved slightly to acknowledge her. "What you been doing?" she asked pleasantly. The noise of the little plastic box streamed between them, rising, falling, soothing, imploring. "Listening." The braying, weeping, jostling went on. "It's the Nicky Doone programme," he offered. She nodded. "You should have come with me," she said, in the jokingly reproachful tone of offering at least some sort of alternative. She forgot that she had not asked him. His long, half-grown hands played with a piece of matchbox. He smiled at her kindly, shyly, without awkwardness, while her own grew until it sounded in her ears as loudly as the radio. She did not go away but she and her son found nothing to say to each other. There was only the voice of the radio gibbering conversationally. At last, in interruption, Jessie said, "I'd better see if Agatha's remembered the meat." Her heart was thumping as she put her hand on the door; she looked at him—she was sure she would speak—but she did not.

The Davises acquired several volunteers for the outing to the mine dances, and while the Stilwell house was finishing late Sunday breakfast, various young people began strolling in. At last they set off in an assortment of cars; the little girls had been waiting, ready, in the Stilwells' old Peugeot for an hour, but

Morgan, who took on the colour of a crowd very easily, went off with strangers.

They drove westwards out of the city and through the settlements of worked-out or nearly worked-out mines that were now being linked to the city by its proliferation : strings of roadside stores, garages, road-houses that seemed to belong nowhere, and to be one with the litter of orange-peel and cigarette boxes thrown from passing cars. At one of the mine properties the cars gathered by prearrangement, and people jumped out to confer about the final directions. Morgan came over to his parents' car. "Didn't Granny live in one of these houses, or somewhere?" "No, not somewhere," said Jessie, setting the words to right as if they were some object knocked over. "On Helgasdrift, on the East Rand."

"Why *is* he so vague. He seems to take a delight in never quite knowing anything," she said, irritated, to Tom.

"He's afraid of being wrong, I should say."

"Jessie, did you really live in a place just like this?" Ann leaned in the car window.

"I did." She added to Tom as they drove on, "Bruno used to take me to see the boys dancing sometimes on a Sunday. We just walked across the veld from our house to the compound."

"I can't imagine Bruno doing an ordinary fatherly thing like that."

Jessie watched the tall gum-trees, the brick bungalows behind their hedges, the traffic circles filled with marigolds, as they drove through mine property. A candle, taken down into the past, swiftly threw light over the bulk and outline of what lay there; and then passed on, to be quenched by daylight.

The cars skirted the compound—a rectangular barracks that presented blank walls to the outside world, and had all its life turned inward towards the quadrangle it enclosed—and came to a scene rather like a fair. A black man who filled out some sort of uniform with the afflatus of officialdom waved them to a level, grass-grown ground where a great many cars were already parked in neat rows. There were two flags flying; the restlessness of a close gathering was in the air. They trailed over the grass and up whitewashed steps to an amphitheatre partly covered by thatch. There were knots of white people about, wearing their city people's fancy holiday clothing—the tight linen trousers, the dark glasses and bright shirts—and others with cameras were prowling and peering. Past a rope barrier there was a less homogeneously-dressed crowd of various kinds and colours—Indian families with their profusion of daughters, all pink and yellow nylon, and plaits of oiled black hair, city Africans with bicycle clips on their trousers and Bermuda straw hats with paisley bands on the backs of their heads, mine-workers who had strolled over from the compound but brought with them from much further off the faces, hairdress and blankets or ornaments of other countries in Africa. Just round the elliptical curve of the amphitheatre, on the left, duster-feathers waved; the backs of another crowd hid groups of dancers who were warming up in preparation for their appearance. There was a small rustic building marked REFRESHMENTS —ALL PROCEEDS TO NATIVE CHARITIES, and a white man at a table under an umbrella gave out programmes.

It was all perfectly neat and clean and orderly. No need for the American and German tourists who, under their guide, obediently occupied a special block of seats, to fear contamination, embarrassment, or the heat of the sun. The Stilwell party filed in where they could; the shadow of the thatch dropped upon them, making them part of the drowned brightness, the blue-dimmed whiteness of those tiers where the white people sat. A hanging garden of faces—black and shining, on the far side of the little amphitheatre—looked on a tarred arena, black where the shade fell upon it; in the sun, a yellow slice of lemon thrown down, startling.

The party twisted and chattered; Ann studied the programme notes and her questions and comments darted like swallows. Boaz kept saying to her, or explaining to other people that he had said to her, "You must realise that you're not seeing the real thing at all." "Oh I know, I know. I don't expect it," she said, the obedient pupil. But she was not ashamed of her eagerness to see the dancing, anyway.

"If they dance, and they enjoy it, why isn't that real?" A heavy-faced dark girl spoke crossly.

Tom said, "What Boaz means is that these dances are usually part of elaborate ceremonies. Here you see them just as fragments, lifted out of their context."

"And changed!" someone added. "Hotted up to please the

34

audience. They've learned to make a performance of themselves."

"The best one's the gum-boot dance. You'll love that."

People related, as people will, unique and wonderful chances by which they had seen the real thing.

"But it's nothing to do with the Chamber of Mines," Boaz was protesting. "The blacks have always done it. The only difference is, it didn't used to be organised for white people to come and watch. Jessie—isn't that right?" The argument deferred to her. "When you saw these dances as a child," Boaz asked her, "do you remember—what sort of impression did they make?"

"Very little," said Jessie, with a laugh. She thought a moment. "I don't know. You know, the mine boys were not human to me. —Like a cage full of coloured parrots, screeching at the zoo. I watched them dancing and I walked home and forgot about them." The black-haired girl raised her eyebrows and looked the other way; she had recently discovered the distinction of professing no colour feeling; she was surprised to find such things said among people in a set she aspired to—she had indeed adopted her present views because she wanted to join it.

Jessie sank into the pleasant, Sunday mood of the crowd; the talk and argument of her friends went on half-heard about her, and her consciousness of self was lost, as it sometimes was when she was surrounded by the common mystery of human faces. The backs of men's necks, the nostrils and mouth of a woman shown beneath the brim of a hat, a young girl tossing back her yellow hair as the fly of vanity stung her—Jessie's consciousness became variously these, as the shadow of a cloud, travelling over a landscape, becomes now the shape of a hill, now the colour of a lake. When the dancing began, though she said to Clem and Elisabeth, who were giggling and scuffling, "Sit up straight and look," she herself was not gathered to attention. A portly African in a white coat and glasses put on an easel a board on which the tribal name of the group of dancers was painted; when they had pranced and yelled and stamped for an allotted time, a shrill blast on his whistle cut them short, and they left the arena, while the name of another tribe was set up, and the next group of dancers came in. So the programme went on— sometimes the dancers began languidly, hesitantly, and worked up to a strong, sustained beat just in time to have it brought down, as if by a shot, by the whistle's blast, sometimes they burst in in the full force of lungs and feet, and swept out again, undiminished. There were men on stilts who wore, rendered harmless by reproduction in cardboard and poster-paint, the terrible fetish-faces of medicine men's masks. There were comedians, hoarse, noisy and tumbling, with the ugly faces of all clowns everywhere, who played to the black gallery, where their quips were understood and brought derisive yells and laughter. There was a choir in white drill pants and satin cowboy shirts who sang while their leader, wearing fringed chaps and boots, released and captured again a small cage of cowed white rats. Now and then the parody of the white man's voice, yelling an order in the jargon of the mines, sent a murmur of delighted recognition through the white audience, who did not know in what light they were being represented, but were glad to be mentioned anyway. Many of the dances were pyrrhic, and the audience and the performers liked these best. With bits of coloured rag tied to old bathing-trunks, lemonade bottle-tops making do for anklets round the legs of those who no longer had strings of rattling seed-pods, and, in their hands, cow-skin shields and wooden assegais, the black men went through the savage motions of warring. They jumped and yelled and shuffled ominously; they found, in their breasts and throats, as the dance took them up, that dreadful sighing grunt that belongs to the ecstasy of death dealt out. They stamped so that a ripple of force passed along the ground under the seats of the watchers.

Jessie registered the succession of dances mechanically, with half-attention; she had seen them often before, not only as a child, but as part of a dutiful "showing around" for visitors. Morgan was sitting not far behind her, but she thought about him as if he were not there, going over the five minutes she had spent with him in his room the afternoon before. The incident went up and down, like a balloon; now it seemed small and unremarkable; then another interpretation made it rise all round her. Yet while she was thinking of other things, her attention began to fix, here and there, upon what was going on before her eyes. There was a man whose muscles moved independently, like a current beneath the surface of his skin; marvellous life informed his ridiculous figure, and shook off the feathers and rags that decked him. Others emerged from and then were merged with the wild line of dancers. They pranced, leapt, grovelled and shook, taking on their own personal characteristics —tall, small; smooth, boy's face or lumpy, coarse man's; comic, ferocious or inspired—and then adding themselves to, losing themselves in the group again. Their feet echoed through Jessie's ribs; she felt the hollow beat inside her. The Chinese-sounding music of the Chopi pianos, wooden xylophones large and small, bass and treble, with resonators made of jam tins, ran up and down behind the incessant shrill racket of whistles. Now and then a man opened his mouth and a shout came out that is heard no more wherever there are cities; a voice bellowed across great rivers, a voice that bellies wordlessly through the air, like the trumpeting of an elephant or the panting that follows the lion's roar.

And it was all fun. It all meant nothing. There was no death in it; no joy. No war, and no harvest. The excitement rose, like a breath drawn in, between dancers and watchers, and it had no meaning. The watchers had never danced, the dancers had forgotten why they danced. They mummed an ugly splendid savagery, a broken ethos, well lost; unspeakable sadness came to Jessie, her body trembled with pain. They sang and danced and trampled the past under their feet. Gone, and one must not wish it back. But gone ... The crazed Lear of old Africa rushed to and fro on the tarred arena, and the people clapped. She was clapping, too—her hands were stinging—and her eyes, behind the sun-glasses, were filled with heavy, cold tears. It was no place to weep, she knew. This was no place to shed such tears. They were not tears of sentiment. They came from horror and hollowness.

She held in her mind at once, for a moment, all that belonged to horror and hollowness, and that seemed to have foreshadowed it, flitting bat-like through the last few days : the night in which she had awakened twice, once to her own sleeping house, and once to that other time and place in her mother's house; Morgan, lying shut away with his radio in the kernel of the afternoon. Her hand went out, and took another's; it turned out to be the hand of Madge, her daughter, who never took her eyes from the dancers, and it was as cold as her own. Yet slowly it restored her to the surface facts of life, and she was able, at the interval, to troop out with the others, exchanging the dazed smiles of those who have just been entertained, and make her way to the rustic hut where the ladies of the mine were selling tea and cake.

After the performance, Boaz wanted to have a closer look at some of the musical instruments. He wanted to see how the miners devised substitutes for the traditional materials out of which such instruments were made. The Africans grinned at him encouragingly while he turned their xylophones upside down, and they burst into laughter when he played one quite creditably. He lost himself; his sallow face closed with complete and exclusive interest. He kept up a patter, not addressed to anyone in particular. "These tins give quite a lively note, in a way. But you lose that light boum! quality, the round, die-away sound that you get from a proper gourd resonator. It's important to find gourds of exactly the right size and shape to resonate xylophones." Ann was taking photographs of the warriors with feather-duster tails. They lined up for the photographers like children in class. "Come on!" she wheedled. "Let's have some life." But they only stood more stiffly to attention.

"The art of making some of these things is dying out, even in the kraals," Boaz said. "Most of them were not originally home-made, in the sense that everyone made his own. There were men who were instrument-makers, and you ordered your *timbila* or *mbira* or whatever it was from them. Now the old chaps are disappearing, and the young chaps are busy acquiring other skills in the towns. In time, no one'll remember how to make certain instruments any more."

"Well, these chaps seem to," said someone.

"Yes, but they come recruited from tribal life—reserves and so on. They weren't born in the locations. And look how the instruments they make have changed! They've had to adapt them to the material they find around them, here. Tin cans. Store stuff. Soon they'll be new instruments almost entirely."

"Ah well, that's all right," said Jessie, speaking suddenly. "Don't you think that's the best thing, Boaz?"

He looked at the woman and spoke almost tenderly. "I don't know," he said with a smile. "In my job, I like to find instruments in their true form . . . But, of course, yes, it must be."

"It was marvellous!" Ann came running up to them. "Wasn't it! I saw you clapping, Jessie!"

"Madge was enchanted," said Jessie. "The other two fidgeted and lost interest after a bit, but Madge never moved."

"Boaz," said Ann, biting on the long, phosphorescent-pink nail of her thumb, and narrowing her eyes, "I want to see the *real* thing. You know? I want to go into the wilds and see—"

"Oh of course," he said. He always parried her, quickly became playful, joked. "Bongo-bongo, savage rites, secret ceremonies."

"What is it that you'd really like to do?" Jessie asked her curiously.

And unexpectedly, the girl gave weight to the question. She hesitated, and then looked at Jessie honestly, and said, with a laugh, "Oh I like to find new things. Things I don't know. People not like the people I know."

"Experience outside what you think you were meant for."

The girl laughed.

"That's just the sort of thing my mother and father said when I told them I was going to marry Boaz and that he was a Jew."

As they walked away, the ancient instruments of Africa struck up the Colonel Bogey march.

THREE

A CREATURE WHO did not exist any more, the girl Jessica
Tibbett aged seventeen, long ago had spent Christmas weekend
away at a resort with her mother and stepfather.

Bruno Fuecht with his European sophistication and Mrs.
Fuecht with the assumption of it that she had got from him did
not have much taste for the Saturnalian side of the festival; as
a rationalist whose only experience of faith had been faith in
the political creeds current in his youth, the true occasion did
not move him, and although Mrs. Fuecht had once been a
devout Anglican, she seemed to feel that through her marriage
to him she had lost the right to the meaning of Christ's birth.
Jessie did not remember ever having been taken to church at
Christmas (perhaps she had gone once, when she was very small
and her father was still alive?) and apart from the excitement
in the air, the coloured lights in the streets and the presents in
the shops, the occasion was simply a public holiday like any
other.

That year they decided at the last minute that they wanted
to get away—the phrase was Mrs. Fuecht's, and implied a press
of guests and gaiety. But the truth was that silent lack of
harmony in the house, the deadly peace between three people
who did not even guess at each other's thoughts, became unbearable at the combination of this time of year and this time of
the girl Jessie's life. Even the most vulgar side of Christmas—
the family booziness and the money-making sentiment of the
shops—was a reproach to them for their lack of human weakness, their disqualification to stand in the comfort of the herd.
And the child's emergence as a grown-up, no longer only victim
but also witness of the unexplained state, was something all three
must seek protection from in the anonymous safety in numbers
of some place, such as an hotel, where they did not belong.

None of this was admitted between them, but it set all three going : Mrs. Fuecht said they should get away; Fuecht intimated that he was agreeable if not much interested, and the young girl got busy eagerly telephoning various resorts. At last, one was found that could offer accommodation of some sort.

When they got there, it was at once clear why the place had room for them. It was a gimcrack building, begun perhaps two or three years before and already falling to pieces before it was completed. The pink colour-wash on the outside was deeply stained with the red earth that spread for miles around it. The windows and doors were set in out of true, and ants wavered along the cracks in a row of brick pillars put up to support an upper verandah that had never been built; a twist of steel cable stuck up out of each pillar like a wick. The dining-room stank of Flit, the lounge was furnished with american cloth chairs showing their springs, and a black pianola. The hotel was full of people like themselves who had not been able to get in anywhere else, and when the Fuechts arrived they were told that there was only one room available for the three of them—an old narrow bed was brought in for Jessie.

The ugliness of the place would have meant nothing to the girl if she had found there the way to play, to begin a life for herself in the grown-up games of the young people seeking amusement. If she were to dance there, to be teased by young men, to learn to use the fashionable slang of the girls, to rush about in the happiness of laughing too wildly and staying up too late, then she would remember it as a marvellous place, the mere scaffolding of joy. She put on one of the sun-dresses she had made herself, but though she looked like any one of the group of young people who already, the first afternoon, had clustered together, she did not know how to talk to a boy, or how to form one of those alliances with a girl that boys seem to find an irresistible challenge—her only piece of equipment was the dress.

Some members of the group actually came from the mining town to which the Helgasdrift mining community belonged, and Jessie knew one or two of them by name. She had even been in the same class, before her mother took her out of school to have her taught at home, with one of the girls, Rose Price. Rose Price was there in a foursome that obviously included her particular boy friend; she waved a friendly recognition from where she sat swinging her legs on the verandah wall, but the greeting did not come from the distance, a few yards of cement, that separated the party of young people from the Fuechts passing on their way to lunch; it came from the distance of the girl's independence and confidence.

There were weevils in the porridge next morning and Fuecht pushed his plate away and lit a cigar, not taking his attention from the newspaper; his indifference to discomfort was not stoic or good-natured but due to the fact that he did not expect anything better of arrangements made by his wife. She was well aware of the hurtful nature of his lack of complaint. Jessie had the cheerfulness and automatic sense of anticipation that were simply there for her when she woke up every day, and she walked out between the unfinished pillars with her mother into the haze of a bare, brilliant morning. The shores of the irrigation lake were flat. Stony veld with the bald red earth showing through over-grazed grass spread to the horizon. Some black children clambered on the wheel-less hulk of an old motor car that had come to rest there; it was picked clean of everything but rust, like the horny shell of a beetle that has been eaten out by ants. A single bird of prey hung in the vacancy of a drought sky. As the mother and daughter stood there, the young people set out in a hired boat, oars waving and yells rising as they exhorted each other to sit down. Slowly distance smoothed out their erratic course and they became a fleck no bigger than the bird.

Jessie and her mother had brought simple evening dresses to wear on Christmas Eve, and, studying the wine list with a look of due consideration for its limitations, Fuecht ordered a bottle at dinner. It turned out to be a bottle that the sort of people who patronised the hotel wouldn't know about, and, probably acquired by mistake in the first place, it had lain forgotten since the place opened. A bottle of wine like that was one of the pleasures that remained to the grown-ups untouched by the tarnish that, for them, lay on other pleasures. Their murmured exchanges on its quality made an unaccustomed intimacy between them; unlike the girl, they were not open to the stir of the dance band—three men with slicked hair and red cummerbunds who began to blow and thump, each looking for the beat like a man searching for a lost bunch of keys.

When the music started Jessie felt a nervous, happy embarrassment, although she knew that there was no one for her to dance with. The young crowd began to slide round the chalk-sprinkled floor in the stylish, skating steps that were fashionable at the time. Married men grasped their wives clumsily by the back of the dress as they went slowly round, and the boys and girls swooped in and out between them like dragonflies. Jessie smiled in complicity with her mother at the married couples; and sipping the glass of wine that was given to her as a treat, she began to take on the lonely superiority that gave refuge to her parents.

But when the three of them went to bed, a secret black sadness came from her and obscured its cause as an octopus hides his enemy from himself in a cloud of ink. She had got into bed first, to let her mother and Fuecht prepare themselves for bed in privacy. But from far away, from that place of hers far from the limping beat and happy shuffle where the dancers were, far from the unfamiliar room with daddy-long-legs on the ceiling in which she lay, she watched her mother and her stepfather silently crossing and recrossing each other's paths about the room. He put down his cigar-cutter and small change and keys; she hung up her dress and pulled out a squeaking drawer. The scent of some special face-cream she used brought a personal, expensive smell into the cheapness and passing-trade poverty of human personality in the room. She was putting the cream on out of sight, but the smell of it, anywhere, was her mother to Jessie; the moment the pot was opened, she was there. Bruno Fuecht appeared in the space of light, wearing only a shirt. His legs, shortish and strikingly male, like the bowed muscular legs she had seen in Japanese prints of wrestlers, held her attention coldly and intensely. She had never seen him like this before, but that was not the reason. She had never seen *him* before—he was hidden from her behind an outward self, a label "stepfather". She was conscious of something forbidden in the way she lay still and looked at those legs; it was the way, as a small child, she had stared secretly at the deformed. She wondered—a flicker on the limits of her conscious mind—if he were her own father, would she see him like this?

Next morning it was raining and it rained for the rest of the time they were there. The young crowd were not seen again

43

after Christmas dinner; they must have decided to go back to town and the possibility of more tempting amusements. The Fuechts sat it out in the hotel lounge. Outside the lake was red with mud and the road was a frothy scum of the same red mud and water. Jessie got up now and then to stare out for a minute and then came back to her book. All the people who had not packed up and gone were held in the unacknowledged bond that, for one reason or another, they could not face themselves at home. Four men played cards in a corner. Wives knitted. Near the Fuechts, a woman was sewing while the husband slept behind a newspaper and their child, a boy of roving, monkey-like attention, clambered and investigated his way round the room until he settled at the pianola. There was something wrong with the mechanism, and his pedalling produced "You are my sunshine" over and over, with pauses of stuttering aphasia. On and on the child played; the intensity of his mother's concentration on her sewing began to distract Jessie more than the pianola did : she watched while the last sentence she had read hung in her mind. Suddenly she saw that the woman was sewing without any thread in the needle. It flashed in and out of the stuff, empty, connecting nothing with nothing.

Jessie occasionally saw the mad woman about town in Johannesburg, more than twenty years later. She was unchanged, for perhaps madness had aged her prematurely when she was quite young, and her hair with its streaks of henna and grey was tied back with the same sort of narrow velvet ribbon she had worn when Jessie was seventeen.

The weekend itself had changed its meaning for Jessie many times before it passed into that harmless state known as for-gotten. Just after her young husband died, when she became aware that a large part of her life was missing, that she had been handed from mother to husband to being a mother herself with-out ever having had the freedom that does not belong to any other time of life but extreme youth—just then, knowing herself cheated, that Christmas weekend had come back to her with revulsion and resentment. There, in that cheap, ugly place, her youth had been finally bound and thrown out into the mud to die, while the middle-aged sat in their chairs. Maimed but living, they sat and held her as one of them, for whom there

44

was nothing but to share their losses of the eye of love, blinded by disappointment or habit, and the leg of ambition, gammy now with self-limitations. Her mother sat there with her accomplice, Bruno, while their hired assassins did the job.

Jessie wept for herself, then, caught in a bell-tower of self-pity and anger where anguish deafeningly struck her hour. She lay in bed in the small room where the baby Morgan slept too, and she beat the pillow with her fist in the night. The death of that young man, her husband, was nothing, in the end, to this : the discovery of the body of her youth out in the mud. Her husband was dead, but she was alive to the knowledge that, in the name of love, her mother had sucked from her the delicious nectar she had never known she had—the half-shaped years, the inconsequence without finger-print, of the time from fifteen to twenty.

Later, when the animus of blame had exhausted itself, Jessie saw that weekend in the critical light of the needs of new growth and shunned it out of disgust for herself as she had been then. Because she had courage now, a passion of self-assertion, she reproached herself for cowardice then. Why hadn't she fought her mother for survival? She drew strength from these reproaches to herself without trying to understand the reasons for the paralysis of the will that had been brought about in her through a long, slow preparation of childhood.

Still later, she saw that the weekend was terribly funny. When she was living with Tom, and she told him the story, they laughed and laughed over it—Bruno loftily ignoring the weevils in the porridge, the woman furiously sewing at nothing, the pianola wheezing out "You are my sunshine". And then it had been recalled too many times to seem funny any more. It lay harmless, an explosive from which the detonator had long been removed.

In Jessie's own house, the Stilwell house, Christmas preparations were elaborate and began early in December with the day when Jessie and Tom met for lunch in town and then shopped for the children's presents. The year that the Davises were in the house Boaz turned up with Tom. Home for a day between field-trips, he had found no one in when he arrived at the house; he had walked into Tom's room at the university.

The three moved from the coffee-bar where Jessie was waiting to a restaurant where they could get a drink with their food. Boaz, in khaki pants and veldschoen, had the happy air of the returned traveller among people who have not left town. "Let's have a bottle of wine. I've been drinking nothing but kaffir beer and I feel very healthy."

"You look it, too," said Jessie. In fact he looked very handsome, his pale opaque skin turned a shiny olive colour by the sun. Although the presence of the Davises made little mark upon the house, the return of Boaz from a field-trip had begun to bring with it each time a rounding-off of the family; besides, both the Stilwells always felt a spontaneous affection for him the moment they saw him, while Ann, although they liked her well enough, had not aroused what was, toward him, almost a family feeling in them.

"Ann's probably eating with Len Mafolo today," Jessie said.

"That's what I suggested," said Tom, "but we phoned the Lucky Star and they weren't there. —She's been very busy with culture and good works, your little wife. Last week she was prettily selling programmes at Jazz of the Year, this week it's a travelling art exhibition in some caravan she's begged off a friend."

"So she wrote. Is there anything good there?"

"Two good Gideon Shibalos—the same two, the early ones he always trots out; I don't think he's doing anything these days. And a few wood carvings—not bad. The rest—" He put a bit of roll in his mouth and chewed it vigorously, disposing of the pictures.

"What would you give a boy of fifteen for Christmas?" Jessie had her list beside her plate, and she laid the problem before Boaz.

"Isn't there anything in particular he wants? Surely there's something he's been longing for the whole year?"

"No," said Jessie, "not Morgan. He doesn't long for anything."

"Not that we can tell," said Tom.

Boaz filled his glass. He did not take Jessie's question in the conversational way it was asked. He often went on thinking about things after the people who had begun to talk about them had moved on to something else. "Shouldn't we talk to Morgan more?" he said now, assuming a responsibility nobody expected of him, but nobody questioned.

46

Jessie ignored the direction of the remark, turning Boaz swiftly back to the immediate and particular. "The present's supposed to be a surprise, anyway. What did *you* get when you were fifteen?"

"I know what I got," said Tom. "A bicycle with the handle-bars turned down. I always let everybody know what I was longing for, no mistake about that. You ask my father. His only worry was that he might buy something that wasn't precisely to my specifications."

"Well, I didn't get Christmas presents, of course. But my bet is you ought to get him something grown-up and smashing."

"You poor little brute," said Tom, with a grin. "I forgot about that."

The waiter arrived with trays and dishes balanced along his arms, and when these had all been correctly distributed, Boaz insisted : "Really smashing. What about a cine camera or a collapsible boat?"

Jessie and Tom burst out laughing. "Yes, why not?" said Tom, lordly. "Or a sports car? Morgan probably needs a sports car."

They bought Morgan a new steel watch-strap and fell back on the choice of a game that Jessie had looked at but not decided upon, because they always seemed to give him that kind of thing. It was a bat and ball affair that provided good practice for tennis or squash, without the necessity for a partner—one of those games you play against yourself.

The Stilwells and the Davises pooled resources and had a very successful party that disposed of three different sets of acquaint-ances in one night : the university people came for drinks and tid-bits handed round by the little girls in the early evening; the friends stayed on to get drunk and eat two great potfuls of hot food; and the friends of friends—hangers-on, people the Stilwells or Davises had liked the look of at other people's parties, invited to come along, and then forgotten—these came and went between midnight and four in the morning. As usual one or two of the Africans were stranded without any means— except their by then unreliable legs—of getting back to the town-ships for what remained of the night, and make-shift beds were provided for them.

On Christmas morning Jessie liked to take the little girls to church, and this year, since Boaz wanted to hear the choir there, it was decided that they would go to a big church in one of the townships instead of the church in the Stilwells' suburb. The church did not have the front-parlour tidiness of the church in the white suburb. Paths worn by the feet of the congregation led up to it on its dusty hill above the township; inside, it was lofty, almost as big as a cathedral, and it smelled of the smoke from open cooking fires that was always in the clothes of the people. But the dresses of the little Stilwell girls stood out in ostentatious plainness beside the frills and pert fancy hats of the small black girls. And the high church service, with incense spreading from the swinging censers, and the white, gold and blue of the priest's robes, and the flowers banking the altar—all this, in contrast to the monotony and stink, the bareness and dunness of the streets outside, was like the kingdom of heaven itself. These Christians had only to walk through the door to enter it.

It's harder for us, thought Jessie. Just then she caught Boaz looking at her, and felt that he knew what had just passed through her mind. He did not kneel when the rest of them did, but all the time sat with repose, listening to the flock of voices that rose steeply around him, or the low sound of prayer. All through the ritual of Christmas, the curious swarming of the human spirit, some of it meaningless, some meaningful. he had given and partaken with zest and a pleasure in participation. Yet from time to time, as now, although she was kneeling and he was a respectful onlooker, she was aware of something that set them apart together. She, a Christian, assumed with her husband and others a common experience of the Christmas ritual, along with other common experiences. But the truth was that for her the common experience was not there. The part she took was not natural to her, in the sense that it was part of a continuity in her life; for her, it was assumed, just as, for different reasons, it was for Boaz. Behind the kissing and the laughter and the exchange of presents, there was his Jewishness, and her forgotten weekend the year she was seventeen.

FOUR

THE HOUSE HAD the look of a trampled garden, after Christmas, and then in the New Year began to right itself as everyone in it again took up a less concentrated way of living. It was the first house Jessie had ever lived in that seemed to die back and put forth along with the humans; this, she supposed, was the organic quality that people were talking about when they called a house a "home". She had lived in flats and houses which, once the reason for which she had gone to live in them in the first place—to be near a job, to provide a meeting-place for a lover—had fallen away, had to be left, like an empty box. This one would take anything.

The last and smallest of the little girls, Elisabeth, was about to begin school, Tom was trying to get in a clear month's work on his book before the university term began, and Jessie was in the process of handing over her job to her African successor. It had been understood that, if and when an African could be found to do the job satisfactorily, this would be done. She was working particularly hard to leave everything running smoothly and to familiarise the new secretary with all the difficulties he could expect to encounter, and at the same time she was conscious of the loose end running out ahead of her. Tom suggested a job at the university that she could have if she wanted it; one of the professors needed a secretary. There would be the advantage that they both would be on holiday at the same time, and they could meet at lunch most days; he saw the idea in the pleasant, comradely light of someone wanting to draw another into the familiar satisfactions and frustrations of his own work. Jessie went to see the professor—she knew him, of course, from various official social meetings—but while they were discussing the job as if it were assumed on both sides that she would take it, it became clear to her in her own mind that she would not take it. Like many decisions, it brought temporary satisfaction.

"I won't go to work for De Kock," she said serenely. "Didn't it go well?" Tom was at once suspicious of the professor. "No, he's a nice man. I'm sure we should get on. Only I just don't want to work there. It was a good thing I went; I knew at once."

She felt a relief at the thought of the city streets at lunch-time, the shopgirls pushing past arm-in-arm, the white suburban housewives and the black factory girls buying hats at bargain counters, the parties of glossy business men filing into expensive restaurants, the black men in the blue boiler suits of the whole-sale firms, making a lido of the pavement, and gambling in the sun. There, she was whatever she might appear to be in the eyes of those whose eyes she met : was it not from the old disabled men who worked lifts and the stocky, impatient-eyed Greeks behind the tea-room counters, who suddenly had stopped calling her "miss", that she had learned something, in the last three months? At the university the transparence of anonymity would be permanently silvered over; the eyes would give back to her an image of the senior lecturer's wife, liberal but not radical, of course; sexually attractive but not immoral, of course; aware of the better things of life but accepting with good humour the inability to afford them, of course.

She toyed with the idea of looking for a highly-paid, com-mercial job this time, a job where she would work for money and nothing else; there was the punch of a kind of honesty in the idea. But once before she had gone to work as private secretary to the managing director of the overseas branch of a famous razor blade company, and she had never forgotten the extraordinary unreality of the life, when she had sat in at board meetings where terms like "faith in the future", "continent-wide expansion" and "the benefits of modern civilisation" all meant razor blades, and nothing but razor blades.

In the end, she took a job that would do until something better turned up—half-day secretary to a company running a private nursing home. The place was only a block or two away from the house, so that she wouldn't need the car all the time, which was an advantage. Once accepted, she scarcely thought about the job again; there was so much to do at the Agency in the meantime—it did not seem that she would ever get through it all. She brought work home every day and sat at it through the mounting incursions of the afternoon, from the hot peace of after lunch, when everyone else was either out or asleep, to the hour before dinner when everyone had straggled in, the grown-ups wanting to chat, or to read aloud bits out of the evening paper, the children wanting to be read to, and the servant asking for instructions about food. She was holding out as well as she could against the division and sub-division of her attention, one evening, and when the telephone rang she ignored it; this was the custom at this time of the day, anyway—everyone was home and everyone waited for someone else to answer it. Tom had just gone inside from the verandah to fetch a lamp, and he might have done so; but he appeared with the lamp and put it on the floor, as it didn't seem dark enough for a light yet after all, and the ringing went on. Presently it stopped, and started again, and Madge was sent to answer it—Clem had abruptly suffered loss of the innocence where such errands are a privilege, and Elisabeth liked to pick up the receiver and listen to the voice inside it, but could never bring herself to reply.

"It's for you," said Madge, in the doorway.

"Which one?"

She looked from her mother to her father. Clearly, she did not know.

"Oh dammit!" Tom drew himself together and got up, going into the house with his arm round the child's neck. She anxiously watched his feet and measured her steps to his.

Jessie began all over again to check a long account of royalties from a record company, and when Tom came back before she had come to the end of it, she held him off with a raised hand.

"Where's Morgan, Jessie?"

The hand dropped and she looked up. "Upstairs. In his room, I suppose."

But the moment she said it, she knew that she didn't know where the boy was : in the hesitation that followed, both she and Tom noticed that the radio programme that sent crescendos of crackling applause out across the garden from the upstairs verandah at this time every evening was missing.

"About somewhere." She had heard the irregular plak! plak! of the jokari ball as it flung itself back at him—when? This morning—or was it yesterday afternoon? Dismay came over her. She felt almost afraid of Morgan. She did not want to have to ask Tom what was the matter. In three days he will be back at school, she thought.

"Do you know of a Mrs. Wiley?" Tom said.

She shook her head, then—"Yes. Must be the mother of that boy Graham."

"Mrs. Wiley on the phone. Her husband has just found Morgan and their son at a dance-place in Hillbrow. A place with paid hostesses. Ducktails go."

Jessie looked at him. Her plastic pen rolled across the papers and fell to the verandah floor with the clatter of a cheap toy. Slowly she began to laugh, but he did not laugh too, as if she had not convinced him that this was the way to take it.

"Our Morgan...!" The little girls had stopped playing, and she said at once, "Go and wash your hands for supper. Go on." Clem and Madge went off but Elisabeth ran into the darkening garden.

"Where was he last night?"

"Why do you ask? You know he went to a film. You gave him five bob yourself."

"Well, he was at that place again." He smiled this time, out of nervousness, with her. "Somebody tipped off the Wiley woman, and that's how her husband caught them today."

A blotch of white blundered up the steps. Elisabeth was talking to a stuffed animal dressed in a floral bathing suit and she ignored them. "I say it's time to wash hands for supper." "But what time is it?" "The time to wash hands." "But what is the number of that time?"

"Blast Morgan," said Jessie, after the dressing-gown had disappeared round the door. "I wish—" It rose with the curving jet of a fountain within her, breaking up the words, toppling them, carrying them : wish he had never been, never happened; oh how to get past him, over him, round him. "He'll be back at school in three days. Pity it's not tomorrow."

Tom said, "I didn't even know he could dance, did you?"

Her lips trembled and she began to giggle again. "Dance! Dance!"

While they were talking the lights of a car poked up the driveway and died back as Ann stopped and got out, coming lightly and quickly towards the house and almost past them, without seeing them. She was singing softly and breathily to herself.

"You haven't had supper, have you? I thought I must be terribly late . . ." They could see her eyes shining and her teeth in the dark. "Did you find my watch in the bathroom, by any chance?" The rhythm of another kind of existence seemed to come from her shape; they felt it, in the dark, like the beating of a bird's wings or the marvellous breathing of a fish's gills.

"Can you believe it? Morgan's been going to some dance-hall," Jessie announced at once.

"Oh, all the kids rock 'n' roll. They teach each other at school," said Ann.

"No, it's not that. He's been going to a place where you pay a tart to dance with you." Jessie insisted on setting the facts before her; if a stranger had come to the door just then, she would have done the same to him. She was sitting at the rickety table in the dark, drawn up in attention.

They could just make out that Ann had bent down, and was shaking something out of her shoe. "Good Lord, that's rather an adventure. I shouldn't think any of the other boys will be able to cap *that*." She laughed, subduedly, straightening, and went on into the house. At the door she turned and added with a polite smile, "Are you worried?"

Tom said, "Haven't made up our minds what to be," and she laughed again.

He put on the lamp. Jessie's face was closed to him in a look of complicity, horrifiedly amused. "Let him go back to school. Ignore it." She spoke with the tone of meting out punishment without regret.

He shook his head, looking at her.

"Then for Christ's sake, what?"

"If we knew what to say to him," said Tom.

"It'll come," she said with distaste.

"From where?"

"I'd like to see this place." She wanted to confront him, the boy, the child—there was an empty shape where the unknown identity of her son should have been.

"Don't humiliate him." They would have to fall back on the child-manual precepts, the textbook rules.

She began to insist on going to fetch him home, but suddenly remembered the thin little neck and the strange big hands—she flinched from the sight of them, exposed in that place. "All right.

53

You're probably right. Let him come home as if nothing's happened."

The rows of figures on the paper she still sat in front of seemed to relate to nothing; in the short interval since she had looked up from them the whole urgency of the Agency's affairs had lost life. She was lying in bed half-asleep at eleven o'clock when she heard Morgan come in. A gentle, tingling curiosity lifted her into consciousness, like a girl aware of the presence of a strange man in the next room.

Morgan, who had always been on the periphery of the life of the house, found himself at its centre. He must have come home with dread in his heart the night before, knowing that the Wiley boy's parents would have informed on him, but at breakfast he put up his usual show of uncertain good spirits—there was nothing unnatural about his behaviour because he was never natural, but seemed always to be behaving in a way that he timidly and clumsily thought was appropriate. At the same time, this kind of selfconsciousness made him extraordinarily insensitive to the moods of the grown-ups with whom he was making a show of being at ease. He would ask Tom (not out of interest, it was clear, but out of a desire to flatter Tom by an interest in his work) questions about some historical point on a morning when Tom had been correcting history papers half the night and was disheartened with the whole business of teaching. When Jessie came home irritated because she had got a parking ticket, he would launch into a long comparative anecdote about an exchange between a traffic officer and a woman that he had overheard in town. When someone said—"Oh Morgan, do let's have a little quiet now," he stopped short without rancour, as if the questions or the anecdote interested him as little as they did his listeners. Between his attempts at entertainment, his presence went unnoticed, though he always kept his face mobile like the face of one of those actors in a crowd scene who, you are surprised to see if you happen to glance at them, have gone on acting all the time the audience has been entirely taken up with the principals. He would never have dared to retire into himself, in company.

Elisabeth would not be parted, that morning, from her newly-acquired, minute school case, and it was constantly in the way

54

among the breakfast things. "We ought to tie it on you somewhere," Jessie said to her, and Morgan took up the suggestion
thoroughly : "You know what you should do, Mum, you should
get a cord and hang it round her neck, like those dogs. Those
dogs who go in the snow with little barrels of brandy round
their necks. No, I know ! Get her a satchel, like I used to have.
That's a good idea—then it'll be on her back. Why don't you,
Mum—" The little girl had forgotten about eating and was
smiling proudly round under this attention. "Let her concentrate
on getting her breakfast down, Morgan, please." "All right."
He finished his own quickly, and slipped away from the table.

In his bedroom, they saw he knew they would come. He had
gone to ground quietly, without hope. The radio was on, softly
howling; it was not really his own ground—in a few days he
would be back at school, and the bed, the portable radio, the
socks lying on a chair and the curling pile of science fiction
magazines and comics would be gone. Tom's filing cabinets and
boxes of papers remained in possession. Tom went over and
switched the radio off, gently, but before he could turn round
again, Jessie had spoken : "What makes you go to that place?"

If only she had started with the expected preamble, given
them all a chance ! What was needed was an explanation, not
the truth. Tom tried to hold her with a look, but she was looking
around the little boarded-in verandah as if the scattered marks
of the boy's tenancy were mysteriously eloquent, like smashed
glass and overturned chairs left witness to a brawl.

Morgan was dead still. If they had put a gun against his ribs
just then he would not have spoken. And then he picked up
some bits of wire that were lying on his bed and began to wind
a loose end of insulating tape round them. He looked at his
mother and Tom, kindly, helplessly, blindly.

"Well?" Jessie could not stop staring at him, roving curiously
over the little thin neck in the open shirt, the lips closed with
nervous lightness over the slightly forward projection of the jaw
(he had nice teeth; what a good thing that was), the shabby
grey trousers folded over like a dhoti under the circle of belt
round his thinness; the raw and tender hands. They were like
the hands she sometimes saw on young mechanics at the garage,
coarse and sad, not yet hardened to the bruises of heavy metal,
and with their pinkness still showing through ingrained grease.

55

"Jessie and I didn't think you were keen on dances and things like that yet, Morgan," Tom said to him. "If you are, there are clubs and places for chaps of your own age, and girls, of course. I should think you'd enjoy those more." Poor little bastard! Healthy recreation, they were offering him; who knew what it was he needed? We can offer him only what we've got, thought Tom.

"You don't have to sneak off to some joint." Jessie made an effort to be friendly. "You could have invited people here, for that matter, if you'd told me. Now it's too late—you're going back to school."

He said, as if fascinated by her voice, "Yes, I know. Only two more days."

They were talking about someone else. Morgan would never invite croaky-voiced jolly boys and petticoated girls to dance to the gramophone. Neither did he have any share of the teddy-boy's animal vigour; the reverse side of cosy home respectability acquired in regular instalments. The interview had come to nothing; there was only the relief that it was over.

Tom said, "He may do the same thing again. I don't see what's to stop him. We'll have to make some plans before he comes home next time."

"He'll have forgotten. You know how children leave things behind them."

"Yes," said Tom, "but he won't be leaving them behind any more."

Jessie was caught up again in the uncomfortable, uncontrollable amusement that had unnerved her the night before. "Tom, Tom, really now, Tom, can you believe that he ever did it, though? Is it real, to you? That little boy? That little pest, with his boring stories?"

It was over and he would be back at school in less than two days, and she accepted that that was an end to the whole ridiculous, queer business. She felt a cold irritability towards the boy and she did not want to talk to anyone about him, especially not to Tom. It seemed to her that Tom had come particularly badly out of the talk with the child, with his totally unspontaneous "understanding"—into which she had let herself be led, too—and his suggestion that plans should be made for Morgan.

56

Plans—there came to mind at once a picture that had had a special appeal for her as a child. It was in a book of pencil drawings of children, dogs, horses, parents and English nannies that was both exotic and comforting to her, and it showed a young woman lying on her side on the sands, her hand shading her eyes as she gazed fondly at the small boy who rested against her big, soft hip, rising in a curve behind him : "What will he be?—A Maternal Reverie."

She had battled to get him into a decent school (you were supposed to be entered when you were born, to get into anywhere really good, but his father had died, she had moved about with him from place to place, and she had not thought it worthwhile to arrange anything until he was almost ready to go). She counted on her mother and Bruno to help with the business of university. She would be unshockable—this she accepted in the abstract, thinking of homosexuality, getting a girl pregnant, running into political trouble, turning Buddhist or Roman Catholic. All this when the time came. But the time was far off; she herself was still in the season of loving and breeding, she had three babies hardly out of napkins, she was filling ever-open mouths . . . what would *she* be, that was the question that possessed her. She was kicking up her own dust.

Morgan was down there somewhere in that cosmic whirl, a particle flying round her. When it settled—ah, when it settled, the atoms would be combined in some other pattern, not her own.

She did not think of Morgan, who was going back to school anyway, but his appearance as a visitation in the eerie grown-up world was like a dream that, not remembered, drains the taste and colour out of the day that follows. Everything was as it was in her daily life, and yet for her it was not the same; she continued mechanically.

As she left the Agency office one afternoon she telephoned the house and left a message with the servant that she was working late and probably wouldn't be home for dinner. She drove slowly through the surge of home-going traffic to Hillbrow and went and sat in a coffee-bar for a long time. It was a big place, that had been decorated with bad abstract murals and African masks and lights shining through the woven strainers that Africans use for maize beer, but it made functional noises that gave it, after all, a certain kinship with the comforting qualities of a kitchen. A stream of bright orange juice constantly rose and streamed hissing down the inner walls of a glass machine, nearly as good as the sound of a bubbling kettle; the espresso dispenser did its work with a hoarse, sizzling chuff, almost like the noise a roast makes when it is being basted with hot fat. The place was empty, and these things were companionable. Then people began to come in. The girls waited with the look of musing world-weariness that she remembered so well assuming herself when she was waiting with wild excitement for some man. The older men, with money and aplomb, read the fresh pages of the evening paper. The young men sprawled back, watching the door, or leaned, tense and pensive, chin on arms, over the table. The immigrants came in : German Jews of the Thirties, doctors of this and that, in shabby raincoats; young Italians of the Fifties, the poverty-civilisation-stunted ones—little men-dolls with lifts on pointed shoes—bold, handsome ones with curly hair, rolling their thighs apart to show off the fine curve of their sex in tight trousers.

Jessie began to pretend that she was waiting for someone, too. Only this was a waiting without anguish, without the possibility of being let down, without a trace of the worst risk of all—that the meeting would go wrong for no reason at all. When the place began to fill up she left with a nice sense of timing. She walked round the shops for an hour, looking with interest at everything, from the rakes and plastic buckets in the hardware shop, and the lilac and silver wigs in the hairdresser's, to the patterns of turkey, duck and chicken corpses laid out at the kosher delicatessen, and the perpetual festival, with its scent of trampled fruit and wilting flowers, of the Indian greengrocer's, banked with purple of aubergine and scarlet of tomato, feathered with carrot and curly lettuce, and glowing with the light showing through the bottles of bright cold drinks on the top shelves. It got dark and she bought herself another cup of coffee. But this time she drank it off and went back to the street at once. She did not know where the place was, but, passing in the car at some time, she must have seen the name up, and now she walked to it with hardly more than a moment's hesitation at each block's end.

There was a flight of concrete stairs set in a narrow passage off the street. As she went up she thought, with the criticism of one generation for another, how what she had sought had usually to be found in cellars.

A woman her own age sat in a booth like the one from which tickets are sold at the cinema. "Yes dear?"

The manner was the shop assistant's one : now, that looks beautiful on you ... The woman, by the adornments she used to disguise them, presented Jessie with a candid admittance of signs she sometimes surprised on her own face. The hair was gaily tinted, confirming as an enduring reality the few white hairs that sometimes appeared, sometimes were not to be seen. A thick coating of make-up defined as final, in two long cracks, the crease running from nose to chin on each side that came out at night, when preparations were being made for bed. The face was realistic, resigned and tough in its assumption of paint and curl; an urban, post-industrial-revolution version of the peasant woman's reliance on the conventions of the various forms of dress and deportment to see her through girlhood, matronhood and widowhood.

Jessie paid five shillings and mumbled something about meeting someone, but the excuse was not necessary. No one was suspicious of her. On the other side of leather concertina doors was a large room lit to a fluorescent pink, with silver-painted globe chairs round the tables. On the walls hung huge photographs of young men with the faces of sulky girls, their lips snarling in song, but the band that was bumping and knocking out the rhythm of some supposedly South American tune was not a fanatic group of jazz-possessed youngsters, but ordinary commercial musicians with the stolid weariness of an endless night in their faces. The people were young, but not noticeably belonging to the teenage cult. Most of the girls must have been under twenty and looked like the bored or head-tossing misses who served in bazaars during the day. There was no hint of sophistication about them and they came from a class too new to the cheap bright benefits of the material to want to ape, even without understanding, its fashionable symbolic rejection by pale girls in black stockings.

A loose-faced youth in a dirty white forage cap brought Jessie a Coca-Cola and a saucer of chips. A few people were dancing, but most of them hung about, the men in chaffing groups around the girls. They looked like young men who had come together in twos and threes from some of the reef gold-mining towns where the pleasures of the city were not available; there was a solidarity about the way they returned to their companions as soon as a dance was over, roaring back in sniggering laughter at each other's remarks. On the periphery of the young men and girls were some of those men who appear, shaven, dressed in their one pin-stripe suit and shining cap of black hair, apparently from the rat-holes of every city. Every now and then one of them would take one of the paid dancing partners on to the floor, holding her with all the ghastly delicacy of a refined finger furled above the handle of a tea-cup. The favourite was a black-haired girl with a queenly, kidding look and a white neck with a crucifix round it. She was not fat but she must have been heavy, for her feet in their pointed shoes came down with an extraordinary impression of force, treading violence, as if they would spear, crush and flatten anything that might happen to fall beneath them. She giggled and nodded while she danced.

One of the men walked twice past Jessie. Then he was there, bent over the table; a zig-zag of orchid-pink light shone on the hair as if on a dark pond. "You wouldn't like to dance, madam?" The fastidious politeness, the obsequious male pride in knowing how a woman likes to think she's being treated lay in a pathetic gloss over the craven ferociousness of the creature. His mean eyes had an objective loneliness, like the eyes of an animal that does not know it was born behind bars.

She did not learn why Morgan had gone there. To do so, she understood at last, you would first have to know where he set out from.

FIVE

Adam, seeing Eve sprung fully-fledged from his side, could not have been more strangely troubled. There was always time to get down to Morgan; he would keep, he was there, whether she liked it or not, and one day she would be able to turn round and take up where she had set him aside. She no longer knew when exactly it was that she had set him aside and it seemed to her that this must have been at the time of her marriage to Tom, but in fact it had been much earlier, when she lay in bed at night in the room where the baby slept, and wept in self-pity and rage for the years her mother had cheated her of. Then the baby, with the enviable bloom of its life untouched by anybody, had seemed something that could well be left to itself in any but the obvious physical needs. It would be safe like that for a time just as its natural immunity from certain diseases, a legacy from before birth, would last for a year or two. Fifteen years had gone by, and now she was confronted with some strange creature : half-man, not-child. Where was the child who had been hanging about her, waiting?

In psychiatric jargon, a man may be spoken of as mentally "completely inaccessible"; in order to survive without the disabilities of the past, without whining, without blaming, Jessie had made most of her past life inaccessible to her rather in this way; she had remained accessible to it, of course, on that level beyond control, the subconscious. She wanted to deal with Morgan here and now, of and in the present. Was that unreasonable? She was trying to put him together as you might a new acquaintance, from the images of the last five or six weeks. He was gone, of course, out of the house again, but he had been there, and, out of an old arrogance of her responsibility for him taken as mastery of him, she set herself out to pick up an easy trail. He was bored; he felt out of things, between the grown-ups and the little girls; he was led into the whole business by his weakness, following the Wiley boy rather than thinking for himself. Or it was the old story of the child who deliberately turns his back on the freedom to develop within the liberation won by his parents, and chooses the rigid and vulgar? Yet Morgan, as he began to fill out in her consciousness as he was— as she had seen him and, until now, not seen him—gave himself away in response to none of these clues. He had nothing to do with them; she could see that. He was not bored—the day she had walked into his room and found him lying listening to his endless radio, what stillness there was about him, a loneliness, yes, perhaps, wrapped soft as content. And out of things—out of things was his place, he had curled up there for years. And just as he had no spirit for resentment (there was shame and a twinge of contempt in her at the admittance) so his weakness would not have been enough to send him so far after the Wiley boy : something more potent than weakness, an initiative of his own, had sent him up the concrete stairs to the pink lights. As for *their* values—her's and Tom's and the house's—she had to admit with a sense of sullen pain she did not know whether they had "taken" or not with Morgan, simply through his being around : that was the only way they might have been expected to have done.

The boy loomed in her mind in a series of outlines that wavered into each other and faded into a thickening oppression. The sight of one of the little girls, coming with a splinter to be taken out of a finger, Clem wanting to chatter or Madge mournful with the desire to be kissed, brought about an instinctive withdrawal. Jessie felt like a dog who sees a raised stick. Love appalled her with its hammering demands, love clamoured and dunned, love would throw down and tear to pieces its object. This was love, that few people could live without, and that most spent the major effort of their lives to secure. And the burden of Morgan, Morgan, hung on her—always she turned in final exacerbation on this. Yet she did not love Morgan, and Morgan —that much she was sure of—did not love her. They seemed to meet over the admittance, looking at each other without expectation or malice, with that space, between the house, where she was, and the school, where he was, briefly blown clear.

The current of her preoccupation moved through the house.

The children stumbled into it, startled, and went on again, forgetful and happy. Tom kept coming into its path, and always with a sense of dismay and surprise—so Jessie was still aware of this Morgan business! He could not for the life of him see why; next time Morgan came home for holidays they would have to make sure that his time was fully occupied, that was all. That was all they could do. It was a matter of finding a few fairly grown-up occupations for him. Tom had made up his mind to see to this when the time came, and Jessie knew that he would. There was nothing else to be done. It might not work, but there was nothing else to be done. Didn't Jessie accept that any longer? Why was she turning the whole light of her being on Morgan now, when long ago, soon after he had begun to live with her (and the boy; the two went together), he had understood that he must give up trying to get her to turn that life-giving light the child's way, even occasionally. She had never been able to do it. Not even then, when it was necessary and there was some sense in it. This business of the dance-hall was the least of the threats that had hung over Morgan.

Tom himself was moving in the inner constriction of his own difficulties at the time. The Bill that would close the university to all but white students for the future was about to be debated in Parliament; and there was talk of a "loyalty" clause being inserted in qualifications for the appointment of staff. The students' council was demonstrating and pamphleteering in protest, and Tom was eager to see them kick up a real shindy, supported by the staff. The issue started off decently clear in his mind, but as the days went by it took on all the stains and nicks of handling, and began to be almost unrecognisable. One morning an administrative official of the university had torn down and stuffed into a rubbish bin some student posters. It was said that this was on instruction from the highest quarters; even if it had been done without instruction, as an expression of personal irritation, it would have had an ambiguous look about it. Tom was beginning to have a sickening sense of the whole affair—that had existed diamond-hard among those few crystal formations of bedrock morality—moving into areas of doubt where it did not belong. He scarcely spoke through dinner that evening and got up from the table while the others were still eating—he had to go to a private meeting with some members

63

of the university staff and students. "Where are my cigarettes? I'd better move on, I suppose."

There was the pause of confrontation with a subject everyone knew too well to want to talk about.

Ann was home for dinner for once, and she asked with the impartial interest she brought to most things, "Was there a big meeting at lunch-time today?"

"Not bad. Only let there be some noise and broken heads so that people begin to see that academic freedom is something to fight over in the street! People feel it's a phrase that doesn't concern most of them, like 'higher income tax bracket'. Let 'em understand it's on a level with their right to their weekly pay-packet, the defence of their wife's good name and blood-heating things like that."

Jessie was moving restlessly about the room as if contemplating some tidying-up activity. "I'll be up," she said, indicating he needn't take a key.

At the meeting that evening a student pointed out that the university never had been truly open to anyone but whites; the African and Indian students had never been allowed to take part in sports or social events. When one spoke of it as an "open" university one was already accepting some of the meaner and uglier evasions by which the colour-bar protected itself. Tom dropped in at a friend's flat for coffee afterwards and got talking to an African whom he had met there a few times before. They left together and as they walked along the street Tom quoted the exchange that had taken place between those members of the university staff and administration who, like himself, wanted to fight the Bill unreservedly, and to back up the students and give them free rein, and others who protested that they abhorred the Bill but that it was foolish to antagonise the Government when it would go through in any case, and the university was heavily dependent on Government grants. In order to keep alive the idea of academic freedom, these people argued, the university must continue to exist at all costs, even that of academic freedom itself . . .

The brown, pock-marked face beside him appeared and disappeared as they passed together under street-lamps. The man turned to say goodnight: "Fight them over this business if you want to, man, but don't think that anything you do really

64

matters. Some of you make laws, and some of you try to change them. And you don't ask us."

When Tom talked to Jessie about it, she had still the clear-cut picture of it that he himself had had at the beginning. She had never cared much for academic people—if she had been married to a business man, she would have cared as little for his associates sworn to the twin gods of supply and demand, for she had the solitary's genuine if slightly jealous dislike of guilds, jokes of the trade, and a soothing assumption of a common lot—and it did not surprise her that some of the university people were now found unable to clap their hands over their revealed careerism and lack of moral courage.

"I don't see that there's any problem. It's only people who're busy taking things into 'consideration'—whether they'll be kicked out or whether Professor Tiddleypush would like them to open their mouths or not—who need give the thing a second thought." She commented on a satisfaction, in him, that she took for granted. Yet this truth seemed to him now flippant and casual. He thought, with a flash of vindictiveness, she sits there in a heap (she had waited up for him) and she has not been listening to me. She's all attention but she has not heard. It was true that he was against keeping a man out of a university because of his colour just as surely as he knew it was wrong to murder. But she knew nothing of the disruption of the working atmosphere by conflict, she knew nothing of the feel of that curious conglomeration of usefulness, waste, inspiration and discipline that makes an institution, shifting and staggering beneath your feet.

He was awake in the night and she was aware of it. She felt him sliding carefully out of his side of the bed. "What is it?" "I don't know," he lied. "I want a cigarette." He lay with his back to her in order not to disturb her, but she could feel the regular inhalations with which he took the cigarette, and the stretching of his arm muscle as he leant to put it out. He ran his foot, curved to caress, over her calf in security, but it was an hour when she could imagine how she would be if she had never met him. She had the actual feeling of herself free, alone, husband dead, mother escaped from, alone, with Morgan. It began to go through her mind in light and colour, a life with Morgan that seemed to have happened. Morgan was a boy of about five and she was pushing him on a swing. Then she was sitting on the swing and he was pushing her. She came toward his laughing face and away from it again, toward and away. Then she and Morgan were on a ship together, they were reading, side by side on deck, and people to whom they never needed to speak walked up and down. (They really had been on a ship together, once, but he had been little and she had put him in the public nursery most of the time, where he had stared down at her on deck in silence from behind wire mesh.) Then he was older, twelve or fourteen, and they shared a flat, orderly, with shaded lights; he poured the drinks for her and they went to the theatre together. They were having dinner, cooking and setting the table for themselves, and talking. She had him with her through crowded rooms, he looked grown-up in a light suit, his big, young, tender man's hand she took suddenly ... At some point these possibilities became a dream and in the dream she was actually looking with Tom at the projection of a roll of old film whose existence had been unknown and which recorded a life that had been forgotten.

Beyond her volition, she began to try whether she might not be able to get at the fifteen-year-old boy through laying her hands on what she herself had been at that age. Out of an instinct that ran away with her, she sought out that girl who had been put away for so long as nothing more than a case history. It was easy enough to see her, going about the mine property and the town with her mother. She did not go to school but was taught at home and she and her mother spent the afternoons on shopping expeditions together. There were the counters draped with bolts of silk before which they were lost for hours, their eyes meeting in considering indecision. The final word hung, inevitable as the curtain embrace. "The blue, or the black and white?" "The blue is lovely, the patterned one has more style ..." Her mother's eyes held hers again. Then the decision : "I need a figured dress of some kind, there are times when—" They were free to go off and drink coffee, breaking the calm after tension by passing some remark, now and then, about what accessories would be right. "Take the stairs slowly"; her mother's gloved hand pressed her shoulder. Sometimes Jessie *did* think she felt the labouring flutter of her heart when they reached

66

the top : she panted a little, with a smile, to show it. When they got home, they rested together in her mother's room.

She was not allowed to play tennis, of course, because of her heart—not an organic defect, and with care she would grow out of it, her mother explained to people. That was why she kept the girl out of school. No tennis or swimming, but she went out at night far more than other children of her age. Her mother and Bruno took her to the theatre and concerts in Johannesburg, and when they played bridge in the houses of the mine, she went with them and was not bored, listening to the grown-ups and helping the hostess efficiently with the tea. She read novels too, whatever she pleased; "I don't believe that girls should be brought up in ignorance of life," said Mrs. Fuecht. The girl looked with fastidious timidity at the great girls in dusty serge gym tunics who had once been her class-mates. She would have been dismayed if she had ever been pronounced well enough to go back to school.

Ignorance of life! Jessie felt no pity for this little creature, her mother's boon companion. She was ashamed of her, repulsed by her sham grown-up poise, her pride in the sense of privilege that had been palmed off on her, her prodigy's smirking acceptance of a dwarf's status in the world of men and women. Thank God she had not lived—done to death with the violence of the truth, when it came to her.

But was that all there had been to her?

Once Jessie began to move down there in the past, once she had forced herself to it, she began to be able to see, like a cat in the dark. Masses crumbled to their components, the detail of delicate structures stood out. All there, all, all, for ever. She came, with great vividness, upon the extraordinary significance, at that time, that was attached to a small painted photograph of her father that she had begged from her mother. She had it still, and for years now it had had no power to stir her; it was simply something she kept, as a gesture of acknowledgement to the man who was her father and whom she could not remember ever having known. But back *there* it shone alive, charged with a force that held her as the little holy image in its dark niche holds the child who passes through an intensely religious phase. The picture had been in a chocolate box of old trinkets that she loved to rummage through. It was a photograph painted to look like a miniature, in a bevelled gilt snap-case meant to be carried in a handbag—the Twenties equivalent of the picture-locket. She was taken, in the manner of girls, more with the fancy case than anything else. It stood on her book-case between cut-out pictures of Beverley Nichols and Evelyn Waugh in bazaar frames. Then, in one of the loud storms that hit the mine in summer, her bedroom lamp fused, and Bruno came in to fix it. He worked by candle-light, quickly and well, as he did everything, and as the lamp came on again and he picked up his card of fuse wire from the book-case, he noticed the pictures.

"Your favourite film-actors, eh?" All his life he had been a connoisseur of women, and he remembered his humble beginnings as a boy with pictures of actresses pinned above his bed.

"They're writers. And that's . . ." She trailed off, because of course he knew who the third one was.

He picked it up. "I don't know the names of these great lovers. You're the age to remember that. Good-looker, eh?"

"Don't you see who it is?"

He smiled. "Oh, it's Charles." It was the curious smile with which he would greet someone who had reason to avoid him. He put the picture back; straightened it. And then it was at once dismissed from his mind; he went out calling to his wife, "I wish you could get the boy to understand that he must not take my pliers to open jam tins or whatever it is that he does to ruin them . . ."

The picture showed a very young man. His grey eyes were fixed slightly askance on something out of the picture, and although he was not smiling you could make out, under the photographer's "natural" skin tinting, the faint bracket-sign on either side of his mouth that showed that he had smiled or spoken immediately before the camera clicked. The just-concluded movement made a starting-point for her. She willed him to life, speaking to her mother. He spoke to her adoringly. And then, very smoothly and easily, it was she herself to whom the strange young man was speaking, it was she whom he adored.

On rainy afternoons she stared at the face with strange and stirring emotions. The features, the ears, the eyes; she lingered over them tinglingly. Her own eyes would fill luxuriously with tears. I love you, I love you, she incantated passionately. He
68

had taken the place of Beverley Nichols, or the young Evelyn Waugh as painted by Augustus John. They held long conversations in bed at night, and they kissed and kissed in the darkness, drawing up into these kisses all the wildly tender, terrible yearnings that swept through her body and sent her mind racing. She was in love, haunted and hounded by a fearful burden of the flesh although she did not yet have a woman's body to fulfil it with, secreting devotion though she had no one for whom to set it working.

Did she ever admit that the fantasy to which she gave all this was her father? Here Jessie came upon the dreadful innocence of inner life, the life dreamt and not lived, that fills but is for ever confined in the globe of the skull. She knew and did not know that the man with whom she rehearsed both the domestic intimacies she had seen in films, and the erotic intimacies mysteriously hinted at in books and strangely understood somewhere in her body—that this man bore the label "father". The truth was that he was a face, a young face, and she had made the face of love out of him. If there was darkness in the make-believe, it was hidden in the dark nature of make-believe itself. For nothing of all this passion existed in the light of her contact with the "real" world where she shopped and talked with her mother.

There were other things behind the self-composed face of the child who moved among grown-ups as one of themselves, like a little ape who has been taught to blow his nose in a handkerchief and eat with a knife and fork. Confronted with them after so long, Jessie took them up, uncomfortable, puzzled—and then came the stab of identity and recognition. The shape of cold terror that used to impress itself on the back of her neck when she turned her back to the dark passage behind the bathroom door at night, bending to wash her face. Had she ever, in the twenty years or so since then, found out who it was that threatened to come up behind her? Then there was the—even at this stage, an old inhibition came back, and she did not know what name to call it—the business of the electric plugs. She had been afraid to be alone in a room where there were electric plugs because she might be impelled to put her fingers into one and turn on the current. The sight of one, brown, shiny and commonplace, fascinated her horribly, and rising alongside the

69

fascination was an equal fear—the two forces possessed her, but to whom could she cry out? Such things did not exist in the articulate world; "there is nothing there," they came in and said, of the dark. Bruno and her mother had what she humbly accepted were "real" troubles—the grown-up ones of stocks and shares rising and falling, that they discussed in the deep dreamy concentration induced by money, in which their differences were surpassed; and the other grown-up ones of which nothing was said, but that anyone, even a child, could sense, dividing the stream of the house's being in two, so that the very cat, coming in the door, paused electrically.

Love and destruction, life and death, were already possessed of the battleground of the mind and body of the child who sat politely, smoothing her new skirt, or hung on her mother's arm, listening with self-important absorption to talk of dress. The courage that the child must have screwed out of herself to maintain this balance appalled Jessie; how was it possible for a creature to live so secret, so alone? Ignorance, of course, the dreadful certainty, hopelessly accepted, that there is no one, not anywhere in the world, like you.

Was it possible that Morgan was suffering like this?

Yet Jessie was now an adult herself, and she was as inclined as any other to be lulled by the commonplaceness of the child. Morgan with his eternal bat and ball, Morgan jumping up with such prompt eagerness when you sent him off to do some piffling errand. Morgan with a front, of its kind, as bland as her own loved and loving daughterly one had been.

"I should tell Morgan how he comes to have his place with us," she said to Tom.

He was trying to write a difficult letter, and reluctantly he roused himself at the sound of the slow, dead voice she always used when she had made up her mind to do something reckless. He stopped writing, put his elbows on the table and pressed his two thumbs against the sharp edges of his top teeth for a moment. "I don't know what you mean," he said at last.

"Tell him more. More about us. Tell him the truth. Why not? Why shouldn't I admit to him that my marriage to his father wasn't anything like this? Tell him that if his father hadn't been killed the marriage would have ended anyway. He ought to know he hasn't missed anything."

70

"What are you talking about?" He looked at her as if he were about to apprehend a crime.

"Why do people always protect children by keeping them on the surface? That's not the way to do it at all. One ought to let them in on everything and make them strong."

In answer to his silence, she added, "We ought to talk to him more—Boaz said it once."

He gave a little weary snort, dismissing that as something different.

With an effort at reasonableness, he began : "How do you think you can go about it?"

"Find—a—way—to—get—at—him," she said. She saw with a thrill of disappointment that she had stung Tom to concealed alarm. "—Well, what have I said?"

He shrugged. "I think the thing for us to do is to stick to practical plans to occupy Morgan. Ease him on to his own feet . . . that's all."

She felt the exchange falling into the pattern of their two personalities and she made an impulsive attempt to break it. "It may be the thing for you, but not for me." She had never before claimed her relationship as the boy's mother, as opposed to his as a stranger and a stepfather. Morgan was something they had put up with together, as best they could.

But to Tom the sudden change had little to do with her actual feelings about Morgan; he saw it as a well-known sign of what he thought of as the amateurishness of her nature. She would want to have a go at something; the single achievement itself obsessed her, with the amateur's disregard for what ought to have gone before in the form of proper preparation, or what might be expected to come after. She was often a brilliant amateur—it was this aspect of her that he had fallen in love with, reaching out in sure instinct beyond the pleasures of their affair to feel the hot flame of her fearful determination, time and again, to achieve a manoeuvre of her own life. How many human beings had this calm and reckless assumption that their life was in their hands? This quality that had deeply excited him and moved him for ever into her orbit turned out to be also, in the long run of marriage, the one that gave him the most trouble, rather as if he had married for a face and the beauty of it had brought its inevitable pain by attracting other men. What he loved most, he came to like least in her. If she was sometimes brilliant in her disregard for the rules, he had also learnt that she was more often dangerous.

He aimed grimly, "Jessie, don't try to catch Morgan in a bear-hug now."

"You think I'm lying."

"I don't think you're lying. I'm sure you're thinking about Morgan these days in a way you've never done before. I'm simply warning you that you can't foist intimacy on to him now. For Christ's sake! He won't know what to do with it."

She kept feeling tears rise to the brink of her voice, awful, easy tears, and she said dryly, with perfect control, "No, let's send him on a fishing trip instead. Let's think like a school-marm, as you're beginning to do . . ."

SIX

A N OLD MAN sat in a hotel bedroom in the city that night. The room was charged with an alert irritability that emanated from him and his movements and then came back at him, electrically, with the bright yellow light that sprang from the walls. The room was too small for the light and it was too small for him. Luggage, not unpacked, stood around him, bearing dangling airways labels with a flight number scrawled on them, the name "Bruno Fuecht" and the destination, "Zurich". He stood in the middle of the room in the concentration of one possessed by what is going on in his own mind, and ceaselessly it went out toward the walls and beat back upon him again. He went to the telephone beside the bed and snapped some enquiry into it, first bringing himself to the state of communication with the world by a sharp cough and a tremor of effort that moved his head unsteadily. He waited, holding the receiver, and the middle finger of his other hand beat jerkily on his knee. He got the information he wanted, and made another request; at last, he heard the telephone ringing in a house he had never seen.

The Stilwells were in the becalmed state that follows a quarrel, when the telephone rang. The quarrel over Morgan had dragged on into a deadly examination of the dissatisfactions and burdens of their daily life, that each took as the unsaid reproach of the other. Each felt the other was known to the bone; there was no possibility that a sudden turn of courage, of frivolity, even, might reveal itself unexpectedly in one of them, and so restore something of the mystery to life itself.

Tom went slowly to the telephone. "Here is Fuecht. Fuecht. Who is speaking?" The voice ended in a crackle.

Tom did not catch the name properly. "This is Tom Stilwell. Who is it you want?"

"This is Fuecht," the voice came back sternly. "I'm speaking

73

from the Queen's Hotel. I was on my way to Europe and the plane is delayed. They brought me to town and gave me a room. Listen, my plane doesn't go till two o'clock." "Mr. Fuecht! That's unexpected." Tom had the embarrassed, disbelieving tone of someone unfairly singled out by a man who had never before paid him any attention. "Can you see me?" the voice insisted. "Couldn't you come into town? I'm at the Queen's Hotel and I'll only be here a few hours, I'm on my way to Europe. You've got a car, eh, Stilwell?"

"Well, the trouble is, it's rather late."

There was a strangely stirring silence on the other end of the telephone.

Why should a man who hardly knew him put such pressure on him? Tom said, "Just hold on a minute, will you, I'll speak to Jessie. Do you mind?" There was some sort of sound of assent.

He went back into the living-room where she was lying face-down on the divan. "Have you heard anything from your mother? Anything you haven't told me? That's Fuecht."

Jessie stayed quite still for a moment, and then she turned round and sat up, all in one movement. "It's Fuecht?" The skin under her eyes seemed to tighten, as it did when she was afraid. "I ought to stop answering the phone altogether," he said, with a feeble attempt at a joke.

"Fuecht?"

"Yes, at the Queen's. He's phoning from there. He says he's on his way to Europe and the plane's been delayed."

She nodded. "Well, that's that. He's threatened my mother for weeks that he'd go." She sat stiffly.

"What shall I tell him? He wants us to go to the hotel. The plane doesn't leave till two."

There was a moment's silence. "I won't go," she said. "Does he mean me?"

The coldness of the quarrel stirred again faintly. "I suppose so. Why should he want to see me? I hardly know him. I don't suppose I've seen him more than three times."

Jessie gave a strange, set, painful blink, like the cringe of an old woman. Tom felt unease, an outsider to the silence between the man on the telephone and the woman bolt upright on the divan. He said, trying to be of use, "D'you want me to go?"

"I won't go," she said, and sat running the nail of her fore-finger rapidly under the nails of her other hand.

He went back to the telephone. "Hello? Mr. Fuecht, I'll be there in about half an hour. Jessie's in bed already. Where will you be?" "In the room," came the voice, suddenly strong— Tom did not know whether it was the telephone, but the voice seemed to fade and rise to strength, intermittently. "Number a hundred and ninety-six, it's on the second floor. I won't go from the room."

Tom drove to town subdued but not too unwilling. A quarrel is better rounded off than left in the air, a miasma. He was doing something now that he wouldn't be doing if he were not Jessie's husband; the relationship was quietly validated by this per-formance of a piece of family business. It was a token perform-ance, of course, just as Bruno Fuecht was a token relative.

Tom had always thought that Fuecht was a strange, foreign choice to have been made by Jessie's mother; the explanation that he was the best friend of Jessie's own father, who had died when she was younger than Elisabeth, certainly seemed the only possible justification. Mrs. Fuecht had the cynical pride of bearing of the woman who has set herself to live out the length of an unhappy marriage. Where Jessie was careless of her appearance, and, in her late thirties, already no longer beautiful, Mrs. Fuecht, at nearly seventy, was dressed in the perfection of cut and matched colour that demands unflagging concentration on one's own person. Tom had never seen her without a hat. Even in her own house, she looked perpetually like a visitor dressed for some occasion to which nobody else has been invited.

"Why is she so cold," he had asked Jessie sometime, struck, on meeting the woman again, with this quality in her. "She loathes Fuecht," said Jessie simply. "She's frozen into the state of living in the same house with him."

Mrs. Fuecht had never been happy with the man, but since he had got old he had become demoniacal. From the coast, where they lived in retirement, came reports, year after year, of his moodiness, his contrariness, his downright devilishness. He was ill and quarrelled with his doctors. He made it impossible to keep servants for longer than a few days at a time. He brooded and threatened to sell up his excellent investments. And when, Jessie said, he had stilled her mother to a state of tight-lipped, despairing consternation at his recklessness—he suddenly burst out laughing in her face, as if all of it, everything, from the refusal to take his medicine to the threats to their security, had been directed to this one end : to make a fool of her.

Tom wondered, from time to time—with the impatience one feels toward other people's troubles—why the old woman hadn't left Fuecht long ago. He meant to ask her, just as a matter of curiosity; but somehow, once in her presence, he never felt himself taken sufficient account of to be allowed such a question.

He accepted that Jessie's relationship with her mother was an odd one, to say the least of it. Apparently she had felt herself passionately dependent on her mother as a child and girl; as a woman, she understood that the truth was that her mother had been passionately and ruthlessly dependent on her. It was clear that her mother had clipped her wings and brain-washed her, to keep her near—the story about the heart trouble was a pretty dreadful one, if you really took a look at it. Before Morgan was born, Jessie had gone to a heart specialist to see if the old ailment had left any weakness that might make a normal birth dangerous for her, and he had told her with emphatic quiet that not only was her heart perfectly normal, but in fact it was not possible that a heart ailment serious enough to keep a child out of school for years could leave no sign of past damage . . . No, better not look into that at all. Jessie told him that as a child she had believed that her mother loved her more than other mothers loved their children. As she had come to understand, through her feelings for her husband and her own children, the free nature of love, her fascinated resentment toward her mother had grown proportionately; yet she supported the woman, at a distance of five or six hundred miles, against Fuecht.

The situation—comfortably chronic and fortunately far away —was doubly foreign to Tom, first because he himself was fond of his old father (a retired doctor who gardened or smoked a pipe on the verandah while he gazed peacefully at the result of his labours) and secondly because there *was* something foreign, in the national sense, about it. As Bruno Fuecht had grown older and more difficult he seemed to have become more and more markedly a stranger in South Africa; his thirty or forty years as a chemist on the South African mines were brushed away and his foreign identity—a Swiss German, a man of Europe—reasserted itself. Yes, Fuecht was unmistakeably foreign, and the emotions of the situation he created about himself were foreign—the theatrical behaviour, the air of aged defiance, the melodrama, for example, of this sudden arrival in Johannesburg. Last week, a letter from Mrs. Fuecht saying that he had gone into a nursing home for observation, this week he's off to Switzerland. What was the sense in hitting out like this, once you were old?

Tom approached the Queen's Hotel with a set mood of almost professional patience—like a paid mourner at a funeral—that did not touch himself. The Monday night streets of the city gaped; there were only a few black men, looking long and steadily into the windows of the outfitters'. The Queen's had the cold sour smell of a drinking hotel—it was not a place where people went to dine or to live. Two or three tables in the bar lounge held up the elbows of men in striped blazers—perhaps some visiting bowlers' team—and an elderly tart was arguing in drunken dead seriousness between two men, in a dingy corner.

When you have your home in a city, it is always a shock to enter the brutal homelessness of a place like this; Tom forgot, for stretches of years on end, that such places exist and are part of the true character of all cities. He went to the desk where a night porter with the deeply suspicious face of his kind picked up a telephone without a word when Fuecht's name was pronounced. While he waited for the phone to be answered, the man moved his left hand strongly over his face, pushing his eyebrows up out of line and then down, rubbing his nose sideways, pulling over his mouth and chin, like the rough tongue of some animal going over its young.

"Second floor. One-nine-six."

Tom went up in the lift, and, with the sense of being let deeper and deeper into places where neither dark nor daylight exists, but only the light of single bulbs gathered like beads of sweat on the ceiling, came out into a passage. Past doors and more doors; before he knocked, it seemed, the door opened, and there was a blazingly-lit room, yellow-walled, with the luggage heaped, as it had been dumped down, in the middle, and the

77

figure of an old man drawn up like an exclamation point before it.

They looked, man and luggage, ready to take off for anywhere. The visitor was ready to back away before them.

"So I wait," said Fuecht, without any greeting. "They will come for me soon."

Tom would not have known him if he had seen him in the street. Was he really unrecognisable? He walked into the room and sat on the bed, under the chandelier that had been meant for grandeur and shone as a merciless inquisition of glare. No, Fuecht must be changed. He couldn't possibly have looked like that; the way he looked was not something that could last for years.

He was ill, of course. But it wasn't that. It wasn't just the usual old men's symptoms of the collar grown too big, the hollow, delicate-looking as the skin over an infant's fontanelle, in front of each bloodless ear. He was blazing behind his line of tight mouth, behind his dark eyes made dominating, in the diminishing face, by his magnifying glasses; he was blazing like the chandelier. Something—a pulse, a convulsive swallowing —agitated all the time in the thin turkey-fold that connected his chin to his adam's-apple.

"They told me a wait of forty-five minutes," he was saying, without a pause. He gave the little unpleasant smile of a man who knows better than to expect efficiency in matters that are out of his hands. "I should get off the plane from Port Elizabeth and then go straight through the customs and so on to the plane for Europe. That was the information. No one would have known. You would not have heard from me, eh? I would have been," he threw up his unsteady hands like a drowning man, but in triumph, "many miles away by now."

"It's very annoying to be delayed," said Tom, but his eyes were on the luggage. "When did you decide to go to Switzerland?"

"Yes! I should have been gone!" The old man took a swift turn about the room. He checked himself abruptly; he moved with the incalculable rushes of a faulty clockwork toy, that jerks into action, moves with wild nimbleness, and then just as suddenly runs down and is arrested feebly in the middle of an uncompleted movement. He laughed, "Switzerland! Yes, begin with Zurich. I was a boy there, a young man, living as young

78

men live. Zurich to begin with, but I won't stay. Don't think I'll stay! I'm not crawling back to Zurich to . . ." He stopped. A close look came over his face, it was not so much as if he had lost the thread of what he was saying as that he had found himself saying something unexpected, something that lay in his mind ignored. He went on, "There are plenty of places in Europe where you can live, still. Well, I should have been gone already, I should have been on the way, eh?" He sat down suddenly, gleeful, shaken, on the chair.

A waiter came in with whisky and soda, that Fuecht must have ordered to be brought when his guest arrived. While the man was in the room, the old man did not speak, and had a curious air of impatient resentment. When the waiter had withdrawn, he made sure the door was properly closed behind the man, and then handed Tom a drink : "Whisky is all right, eh?"

"And Mrs. Fuecht—?" said Tom.

The old man drew the whisky round his mouth and then put the glass away from him. "I'll tell you something," he said. "When she wakes up, she'll find there isn't a penny. I've got all my money out. Here, in my pocket—here's a cheque book for the Zurich bank. I've taken it all out. There are ways, you understand. I know people, I managed it—never mind. It's all there. All I have to do is write out a cheque."

"It sounds as if someone's going to have a good time." It was impossible to remedy this conversation in which both were talking of different things, although their remarks appeared to follow one on the other in the parody of communication. Oddly, Tom was reminded of times when, talking to Jessie, he became aware that they were not talking about the same thing; she sometimes went through the motions of communication with her lips, while what she really was doing was to hug further and further into herself what it was she had to communicate.

"I'm sorry about Jessie. She wanted to come, she would've . . ."

Suddenly the old man seemed to realise Tom's presence; he smiled a slow, grudging recognition, and the lie lay exposed between them.

The old man took up his glass of whisky and finished it at a gulp, getting it over with, like medicine, and his other hand was raised, calling for attention, promising. "*She* doesn't know I've gone, and when she finds out—well, too late! That's all."

79

"Jessie had a letter from her last week. She said you were in a nursing home."

"That's all right!" said the old man, swaggeringly, grim, shrugging. "That's right! They wanted me in a nursing home. But I tell you"—he stopped and leant forward as he might have done if he had wanted to use the name of someone with whom he had entered into conversation in a bar, only to remember that the man was a nameless stranger to him—"I tell you, they won't get a penny from me, just the same! I'm going to spend it all. D'you follow me? I may not be young, but I've got money, and a man with money is never lonely. There'll be women—you understand? I'm not finished with it all yet!"

His voice rose powerfully, as it had on the telephone, and came ringing back from the four walls of the room, shocking, so that it silenced even himself.

He sat back in his chair, fixing his eyes on Stilwell angrily. He looked once or twice round the room, like the circus lion puzzled and restless on its painted barrel. And then he said again: "Women. There are women who won't say no to my money."

The middle finger of his left hand beat continuously against the chair-arm. Tom saw him notice it out of the corner of his eye, as an animal looks up, helpless, to see its rump twitch against the attentions of a fly.

Tom spoke. "I wonder if you're well enough to go."

The old man's mind darted at once to the real meaning of this. "What's the use to stop me," he said. "I've told you, there's not a penny here. And she can never get it into the country again without my signature. I'm not going to be buried yet."

Some hostility stirred between them. "Jessie should have come," said Tom, almost crossly.

"They will get nothing, either of them."

"Mr. Fuecht, you must know that Jessie has never had any hopes about your money."

"I didn't expect her to come. She's never been much like a daughter. Well, that's an old story. Never mind."

Tom smiled. "Well, she's only a stepdaughter."

"Yes, her mother kept that up. For the memory of poor Charles, she said. We both loved poor Charles. Only she couldn't have loved him so much, could she? Eh?"

Tom was bewildered by the old man's wry grin, the surly, sly self-contempt that sounded in his voice.

"Charles?"

" 'Charles' !"

"Jessie's father?"

The old man nodded with exaggerated vociferousness, like someone satisfying a child with a careless lie. "All right, Jessie's father. My friend Charles. Only I couldn't have been such a good friend, after all, eh? She makes a great fuss, she bursts in tears when I bring up the name of Charles. Because we both loved Charles, she says. What's the difference; the girl and I never had much to say to each other, anyway." His mind turned back rapidly to the obsession of the present; he looked at his watch for the fourth time since Tom had come in, and said, with the fierce satisfaction of time passing : "Tell them what you like. Tell *her* what I said about going to Zurich and what I'm going to do. She'll be on the telephone tomorrow. You'll see. Well, you can tell her I've gone—what you like—you understand? You tell her I'm not finished yet."

Tom suggested that they should phone the airline and find out when the plane was expected to be ready to leave; the truth was, he felt he could not stand waiting shut up in the hotel with the old man indefinitely, and a drive to the airport would fill in part of the time. When Tom could decently say that they had better start off, Fuecht watched with glittering eyes while the luggage was being carried from the room. Then, with one strange look round it, a curious look of blind courage, he snapped off the blazing light and walked out.

He did not speak in the car going to the airport. He seemed exhausted, or resting, or husbanding himself through the drive in the dark. At the airport he became talkative again; the strength of his desire to be gone, the desperate glee of his going, trembled through his body ecstatically. Now and then he said : "Let them both look for me. Not a penny. Not a penny. I'm going to spend the lot, you understand."

At last he was called. The number of his flight echoed and re-echoed through the airport halls, and Tom watched him walk down the brightly-lit ramp to the dark runway. He did not look back or wave. He walked slowly but the extreme lightness of his body, hardly there at all inside the tailor's shape, suddenly came to the young man watching. Tom noticed for the first time that he was immaculately dressed, like a corpse laid out in new clothing for its long journey. There was a moment's last glimpse of the face; the mouth was stiff, a little open, the eyes looked straight ahead into the dark. Then the figure came out in the stream of light from the aircraft, and was seen climbing, through the shafts of moted light, up the gangway.

Jessie woke the instant Tom moved into the room. She put up her hand and turned on the light, full in his eyes. Frowning, he moved the lamp's neck.

He began to describe to her how the old man had been, standing with his luggage, ready to go, in the hotel room. He did not know how to convey the queerness, the dread, the sickness, defiance—madness, perhaps, in that room. But she seemed to know at once exactly what he had found there. She pressed her fist into her cheek and cried out, from something in herself : "He still wants to live ! Isn't it terrible ? He still wants to live !"

Tom's mind turned, like the needle of a compass coming to the north, to one utterance among all the nightmare mutterings of that night. "She's never been much like a daughter." There it was; he could not leave it alone. It rose out of the jumble of ravings, boastings, imprecations.

Other phrases came to join it. "Only she couldn't have loved him so much, could she ?"

What else had the old man said ? Suddenly, because it became important to Tom to remember that part of the evening, he could not; it was all muddled up with the other things that sounded through his head in the old man's voice. "Jessie's only a stepdaughter"—he could hear himself offering, platitudinous, soothing; he had been so busy treating the old man like an invalid or a lunatic that he had not listened properly. What was it the old man had said ? "That was kept up, of course" or "Her mother kept that up"—something like that. Again and again Tom sounded the same note, like a piano tuner looking for true pitch : "The memory of poor Charles . . . only she couldn't have loved him so much, could she ?"

He watched Jessie when she was unaware. What would it mean to her if she knew that she was Bruno's daughter ? Was she Bruno's daughter? And at times it seemed to him : she knows she is really his daughter. It would be like her mother to have told her, when she was a young girl, perhaps, or half-child, half-girl, and to have made her see at the same time the necessity for conspiracy to conceal the fact, for her mother's sake.

He felt an obscure danger in the possibility of asking her. Suppose she did not know? Suppose it was true and she had never known?

Days went by and soon he knew he would never ask her. He would never tell her the things Fuecht had said; or seemed to say. Yet he continued to think about it all, to be aware of this twilight tunnel of his wife's life, walled-up, lost and over-grown, an extension of herself, hidden, or perhaps unknown to her.

A week later they knew that Bruno Fuecht was dead. He had died in a hospital in Rome. They never knew why he had left Zurich. Of course, he had not taken "every penny" with him, after all; he had transferred considerable sums to Switzerland, but there were still a number of investments and a substantial sum of money in South Africa. His mental state must have been such that he believed he had done what he had said; or perhaps this discovery, after his death, was contrived as just such another malicious laugh as he had sometimes had at his wife's expense when he was alive?

Mrs. Fuecht was in the Stilwell house, come upon strangely, at all hours of the day, sitting on the verandah, or in a corner of the empty living-room, with her hat on. She had arrived from Port Elizabeth two days after Fuecht disappeared. Jessie treated her with quiet consideration; it was understood that, although she could not be said to be bereaved, she was certainly more alone. She had outlived two husbands, and was old. The two women talked of Bruno Fuecht as of some practical problem, a condition of life that had existed, and that, in its passing, had left things a certain way; there were ends to tie up.

"I wonder if it would be best to sell his car in Port Elizabeth or have it railed up here."

"He'd had it reconditioned just the month before last. Heaven knows why, if he was going away. New seats, all real leather. I don't suppose it'll fetch anything."

But Tom, coming upon mother and daughter talking like

this, as he often did during those days, was filled with tenderness for Jessie. He was overwhelmed with pity for the lack of grief in this death. He sat on the verandah with the two women night after night, and their quiet words fell upon him like stones. Suddenly one evening he found it in himself to ask—an impulse of curiosity, idly remembered—"Bruno Fuecht—why did you never leave him, I often wondered?"

Mrs. Fuecht said without a pause, "I gave him my whole life; I did not think I could let myself lose his money, as well."

There was a silence; if the jangle of the dinner-bell, that Elisabeth was ringing for Agatha, had not broken it, it might have gone on for ever—there seemed to be no words that could have ended it. Tom touched his wife, and she turned, awake, with a slight smile. They rose like lovers; for lately the sense of strangeness that one being has for another had come back between them.

Mrs. Fuecht went home to the coast to settle her affairs. Jessie felt that an immeasurable lapse of time separated her from the friendly comings and goings, the odd hours and long gossips of her days at the Agency office. Her job in the suburbs and the presence of her mother in the house had kept her away from familiar haunts. The arrival of Fuecht, that night, was something she seemed to have called up from the descent into the past that Morgan had forced upon her. The man had come and gone, and she had not seen him; would never see him again. Yet the shock of his coming *when he did* had established a connection. The connection existed in her mind alongside the answer that her mother had made to Tom's queer question : "I had given him my whole life; I did not think I could let myself lose his money, as well." The past rose to the surface of the present, free of the ambiguities and softening evasions that had made it possible in the living. Her mother spoke as someone who has accomplished her life, however bitterly. Nothing could be more extraordinary to Jessie than the discovery that, however remotely differently arrived at, this, her own need, had existed in her mother.

A day or two after Mrs. Fuecht had gone, she left the nursing-home office at one and went to the western end of town to her old lunching-place, the Lucky Star. She had not been there for six weeks or more; there was the old smell of curry and chips, and the board in the doorway still said, "Try our famous Eastern delicacies, grills and boerewors." Uncle Jack, the proprietor said, "How've you been—that's nice," as he always did, his sad Levantine face, produced by some alchemy of white, Indian, Malay and probably African blood, appearing to look up from his little gambler's notebook, but not pausing in his calculations, and she turned to the tables with convalescent ease, ready to sit placidly over lunch with whoever was there that she knew. It was then that she noticed Ann, facing her at a table in one of the booths, with Len Mafolo's back to the room. She went over to them and as she did she saw that the man was not Len. "Just push my things on to the floor" Ann's face was flung up at her, brilliant. "Will you have a delicious coke, that's what we're drinking." "Pretty heady stuff. Wait, I'll order some more," the man said, swivelling round in his seat to summon one of the Indian waiters, and Jessie recognised Gideon Shibalo, the schoolteacher, the painter. They had met somewhere, years ago.

She doubted if Shibalo could have remembered her; yet Ann talked to them both as if they had known each other intimately for a long time. "You'll be relieved to hear that we won't have to trot out those same two old pictures of his on our next exhibition —she's one of your most faithful deplorers," she added, to Shibalo. They might be drinking coke now, but they had been drinking brandy. There was a heightened tempo about them that made Jessie aware that she was too sober.

"As long as she's faithful, that's what matters." Shibalo had a low, chuckling, snickering private laugh, with which he prefaced such remarks; it was directed at himself. His yellow-brown face, older than he was, had little whorls of uneven black wool sticking here and there between chin and ear—perhaps not a beard, but laziness about shaving over the past few days. He was dressed in a shabby way that suited him, with a red and black checked flannelette shirt, and the end of his trousers' waistband tucked in against his belly.

"What sort of things are you doing?" Jessie asked.

"Come and see." He woke up to the full plate in front of him, began to press and turn the rice and meat with his fork as if it were some plastic material rather than something meant to go into his mouth.

"Still the knotty stick-shapes and the sky with dust hanging in the air?"

He smiled in acknowledgement. "Ah, that's out." He put down the fork after a mouthful or two and took out a cigarette. "I'm in a different mood, these days. I hadn't painted for so long my fingers creak." He clasped his hands and cracked the joints.

"Serve you right," said Ann, taking a cigarette from him and beckoning for the matches : *"Please!"* "Oh, sorry !" They smiled at each other. While Ann talked and ate she kept looking out round the room, neck held high, excited and assertive. "Len thinks we can get a bigger caravan. Not borrowed, but hired. We'll use it part of the time, and we'll let it to the Boys' Club, and things like that, to cover the cost."

"Pity you can't buy one. We'd hire it from you to go on holiday—Tom wants to go to Pondoland in July . . ."

They talked trivialities with ease, but from the moment she saw Gideon Shibalo's face Jessie had become aware of a sense of intrusion so strong that she felt it physically—her hands were awkward as she used her knife and fork. She talked, but she was in retreat behind every word as if to efface herself from the company.

She did not wait for coffee. "Oh Jessie," Ann was quite effusive, "would you find out from Agatha whether my blue dress is back from the cleaner's? And if not, would you be a dear and phone them about it?" The sudden request had the trumped-up ring of the little chores that Jessie herself often invented to distract one of the children.

"Of course. —I'll look forward to seeing the new Shibalo," she said to the man.

"You won't like it." —In the superior way that painters refer to a new trend in their work.

The open street, jagged with light, and small hard shadows of a hot day, broke upon her. They're lovers; they're lovers : she thought, and felt herself abruptly returned to the life around her, that had been going on all the time.

PART TWO

SEVEN

Ann Davis had not thought, when she left England, that she would be spending much time in Johannesburg. She enjoyed the feeling that she had left behind the risk of the Chelsea flat or Hampstead or Kensington house from which so many of her friends looked out, captured, unlikely to get at the world. Marrying Boaz, she had been admitted to the select band who returned only at intervals from teaching jobs in Ghana, study grants in America, or one of those world organisations, born of United Nations, that seek to make deserts bloom here, and limit teeming population there, in the more fatalistic wilderness of the earth. She thought of herself as lucky; and no one could suggest, even, that a return to South Africa, for Boaz, was a condonement of the white man's way of life there, for he was returning only to do something that could not be done anywhere else—to study the black man's music, part of the heritage that was becoming as much of a cult as it had once been culturally discounted. This was important to her, socially; she accepted it just as, if she had belonged to another set and another time, she would have accepted that it did not do to be in trade. She was not really concerned with politics. The surge of feeling against the barriers of colour was the ethos of the decade in which she had grown up; her participation in it was a substitute for patriotism rather than a revolt. She had no lasting feelings about the abstractions of injustice; like many healthy and more or less beautiful women, she could only be fired to pity or indignation by what she saw with her own eyes.

The field-trips with Boaz had not been a disappointment to her. She was seldom disappointed, anyway, but the very freshness that all things had for her tempted her away lightly from one to another. She played happily with the Pedi children, making stick boats to sail in the muddy river, and she got on well with the women despite the language difficulty. She had an intelligent grasp of the fundamental pattern of tribal life that the people tried to confuse—through secrecy, shyness, or a mistaken desire to please—before the eyes of strangers, and her good memory was often a help to Boaz. When she sat in the tent, under the lamp's circling galaxy of insects, making fair copies of his sketch-notes of musical instruments, he was aware of no difference between her absorbed interest and his own. But the fact was that the day's task was sufficient to her, while for him it stretched on to the distant end of his life, old age or death would interrupt him at it . . .

She began to stay behind in Johannesburg more and more, simply because there were so many things she was asked to do, and they were all new to her, just as the field-trips had been. The idea of living in the bush was somehow never unpacked, like one of those apparently essential garments that turn out not to be needed for the climate after all. When Boaz came home for a weekend, there was so much to tell him—they lay awake for hours, smoking in bed. He smiled in the dark and stroked her smooth, cool arm while she talked.

Patrick, their photographer friend, and his wife Dodo were a pair whose enthusiasms bloomed like daisies—hardly a week went by when she was not caught up in their activities, which invariably concerned some rearrangement of the physical world that contained them. They dug a swimming pool or knocked a wall down, lugged rocks for the garden, and swopped a two-seater for an old caravan; the house they lived in, the disposition of walls and chairs, car, trees and even landscape—these stood around them like a set of blocks that, in the hands of children, is constantly changing shape. Ann joined in this game of house with enthusiasm, enjoying the dirt and the mess and the picnicking that accompany amateur undertakings. She often thought that it would have been fun if she and Boaz could have lived with Patrick and Dodo instead of with the Stilwells, but of course Boaz thought the earth of the Stilwells. It didn't much matter, anyway. She was free to do as she pleased and the Stilwells, nice enough in their way, did not bother her. Although she got on well with Jessie down at the Agency—indeed, it was through Jessie that she had got to know Len and thereafter, through Len, the city world of young black men and girls where she found herself so pleasantly accepted—Jessie at home was often, so to speak, out of sight for her. Just as, in a musical work, there may be whole phrases that are out of the range of your understanding for one stage of your life at least, if not for ever, so there are sometimes people whom some stage in one's own life, or composition of one's own self-hood, prevents one from following all the way. Ann saw the Stilwells' life as a set of circumstances—children, the queer elder kid from some other marriage, ugly old house, not enough money. There it was, remote as old age. She did not think of it as something that had begun somewhere different and might be becoming something different. The present was the only dimension of time she knew; she woke every day to *her* freedom of it.

It was awful the way Jessie appeared sometimes, like a ruin. She could still look attractive, when she took the trouble. She did not seem to know or care that at times her face was stripped, more brutally than the gradual methods of ageing would ever come, finally, to do it, by the violence of the spirit over the flesh. There was always a great to-do, in a delayed-action, muffled sort of way, over anything that happened in the house—queer things did seem to happen to the Stilwells, like the arrival of the old man, that night, and then his dying somewhere in Europe, but even quite ordinary incidents did not pass off and get forgotten in the usual way. Most of the time, she, Ann, really could not say what it was all about. Some incident that would appear to bear no particular weight at the time, and that, if she noticed it at all, was out of mind next day, would apparently lie gathering force in some dusty corner of the shabby old house until one day, coming in out of the sunny world outside, the girl would suddenly become aware of a great rumbling disturbance passing through the human conduction system of the house—snatches of talk, looks exchanged—and would be astonished to recognise the tiny motif of the forgotten incident, now fully orchestrated. Who did this? Jessie, she supposed. Who else? Not much interested in the whole business, there was still a feminine tartness in this uncritical conclusion of Ann's. Once Jessie's attention was on something quite ordinary, it was lit with fancy lighting. There were shadows denser than objects and the gauze curtain of appearances melted away ... If Jessie hadn't looked at it, you would never have seen it like that. The evening she, Ann, had walked into the fuss over the kid Morgan—the way Jessie called out what had happened in that intense, ringing voice : she made you feel she expected something, some response that you didn't have. Honestly, one did not know what to say to her. It simply didn't seem very terrible that the poor kid slipped out to go dancing; only funny, because he was so nondescript. And, of course, it all blew over in a day or two.

The Stilwells' friends and such of Boaz's old friends whose affinity with him had survived a ten years' absence provided her with the sort of company she was used to in England, but it was Len Mafolo who let her into company where she could shine. When she walked in among his white and black bachelor friends and their girls, it was as if she had been expected. With her looks, her kind of liveliness, her impatience with the limitations of a mapped-out way of life, and her background with Boaz, she would not have fitted in with the night-club and country-club set of the rich white suburbs; and among the office drab of people who mixed with blacks on a philanthropic, religious or political basis she would have been a note of scarlet. But among the show people, whose spendthrift vitality she could match, and the small group of black men who found life most approachable late at night, through talk, through music, through drink, and in the company of whites like themselves, she was at home.

For she was that new being—beginning to appear, here and there—for whom the black man in a white city waited. In her, the kicks and the snubs and the vengefulness and the hate met, complemented and merged with each other, two terrible halves of the vicious circle become whole, and healed. She was white, top-class beauty, young; young and beautiful enough for the richest and most privileged white man. She was not a woman who could not find a white man, nor was she one of the nuts, hankering for a black man as a shameful sexual aberration. Neither did she merely offer friendship, understanding, and fellow-feeling. The truth was, she looked the kind of girl who would call you Jim Fish, but dancing with her, sitting talking to her, you were man to her woman. The laws had not changed, the pass was still in your pocket; this simple miracle happened in spite of these things and far beyond them, in a realm where their repeal would have been powerless to release you anyway. It was not worth much—yet it was beyond price.

Ann took an innocent pleasure in her success. When she pushed her way into a crowded township room admiration and attention turned on her, warmly, familiarly, with all the jokes and liberty-taking that go with appropriation. There were one or two other white girls like her; not slumming, but full of joy, they could dance nearly as well as the black girls. But Ann quickly became as good as the best of the black girls; like them, she could dance with her whole body and use muscles that most white women do not know are theirs to command. Sometimes the other dancers would fall back around her and the young man who was feeling the aura of her shape in the air as they circled and stalked each other. A thrilling awareness of movement caught up the spectators, as if they suddenly could feel the world turning them in space. "Great kid! She's terrific, this girl," they would tell her, patronising, celebrating. The repetitive music, the coming and going of people, the animation of movement and the passivity of being available to whoever drew her into the dance made her tireless. She could have danced until she dropped. Once, on a Sunday afternoon when she had gone with Boaz and Len to have tea with his sister in her respectable Orlando house, she drew Boaz with her into a group dancing round a couple of penny whistle piccanins in the yard outside. The gathering spread into the township street and a journalist on a black paper got a picture of her, a white face whirling, and Boaz, knees splayed, among the crowd.

Len Mafolo was not much of a dancer but he liked to talk, comfortably shut in by music and noise. He would be in the same corner from nine or ten until one in the morning, drinking, but not too much, and arguing in a slow, lofty way, as if for him getting at the truth was like picking one's way breath-holdingly, toe-hold by toe-hold, down from some dizzy spire on which one found oneself stranded. He had almost at once forgiven Ann for going to the mine dances; it was a joke between them now. He understood her not very fastidious enthusiasm for anything new to her, and she understood his distaste for tribalism. He described her as a "wonderful kid" : with a pause and a shrugging snort to follow the impossibility of defining her. He liked white girls because those he knew were good to talk to as well as beautiful; *she* was also extraordinarily easy to work with, undiscouraged by the slowness and difficulty of getting people beyond the planning stage, tackling everything without fear of failure because she found it fun. "Don't be so limp, Len," she would say, fretting at his pessimistic objections.

The idea of taking round an exhibition of African paintings and sculpture—that was something he had been talking about for years, ever since he'd been a clerk at the Institute of Race Relations and had been put on to packing orders for their special Christmas cards every year. But the moment he talked to Ann about it, it began to take shape out of all sorts of impossibilities. There were not enough halls, particularly on the Reef, where the exhibition could be seen by white as well as black; "I tell you what—you need a caravan!" she said, "We'll borrow Patrick's—that's it! They've just traded in their station wagon for a caravan." And when he objected : "Who's going to drive the thing around?" "Us!" she said, "You and I, of course."

And so the impossibilities were changed, one by one. She was marvellous with the people they got to exhibit, too; if someone sent in something disappointing, she would stand looking at it with Len, and just as he was ready to say he supposed it was all right, an obstinate look would come over the bottom half of her face : "Let's go and see him and make him dig up something better. Where does he live? Let's go now—"

She called Mafolo "old Len" : the epithet for the childhood companion, the family friend . . . He got used to her, but sometimes when he looked at her and saw how she was like some lovely creature in its glossy coat, perfectly equal to its environment, he was seized with anxiety and hope. It was almost as if he were already reproaching himself for having missed something that, at the same time, he really knew never would be offered him.

The caravan exhibition was exactly the sort of venture that occupied Ann most happily. She knew a little bit about displaying works of art—in the fashionable sack-cloth-and-space way—because, although she did not take her attempts at various careers seriously, it was true that she had worked for a time in a small London gallery. She flew in and out of the house for nails, boxes, lengths of rope—all kinds of things—during the preparation of the exhibition. She was always running into Mrs. Fuecht, Jessie's mother (who was in the house at the time), with the sort of object in her hands that must have appeared to require an explanation—the bathroom mirror, once, and another time a cooking-pot with an old sheet bubbling away inside it in a soup of purplish dye. The old lady showed no surprise, however—she was quite a surprise to come upon suddenly, oneself : rather an impressive old lady, slightly dotty, with the tragedy-queen air that Ann noticed often hung about aged women who were probably very attractive when young and who had given the greater part of their energies to love. "Your mother has been a beauty; she must have had lots of lovers, I suppose," Ann said to Jessie. But Jessie laughed, and said in that menacing way of hers : "No, she was in love with me." Perhaps Jessie was jealous of the old lady; certainly she had none of the old lady's air. Ann always stopped, in passing, to exchange a few words with her; at least, that was what appeared to happen; what was really exchanged was a brief kindling of each other's beauty, a flutter of recognition across fifty years. Once, the old lady seemed on the brink of beginning to talk to her—but it was not possible, that day. And one day her visit blew over, too, and she was gone.

Ann met Gideon Shibalo when she and Len were invited to take their travelling art exhibition round African, Indian and Coloured high schools. She had heard all about him before, of course; he was the man whose painting had attracted attention overseas and won him a scholarship to work in Italy, but he hadn't been able to take it up because the South African Government refused him a passport—he was involved in politics, the African National Congress movement. He came in during the school break and stood looking at his two pictures with the removed yet fascinated air with which one glances through an old photograph album. "Talented chap," said Len, at his elbow.

"That's a fact." They burst into laughter and pushed each other about a little.

"My partner in crime," Len indicated Ann.

"Again and again, I've wanted to see if we couldn't get something more from you," she said to Shibalo, "but he said it was hopeless, you don't paint any more."

Shibalo chuckled, considering himself. "Hopeless. Quite right." He and Len had an exchange, punctuated by laughter, in Sesuto. "You should have come to see me anyway." Shibalo turned to Ann.

"Why?" she said cheerfully. "Any hope? We'll come if you've got something for us, any time."

"I've put away childish things," he said.

"Don't you worry, he can still knock out a picture if he wants to," Len encouraged and reproached, resentfully.

"Do you dislike being probed about not painting, or do you enjoy it?"

They all laughed. "Good God, I live on it. Where has my inspiration gone? Don't I feel light, shape, colour, thickness, thinness, what-not? Don't I want to express the soul of Africa? Don't I want to make the line vibrate? Don't my guts wriggle and send new forms to my finger-tips? That chap Gauguin started at forty, I've stopped long before."

He scarcely looked at the other pieces of painting and sculpture that Len and Ann were modestly proud of, and when he sat drinking coffee with them remarked that the exhibition was really "a waste of time". "The shock of modern art—we don't need it around here, man. You can't shock my kids in there, in my class we've got three who smoke dagga, and two pregnant. Not bad, eh? And they're not even in matric yet."

"Sounds like a very advanced class," said Len to Ann.

She wagged her head : "He's done wonders with them."

But Shibalo's tone changed suddenly and obstinately; he stood up now, apparently bored, and made some excuse to leave. "The ah—the headmaster wants to talk to me. I promised to drop in. About sports day." He didn't seem to care about them being aware that he was lying; he looked the last man in the world any headmaster would choose to organise a sports day.

As he left he said : "I might change my mind."

"About what?" said Len.

"Painting something."

"Oh, really?" said Ann.

"Under certain conditions."

She was alert to amusement, but unsure; his voice was serious, impersonal, bargaining.

"I might paint you," he said. And stooped his head under the doorway, and was gone.

Ann was used to the admiration and interest of men; it was only the absence of these things that she noticed. Ten days later, when the exhibition was at an Indian school, the headmaster

96

invited Len and her to tea in the staff room, and introduced Shibalo among the other teachers. Shibalo did not say they had met before.

"What are you doing here?"

"Inter-school sports. Some arrangements have to be settled."

At lunch-time he was still there, and they saw him coming slowly across the field, smoking, and blinking as if the sun hurt his eyes. Len went and waited in the doorway for him. He sat with them and picked at the ham rolls they had bought on the way out to the school, and drank the coffee Ann made. He had the confidence of someone who is wanted everywhere, the moody ease of the man who pleases everybody but himself. Within the week, he turned up again; he had happened to meet Len in a shebeen the evening before, and had taken him on to the Bantu Men's Social Centre to provide an audience for his snooker game. Len had then had a lesson from him—Len's first. The casual chances of city life had thrown the younger man into the company of Shibalo, and Len was rather proud, as quiet, studious people invariably are, to be taken up by someone bold and amusing. He described his efforts at the billiard table, giggling apologetically, rather enjoying the new business of making a fool of himself. "But when you pocket your white ball does that wipe out your whole score? Or what?"

"No, no, boy, don't you remember, last night, when Robert Duze pocketed his, he just lost the points he should have made with that shot —It's a good thing I'm a born teacher," Shibalo complained to Ann.

"Good Lord, to think I had to come to the townships to get into the company of clubmen. Len—you know I do believe there's a billiard table lying around somewhere in the Stilwells' house. At least it looks like a billiard table, only very small."

"Yes, yes, they do make half-size ones." When she talked, Gideon Shibalo watched her rather than listened.

"Where did you see it?" Len was deeply interested and sceptical.

"In that sort of cellar or boot cupboard under the stairs. I'm sure they don't want it—you know what that house is like. Perhaps you could buy it from them?"

Len and Shibalo laughed. Shibalo was delighted. "Can you see it? A donkey cart comes along 16th street in Alex and delivers a billiard table to his house. First they take the door down to get it in. Then they take down the inside walls . . . Then his landlady comes home . . ."

"Then they use the billiard table for a floor and build the house again on top. —But we could go and look at it, anyway?" said Len.

"I'll ask Jessie what they think of doing with the thing, if anything."

"You want to come and play tonight?" Shibalo asked Len.

"Thanks—I'm going to a concert with Ann and Boaz."

Gideon was wandering about the caravan, quite at home now; he took down two pictures and exchanged their positions. "I might be there. I'm supposed to be there. —Who's this guy out of the Bible?"

"Ann's husband."

"I'd like to meet your husband."

She grinned at him. "He'd like to meet you."

He had already turned to something else, in the manner of people who do not want to make the effort at real communication but toss a remark, like a small coin, as a signal of passing attention.

At the concert at the university they saw him on the other side of the hall, tall and carefully dressed, with a white woman whose short, flying grey hair and high pink brow made an authoritative head. He bent with her over the programme and seemed another person in this company.

Ann pointed him out to Boaz: "*That's* Shibalo over there." Boaz twisted in his seat to see; he knew the story of Gideon Shibalo's scholarship and how he'd had to give it up for political reasons. There were quite a number of people that she knew, and her attention was caught, this way and that, as people came down the aisles. "Callie Stow, with him," said Len. At intermission they saw the backs of Gideon Shibalo and the woman, in a group that rather held the floor. He did not turn his head.

Next day he came to the exhibition—which had moved on to another school—at lunch-time and brought a large bottle of beer with him. "What about some cheese for a change?" he said, looking at the ham rolls.

"How'd you like the music?" Len wanted an opening in order to give his own views on it.

"Wasn't there."

"We saw you." Ann laughed at him.

But he was unperturbed. "One can go to a concert and not be there. Sometimes you just don't hear the music." He shrugged.

"Well, you missed something good."

"No doubt, no doubt." He was overcome by weariness at the reminder of the evening, and slid his legs out across the small space of the caravan. Ann was obliged to step over them to get past.

He began to appear sometime nearly every day. Len bought cheese rolls, and if he were not there by one, the two of them sat smoking and talking without a mention of lunch. If he had not come by a quarter to two, one of them would say, at last, "Well, I'm hungry," and then they would eat hastily, as if they had forgotten the meal.

One night the three of them went to a boxing match together; Ann had never watched boxing before. "Put on your best dress," Shibalo ordered. "I mean it. A woman's got to look like it at the ring-side." They sat in front among the black promoters and gangsters and their girls. The girls in their drum-tight dresses, heels thrusting their haunches this way and that, swaying ear-rings beside brown cheeks and full red lips, made a splendid, squealing show; Ann pounded her knees with excitement like a schoolboy. Shibalo held her elbow as if to hold her down and explained in a swift and urgent commentary all that was going on between the two forces struggling in the ring.

Shibalo had seats for a match in a nearby town, and they went in Ann's car to see it. Ann was delighted with the extravagant descriptions of the fighters on the handbills and posters. The brutality of the sweat-slippery black bodies, colliding and heav-ing apart, the bloodied eyes and the grunts of pain had for her the licence of a spectacle; she enjoyed being swept up, bobbing and buoyant, in the noise and show-off of the crowd. They went a third and a fourth time, following the African boxing promotions from town to town. Then Len said, "I've had enough of this craze—no thank you." Ann and Gideon went anyway, on their own. "You won't leave me stranded in the middle of the night in Germiston location, or wherever it is?" she asked, smiling at him. "Come on. You'll be all right." He made no personal assurances.

She had dropped the joke of dressing-up by now and looked even more conspicuous in the black crowd, in jeans and a leather jacket. There was a dirty fight, and a close one, and the crowd first snarled and reviled and then celebrated wildly. Gideon Shibalo got his tickets free because he knew the promoters, but apparently he considered this sufficient honour for them and never spoke to them. He pushed a way through the crowd as if he knew they would make way for him; but his indifference was met, as he and Ann passed, with glances and remarks of recognition : the regulars had seen them before, now; the white girl and the teacher were part of the circus. A brazen little caricature with stiff straightened hair darted out long red finger-nails to feel Ann's coat; someone smiled into her face.

The looks, the casual remark of faces in the crowd, set them together; it was a picture imposed from the outside, like a game that partners off strangers. Shibalo drove the car home that night. They laughed and talked all the way; neither had ever been so amusing when Len was there.

Next morning Shibalo telephoned her at the Stilwells' house. Oddly, she was greatly surprised when she heard his voice; with Africans, she still expected to take the initiative in any attempt to keep up a friendship : they seldom did, perhaps to show you that they didn't need you.

"Where're you having lunch today?"

She was supposed to be out with the exhibition, as he must know. "I don't know, Gid, I've got to go into town to do some shopping this morning." "What about the Lucky Star or Tommie's, then." Those were the two places where coloured and white people mixed. "Oh, Lucky Star, I think." She at once chose the one where she went often, where everyone she knew went and was seen.

She simply did not turn up at the Agency office, where Len usually picked her up with the caravan. At half past one, rather late, Shibalo came into the Lucky Star; she left the people she was talking to and went to him : "Come—" They had something so important to discuss that there was no need for pleasantries. He went swiftly to a table at the wall. "I felt bored stiff at the school today. Ugh, the smell of the place gets me down, the ink, the musty old books." "Let's have curry, then, Gid, that's a good smell." He looked at her slowly, resentfully, with a smile that was an open, blatant declaration, cock-sure of welcome, full of guile. "You're the one that has the good smell. Everything you touch in the caravan is full of it. Even the coffee-cup. You hand someone a cup of coffee, and as he puts it up to his mouth there's the smell of lilies."

She gave the laugh that is as female as the special note that birds find when they want to call to their young. "Remember, lilies that fester smell far worse than old books."

"Oh, I remember all right. I'm always careful not to keep them too long."

They began to go about together. It was another craze, like the boxing one. Every day they ate at the Lucky Star; there was not much choice of places where they could eat, and the food was crude, but this did not worry them : they chose the same table each day, and had their tastes anticipated by the waiter just as, in other circumstances, they might have done at the smartest restaurant in town. And the habitués noted the beginnings of a new grouping in their composition, just as, if Ann had lunched with a white man at the Carlton Hotel, the daily presence of a champagne bucket at the table would have made the necessary announcement. There are certain human alliances that belong more to the world than to the two people who are amusing themselves by making them; this diversion taken up by Shibalo and Ann was one. She was not the first white woman who had been interested in him, but she was perhaps the best-looking, and certainly the least discreet. The open flirtation, for the fun of it, meant more than going to bed with a white woman who was frightened to be seen with you in the street.

Ann was scarcely attracted to him at all, in the strong and sudden way that she had felt matters settled beyond protest between herself and other men. Yet when she saw that he was aware of her, keenly but casually, granting her the power of her sex and beauty but in no way over-valuing her—she was like someone who has no intention of playing the game but finds his hand go out irresistibly to return the ball that comes flying at him. Her sex and her beauty were her talent, her life's work, the grace of her being that other human beings felt in her; whatever else engrossed her was, in all innocence, mere pastime. The vivid sense of life that she felt when people saw her walk in with Shibalo, laugh at private jokes with him, drive away with him in her little car, came as much from a subtle use of her gifts as from his company. It was a new and amusing variation of their employment to show other men, simply by a companionable silence with Shibalo over a cup of coffee, that she could ignore them for a black man, if she pleased, in addition to all the other incalculables the hazard of her desirableness contained. Even in the restricted clandestine fringe of the city's activities that was open to Shibalo and her, this was an attitude that carried some subterranean force and audacity, and was seen in the context of the white city, to which, after all, she belonged, and to which she could return whenever she chose.

One afternoon Shibalo remembered the billiard table : "What have you done about it?"

Len made a gesture that suggested the idea had never been serious.

"Ann, eh? What's happened?" Len seemed always in a lower key than the other two, now, and Shibalo instinctively tried to counter this by an impatient quickening of his own vitality.

"I forgot all about it—so did you," Ann said to Shibalo.

"I want to have a look at it. Come on, let's go."

They were packing up the exhibition; Patrick wanted his caravan back. Everything was dismantled, and lay about, ready to go into the crates. The sun made a structure of hazy blue bars out of the cigarette smoke.

Ann was examining her dirty hands with absorption. She looked up at the stacked pictures and the mess, from Len to Shibalo.

"Come on." Shibalo was on his feet.

A mixture of opposition and indulgence characterised Ann's response to him : "I haven't said a word to the Stilwells, you know."

But though Shibalo took it for granted that the whole interest in the billiard table was on behalf of Len, and Len found himself suddenly assumed to be taken up again, he would not go with them. "Look at this"—his satisfaction in the work to be done was obstinate.

As they were driving, Ann said, "You know Jessie Stilwell, don't you?" "I suppose so." When they got to the house there was silence, anyway. Not even the children were there, and the servant was in her own quarters. Ann's voice sounded through the rooms and up and down the stairs; Shibalo's was a murmur behind it. She lugged aside broken toy wagons, frayed baskets, mud-stiffened gardening shoes and an old chandelier, and there was the billiard table, wedged against the wall, on its side. "Match size. That's what I thought. Most of the felt's finished." They tried to pull it upright, but there was no room to turn it over. "I'm sure they'll be glad to get rid of it. Would you really take it?" She knew that he lived in Alexandra township, but she had never wondered how, in what sort of place, though she knew the cabins, shacks, backyard rooms and occasional neat houses of Alexandra. His shoulders hunched with his inward chuckle. "I might."

"Have you got somewhere to put it?" On her haunches, she smiled at him in the gloom. "I've got a place—maybe. There's a flat in Hillbrow." "Hillbrow?" It was a white suburb. So often she felt he simply gave her an answer, any answer, while he was thinking of something else. "Yes," he said, with a touch of reserve, "Couple of chaps I know. I stay there sometimes." He chuckled again : "It might be a good idea to give them a present of a billiard table." "It's supposed to be for Len." "Oh of course, I can take anyone there I like. *They* don't play."

They pushed the table back into position, grunting and laughing; Ann was in her element at this kind of headlong activity. A splinter from the leg went into Shibalo's thumb, and though he said nothing beyond the first exclamation, when they came out of the storage-place she saw that his hand was trembling with pain. "Oh look, it's an awful one."

He held up his hand; the splinter was driven like a wedge into the smooth dark skin beside the second thumb joint. She tried to get it out, and while she did so, concentrating on the broken butt of wood that could be felt sharp, dead and hard against the live, cold thumb, his hand came alive to her. This was he, this big slim hand half-curled and slack, like a living creature itself. The fingertips throbbed faintly, their skin showed their own unique engraving of whorls. There was an expression in the set of the fingers as there is an expression in the features of a face.

For a moment the quality of the reality she was experiencing underwent a swift change. It was as if she woke up from an idle day-dream and found herself holding some unexplained object brought with her from a dream-world.

When the splinter was out they went into the living-room and had a drink. She had never had the house to herself before, that she could remember, and she felt herself in possession of it in a special way, as a child does when she creeps into a deserted house through a broken window. She took him upstairs to show him a woodcut in Jessie's room, and some carved figures Boaz had picked up in his wanderings. Their movements from room to room, pauses in their chatter, had the rhythm of a dance through the house.

They were about to drive away when she found she had forgotten the car-keys and went running back into the house. As she raced downstairs again, she suddenly saw the profile of Mrs. Fuecht's seated figure, through the open doorway into the dining-room. She stopped; in the moment, the old woman turned her head. The girl was drawn across the entrance hall, through the door, to the window where the old woman sat.

"Hullo. All alone?" The girl's face had the blind eagerness of a face in a high wind; nerve-endings alive, responses on the surface, like the flash of sun or the shiver of wind on water.

The old woman scarcely existed in the moment. Her carefully powdered face was a mummification of such moments as the girl's; layer on layer, bitumen on bandage, she held the dead shape of passion and vitality in the stretch of thick white flesh falling from cheekbone to jaw, the sallow eyes and straggling but still black eyebrows holding up the lifeless skin round them, and the incision of the mouth. The lips showed only when she spoke, shining pale under a lick of saliva :

"It seemed I never would be."

The air bridled between them. "Can I get you anything?" said Ann.

The old woman smiled. "What?"

"I just wondered . . ."

"Oh, I know. Now and then one notices other people and is at a loss."

The girl laughed and the old woman took it like a confession. But it was an exchange of confidences : she said, "As time goes by there seem to be more of them—other people. And then, all of a sudden, you're one of them."

Ann sat down on the edge of a small table.

"Weren't you on your way?"

Their eyes met, blank and intimate. She got up. "I'll be going then." She paused, a bird balancing a moment on a telephone wire. "Goodbye."

The old woman did not change the angle of her head over her book while the front door banged and the clip of heels faded down the path, but when the house was silent again, the alert spread of her nostrils slackened. The silence where the voices of the girl and the unknown man had sounded was the silence within her where many voices were no longer heard.

The day Jessie met them at lunch they had been moving Shibalo's painting things from the back-room of a shop to the flat in the white suburb where he came and went as he pleased. Ann had not been there before; the tenants, two young men in advertising, were at work, but Shibalo was supplied with a key, and everything in the flat was in the natural state in which the owners' continuing activities had left it—he constituted no interruption. There must have been some prearrangement between them, however, because he stacked some canvases in the wallcupboard in the bathroom, and pushed two easels in beside the ironing-board in the dingy kitchen before he dumped the rest in the living-room. Ann was deeply curious about the canvases and stacks of drawings gathered in newspaper—"all old stuff," he said; whenever one was revealed she would stop dead to look at it in searching silence. She showed, too, the possessiveness on behalf of the artist that attacks ordinary people once they get to know a creative person; she began moving various objects out of the way to make room for pictures, and was irritated by the screen that was carefully placed as a target for a projector. "Why can't that thing be rolled up somewhere? They can't be using it all the time."

Vanity made him ignore this partisanship out of embarrassment; like most artists of any kind he thought himself far above the measure of privilege that ordinary people might think it necessary to claim for him. He put a record on the player and sat back to listen; he watched her, as if he were lazily following the movements of a bee or a moth about the room.

She put down a canvas she had pulled free from some others.

There was a flurry in her busyness. She looked at her hand, picked up the canvas again, and then put it back.

"Look," she said, coming over to him.

On her forefinger, with its slender tip that bent back supplely as she stiffened it, there was a streak of fresh wet paint.

He pulled a face of concern and, smiling, leant out to pick up the turpentine bottle. He took his handkerchief and used it to clean her hand; then he leant out again and got a sheet of paper between his fingers and put the hand flat down upon it on the chair-arm, twisting her arm awkwardly as she half-sat. He drew round the outline of her hand with a stub of charcoal. The triumphant, challenging set of her face weakened; she kept her eyes down on her own hand. He picked it up and gave it back to her.

He jumped up from the chair and began to fool about with spontaneous energy. "I must do the honours of the house. Forgive the informality of this humble abode. It's the girl's day off. There are no snacks prepared. The champagne isn't cold enough. But in the kitchen you'll find the glasses, and somewhere"—his head disappeared into one of those unidentifiable space-saving cupboards that might store anything—"we'll find the brandy."

She took off her shoes and drank her fingerful with ginger ale, stretching herself on a plastic-thonged chair on the balcony. He had taken out a big, hairy white sheet of card and sat in the shaded doorway of the room behind her, drawing. "Let me see." He took no notice so she got up and went to look. It was her profile, glancing over a naked back.

"How do you know that's how I look?"

"You're all the same," he said, "that's the beauty of it."

She went back to the sun and sat on the balcony ledge, the sun contracting the skin on her back, her bare soles just in contact with the grooved tiled floor.

"One push," he said, looking and looking at her.

She crossed her arms over her stomach, balancing carelessly. "Why not?" A reddish warmth from the tiles was reflected in her skin. Death never occurred to her except as a thrill in life; the drop behind her brought a special smile to her face.

When Jessie left them at the Lucky Star after lunch they went back to the flat. There was suddenly nowhere else to go, nothing else to do; the whole city seemed to let them pass unnoted as if some intense preoccupation between them made them invisible. They sat in the room with the curtains pulled against the sun, facing each other. Ann was not thinking of Shibalo but was filled with consciousness of Jessie. She was aware of her in broken images from their association, that was unimportant for her and had gone by, irrelevant. This strong awareness of the other woman made her roused and shaky inwardly, as one feels after an exchange that has left one goaded at the point of the moment to speak.

She went to the bathroom and did her hair and her face in a trance of skill; the smell of her trailed across the room. It was five weeks exactly since he had walked into the caravan. Time went so quickly for her; it had brought her here, now, quite suddenly. No good thinking of anything else.

They began to kiss and please each other with some rivalry, like a pair of peacocks showing off their feathers. If there was laughter, there was also fascination. At last there was solemnity too, but it was the hectic solemnity of surprising passion.

EIGHT

Because he was not much interested by her, Tom Stilwell made an effort to talk to Ann when he found her about. There were gaps in his attention to as well as his knowledge of her day-to-day life, and usually his attempts were of the well-how-are-you-getting-along-with-such-and-such variety. He asked her about the travelling exhibition one evening when she happened to be in to dinner, only to hear it had just closed. "Oh my God, everything's always over before I get to see it. I suppose that Japanese film's off by now too, darling?" he added to Jessie.

"Of course" she said cheerfully. "But there's a new place to eat opened up where the old Bella Napoli used to be. We could try that before it goes bust, perhaps."

They passed from this to discussion about whether, in general, group shows were more or less satisfying than one-man shows. "In any case, I imagine there isn't anyone among the group you showed who could attempt a one-man show—except perhaps Shibalo."

"Of course, yes. And he can get a gallery in town, any time he wants to," said Ann.

"What about talking to Patrick Bold about the caravan now?" Tom said, half to Jessie.

"You can," said Ann. "His brother's taking it for the next six weeks or so."

"We wouldn't want it until about July—Jessie?" She had the component parts of a small doll beside her and was studying them between bites of apple. Her eyes hesitated over the coupling of this piece to that with obstinate enjoyment of the difficulties created by her ignorance of the principles of construction involved. "I'm not so sure." She was not referring to the time, but to the fact that a house that was part of Fuecht's estate might be available to them soon. It was a house at the sea where she had stayed as a child.

108

"How many would the caravan take?" The possibility of the house, vague as it was, stirred some opposition in Tom, as will any proposition that appears to bring to the active surface something one dislikes in the nature of someone one loves. He had the unexpressed knowledge, based on no facts and requiring none, that Jessie wanted to use the house because Fuecht was dead; perhaps to demonstrate that he *was* dead.

"It's huge. Oh, six can sleep in it, easily," Ann assured him at once, with the confidence of a butterfly telling a bird how to build a nest.

"The kids could double up, anyway. And one could take a tent as well. How about you and Boaz bringing along a tent?"

"Marvellous. But it depends when. Boaz is supposed to go up into Moçambique in the winter." Ann was drawn to the problem of the doll. "Wait a minute, why don't you try getting the head in first—then that bit"—she took up the torso irresistibly—"hooks in there. Ought to."

Tom, too, picked up an arm, like the piece of a jigsaw that the passer-by feels sure he will drop into place unhesitatingly. He fitted the wire spring to the truncated shoulder and pushed it through one hole in the pink plastic body. Jessie watched with the silence of one who has tried all this before. The spring was too short to project through the hole on the other side, where the other arm was supposed to connect to it, and the hole was too small to allow fingers to enter and pull the spring through. "You need a bit of wire. Or tweezers would do."

"Eyebrow tweezers? I'll get mine," said Ann, and left the room for a minute.

Jessie said to Tom softly, looking up over the doll. "She's having an affair with Shibalo."

Her tone was curiously reassuring and unconvincing.

"What on earth makes you say that?"

"I know. I was mad not to see it before."

"Does Len say so?"

"I had lunch with them at the Lucky Star the other day."

There was the almost dreamy quiet between them of a man and woman who have been sexual partners for an unbroken communion of some years. Like rain and tempest watched through the window of a warm, light room, they remembered wet and wildness out there.

Even while they were speaking, Ann's voice, da-la-la-ing a phrase of a jazz song she liked, cut across theirs. In a moment she was in the room again, calling out, "This'll do it," and attention to the doll continued unbroken, each impatient of the other's attempt to get it together.

Boaz came home that weekend, but as he arrived while the Stilwells were out, on Saturday night, the first they saw of him was on Sunday morning, when he and Ann emerged from the house about eleven o'clock and joined the others on the lawn. They were both still in pyjamas. Ann wore a short gown over the cotton romper arrangement in which she slept, and Boaz's brown hand, dangling round her neck, stirred now and then in her tousled hair.

Jessie was lying on her stomach reading the papers and she turned dazedly on to her side, elbow propping up hand and head, at the approach. The lawn sprinkler was circling to provide a fountain in which the three little girls, Elisabeth naked and the other two in their pants, played. A couple whose sole claim to friendship rested on the exchange of such visits had dropped in on the Stilwells to drink some beer. Boaz agreed to have beer for his breakfast, and he and Ann settled themselves on the grass. Boaz was unshaven but looked handsome, squatting like an Arab with the planes of his olive-pale face shaded in by beard; the limits of its growth were clearly defined, like the markings on the face of some deer. As usual, since he was so often the returned traveller, talk took its impetus from him for a while, though he in no sense dominated the conversation but simply shared, in his friendly, serious way, what he had to say. He had lost a camera and given some other things of his a good dunking, getting through a swollen drift, and as he told the story now the mention of the district where this misadventure happened prompted a question from Redvers English, the visitor, about oil prospecting that he'd heard was going on there. Boaz had got mixed up with an oil-prospecting crowd the other day, and had an amusing story to tell about them; this led the talk out of his single stream into the general pool where everyone's opinions, questions and desultory comments about what would happen to the tribes in the reserve if oil was found, made overlapping rings. Ann did not bother to take part in the conversation; only her laugh rang out now and then : she had pushed up the gown into the elastic legs of the romper and lay rolled over on to her back in the sun in feline laziness. The smooth skin of her knees soon took on a tight shine and the grain of her thigh-flesh came up rosy. She was not pensive, not "quiet", not, perhaps, content. Nothing was projected from her. Jessie thought: she exists.

The pitch of the group rose a little with the beer and the hot sun. Olga English had one of those weeping laughs, maddening as the repetitive cry of certain birds; Jessie began to be irritated by her but Tom, though he did not like her very much, was in the sort of mood when one enjoys drinking and talking not particularly witty nonsense rather more with people one does not care much for than with friends who draw more strongly upon one's personality. They had sent the children for biscuits and cheese, but although the sprinkler was deserted, the children had not come back. Warmed by beer, Tom in passing leant over Jessie with his arm round her and half-whispered, half-showed off, "Are you gloomy this morning, my love..." It did not matter what he said—he knew that increasingly over the last year there had been times when she was not carried along with the mood of the company; he liked to give a sign, any sign, that he was in touch with her. She had merely felt rather impatient for the Englishes to go, but the softness of the gesture suddenly did make her feel sad; she saw out of the corner of her eye—the small movement that betrays the presence of an enemy—a lover's knot of raised blue vein showing on her left calf. In this full light it was obvious—she bent to examine the skin intently and saw that thin red-blue lines were spreading and branching from the vein, a faint map recording the advance of an invader. Madge and Elisabeth appeared at this moment, their dresses on but unbuttoned and with sashes hanging stringily. "About time, good heavens!" Jessie sprang up briskly. But they did not have the cheese with them, they had forgotten all about the cheese. Madge was crying. She held Elisabeth like a bailiff with his hands on a poacher. "Look what she's gone and done."

"Oh that blasted doll again. No, I can't, I can't," Jessie held it up tragically, while the others laughed, though (since Ann's eyes were closed) only Tom knew what at.

"Now the eyes have fallen back into its head."

"Give here," said Boaz. "Don't worry, Madge, we'll fix it for you," and Madge went over at once to her new victim.

"If you knew the struggle we had with that thing the other night; Tom, Ann and I—we were all working on it."

Tom's and Jessie's recollection of something else met suddenly over the bent heads of Boaz and the child. Ann rose up into the moment, stretching, smiling, yawning, "I'd better put some clothes on." Moving sluggishly from hip to hip, she was arrested in her trail towards the house by some remark, and paused to stand talking to Olga English.

"Boaz doesn't know, anyway," Tom said. They had returned a number of times since the evening when Jessie first spoke of it to the business of Ann and Gideon Shibalo. They never talked about it for long, nor very fully; what she did was none of their business—not in the trite sense of minding one's own business, but in the real sense that although she lived in the house they had nothing of the involvement with or concern for her that is the real reason for one human being being another's keeper.

"She hasn't told him." It was a conclusion; this was an affair on the side (perhaps not even the first?) and not intended to break the marriage.

"It'll be all right if only she goes on resisting the temptation to tell him," said Tom.

"Quite."

Tom felt sleepy after Sunday lunch and was lying on the bed in his clothes. "She takes it all very calmly," he said, with a slight hesitation.

Jessie was pushing open all the windows and drawing the curtains closed; she turned her head to him and laughed.

"D'you think she sleeps with the two of them?" He was diffidently curious, with a touch of male fear of the female.

"She must. —I should think so, at the beginning, at any rate. The one may have become awfully familiar—you know—it may not seem like the same thing, perfectly harmless. —You never liked her much, did you?" she said, taking up the tone of curiosity.

"I don't know. I was pleased that *he* was so thrilled with her—"

As he was dropping heavily asleep, Jessie's voice woke him: "There was something wonderful about her today, though." The quiet, ordinary voice startled him convulsively and his hand as it jerked out came into contact with the bony yet padded eminence of Jessie's pelvis. In the dark behind his eyelids it was at once a skull turned up by a boot, and a grassy bank.

They went to a party, in the week that followed, with Ann. It was one of those shapeless parties that people give to introduce foreign visitors to a succession of faces they will never see again. Tom got trapped in a corner with a bore who always lay in wait for him at such parties, and Jessie drifted ruthlessly from group to group, finding herself talking to people whose identity she ought to have known, since they appeared to know her. The only liveliness came from the small company where Ann was. She herself held the same glass of gin and tonic the whole evening, but her presence roused an appetite for pleasure in the others around her, so that there was constant traffic between their corner and the bar. Laughter, raised voices and general animation surrounded her yet appeared to emanate from her; she was not looking her best that night, her hair was in need of a shampoo and the dress she wore was not a really good colour, but she had, Jessie recognised, the attraction for men of a woman who is excited by some private amorous involvement. It was a state both helpless and powerful. The attention was not something one set out for; but the power! The power came from the brief time of balance between two men, the extraordinary moment before guilt, shame or regret set in, when one gave to and took from each of them an identical pleasure. Jessie remembered with something of a shudder the discovery that one could make love to one man one night, and another the next: the taboo that had lived in one's mind as a hoop of fire—and simply fell apart, as one jumped, a thing of tissue paper.

Tom was coming home one afternoon when he saw Ann's car draw up outside the gate, Ann get out, and a man with a beard, whom he recognised as Gideon Shibalo, drive off again. When she caught up with him along the path, he said, "What's happened to your car?" She laughed, gave him a look of surprise that might have been a rebuke. "I've lent it to Gid Shibalo."

The initiative seemed to have changed hands swiftly, so he said, "What is he doing these days?" They went up the steps together. "Teaching." She smiled at him as he pushed open the door for her to enter; her hair was wet on the ends, she must have been swimming, and the powder had rubbed off her face on the cheek-bones and nose as the bloom rubs off the round prominences of a fruit. She never had the dazed look that, paradoxically, clouds the face of someone who has been doing intellectual work, she never carried the dull smell of smoky rooms, the staleness of ink, papers or cooking. She did not bring an ether of cold perfume, either. He felt it almost as an insult that he was unmoved by her living beauty. He went upstairs and said to Jessie : "So he's driving around in Boaz's car, now."

"Oh, several times lately." She answered with the impatience of someone who has something else to say.

"Didn't he have a long-standing affair with that woman Callie Stow?"

"Mmm. A few others, too."

Tom felt vaguely reassured; the thought of Boaz, whose name gripped his mind in unease, slackened and let go.

"My mother says the tenants are definitely going to be out by the end of May," Jessie said, beginning to put papers and photographs steadily back into her dressing-table drawer, so that she could ignore any reaction he might be showing. She was talking about Fuecht's house.

He was careful what he said. "But what's it like? I mean have you any idea whether there's enough furniture and so on . . .?" and while they talked Ann's heels went lightly, loudly about the old wooden floors, and clattered away from them.

Although Morgan had gone straight from school to a farm— Tom had arranged for him to join the three sons of the professor of botany—the little girls were at home for ten days at Easter and Jessie felt obliged to come home to lunch with them every day. It was not so much that they needed her; the reprieve of responsibility for Morgan usually produced some compensatory piece of dutifulness towards the other children. The second day she found Gideon Shibalo sitting in the garden. The angle of the two chairs (they were set slightly awry, as if their original intimacy had been put out by the restless movement of occupants in tense discussion), the remains of some clumsy sandwiches, the torn lace of beer-foam dirtying a glass, the litter of cigarette stubs—all these conveyed to her a sudden hope of signs of crisis. But when she came down into the deep shade where they might have isolated themselves in a deadlock of reckoning, she was at once aware that her high pitch was wrong : there was nothing to meet it. Gideon greeted her and belched, raising his eyebrows at himself. He had the slightly out-of-place look that she noticed Africans sometimes had in a garden. Ann had kicked off her shoes and sat pinching up grass blades between her toes. The children were playing house not ten yards away, in the curtains of the pepper trees.

"Was there anything to eat?" Jessie asked, falling back on hospitality. Ann assured her that it was all right, they had found something. An air of normality, of commonplace almost, prevailed between the three of them; Jessie felt that she ought to throw it off, but she was hampered by what now seemed to her the impossible code of personal freedom by which they lived. How could she suggest to Ann that she did not want Gideon Shibalo there? *Why* should she not want him to come? Was Ann in the house as an appendage of Boaz? If—and it was unthinkable, with the concept of individual dignity that the Stilwells held, that it should be otherwise—she was nothing less than herself, then that selfhood was entitled to determine its own actions, and they should be seen *as such*, and not at the angle at which they lay across Boaz's being. Why choose Boaz, and not her? Oh it was all right to choose him, for oneself—but one could not put a finger out to flick her direction to suit his. Jessie had a horror of the attempt by a third person to deflect the life of one to serve another; without God, the unquestionable existence of this horror beyond the strength of a moral sense was a scrap of torn paper from the difficult documentation that might put together his existence. Any influence directed by consideration of Boaz's life should come only out of a private covenant—and, to Jessie, this did not mean marriage—between Ann and Boaz.

Yet she was resentful in some constant, concealed part of herself at Shibalo's presence, as at the awareness that he was at the other end of telephone calls, and the regular sight of him driving the car—"Boaz's car" as she and Tom referred to it lately, although Boaz had bought it for Ann. She was resentful and yet she sat and talked with them amiably, because she liked him. He treated her in a good-humoured, dry way, certain they would get on. Ann again did not talk much, though at least her air was animated. When she did say something, it was invariably a corroboration of, or corollary to, what Shibalo was saying : "He really did. You should have seen the faces of the others." "—And then that was when you met him alone and said to him . . ."

"Look at your children," Shibalo said at one point, pulling out a sheet of cardboard from under his chair. It was a sketch of active angles half-recognisable as legs and arms.

"*Very* smart." He must have been there the whole morning, then.

He took it without rancour. "I'll come and do one for you one day. I'm pretty hot on drawing kids these days."

"Like circus dwarfs," said Ann, with the intimacy of a repeated bait.

Jessie was conscious of being drawn into their ambiance as a privilege which she had not consented to accept. Once she had been let in on them, they could not let her go without the temptation to make her party to themselves in some way; she was the outsider who stumbles upon the secret and is offered, as the price, the excitement of sharing it.

There is a magnetic field in the polarity of two people who are conducting a reckless love affair; the insolence, emotional anarchy, uncalculatedness have the gratuitous attraction of exploding fireworks even for those who regard the whole thing as a bit ridiculous. Something of the showy flare caught Jessie, and, in a mood that had risen to sharp banter and some laughter, she went off with the two of them to take up Shibalo's old casual invitation, given at the Lucky Star that day, that she might come and see what his new work was like.

Ann was gay, in the car, and leant forward with her elbows on the back of the front seat so that she could chatter to the two in front. Gideon was driving. For the first time since she had come to live in the house, Ann treated Jessie as her equal : equal of the freedom of her youth, her lack of conditioning responsibilities, her unreflective responses that made her flat "I love that", "I hate this" an edict.

"Stop at the corner, Gid."

"What for?"

"That shop has nuts. I'm dying for some walnuts."

She dashed out of the car and back again with the supreme and arrogant self-consciousness of someone who feels she may be mentioned in her absence. Jessie saw her go straight to the counter to be served before others who were there before her, taking no account of them. She paused at the car window, on Gideon's side, before she got in again. "Have one"—her face was beseeching, a big smile with the corners of the lips tensely pressed down, her forehead flushed like one of the children's before they began to cry.

The flat that they went to was like many of those in which Jessie had lived. She looked at the draughty entrance with its list of occupants, under glass, its trough of pale plants, its one maroon and two yellow walls, and gave a grudging smile. The urban education : if someone managed to get out of the townships it would be to a place like this.

"How d'you find it, working here?" she asked.

"It's just like having my own place," he said, giving her the freedom of it grandly. "Nobody's there all day and I can do just what I like. I'll meet you up top—" He took the back staircase instead of the lift because he had to take care not to attract the attention of the caretaker; she must not suspect that her tenants were allowing a black man to use their flat. When the two women got to the flat door, he was already there, inside. "Come right in, just step over the mess"—he kicked away a parcel from the dry cleaner's and a cardboard honeycomb of empty bottles. He pulled open the curtains in the living-room, picked up some letters, put a noisy Greek record on the gramophone, talking all the time with the relaxed busyness of someone who has just come home. Ann ripped the paper bandage off a magazine that lay among the letters and began to look through it. The purpose of coming there seemed to be forgotten. Jessie, kept standing by the presence all round her of objects meaningful to the lives of people she had never met, began to wander curiously around the room, touching this, glancing at that. She put her hand out to turn canvases without asking permission, for she had been asked twice to come and look at them. The third one was upside down; she righted it. It was a nude, Ann, flung down alive on the canvas as if on a rug. She turned another and another. They were all Ann, only in several she was black.

Gideon Shibalo came up beside her, professionally. "It's the subject that takes your breath away, ay?" He laughed. "It's not my new technique." He began to put up for her, one by one, without comment, charcoal drawings and oils of children, friezes and splashes of children, old with the life of the street.

NINE

GIDEON SHIBALO SOMETIMES had the use of a car, and sometimes had not. There were various complex arrangements, from time to time, with friends or relations. When he said, "I've got my car round the corner", it could mean his own old black Studebaker that he had sold to his brother-in-law two or three years ago, or a Citroën that he was only keeping on the road until he could find a buyer on behalf of the owner—a friend who had gone to Nigeria—or even the little shaky "second car" of some white friends who didn't need it over a weekend. At one time he had had Callie Stow's car practically permanently; a tiny beige Austin with a feather duster on the back window-ledge, and a yellow duster, street-map and snake-bite outfit in the glove box. When he did not have a car he went back to the bus queues and the trains at which the people hurled themselves in the echoing caverns of the city station or the open veld sidings of the townships, marked by a single light that was still burning at dawn.

The black car was sold when he was going to take up his scholarship, that time; his sister's husband had given him a hundred pounds down and hadn't paid off much more in the three years since then. The hundred pounds had gone towards the air ticket to Rome. He had got the whole fare back, of course, but he hadn't kept it; some of it had gone into politics, but most went during the months when he hadn't worked, and drank and gave it away. He was teaching now and he could have bought some sort of a car again, but he did not think of it; it did not irk him to depend upon the chance offers of others, in fact he took them all for granted in the manner of a man who is fobbed off with an abundance of things he does not want.

For the past two years—longer; since the scholarship—he had been made free of a section of the white world, and had lived as much there as among the people in whose midst he was born.

He did not have the obvious freedoms of the street and public places, of course, but was a frequenter of those private worlds where the rules of the street, the pronouncements of public sentiment, are disembodied voices shouting out of a megaphone —here, between four walls, the rules are quite different, and the sentiments diverse. He had never sat in school beside white children, or in a bus among white men and women, or shared with them any of the other commonplaces of life; he simply found himself taken right into their most personal lives, where all decisions are upon personal responsibility, and even punishment is self-meted. The first time he slept in a white man's house was after a party, in the studio of a white painter who had liked his work and wanted to get to know him; there was a noisy quarrel, sometime towards morning, between the man and his wife, and the wife had rushed into the room and dumped a sleeping baby boy out of the way on Shibalo's couch.

During the months when he was trying to get a passport he saw a great deal of the liberal and political whites who took up his case and introduced him to the moral twilight zone of influence; from a people without power, he had not known that even among those who made and approved the laws that prevented a man like himself from going where he pleased, there were men who might have been able to help him, not out of a desire to do so, but in response to pressure on some tender spot in their own armour of power-survival. You touched the right secret place and the spring flew open somewhere else : it hadn't worked, as it happened, for him, but there were others for whom it had.

Every contact with whites was touched with intimacy; for even the most casual belonged by definition to the conspiracy against keeping apart. It was always easier to be drunk than sober, to exchange a confession than have a chat; even, he found, with amusement rather than surprise, to have a love affair than a friendship. He had found easy and mutual attraction between himself and several of the women. The affairs were short-lived, and, like dreams, never emerged into the light of day. This was not to say that they were nothing but sexual encounters—these were always far more than that, for even the most ordinary of sexual encounters was also the reaching out of two mysteries—but that they carried over nothing into the world of streets and public places. Nothing, nothing; if the two met in the street next day it was as if they had not met.

Callie Stow was something else again. The very first time he remembered seeing her face was in the confusion of that stage at a party when faces, furniture, objects began to present shifting levels for which his eyes could not make a sufficiently quick change of focus. As if he were on a trampoline, people now rose, now fell before him. He had seen her quite often before, but it was only when she became part of the onset of nightmare that he remembered her. She was a Scotswoman with a Scandinavian mother, and in her soft voice with a slight Glasgow accent she was talking to him as if he were perfectly sober. She told him that he had made a discovery, that was all, a discovery that would have had to come to him sometime, anyway. "There's no time to go after what you want for yourself, you've got to be one of the crowd if you want your life to have any meaning to you," she said. She had short, very clean hair that might have been blonde or already white, and the fine fair skin that those sort of Englishwomen have (he never did understand that Scots and English were not the same thing). She could have been any age; his grandmother, for all he knew; an Englishwoman with a skin like that, and blue eyes and no lipstick, might turn out to be anywhere between twenty-five and fifty. (Some sort of flowered dress, and a string of small pearls.) He thought about the matter-of-fact way she had spoken of the wall that reared up before him, although he was hazy about what she had said. When he met her again in someone else's house less than a week later, he at once asked, "What was it about finding something out?"

She said precisely, "I said that you'd have had to discover sometime that you can't do anything for yourself, and perhaps now was the time—that's all."

He gave his chuckle, and said sourly, "Thank you very much, but I don't feel particularly philosophical about not being able to do anything for myself. Whether it's the time or not."

"No one would suggest you should," she said. "It just seems to me that now you've had clearly shown to you that the only thing that means anything if you're an African is politics. You've made the only choice. You don't need philosophy; you've got necessity."

"You're not a painter," he said.

"No, I am not a painter—" the tone of her voice granted a

demand she respected but could not share. "What's the good of saying that it's terrible that you can't be one? There it is. You've got politics, that's all. Why drink yourself silly, mooning over the other? You're a man of your time. Different times, there are different things to be done, some things are possible, some are not. You're an African, aren't you?"

He laughed but she pressed her chin back firmly : "Having a black skin doesn't automatically mean that, you know."

As he got to know this woman he made another discovery—one that she would not have been aware of, since she had no more self-consciousness than vanity. Although she shared a kind of life that was familiar to him, some outward identity of outlook as manifested in their being present together in the same room, smiling at the same remarks, at a party, for example, or sitting at the same conference table (as they were later to do) on a political action committee—this outward identity of outlook gave no indication of her control and direction by forces of whose possible existence he was not even aware. He had never known anyone before who was a rationalist by conviction and education. He was aware, dimly, that his actions were moved by the huge wheels of the need to create, to be free, and, clearly, the small wheels of wanting and taking. But for her nothing was empirical, no instinct was without sound objective backing, no action ran wild and counter to herself. All was codified, long ago, beginning when, as a child, she had listened to discussions between her free-thinking, Victorian socialist grandfather and her missionary father. As children are said to select automatically the foods that their bodies require, she rejected the faith of her father for the tenets of her grandfather, and went on to university to read political philosophy. Then she had studied labour organisation in England, and economics in Sweden. She was one of those who take an actual hand in rigging up the framework of civilisation; she had worked in refugee camps in Europe after the war, and in North Africa later, and had run an adult education scheme among African farm workers in Rhodesia. In South Africa she had written surveys of indentured and migratory labour for a world organisation, and was a standard figure among the organisers of various campaigns for civil rights that came into existence time and again, sometimes comparatively flourished and sometimes did not, and at last were banned, anyway. She had taken out South African papers at the beginning of the Fifties and so could not be deported; but she had had, of course, a spell in prison during one of the States of Emergency declared in times of African unrest.

There were books in her house on butterflies and architecture, cave paintings and birds, as well as the sociology and history and politics you would expect. It seemed to Shibalo that she had books on everything; for her it was not that the birds were simply there, flying around, mushrooms came up in the veld after rain. She possessed the world twice over; once as a natural phenomenon, a second time as a filing cabinet in which all creation existed again in the form of a name and description, all concurrent, all within the compass of one man's experience. He was aware of this second possession as some kind of power over life; one he didn't have, though he'd got his B.A. at Fort Hare, years ago.

Callie Stow darned his socks and thought nothing of waiting for him on a public street corner; but who would have dreamed that this woman with her tweed skirt and sensible shoes, and her calm white head (he thought of it, all his life, as "the professor's head"), was getting into the small beige Austin driven by her lover? He was not unattracted by her, either; it was again a first time, the first time he had desired a woman mentally, been drawn to her through the processes of her thinking. In the end, the very thing that had made the open relationship possible killed it off, for him. He did not feel like her lover; she came out of prison and he came from "underground" where he had been lying low for a while, and she said, "Hullo my dear, it's good to see you," with the "ui" sound in "good" that he remembered so well. It was all right to say it, but he suddenly felt cheated and disappointed beyond words. He did not know what he wanted; he had not known it was not this. He moved away from her, taking with him a certain discipline of mind, an ability to get at arm's length from himself, that he had got from her but that he could make use of only intermittently, since it was acquired and not inherent; it continued to be most easily at his command only when he found himself in her company or in the set within a set in which he had moved with her. In time he began to see it as an act that he could do to show how easy it was, really, to belong with them.

White friends like the young advertising men at the flat, who were not much interested in politics except as a subject for argument, enjoyed a black man's joke at their own expense, and in several places Shibalo had quite a success with the well-timed remark, confiding, marvelling, assuming a naïvety they knew to be assumed : "I knew a white woman once who kept a snake-bite outfit in her car." Pause : "Never drove through town without it." (Of course he knew quite well that Callie Stow kept the snake-bite outfit in the car because she used to go climbing in the Magaliesberg on Sundays, with a woman friend.) They would laugh, but he would keep looking at them straight-faced and questioning : "I mean, a snake-bite outfit? The needles? The stuff in the little bottle? The knife to make the cut?" He shrugged and looked impressed. And they laughed indulgently at the calculatedness of the white man's way of living.

He emerged from the mat of people on one side of the street, darted across, was taken in at once in the line of the bus queue. He had spent two or three nights at the flat, and now was lost to his hosts, with their casual friendliness and the excess of equipment which even the most modest or hard-up white person seemed to find it impossible to do without. Ahead of him a woman sat on the kerb unravelling her baby from the wrappings it had worn on her back; it had a hot, wet, but not a bad, smell. People were eating single bananas, bought for a penny from an Indian with a push-cart. The intersection at the corner was one of the main exits from town and great processions of white men's cars and buses pulled up face to face. As the lights changed and the press began to move on, a drunk brown boy walked almost into a bus. He had straightened hair in a crew cut, wore a loose jacket, and carried at the end of his long arm a transistor radio covered with imitation crocodile skin. He wove through the sluggish cars, swinging back from one to bump the nose of another, and shouting modestly all the time, "Ya fuckin' bastard . . ."

The bus settled low on its wheels as it filled up and then pushed a way into the traffic. Gideon Shibalo's body adjusted itself to the pressure and jar of other bodies like the automatic accommodation of muscles to a bed whose discomforts are so familiar that they have acquired a certain comfort of their own.

He read a column of newspaper between the angle of someone's jaw and a dusty shoulder. The shriek and chitter of penny whistle music came from a loud speaker down on the heads of those, like himself, who occupied standing room; he looked up from the print along the lightly bobbing heads, seeing the amber of stale afternoon sun show dusty on the wool of the bareheaded ones; he thought : like the pin-heads of mould. If you saw us from high enough we would populate the earth like the furry patch spreading on a bit of cheese. He was smiling as he turned back to the paper. The smells of cheap soap, dirty feet, oranges, chips, and the civet smell of the perfume on a girl spooky-faced with white women's make-up, were soon overcome by the warm, strong sourness of kaffir beer, given out from the pores of the men and shining on their faces like a libation.

As he walked through the township he called out to people he knew, stopped to talk, and, as the home-comers dispersed along the streets, passed for whole stretches, before houses, boarded-up shops, a church with uneven windows, a dry-cleaner's, a coffin-maker's, a men's hairdresser's, the insurance agent and the herbalist, without seeing what he passed, though he avoided surely the sudden ditches that sagged down beside the streets, the zig-zag of brats and dogs and the occasional mule. He did not see all this, but he could have sat down in a room anywhere on earth and drawn it. If it were to be pulled down, bulldozed and smoothed flat for other occupants, he would not see it any less clearly, or forget a single letter of the writing on the hairdresser's sign that got smaller as space on the board ran out. For years, up until the time the passport was refused, he had hated all such places, but once the passport was refused, once he began to spend most of his time among whites, the strong feeling died away. The passport had slammed in his face; lethargy can produce an effect outwardly very like content. He was drinking a lot then, and the township, with what he had thought of as its muck-heap tolerance, its unbearable gregariousness, its sentimental brutality, sheltered him. You could die of self-pity in those places; no one would harry you into feeling ashamed, or flog you on to your feet with bull about what you owe yourself, the way whites do to each other.

His relationship with the Stow woman was one that laid great emphasis on self-respect, and yet for him the real fillip of self-respect came when he was finished with her; it seemed possible to live again quite simply, without making a lot of talk about it. He was back at his teaching job, his lousy job; the crowded faces of hungry children facing his own every day; the timidity, earnestness, self-importance and pomposity of the other teachers in the staff-room, with their consciousness of themselves as "educated". They were very conscious, too, that he was an "artist", and reminded friends that he was a colleague of theirs. Hadn't he competed with white artists and won a scholarship to go to Italy? In the city, too, in the white houses and flats where he was welcome, he was always accepted as a painter—"the one who was supposed to go to Rome". He did not paint any more but he realised that this did not matter. It would not matter if he never painted again; he could live for the rest of his life, in the townships on the fact that he had once painted something that competed favourably against white artists, in the city on the fact that he was both a painter who had achieved notice overseas and a black man. The idea coldly frightened and fascinated him. It seemed the real reason why he could not paint. He chuckled over it and at the same time the fact of his amusement was the confirmation, the finish—let him laugh; he would never paint anything again.

After he had turned away from Callie Stow, like a man who goes out for an evening stroll and never comes back, he had come to see his own old view of his home as as inaccurate as hers : she thought of the townships as places exalted by struggle; like treasure saved from the rest of the plundering world in a remote cave, she believed the Africans kept love alive. He went about the townships again now almost as he had worn the coating of streets there as a child, without any moral or spiritual conception of them. He went in from the white world like an explorer who, many times bitten and many times laid low with fever, can go back unthinkingly into territory whose hazards mean no more to him than crossing a city street.

His room was far down from the terminus. Shoes scuffed and twisted against the uneven ground so that by the time you got there you had taken on again the dust and shabbiness of the place, you were given protective colouring. The room itself was in a row added behind a house that was solidly built for a location, a brick house with a verandah. A piece of bald swept ground before it was fenced in with scrap—railway sleepers, bits of corrugated iron, chicken-netting—and a dog on a chain attached to a wire that ran the length of the fence raced barking from end to end of the scope of its existence. The owners of the house, the old woman and her husband, sat on the verandah behind this fierce frieze and added figures on bits of smoothed sugar bag. There were tins of fire in the yard and the small children called out, some even in English, "Hello", while the bigger ones, who were no longer friendly and had not yet learned the substitute of politeness, took no notice of who came or went.

Ida was in the room; he heard her gentle, breathy voice with the sound of agreement in it as he put his foot on the thick doorstep. Some shirts and socks were lying on the bed; she had a key and must have brought his washing. Sol was there too, a friend who drove a dry cleaner's van. He challenged, with pleasure : "You're not easy to get hold of, man! I've been here twice, everything locked up. I met the old man and he said he hadn't seen you for two days."

"Yeh, I know." Shibalo grinned. He was looking round the room with the roving interest of one who wants to keep up with whatever life has been going on in his absence. "Did Bob do anything about the record player?" he said to the young woman.

"Well, I don't know. I haven't heard from him. He might have tried to get hold of you."

"Night duty?" he asked her.

She shook her head and moved her feet so that she could admire her patent shoes. "Day off."

"Where're you people going to eat?" Sol asked.

"I've eaten at my sister's already," the girl said.

"Well, what about it, then?" Sol gestured as if to set her about preparing a meal. She laughed, "I don't think there's anything."

The room had the disturbed look of a place that is subjected to quiet neglect alternating with vigorous raids on its resources. A suitcase stuffed with papers had burst a lock on one side, there were paper-backs embossed with candle-drippings beside the bed, four or five different tobacco tins, some bottles of pills and a broken chain that had once been on the door. Sol sat in a smart yellow canvas chair shaped like a sling; it was of the kind

127

advertised for "modern leisure living". The black iron bed, book-shelf sagging under canvases as well as books, the cupboard where the girl Ida unearthed a tin of pilchards—each held objects that had been turned up in the rummage for something else, and never found their way back where they belonged. The window was overgrown with a briar of strips of wire and tin provided as burglar-proofing by the landlord, and as it gave no light or air anyway was covered with a strange little wool carpet. A primus, a basin of pots and dishes, and a big old typewriter, filled up the space between the legs of a table; there was a clean square on the top where the record player usually rested. The back of the door was covered with a huge travel poster reproduc-ing a Romanesque madonna, and magazine cut-outs of Klee, Picasso, Jackson Pollock, Sidney Nolan and the Ife bronzes curled away from the walls. When they fell in an autumn of their own they were replaced by others, but the cutting of a photograph that had appeared in a newspaper when the Italian scholarship award was announced was stuck back again, and was already yellowed and brittle.

Ida went to the corner shop to get bread and polony and Shibalo took out the brandy bottle. Sol was talking politics—it was about some point that was going to come up for discussion at a meeting that he had wanted to canvass Shibalo—and look-ing over Shibalo's newspaper at the same time. "There you are" —he chopped the side of his hand against a column. "There you are"—he took the glass of brandy and began again—"they want a conference. 'Liberals and Progressives urge consultation with all races.' There it is. What do we want to talk about, for Christ' sake? Jabavu talked to them, Luthuli talked to them, talk, talk, what do we want to talk for when we've got the whole continent behind us?"

"A long way off," Shibalo suggested. "Rhodesia, Portuguese East in between—" Sol stared at him to indicate that he knew better, whatever he might be saying: "Going, going, man."

"You think Nkrumah's going to sail round to Cape Town and land troops?"

"*No,* man. I didn't say that. You know what I think. I think the guns are going to come in through Bechuanaland and Basutoland and the U.N.'s going to take over in South West."

He stopped at the obstacle of his own impatience because these things had not happened already.

"And the guns are going to come in from Southern Rhodesia and the Portuguese to blow those guns out."

"So what do you want? You think we'll have a nice talk to the whites and they'll push the Government out and hand over to us?"

"Look—even when you're being smart, you don't get it straight. Most of the whites don't want to talk to you, they wouldn't be ready to talk to you until you've opened their brains with a panga. Make no mistake about it, they won't waste any words on the blacks. They don't want any palaver with black leaders because there are no black leaders so far as they are concerned, understand? *They* are the ones who decide what's going to happen to us. Where we're going to live. Where we're going to work. What bloody stairs we'll put our stinking black feet on—talk! My God, it's only a miserable handful without a place up there in the Government between them, who want to *talk*. The others want to shoot it out, man, once they can't wangle it out any longer with shit about homelands. But when it comes to shooting it out, stop dreaming, that's what I'm telling you chaps. We may need sticks and stones and whatever we can lay our hands on, as well as the promises from our brothers out there."

Sol, who spent his nights in such talk, could not lean forward in confirmation of points as he wished to, because the yellow chair was one that held its occupant rigidly back in repose, and tipped him out if he tried to make it more accommodating. But his face broadened in the relief of agreement, now and then, and now his lips lifted away from his big, uneven teeth and his mouth opened in a gesture of receptiveness, warm, encouraging. He and Shibalo held one another's eyes for a few moments, drank the brandy, and felt the comfort and reassurance of an old complementary friendship. When Ida came back with the food they were loud in talk again.

"I don't want blood! I don't like blood!"

". . . no, be honest, man—what's the real reason? Why have you stayed with Congress, why have I stayed? No, it's not because of non-violence—"

"I don't want blood! I don't like blood!" Sol got carefully

129

out of his chair and took another brandy; this was one of the interjections he always murmured.

"We want guns, like everyone else. We're prepared to fight with guns. We're waiting here for guns, like manna from heaven. We've got round to feeling we can't do anything without guns, isn't that so? The only difference is that Congress doesn't say this out loud, and the Africanists do."

"Wait a moment, wait a sec . . . we don't want to have to use guns, that's the difference, but they don't see any other way—"

"But *we* don't see any other way, either, do we? Isn't that exactly what we've been talking about all this time? We're a banned organisation, man—you can get arrested tomorrow if you hold up your pants with a Congress badge."

The young woman cut the bread and the meat. She did not take part in the talk, except to laugh occasionally, but she listened with the air of one who hears her own views expressed, and when she was in other company she always repeated what Shibalo said. She was a nurse, which, along with school-teaching and social welfare work, had been the ambition of most African girls with intelligence and drive above the average until a few years ago; now such girls wanted to be models or actresses. Influenced by them, she dressed in the latest fashion to filter down to mass-production, but had not straightened her hair and wore it grown long into a high bun on top of her head. There was no indication in her face of how old she might be; it was simply a statement of adult womanhood, that would last fresh and firm for a comfortable time. Shibalo had paid a lot of attention to her at a party one night, and then people had begun to ask them to parties together, as a couple. He was always affectionate with her at parties; there was something about her that fitted in with a light mood, that demanded that one should tease her about her gilt choker necklace and put one's head on her shoulder after too many drinks. She knew that this display was misleading; they were not really a couple, that she could tell, though she had lived with him on and off for a year, and she did the things—like taking his washing away for him—that a casual bed-companion does not do, but that a woman does for her man.

"Ida—you want to sit here?" Sol made as if to get up when she brought him a plate of food. "Stay there, stay there—" she sat on the bed next to Shibalo. She felt very friendly and easy and fond, with Sol; to be one of them produced a welling-up in her, relaxing and secure. If they joked, she felt witty and lolled back on the bed; if they were at each other, hammer and tongs, she was excited; when they spoke of what she thought of as "taking over", she felt an intoxicating superiority, the stiffness of face of one who has witnessed prophecy.

Sol was made slightly anxious by a certain shift in Shibalo's thinking that he himself had not caught up with; this was how it occurred to him, but he was also aware that it might mean that Shibalo was moving off, abandoning a position that he, Sol, had thought was as immovable, for both of them, as the earth they stood on. He continued to argue disbelievingly : "You're not serious about wondering why you've stayed with Congress? If you just like to talk, man, then it's all right."

Shibalo settled himself quietly and patiently. "I'm used to the people I work with. We've gone through a lot together—there's this business of loyalty, eh?"

"Sure, sure." Sol was warming, but wary.

"Right. But I didn't begin to work with Congress as a friend-ship club, eh? I wanted to work to get things moving for us, eh? So why should I, or anyone else with an eye on the real objec-tive, the only thing that counts, stick with any crowd if I see that some other crowd is getting something done? What does another name and another slogan mean to me? I've got no ambitions to climb up a party ladder, Sol. I just want to see the blacks stand up on their hind legs, that's all. I don't care if they give the thumbs-up or bow three times to the moon. The chaps in the street have got the right idea, man; I used to get wild when I'd see them join any campaign that looked like scaring the whites. If it was a Congress thing, yes, they were Congress men; if it was a PAC thing, yes, they were Africanists. But why not? I'm not sure I shouldn't do the same thing.'

"Ah-h, you're crazy," Sol said disgustedly; his voice touched upon the idea again, the toe of a boot gingerly up-turning a dubious object. "What do you call that?"

"Guerilla politics, that's what it is."

"Again you talk as if there were no principles. Do I have to spell it out for you?"

Shibalo handed the brandy bottle to him. "Good God, Sol,

no one's going to care a damn for our principles in this business, in a hundred years' time. They'll simply write it down—they took control at such-and-such-date. They made a go of it, or they made a mess of it."

"I don't know what's wrong with you. You used to go on about ends determining means, now you only scream for results. What about the difference in principles between the Africanists and us?"

"There isn't any in the long run. There won't be any. They want to get rid of the white man any way they can; Congress wants to submerge him in a non-racial state without cutting his throat first. The Africanists will find it necessary to hang on to the white man and employ him and his cash, Congress will find that he won't come quietly. See?"

Sol began to laugh with savour at the neatness of it, and they laughed together. He felt that they had landed up side by side on the solid ground of accord, and said again, as they ate, "My God, it *is* something to feel the whole continent of them free up there—whenever I pick up the paper, man—"

But the death-embracing surrender of his will to paint had given Shibalo, in some unsought exchange, by a law of balance, a firm assurance and detachment in his approach to other things. He had gone through a form of submission so final that he could manage very well without illusions of any kind about the other circumstances of his life. He said serenely, "My brothers. My brothers. I'm not so sure about that."

Later the two men went out to the house of a third friend. He was out, at the house of a fourth, and so they went on there. It was a night like others before and after, that ended neither late nor early, since no one thought of such conceptions; eventually, no one came in or out any more, and the last knot of talkers dissolved into the dark.

One evening some months later, when Ida was packing Shibalo's dirty clothes into a department store paper carrier of the kind she carefully saved for this purpose, she found paint on a shirt. She said nothing; only wondered, in her practical way, how she would get it off.

TEN

In the Easter holidays, Shibalo was free all day. There was nowhere they could go together in town. Ann drove him out into the veld, kicking up a wake of dust in the face of the city where everyone was droning away at their jobs, and sending the little car scudding along the empty, week-day highways and lurching over dust roads and farm tracks. They never knew where they were making for, only what they were looking for, and if they saw a kloof, or the concentration of trees along a declivity that meant a hidden river, Ann found a way to it. They were safe from other picnickers during the week; only once a little troop of passing piccanins stood on the further bank of a river and looked with dull astonishment on the sight of a white girl and a black man eating together.

Ann was seized with the desire for water and grass and willow trees, sun and birds. She swam in the brown rivers, waving to him where he lay sipping beer; she emerged seal-wet and dried off in the warm smell of water-weed rising from her skin. She picked the fragile and sparse flowers of the tough veld with enthusiasm and then let them wither, and she brought a book with her that she never read. He watched her activities with the amusement of novelty. He was born in the townships and had never lived the traditional African life of raising crops and herding cattle, neither had he known the city white child's attachment to a pastoral ancestry fostered from an early age by the traditional "treats" of picnics and camping. He belonged to town life in a way that no white man does in a country where it is any white man's privilege to have the leisure and money to get out into the veld or down to the beaches. He could not swim, and felt no more urge to get into the water when she did than if she had had some special equipment for the environment —gills or fins—that he did not naturally possess.

Intense physical silences arose between them. Her smile, his lazy voice filled space no longer fretted and pressed in upon by the jostling of others outside the walls of the flat. The vision of each for the other was not broken up—like a pack of picture cards thumb-shuffled in quick succession—as it was in the clandestinity of the streets. And they had the touch of lordliness of people who are breaking the rules out of no stronger reason than mere inclination.

Yet even in the innocence of one of these Edens each retained something watchful of the other. When Boaz's name came naturally into her conversation, neither paused; once when he mentioned something about his child, she betrayed no curiosity about the child's mother, but only asked, with affectionate interest : "What's he like?" The one time when each was not making an amused and attracted audience of the other was when they talked of the possibilities of his going to Europe to study and paint. The basis of an exciting sympathy between two people is often some obstacle that lies long-submerged in the life of one; he thinks he has accepted it until the resurrection of fresh feeling, the swaggering assertion of self, that comes with a love affair. She heard from him again and again, in the piece-meal way of such revelations, details of the story about the scholarship he had been unable to take up in Italy, because his record of political activity had prevented him from getting a passport. At the time he had turned his back on the alternative of signing away, on the exit permit that was offered him, his right to come home again. He had decided that he did not want to be a painter at the price of giving up his right to fight the system that demanded that price. He had made the decision long ago, in all the ways that a decision like that is made and ratified and accepted and forgotten—except by the one whose life is ringed by it as a tree is ringed, so that as time swells it must be taken into the flesh. He had talked it out in the fire of approval that warmed the group he worked with in politics. He had entered, through it, the solidarity of the wronged, with their pride in their formidability; he had been the *cause célèbre*, in demand at parties at the homes of leftist and liberal whites; he had boasted, drunk, when everyone was tired of him, and the others around him in the shebeen didn't even know what he was talking about, of his defiant sacrifice. But lying with her head on his arm in a eucalyptus plantation while she described a life that might be possible for him in Italy or France, Greece, perhaps—he did not pay much attention to the geography, and she did not always identify the strange place-names—the whole balance of his existence seemed to fall on that side, and the weight of a struggle that was other people's as well as his own did not count against it. He forgot he was an African, burdened, like a Jew, with his category of the chosen, and was aware only of himself as a man who was one of those who, even if they are only drawing pictures on the pavement, choose for themselves.

The eucalyptus plantation was not more than twenty minutes from town; it belonged to one of the dying gold-mines near Johannesburg. Ann was sure they couldn't be seen there, though, leaning on her elbow, she could see men cross the veld from the shafthead not far away. The little old houses of the white married quarters near by were not lived in. She got up and began to pick the narrow leaves from her dress. "This is a good place to dump a body," she said, with a laugh. "You know. You see those photographs on the front page with an arrow next to a tree—that's where it was found after a three-day search."

The dry, clean smell of the eucalyptus was strong; under the trees it was cool as menthol, in the hot sun it had the live fragrance of burning wood. There was no stir in the air but the leaves moved silently in the evaporation of heat as if unseen insects clambered among them. A dove throbbed regularly in the heart of the man-made wood. The city was so near they might have put out a hand and touched it.

"Do you think you are the kind that gets murdered?" he said proudly.

". . . Nobody ever thinks they're the kind. Who does get murdered anyway?" She appealed to him when she talked; he challenged her—that was their game of communication. Her eyes were lazily following the blanketed figure of a man on the veld path; he bent to pick up something, probably a safety pin he had dropped, and then took off the blanket, cast it out round himself, and secured it closely under his neck. They were both watching him now, and they laughed. "That'll keep out the cold." "He's come up off shift," Shibalo said. "It's dark and wet down under the ground and now he's going back to the compound for his *phuthu* and his *nyama*."

"I wonder where he comes from," she said. "These mines are

worked out, or just about. We came this way one day when I first arrived—with the Stilwells and everybody. We saw them dancing at one of these mines." The man walked on, unaware of their eyes on him, and disappeared out of sight round the yellow pyramid of a mine dump.

"People get murdered for money," he said, lying back. "Where I come from it's money. And women get murdered by men," he added.

She looked at him, and smiled, and gave a brief toss of her head, to settle her hair and liven the angle of her neck.

Presently she came over and squatted beside him as if she were making herself comfortable at a fire, and said, "Boaz is coming home soon."

"Wasn't he home last weekend?"

"I mean he's coming home to stay. For a while."

"Your husband is your affair," he said, stroking her ankle.

She liked to be free, but not as free as that. She smiled brilliantly and her forehead reddened. "I know," she said, with an uprush of confidence and gaiety. Then suddenly : "Let's go and buy lunch at Baumann's Drift Hotel."

"Oh yes," he said, "I'm sure that would be lovely."

"Why not? I mean it. I can go in and tell them I want lunch packed up to eat on the road, and a bottle of wine."

"You can send the boy in to get it," he said, grinning.

"That's right."

They got into the car and drove off over the veld to the track; the man they had seen, or another in a blanket like his, was sitting on an old oil drum, smoking a pipe. He was talking to another man who still wore his tin helmet and yellow oilskins from underground, and as the two looked up, unhurriedly and incuriously as the car brushed them, Shibalo slowed down and hailed them. They were suspicious and startled, and then their faces opened in delight. Whatever it was that he said seemed to shock them and make them laugh; they called back after him, still laughing. Ann was excited by the ease of this communication. "How did you know they'd understand?" "I talked to them in Shangaan. It's the first language I ever spoke, up at my grandfather's place. I could see they were Shangaans, they're chaps from Moçambique. They were very polite." "Did you see, the one had clay ringlets in his hair," she said, her eyes

136

shining. "Of course, that's the right thing for a young man." He was laughing with her, in a kind of pride.

They stopped just off the main road to eat the lunch they got from the hotel, and sat under a tree where any passing motorist who looked twice might see them. Neither mentioned the dangerous carelessness of this, or suggested that they might be more discreet. Ann met with the insolence of disregard the outraged curiosity of a woman who kept her face lingeringly turned toward them from a car window; she must have drawn her companion's attention to the sight, for the car faltered before taking up the speed of its approach again.

That evening, on the way home from a party, some white friends that they were with tried to get Gideon into a night-club with them. Someone's brother was a member and had a bottle there, and there was a black cabaret act : these were the grounds on which, rather drunk, the party thought they would bluff their way into admittance. The story was that Gideon was a singer himself and brother of the leader of the act. "He'll sing for you, you'll see"—the amiable insistence of one of the young white men produced in the manager, who had been summoned to deal with the crisis, the special shrewd sternness, the clench-teeth lunatic tact, of the man who smiles in the patron face all his life and loathes and despises it. The party stood round him in the dim entrance among gilt mirrors, cigar smoke and muffled music; their appearance, the pretty, animated women, the authoritative, light-hearted air of the men, was like a distressing caricature of the scene inside, where such people were being subserviently tended, and where drunken whimsicality, fumbling sex, and argumentativeness, were respectfully condoned.

"You'll understand, Mr. Solvesen, sir, I can't do it. I'd lose my licence. I dare not even let the artists sit down at a table after they've been on." The man's eyes were dead with rage against these arrogant young fools who pretended not to know the vast difference between natives employed to serve or enter- tain and some educated black bastard sitting himself down, like one of themselves, among the members. He wanted to throw them out, but a long discipline of sycophancy held him back : he had an idea that although the brother was an insignificant member he had been introduced by and sometimes was in the party of a wealthy and important financier.

Ann, who was leaning amiably against the red velvet wall and pinching the plastic laurels of a fake Caesar on a cardboard pillar, said, "Oh, poor little man, let's leave him alone."

The group left quite calmly, exchanging private jokes. The girl who had spoken was good-looking, sure of herself; could one understand them? Suddenly, for no reason at all, the man in evening dress felt like a lackey—but *of course*, a black man was good enough for them to laugh with and slap on the back.

Boaz came home at the weekend again; he had been moving about as much as he could in the Eastern and Northern Transvaal, but the summer—the rainy season—was not a good time for field-work, and at the beginning of April he meant to come home finally to prepare for a long field-trip during the dry winter months. He brought a bottle of aquavit with him, and although it was still warm enough to sit on the old verandah in the evening, he and Ann and the Stilwells drank it instead of their usual gin or beer. Two small glassfuls each produced that stoking-up of social responses that the neat liquor of cold countries is famous for, and by the time the servant Agatha called them to dinner they were ready to open a big flask of chianti that was being saved for a special occasion, and to make a banquet out of the stew. Jessie felt too lazy and disinclined to absent herself from the others to put the little girls to bed, and they ran in and out as they pleased, left out of, but nevertheless infected by, the grown-ups' mood. Only Morgan, who had arrived from his farm holiday the day before, remained unaffected. "Give him a glass of wine," Jessie said. But he did not want it. "For God's sake, you're old enough now," she said. "It's wasted on me," he said, with a smile. "I don't like the taste." He was innocent of the despising look she rested on him. He was going back to school in the morning. His hair was sunburned along the hairline and shone phosphorescent there; brown skin made his face more definitive but his voice was finally breaking and the awkward uncertainty of its pitch seemed cruelly appropriate to him. He made her restless, like a piece of furniture that never looks right in any room. The conversation was lively with anecdote and mimicry and the broad verbal

138

gestures of vigorous people among their own kind. The atmosphere was not cosy, stressing the relationships of the four men and women to each other, but independent : each individual enjoying the licence of an adulthood that had no rules except those of personal idiosyncrasy. Morgan sat quiet, as the bewildered will; he thought that he could think of nothing to say, but the fact was that he had nothing to say in the context of talk that, as usual among grown-ups at home, ran counter to the tenets of adulthood that *they* taught *him*. In order to qualify as an adult (they said) one had to be kind, controlled and respectful of human dignity. Yet they criticised their friends and the people they worked with, laughed and shouted each other down, and referred with veiled bawdy cynicism to love. He was afraid to admit to himself that the rules they thrust on him were merely some kind of convenience, some kind of fraud by devaluation; and he had no way of knowing the inner disciplines by which they lived.

He admired and was amused by his mother, as, bare-footed and flushed-faced, she cha-cha-cha-ed round the table with Boaz, between the stew and the fruit salad, or, with narrow eyes and a challenging grimace, forgot her food and waited to make a point. He was afraid to show his pleasure; he knew it so quickly grew into the pawing attention that irritated everyone.

All Jessie's animation, that evening, was for Morgan. She was conscious of a picture of herself, as a woman is conscious of a picture of herself for the eyes of a lover.

When the Stilwells had gone upstairs to bed Boaz and his wife hung about a little longer. Boaz had the true scholar's tendency to turn furtively, as to a secret assignation, to his work, to "finger it over", as Jessie had once described it, after any sort of break from it. Quite naturally, for him, the boisterous evening ended in a quiet hour of the night when he might as well play over a few of the new tapes he had made in the bush. He went upstairs to fetch the portable player. Jessie, coming from the bathroom, said "I've left the alka-seltzer out." They both thought of something they had been laughing over earlier and burst out laughing. Tom called from the bedroom "Good night", and Boaz said, "I'm going to have a little music first."

In the living-room, Ann lay on the divan watching him come

in and said, automatically, "We ought to go up." But she did not move, except to roll over on her stomach and rest on her elbows. Drumming and nasal humming began to come from the player, and she swayed and began to fit the words of a jazz-jargon song to it. "That's it, that's it," he grinned as he went through a box of tapes. The tape in the player snapped and at once he was busy, exasperated and absorbed. When it was fixed, and the music began again, he said : "Come on?"

She had begun to examine her finger-nails; again and again she pushed down the surrounding skin and looked at her hands. She was frowning in deep concentration, the concentration of keeping something out, rather than in, but one of the pen-ultimate ripples of drunkenness reached her and suddenly she rested her outstretched chin on her hands and flung her head back, smiling brilliantly, sleepily, uncontrollably.

"Isn't this a good one?"

"So tender ! What is it?"

"*Makhweyana* bow accompaniment. Zulu woman. It shouldn't be on this tape, with that other snake-charmer thing, but I was short."

"Gorgeous !" she said again, as a particular phrase in the song was repeated.

"Pasty-face," he said. It was an overture of affection, to show he noticed her. In the generous outpouring of trivial intimacies when they first fell in love, she had told him how this had been a hated nick-name at her first school. He used it whenever he wanted to tell her he found her beautiful.

She did not attempt to brush the acknowledgement aside; as always, the temptation to accept it overcame her; denial would have been guile : the acceptance was innocent.

The mood between them was affectionate, and the mood of the evening behind them was one that suggested that men and women were neither good nor bad, happy nor unhappy, but taking pleasure here, suffering there, as they tried to live; rash, occasionally exalted, often funny. To be human was to bear with one another through all this. He was looking for another tape that he particularly wanted to play to her and telling her how he had come to make the recording, when she said, with obstinacy and even a little humour : "You know, this business of going about with Gideon Shibalo. I've been having a sort of"

—she did not pause, but interrupted herself with a quick lurching sigh—"love affair."

The second sentence was something she forced herself to say,
for herself. He knew the moment she said Shibalo's name; she
saw it at once in the slackening of muscular tension in the line
of his neck from ear to shirt collar. His ears went scarlet, like a
girl's. She watched these things although she didn't want to.
Boaz had a waxen, oriental skin in which the blood never showed
unless he cut himself.

She spoke again before he could say anything. "Did you have
any idea?" At the dinner table, she had told—very well—the
story of the incident at the night-club. Now she tried to let herself off lightly by believing that she had really confessed then,
in a way, in a general context of the culpability of experience.

He was frowning, to ask for time; he stayed her. He said,
above some tumult, "You've made love to Shibalo?"

"I've told you."

There was a silence; the first real silence of their lives together.
She was sober, but the ultimate ripple of the wine's tide just
touched her, once more. Without meaning to, she made the
funny, doleful smile, lips pursed down at the corners, eyebrows
wide, that she used to draw his attention to, and make mock
excuse for, some trivial blunder when she was doing drawings
for him.

He smiled slightly, slowly, fascinatedly; it was as if she had
done it on purpose, to play with him, to demonstrate a power
over him, and from that moment she did begin to feel
power.

He came and stood above her. He faced her without weapons
and in an honesty as different from her own as his conception
of work was different from hers. "What's it all about, though?"
he said.

"I don't know."

He nodded. She spoke the truth, for her.

"It's just one of these things that happen. Before you realise
it . . ." She was ready to embroider, to invent, now, but he
stopped her by squatting on the floor beside the divan and
putting his hand in a sort of muffling caress over her face. "Poor
Pasty-face."

She sat up, offended. "Don't you believe me?"

"Of course I believe you."

"I mean don't you believe about him and me?"

She felt that it was her eyes that made him walk about the room; they did not follow him so much as propel him.

"Yes, but you don't know what it's all about. You don't tell me it's because he talks to you, or because you admire him, or because he's great in bed, or because you wanted to try a black man—I mean, it's like a child picking daisies. . ." He was patient but distressed, and she was alert to the feeling that the distress was a moral one that by-passed her. Like many people who do not mean to wound but want merely to draw attention to themselves, she found it might be necessary to make her mark draw blood.

"Why should the reason matter?" she said, smiling at him. The unspoken "to you" stopped him as if she herself had risen from the divan and stood squarely in his way. How could she force him to say, in the debased verbal currency of the film close-up, do you still love me? Don't you love me any more? The cat's whine repelled him. He tried, in the moment, in his mind, to jumble the mumbo-jumbo so as to get sense and reality out of it: Is it me you still love or is it because you don't love me—the worn units were idiotically unusable.

They talked a little while longer, but as though musing gently on something that had come upon them without volition—the inexplicable behaviour of friends, or a venture that had gone wrong through outside circumstances. "I suppose I ought to have come with you more." "Nonsense. You can't run away from these things."

"Have you really never wanted to make love to anyone else since we've been living together?"

"I don't think so. Oh, perhaps once—"

"Viveca, that time at Ellman's?"

"Yes, well, she hadn't changed a bit, she was as crazy as she used to be—" But it was still only just after midnight; the night stretched long as soon as their voices gave way to the creaks that went over their heads as the house eased itself.

They went upstairs with loosely linked hands. Castaways thrown together on the unfamiliar island, they moved about the room with a show of being at home, secretly watching each other. He never had asked her if she was still in love with him.

Lying in bed she felt a lust like sudden generosity toward him, and longed to touch him.

Yet in the morning, when the whole business hung in wait with the smell of last night's drinking in the house, and he asked, "Are you going to see Shibalo this week?" she wrapped the hair-combings from her brush round her finger and said, "I suppose so."

Ten days later Boaz came home. There were sheafs of notes, drawings and photographs in the bedroom, and instruments and various African cooking utensils (these had nothing to do with his studies, but he picked them up anyway) littered the upstairs landing. He was in the house surrounded by these things all day and would have come downstairs perhaps only to the smell of dinner, in the evening, if someone had not broken in upon him from time to time. One of the children would stump slowly up the stairs, sent to say that lunch was ready, if he wanted some. Agatha would shout up the well, "Telephone for Baas Davis!"

Jessie appeared with a bottle of beer wearing a glass over its neck. "Still in a muck. How long is it going to take you to struggle out of this? I'd almost forgotten your existence." "Oh, I've only started unpacking. Wait till I start editing my tapes; all sorts of horrible noises—you'll remember I'm around then, all right." He pushed at the papers before him with a gesture of washing his hands of them. He wore an old pullover as if he didn't know that it was an exceptionally hot day, for April, outside. The beer seemed like an offering for an invalid. He took it from her and, fishing with one foot for his sandals under a chair, said, "You know about it, of course."

"Yes." Jessie stood blinking slowly, wary.

"What's he like?"

"I like him," she said.

He smiled. "That's all right, you don't have to worry about it."

"I thought everything was fine with you two. Of course it may still be, you know. It may sound a vulgar way of putting it, to you, but these things blow over. You forget about them if you live together long enough."

"Three years."

143

She said encouragingly, "Not a bad basis. The trouble is that one always begins to think one owns a person. If you really could, you wouldn't want them any more. I don't think that's bitchiness or neurotic; it comes from the destruction of polarity, and the tension of attraction that goes with it. Well, sex—love, whatever—apart, you have to let the other person live as he must. I don't know why we always talk about power as if it were something generated by and operating only in politics. It's a ghastly thing to resist taking hold of, anywhere. Oh I'm scared of it," she shrugged in distaste, "and I'm always fondling it, like a dirty habit."

They laughed, and went down to lunch. Tom was home, too, and the talk was of other things, not as if Shibalo did not exist, but in acceptance of the fact that he did, indeed. It could not be expected that the whole household should be stirred by his existence; Tom, Jessie, Elisabeth, Madge, Clem—Boaz had the pull of other lives about him, and felt comforted, and lonely.

The life of the house seemed to go on as usual for the next few weeks. The situation became, astonishingly, as impossible situations often do, part of the everyday comings and goings of eight people. The coarse, elastic fibres of being, that sustained so much, matted in the new tension.

Ann left the house, alone, three or four nights a week, and was often out all day. When she was at home she helped Boaz assiduously with his work, and would come swiftly downstairs every now and then, full of enthusiasm : "Look at this ! Boaz copied it himself, made it himself from reeds. Look, he had to find the right grasses to bind it together, and everything !" Sometimes, when they were all in one room, she would seem to put herself apart from them—Boaz, Tom, Jessie—abandoning her usual way of lounging or squatting where she alighted, and holding her profile clear. Whenever she came upon Jessie in any part of the house she would take the initiative of a big, blazing smile—though, as Jessie remarked to Tom, ". . . I'm not going to ask her anything, for heaven's sake."

The Stilwells supposed the affair was tailing off, in the civilised way. There were two ways such adventures died, once they weren't going to bring about a divorce : one, the primitive catharsis, with tears, threats of suicide, and a highly emotional reconciliation; two, the civilised way, with three-cornered talks, plenty of drinks, and an exaggerated courtesy. The Stilwells had heard Shibalo's voice upstairs one afternoon; he was being shown Boaz's collection of new instruments. Soon all three of them, Boaz, Ann and Shibalo, came down, and Shibalo stayed to dinner. He was charming, rather like a visiting celebrity determined to be natural.

ELEVEN

Every day when Ann went to meet Gideon she held in her mind a frame of awareness that might fall into place and mark it as the last time. There did not need to be an event or a decision, merely the word or the look, the turn of mood that would give the affair its meaning and the grounds for its destruction contained within the meaning. She neither dreaded this nor was curious about it, but it lent intensity to the inanimate witnesses of her movements—the grain of tables that she scratched with a finger-nail as she talked to Shibalo, the colour and heat-tacky texture of the plastic covering on which she sat alone in the car waiting for him at mid-day. People's faces she scarcely saw, for she was aware only, in the house, of what they might be thinking of her : a scribble of fears and impulses scratched them out, like the faces in the children's picture-books that she saw lying about upstairs.

She could not stop seeing Gideon simply because Boaz was home; it had never occurred to her that she might not stop whenever she felt like it, but after she had told Boaz that night, she knew that this was not so simple : if she gave up seeing Gideon because Boaz had come home, it followed that she had begun a love affair with him only because Boaz was away.

The day after she had talked to Boaz, Gideon saw her standing on the balcony of the flat watching him as he came up the road. She stood there with her arms open, hands resting on the balcony rail, and he could feel her attention on him long before he could make out her face clearly. She smiled suddenly as her face came within distance of recognition, and turned and went into the flat, leaving a single trail of cigarette smoke moving gently, like a water-weed, in the air where she had stood. He hurried instinctively. In the flat she had arranged flowers that she had brought; she must have been there some time, but she wore a coat, as if she did not intend to stay. The coat came to his eye

146

and suddenly created the status of a past tense between himself and this woman; how many times had he seen it, flung on the back seat of the car, hanging from her shoulders with the sleeves empty! He had slept with it rolled up under his head, under the blue gums. He said to her once, "Your coat'll get dirty," and she said, "That old thing—nothing harms it." It had been to Norway and Turkey and Italy, this coat, that was shabby-smart and designed to make a girl like her look lost and in need of no home.

"Where're you off to?"

"Nowhere." She stood in the middle of the room.

He came over to her kidding, tenderly, lingeringly, "I ought to paint you in that coat. Trench warfare." He touched the belt, fiddled with the buttons and slid his hand down into hers. They began to kiss; when she felt him about to release her she held him and when he felt her about to draw away he enticed her closer. "You'll find another model," she said. "What about a picnicker—wha'd'you-call-it, an open-air companion." "That too, I suppose."

The game of renunciation began. In it they felt the parenthetic closeness of two people who have shared an experience outside the separate involvement of each in his own background. The Stilwell house, that held every vibration of her voice and laugh, and had seen her every gesture, did not know her as she had her being among the objects and with the person in the flat. Like two men who have been stationed together in some foreign region, or a pair of children who return to family meals from an imaginary country, there was an existence in which they knew life and each other as nobody closer to them did. It became a refuge, too; doubts and decisions did not operate there, any more than public notices specifying enchanted circles which a black foot might not enter. As soon as she sat smoking in one of the chairs belonging to the two young advertising men she had seen only twice, and following, now with her eyes, now with the sense of an intensely-known presence, Gideon as he moved about the room, Boaz's "What is it all about?" was dislodged and fell harmless.

She said, "I want you to come to the house. Meet Boaz."

They were eating grapes, sitting in the car. He threw a couple into his mouth, ate them slowly, and spat the pips out of the window. She had no idea what he would say. Their relationship was a pure one, without questions or importuning. "If you think he would want to."

"He's nice," she said. "It seems idiotic. I mean, we always both know people—" She spoke as if the affair had already died and become a friendship; while she was speaking she believed that, *from that moment,* it really had.

He did not know if what she said implied that her husband was used to her making love to other men; he felt himself, as he occasionally was, lost in this particular world, like a foreigner who speaks the language perfectly but is sometimes floored by some esoteric colloquialism. He was off-hand : "All right."

She said no more about it, though several times she talked of Boaz when they were together, held him off at arm's length and considered him. She seemed touchy that Gideon Shibalo should appreciate Boaz. The references, the anecdotes were not ones that reflected the personal relationship between Boaz and herself, but showed him, a figure on the horizon, against an impersonal light. Once Gideon was describing an acquaintance who had a special kind of perception : "He'll see you walk in the door and he'll know at once you haven't eaten yet today and are not up to much. Or he'll catch on from something you let slip without knowing it that you're about to lose your job. He smells you out and then uses what he's found out ... Not always to do you any actual harm ... but to make you feel afraid of yourself ..."

She agreed about the existence of such people and remarked, a footnote in the flitting silence before they turned to something else, "Now someone like Boaz is just the opposite, you know." She paused. "Just the opposite. He's always amazed when you point out some weak spot in a person. He's very self-absorbed, in a way, and he treats everyone as if they have the same standards and so on as he has himself. You can see a mile off that someone's lying, or a perfect mouse, but he'll treat them as if important work can be expected of them at any moment. Sometimes it's just funny, of course, but at other times it's wonderful. He never exposes people."

One afternoon after they had had lunch together at the Lucky Star she began to drive across town in the direction of the Stilwells' house. "Where're you going?" "Home," she said. "Drop

148

me off somewhere?" "Come in for a bit." She had the faraway look that seemed the nearest she ever got to depression; in the Lucky Star she had sat quietly, smoking, her hand secretly covering his every now and then to exclude him from the distance she kept from the rest of the room. Once at the house, she was cheerful and humorously at ease; how beautiful she looked, clipping across the floor in her high heels, the slim strong tendon to which her ankle narrowed at the back hollowed away on either side. There was no getting away from it, no black girl ever had ankles quite like that.

He had not given it a thought that the husband might be there, but when, after they had had the inevitable cup of tea and listened to a new record that Tom Stilwell had left in the living-room, she said, "Come up with me to see what Boaz is doing," he felt no nervousness but a calm amiability to match hers. They went upstairs, talking. She was breathy, hospitable : "Mind your step there. Jessie's children take a delight in creating hazards on the stairs. Oh, just look at this a minute—this is a wonderful *timbila* Boaz found, we're trying to fix it—" They were standing on the landing, looking into a half-unwrapped parcel of sacking and newspapers, when Clem and a grubby friend appeared in one doorway and Boaz came along the passage from the bathroom. "Boaz, this is Gid," said Ann. "Are you busy or can I bring him in to look at a few things?" Boaz had rigged up a darkroom in the bathroom, and his hands were full of wet prints pegged to a string. "Come in; let me get rid of these . . ."

Boaz had the great advantage of being on his own ground; the room, that Gideon had seen once before, briefly, was filled with the authority of work; the bed, the personal possessions and clothes scattered about were no more important than a few human necessities set up in the corner of a laboratory. Boaz pointed out various instruments, drawing attention, with the diffident modesty of a particular pride, to those he knew to be treasures. "This is quite interesting. The only thing I've ever seen at all related to it comes from Bangui, what used to be French Equatorial Africa . . . and this I think may be the only one left of its kind—beautiful, eh? It makes a mewing sound, rather disappointing after you've looked at it." He paused and said half-questioningly, half taking it for granted, "I don't know

149

whether this sort of stuff means anything to you." "Ah, it's all Greek to me," Gideon reassured him and laughed. "I remember a bit of tissue paper over a comb, at school. The kids hadn't even begun the penny whistle craze in those days." "Didn't you have an old grandmother who sang you an old African song occasionally?" Boaz could not resist a flicker of professional interest. "No, no. I'm afraid not. I was brought up by an aunt, she was great on hymns." Ann gave her usual performance, calling, "Wait, I can play this," and determinedly producing a note blown out slowly as the thick bubble of a glass-blower. She drew them together in amusement, watching her. Boaz said, "But seriously, it's quite amazing, you know. She's intensely musical. She can sing almost anything. I mean, in African music the melodic patterns differ from area to area, according to the tone pattern of each tribe's language—but she can sing accurately a song composed in any melodic pattern. And with wind instruments—a *shipalapala, kwatha,* anything like that— she controls her breath like an experienced trombone player!" They got down to the principles of construction of a group of instruments : Gideon challenged some of their features—"Why that bit of wood there? Seems crazy—why not the other way round?" and Boaz took the harp apart and, surrounded by bits of it, on the floor, demonstrated—"You're way out. They know what they're doing—you see, that conducts the vibration from the strings into here—like that. And if you put it anywhere else at all—see? It's the principle of sympathetic resonation." He looked up, intent and smiling. There was the atmosphere almost of gaiety that came of a new presence among extraordinary things that were familiar to the Davises. Ann, achieving a perfect balance between the two men, had a weightless freedom; she hummed, touched this and that, made a remark that brought the attention of both of them finely to her, like the eyes of runners breasting the tape—and came not so much as a feather's breath down on the one side or the other. After perhaps half an hour, the three of them came downstairs, and, finding the Stilwells, joined them for drinks.

For Ann, all that was necessary would have been over, now; but Gideon hung on in some sort of perversity or fascination, and then it was dinner, and of course he stayed. As the room upstairs had been, another cell of the house was roused to the hum of company. Tom and Jessie not only seemed determined to take Gideon as just another guest who had dropped in—they appeared actually to regard him as one. He and Boaz were at the centre of the talk, all through dinner. Ann knew that Boaz was impressed with him; with Gideon and Boaz both at the table with her, she was expansively charming to everyone.

"Is it a fossil you're preserving, or is it something living, that's what I'm asking," Gideon said, of Boaz's studies in music.

"Both," said Boaz, with a look that suggested this must be self-evident for two people like themselves. "The instruments will disappear altogether very soon. But the impulse to make music won't die."

"But can the drums and flutes and xylophones provide a tradition for chaps who're now going to be playing the piano and the trumpet muffled with a tin pot—all right, then, say even the violin or the organ. You come to Schoenberg via Bach and those boys; can an African arrive at the same point straight from the talking drums and the rain-making dance played on an ox-horn covered with python skin and strung with monkey-guts?"

Jessie and Tom and Ann laughed, but Boaz was excited : "Now you're getting to it. Once an African acquires all that the white civilisations have learnt about music, can he make use of a tradition that had not reached the same culmination, and perhaps was reaching in another direction?"

As usual, Gideon moved the food about his plate without eating it. He leaned back against his chair with a cigarette burning down in his hand and said, "The whites took away the African past; once we accepted the present from them, that was that."

"The past is accomplished, living in your bones, you can't lose it," Tom said.

"No, you must lose it. When we accepted the white man's present, of industrialisation and mechanised living, we took on his future at the same time—I mean, we began to go wherever it is he's going. And our past has no continuation with this. So it is lost. For all practical purposes it is lost. I don't know if perhaps a musician or a writer or somebody might be able to make use of it still. And, of course, though you can sign on for somebody else's future, you can't share their past; that's why we haven't got one." He seemed to be showing off a little now, but merely to divert. He looked down over the slope of his slouched body like a man who exhibits a stump where an arm or leg should be. "That's what's wrong with us."

Jessie was suddenly listening, as if she had been absent from the company and had returned, but before she could speak, Tom said "Peoples have survived a break with tradition before," and Boaz said "What if the break had come from within?"

"It always comes from there! Doesn't it? Doesn't it?" Jessie called to Gideon. But he seemed to move a step out of their claims on him every time; he murmured, "Christ came from inside. Yes. I suppose you could say that. I don't know whether something like that would have happened to us. If we hadn't signed up."

He had never talked with Ann as he was talking that evening. Her impression of his presence came, not direct from himself, but as made by him upon the others. The least self-esteem demanded was a jealous, immediate assumption of the new valuation of him she saw in them. She was goaded to possessive pride in an aspect of the man, and therefore her association with him, she had been innocent of; she could not admit that while *they* found these things at once she had missed or ignored them.

She began to see something that it might be "all about".

When she sat beside him in the car, now, she was aware of her distinction from the white faces passing in the street. They merged into a white blur, down there. Gideon became a black man to her; the black man that everyone pushed away, and that she, she, put her hand out and touched.

TWELVE

THE WILLOWS OUT in the veld where Ann and Gideon had picnicked a few weeks before were yellowing, but the garden was still dark and heavy. The tide of green had risen and risen with each rain; new growth overlapped old, the grass stood thick and soft. All around and overhead the leaves, layer on layer, shadow on shadow, swag on swag and tier on tier, were holed and lacy with the feasting of insects. Jessie sat reading, in the afternoons, among the remains of the banquet.

Recently she had begun reading again as she had done when she was seventeen or eighteen and it was possible for a particular book to influence her as the mind of no person she knew in the flesh could. The opening of a window or the snatch of some weird music from the house behind her kept her reminded, on the surface, where awareness of environment is automatically recorded, like a message taken in one's absence, that Boaz was usually at home when she was. She felt not curiosity, but a shrinking away from what might be going on in him; she wanted to be left alone to no demands but her own. This adventure of Boaz's wife would work itself out between them like so many others; since she (Jessie) was fond of him, she was slightly ashamed to find how now, once he knew, she felt herself disengaged from friendly involvement. She had been mixed up so many times with friends whose marriages or love affairs went awry because of another man or woman; the situation between Boaz and Ann was the same as the others—except that Gideon Shibalo was black, of course. That was the only difference. It was a difference that she assumed had very little significance for people like themselves—the Stilwells and Davises. It did mean that there was some element of calculable danger in the whole business for Ann, she supposed—making love to Shibalo was breaking the law—as against the incalculable dangers of pain and disruption present in every love affair.

But Boaz came down sometimes for a breath of air and his casual yet intimate presence, stretched on the grass beside her, or leaning forward in one of the old deck-chairs he had dragged up, brought them to the point when naturalness made it necessary to talk about Ann. Jessie did not ask him what was happening, but felt obliged, out of the only politeness she cared for, to acknowledge the subject of his silences. They were talking of Fuecht's house at the sea; Jessie said, with the open-eyed assertion that was directed against Tom's unexplained resistance to the place, "We can't afford to turn up our noses at a free holiday. As I remember it, it was miles up the beach, which is nice. But it may be more built-up along there now, I don't know; my stepfather had it let permanently for years, we were never offered it."

"You want to go next month, you said?"

"If Tom definitely makes up his mind he won't go in July. Are you going to Moçambique?"

He said, in an ordinary voice, frowning at her, "I don't know what to do about it."

"Is she not going to go with you?"

They looked at each other. "I haven't asked her." He added : "It may sound mad."

"Oh no."

"I don't want to force her to decide. —Anything."

"Yes?" Jessie spoke with her hand over her mouth.

"I've got to wait to see how she feels. I'd expect her to do the same for me, as long as she was interested enough. —I am," he added.

"Well, that's fine. It makes me sick when everybody's playing. People show off so much in love affairs. You know, Boaz, I sometimes get afraid that everything we think of as love—even sex—is nearly always power instead. You know what I mean? Most of the time people don't really want each other, they only want not to let go."

He smiled. "Well, how are you to know?"

"Oh I know—you don't. Certainly not when you're in it. But so much of your life goes in this business of sex and love. It's horrible to think that you may find that love wasn't in it at all. You've just been *manoeuvring*. Like a pile of crocodiles on a mud-bank. Feel the sun and simply climb up on top of one another to find yourself no nearer to it when you get there."

He was listening to her with the mixture of wariness and curiosity with which people see through a crack into another's wilderness. But his whole being was tethered to the thought of Ann, himself and Shibalo, and he felt always the tug on his attention, pulling him back to it. Jessie said, and was ashamed of the obviousness, the lack of real concern, in the suggestion, "You don't think that she wants you to kick up a hell of a row? Some women want to be beaten."

"Ann's not the sort who gets her kicks out of punishment. She's a tremendously happy, pleasure-finding person. You know how she is."

"I don't know her *at all*," said Jessie. "That's it."

"She can't bear threats or rows. She knows nothing about the joys of crawling on your stomach and feeling remorse. She hates all that slimy stuff. Oh, you know how she is."

Jessie kept smiling and shaking her head.

After a while he stood up, the movement bringing the grass around his feet alive with minute hoppers that exactly matched its brilliant green. He looked up at the house and at the sky, his long eyes shown by the unconfined light to be green, like black water where the sun strikes deep. The sky gave his face a blind look. He said under it, trying to see, "I ought to go to Moçambique. There's that grant, you know; it's practically sure I'm getting it." She said, "Perhaps you can go a bit later. I don't know . . . perhaps you ought to go anyway."

"He's an interesting chap. Hell of a lot going on there, I felt. He talks a lot and so on, but he's really alive in secret behind that cover activity." He drew them back to the evening a week ago.

"I like him," Jessie said, meaning that she had admitted this before.

"Exactly. Not the sort of person you'd choose to play the fool with. Too vulnerable. You'd think twice."

He went into the house and left her. His cigarette ceased to smoke in the sappy, succulent grass, but she saw him, his olive tan faded, with so much indoor work, to that smooth oriental pallor, his sallow hands and bare feet showing that hollow beside the tendon of each finger or toe that gives an impression of nervous energy. How bungling this beauty was, his and Ann's, that had brought them senselessly together and given them the appearance of happiness in each other, both to themselves and onlookers. Take away the running blood, the saliva, the animation of breath, let the beauty harden into its prototypes, and even this would be found something they did not have in common, but that was diverse in the kind of consciousness that shaped it. He was opaque, his expression and posture the Bodhisattva's outward cast of an inward discipline. She was one of those clay figures made by the Etruscans, grinning even from the gravestone.

Jessie began to write a letter to Morgan. She had brought a pad and a ball-pen out with her book, but had not used them. She wrote quickly now, tearing off one sheet after another, and looking up from time to time with her mouth parted. A barbet somewhere in the garden went off continuously like a muffled alarm clock. The afternoon was borne away steadily in the sound. She felt it going, left the letter for a moment, and when she looked back at the pages covered with the thinly-inked pattern made by the bad pen, suddenly thought : who is this for? It was one of those incoherent letters that, when you get one, causes you to remark that so-and-so seems to be in a queer state. So-and-so has not been censored by the usual wish to amuse or impress, to give a certain idea of himself.

". . . little girls are always over at Peggy's. I have the place to myself, except for Boaz, up in his room working. Everything disappears. It's like it was when I was at home in Bruno's house waiting to begin an imaginary life. I don't seem to have had a second in between when I wasn't completely concentrated on some person, blind, deaf, and *busy*. You remember those silkworms, their jaws never stopped and if you were absolutely quiet in the room you could actually hear them going at it? —To have been so hungry, and not to have known why."

"But then they were full, and suddenly knew how to spin silk."

It would be idiotic to send it to Morgan; a nervous, hostile embarrassment came over her—it was a grown-up's letter. She closed her fist on the sheets, squeezing them into a ball. They lay slowly opening on the grass while she dashed off the kind of note, full of studied friendly interest, that she sent to him every few weeks.

The children came home, and then Tom. "Why doesn't Josias cut the grass?" The sun had gone down and the swells of growth made gentle troughs of shadow. Jessie answered as if to some criticism of one of her children, "It'll be brown underneath. It's nice." "Yes, of course it would be brown, it's been allowed to grow much too long."

Madge edged herself on to her mother's chair, pressing against her thigh. "State your case," Jessie said, and smiled. "Oh *Mummy* . . ." the child scowled at her impatiently.

"I got good seats for Friday."

"How many did you take?" A trio from Brazil was to play at the university hall, and Jessie wondered whether Boaz might not want to go too.

"Well, I took three . . . I didn't think she'd be coming. But I suppose it looks funny not to ask." Tom looked doubtfully at Jessie.

She smiled intimately, parenthetically. "She'll probably be there with Shibalo."

"I know. That's what I thought."

He squeezed her hand. Jessie turfed Madge off her chair like a bird pushing its fledgling out of a nest.

"We'd better not ask him to come?"

She murmured, "Difficult. Don't know."

She added, speaking low because although it was out of hearing the window was up there in the house behind them : "He really does seem to like Shibalo. You know how it is when the man really likes the other one. Everybody being so considerate, and no hard feelings. My heart sinks. It'd be much easier if he thought he was a louse and wanted to kick him in the backside."

"Well of course that's impossible this time."

"Only because Boaz is so fastidious about everybody's feelings, and wants her back a hundred-per-cent off her own bat! No coercion whatsoever, like a unicorn that you have to wait to have come and put its head down in your lap. It's a lovely idea, it's how it ought to be . . ."

"No, I mean because this is not a white man."

Jessie shook her hand out of his and sat forward. "What has that got to do with it?"

"A lot. Quite a lot."

"If you'd said that it had a lot to do with Ann I'd understand it. She wants to prove she can do exactly what she likes! She wants—well, then I'd understand it. From her point of view the whole thing has everything to do with his being a black! But Boaz, *Boaz*—? You know that Boaz truly never thinks about these things, he has no feeling about it at *all*, you've told me yourself that he was once keen on a black girl, he's slept with black women—"

"Yes, yes—" Tom said for her in conclusion. "And Boaz cannot kick a black man in the backside."

Jessie began to speak but she saw the expression on his face change to acknowledge another presence and realised that Boaz had come out of the house. The Stilwells tried to treat him without any obvious special consideration these days, but a certain concerned brusqueness sometimes crept into their manner. "I met John Renishaw today, he wants to know when you're going to see him," Tom said as Boaz came up.

"Christ, I want to know too. I promised weeks ago."

"Well, you better do something about it, because he's going to Cape Town for six weeks. —Hey, what have you got there—"

Clem and Elisabeth had smoothed out the sheets of Jessie's crumpled letter and folded them into shapes that would hold water. "Water-bombs! Water-bombs!" Elisabeth shrieked and boasted, throwing hers, that she had filled at the garden tap.

"Don't leave the water running," said Jessie, in a voice of patient repetition.

"They've used some letter of yours!" Tom's voice rose.

"I know. I'd thrown it away, anyway."

"Why on earth . . ." He looked at her with amused, slightly aggressive curiosity.

"It was wrong." She waved a hand to dismiss it.

While she returned to what she had been saying to Boaz, Tom glanced at the wet paper-shape covered with words running into each other. "Who was it to?"

"—Morgan—" she said in quick parenthesis.

"Why on earth write a long letter to Morgan and then throw it away."

She looked at him for a moment to make him see that he was putting her to the trouble of providing an answer. "Haven't you ever written a letter that had to be torn up?"

"But to Morgan?"

"Why not?" said Boaz.

Jessie smiled to discount his objection and opened her hands and clapped them loosely together before her again in indication of her own crazy lapse.

"You do that with love letters," Tom said. "Write them and tear them up and write them again. What was it all about, though?"

"Oh nothing. Nothing for Morgan. Nothing that would interest him, that's all."

"But what was it about?" Tom was encouraging, cornering her.

"Well, if you really want to know." Her face was a mixture of annoyance and the reluctant pleasure of giving oneself away. She said matter-of-factly, as if repeating something that she had heard or read, "I was just thinking how sex fills one's life for so many years. Sex in its various aspects, I mean; looking for men, securing to yourself the chosen one, seeing children as the manifestation of the bond. It's only when and if you've fulfilled all this that you begin to ask the purpose of it all—*for yourself*, not the biological one—and to want an answer with a new kind of passion."

What she had just been saying brought her into two separate streams of unspoken communication with the two men. Boaz recognised the mood of what she had said when they were talking alone together earlier, and it sprang alive in silent reference between them. Between her husband and her were the tremendous attempts at knowing each how the other lived, and the knowledge that the measure in which these failed or succeeded is never known. "That wouldn't be the accepted idea of fulfilment, simply a making-room for another want," Tom said.

Sometimes they were all at home at this time of day, even Ann. She would hear the Stilwells' talk as the Stilwells heard the children's—half-listening, preoccupied. What were they saying? Always the same sort of thing; a drain was blocked, someone must take the car for servicing, who would pick up Clem from her swimming class, and had the renewal of the newspaper subscriptions been remembered? The enduring surface of marriage seemed to be made up of such things; they had little meaning, no interest, and they matted together as monotonously as a piece of basket-work. Her eyes rested often on Boaz. She liked him.

They had always managed almost entirely without any paraphernalia to hold them up. She wondered if, in fact, he really liked living like that. It might have been to please her. She thought, with resentment making a quick fist inside her again, he would do almost anything to please her, but he could ask, as if prompted by the knowledge of some inadequacy in her that he did not admit, "Do you know what it's all about?"

Gideon was doing a tremendous painting of her. It was larger than life and the incised line along the solid brush-strokes released the figure from the flat background. She kept going back to look at it while she was in the room with it, not as a woman admires herself in a flattering portrait, but in an excitable and terrifying curiosity : there was no surface likeness to provide reassurance; she knew it was the likeness of what he found her to be.

She had an awareness of him as a single creature unrelated to any other. She did not know his parents or his brothers and sisters, who might have shown less attractively the looks and movements she thought of as his alone, neither did she know his real friends (Len, she suspected, did not count as one), who might have exhibited views and opinions that, although she thought them entirely his own, in fact he shared with others.

She brought this awareness of the man she had just left into the company of the Stilwells and Boaz as unthinkingly as a dancer carries her posture from the rehearsal that has occupied her afternoon. They chatted as they had always done, sometimes joking, sometimes silent, often interrupted by children, now and then rising to an argument, or getting into a discussion. She was reassured, not only for herself, but also, oddly, for them all, by the ease with which she could resume her place among them. It had the same effect on her as the sight of one's feet in familiar shoes may have when one sits down, rather drunk, among the press at a party.

She was hardly aware of how she was going or what direction she was taking. The only conception she had of her life at that time came one evening when they were sitting outside after the sun went down. With her head tipped back over the hard rail of the chair she saw the upstairs windows of the house, open to the sky, space shading off into the high, last light. All the meaning of the almost-past summer gathered for her in the vision of

Jessie's old house—ugly old house—as it was this evening and had been so many evenings, with the windows open like hands and a first bat fluttering without sound, wandering and rising. None of the others saw the creature; it was only the acute angle at which she had let her head fall back that let her see it. It was in the air above them all, soft, deaf, remote, steered by warnings and attractions they lacked a sense to apprehend.

Boaz said to the Stilwells, "If I go to Moçambique, you don't mind if she stays on here?"

"Naturally. If she doesn't go with you." There was a pause after Jessie spoke. "I must get started sometime," Boaz said. "My whole organisation up there'll break down if I don't."

Tom said, "And anything can happen—there could be a political blow-up at any time, you might not be able to get in."

Behind this sensible talk the Stilwells saw that Boaz no longer assumed that the house was also Ann's home whether he was there or not: it sounded as if he were already considering her life as separate from his own.

But he said, "If I'm not here, there's no one who can do anything for her. At least if she's living here she's got some sort of a base...?" He added, "Without being unfair to Gideon Shibalo, he can't actually look after her much."

Jessie was not looking at him; she had her left elbow supported in her right hand, the left hand covering her face below the nostrils. He said to them, almost exasperated, with a little laugh, "I can't say anything to him. And I can't just leave her to it. Not really. I want to let her do what she has to, I mean she's free to live her own way...but I can't leave her to it—as things are."

Tom's father was spending a week in the house and Jessie went now to give him some newspaper cuttings on indigenous bulbs that she had kept for him. He had just come in from the garden, an old man whose weakening eyes always had happy tears in them, and he was full of pained shock over the condition of the rose bushes, the enjoyable shock of one eager to prescribe—"My dear, I find it difficult to credit...just shreds of leaf, shreds. What you want is to go out there of an evening with an ordinary bowl of water and a strong torch. You'll attract those beetles in hundreds, simply fall in and get drowned, that's all."

"Really, Dad? Will they?" It was true that Gideon had nowhere to take Ann to.

". . . done it time out of number. An ordinary mixing basin will do . . ."

Where did he come from, when he was not living secretly at that flat? Somewhere there was a wife, children, old friends, a kinship—a man's life couldn't be lived by permission in the hours when someone else didn't need a flat.

". . . when I was a boy, it was a paraffin flare. Tom's got a strong torch, of course?"

"Oh I think so. Clem's got one. From last Christmas—if it's not broken." They couldn't go away together. He couldn't keep her; not on an African schoolteacher's earnings. Did it ever come to that? Jessie thought of the other white girl she knew who had fallen in love with an African; the girl had kept him, and saved the money to get them both to Ghana or Nigeria or somewhere. Shibalo, for all his talent, no matter what he was, was on the receiving side, and the receiving side was always at a disadvantage.

"A tin basin will do."

She turned her attention to the old man with a special softening of desire to please, because she had not been listening to him. He seemed to her, as the old often do to the young, endearingly innocent. Children were supposed to be, but she seldom found them so. There was Morgan, apparently born with all kinds of terrible knowledge. What she thought of as innocence was the lack of evidence, in another, of the things she mistrusted in herself.

Gideon came to the house with Ann on Saturday afternoon. He brought sketches he had done of the children, from memory. He gave them in a negligent, off-hand way, but Jessie thought that they were purposely "interesting". She felt sorry for him for the necessity he felt to try to put in a word for himself with her by flattery, even so obliquely. Again he stayed for dinner—or rather for a cold supper, for that was what it was. Old Mr. Stilwell had never mixed with black people socially in his own life, but he understood that his son "looked at things differently", as he put it, and was rather proud of the open house

162

kept by his son. He liked to shock acquaintances of his own kind and generation by swanking about the way he often sat down to dinner there, without blinking an eyelid, between black guests. In fact, the only black guest he had ever met there before was Len. Len was present again, and called him "sir" in the way that he liked young men to do. The old man lived alone and was excited by the company of young people and children, the wave of life caught him up roughly again. Laughter, raised voices, interruptions, things begun and not finished, things that never got said : this was the way it was; only when one was alone and it was over did the sentences get completed and end in silence.

His second gin (he had two every evening) warmed the impulse that is always there—to explain to the one in whose presence you have been silent all your life what you really have been thinking all the time. It was not truthful, but was simply the impulse made audible in phrases that would hold it harmlessly. He had cornered Gideon, and was saying with some of the charm he must have had when he was young, "I've always had a lot of respect for your people. And I've always found them show respect in return." Later he became bolder, and more consciously candid : "After all, it's nonsense to talk of marrying and all that—politicians' scare-stories, I tell people. I'm sure none of us thinks of that. But you can't tell me there's any good reason why you and I shouldn't be having a chat together in a drawing-room if the mood takes us." Gideon listened to him with carefully narrowed attention : his head inclined as if he must be sure to be wily enough to miss no word of a daring and debatable argument. Tom said between closed teeth, "Oh Christ." But Len, who got up to renew the old gentleman's drink, was almost primly reproachful—"He's a sweet old man"—and a spirit of outrageous undercurrent amusement suddenly took over the company. They drank quite a lot and the need to be tactful disappeared. Jessie no longer felt it necessary to bother whether, if Boaz found himself at one end of the table, while it had somehow come out that Gideon was sitting next to Ann at the other, it would look ominous or odd. Boaz and Ann, reminded by a turn of the talk of some old private joke, caught each other's eyes and giggled.

"We never going to see you down at the office again?" Len

said, turning to Ann. When he met her nowadays, he talked to other people, as if the two of them had quarrelled. He bore the slight that, so far as she was concerned, nothing had changed, she felt no less interested in him than she had ever done.

"Lennie, I'd love to get started on something. What's new there for us?"

He looked pleased in spite of himself. "Always *new*. You're a damned good unpaid worker, but like all people who don't get paid you're unreliable. Disappear in the middle of things, man."

Her indignation was flirtatious. "I like that! There wasn't a school or a hall within seventy miles we didn't lug that caravan to."

"Won't you give me my job back?" Jessie called out. "As a paid worker, needless to say. I think I'll leave the mortuary at the end of this month, I can't stick it any longer."

"It's not our policy to employ whites where blacks will do."

"Ha-ha. Don't we know it; unless they're unpaid and unreliable, eh?"

"Are you really giving up?" Boaz said to Jessie.

"Oh I must. I'm sick of the dying rich. Trouble is, what to do. The Agency job really did suit me down to the ground, you know. Useful, gregarious in a surface sort of way. Anonymous."

"Work for me. I mean it," said Boaz. "My things are in a hell of a mess. I must get someone to catalogue and type notes and so on."

"Oh no," she laughed and drew back, vehement. She sawed away at the leg of lamb with a rather blunt knife, while he went on, "Personal, convenient, learn in your own home. Write now for illustrated booklet." She laughed but she felt in herself the symptom of a disease she had feared and forgotten, the set of opposition she had discovered nearly a year ago, when she and Tom first discussed the possibility of having the Davises to live in the house. It was just what she had been afraid of—the presence of strangers was influencing the way they lived, turning them to distractions that required the posturing that another pair of eyes on oneself demands. The Davises were drawing everyone into their own charged air; the whole house was the way things looked within such an atmosphere. Now came the suggestion that she should work with him, put herself in danger of assuming jealous concern for his research, of standing in a comradely working alliance with him as Ann was not. They would end up going to bed together, maybe? She felt a wild and stirring indignation, a struggle for life. No, no, she wanted to say to him, it would be too nice, it would be too convenient, it would be the *end of me*.

She did say, with the rudeness of fear, "I don't want to be private secretary in my own house, Boaz old dear."

"Len, I suspect you've got your shoes off under the table." Tom was referring to a report in the morning paper that Rhodesian Africans had started a campaign to give up wearing shoes because "that was the custom before the white man came".

"Why stop at shoes? My ancestors didn't wear trousers either." He buttered a piece of bread as if it were the object of bored distaste.

"That's why I don't understand politics," Jessie said. "They never function at my level. Whatever goes on is either rigged by big money and diplomats or clowned about in the streets. Nothing in between seems to work."

Ann pretended to lift up the cloth : "And he's got knobbly toes, into the bargain !"

"Shaka's warriors certainly wore sandals," said Tom. "I don't know about any others—Boaz? What d'you say?"

Gideon's voice, once he had begun to speak, went on through interruptions without emphasis and with an indifference to whether it was lost or not. "People must have something, something not hard, that anyone can do. It may be meaningless ("Not meaningless, this," Boaz said) but that doesn't matter much. Take off your shoes. You don't have to be able to understand what goes on at a meeting. You don't have to read about it. You don't have to pay two and six membership. Useless, harmless, but you feel you're doing something."

"It's not harmless," Boaz said across the voice.

"Take off your shoes. People can afford it. You don't ask too much of them. You hold them together."

"Whenever you talk about people—the people—I have the feeling I don't know who you're talking about," Len said to Gideon. "You don't mean yourself, do you?"

"Can't ask them all the time to trust you, trust you. Let them have something they can do by themselves. Even if it's meaningless and harmless."

"No, you never mean yourself."

Boaz leaned out across the table like the figure-head of a ship, his clear-cut lips shining wet from the gulp of wine he had just taken. "Not harmless. You know that. You know quite well what it is."

"Take off your shoes." The voice said it to himself, for the sound of it.

"Oh yes, not harmless at all. Exactly the same meaning as burning down a church or a school or a clinic or a cinema."

"Take off your shoes." Gideon smiled at no one in particular, then gave his little chuckle, and fixed his consciousness of the room on Boaz, like a drunk choosing a point of focus. He said, suddenly, "An act of pure rejection."

"Exactly."

His cigarette was burning down in the crumbled bread on his plate and he picked it up, saw that it was almost dead, and brought himself back to the company with an effort. "Beautiful, stripped, pure—" The words were unsheathed, one by one, like a man giving up knives.

"A pure rejection."

The phrase held for a second; and then all the talk round the table piled upon it and buried it. "Not harmless to the people who do it, I mean; I'm not talking of the act itself—" "An anomalous glorification of the past, *qua* past..." "Damned silly to identify..." "More than that, dangerous, you can't substitute magic for political power ..." ". . . step out of his shoes and out of his power, I suppose." Everyone said what he always said, in one form or another, in every context, seizing automatically on what there was in the subject for them. For Tom it was institutions—the difficulty, for new, intensely nationalistic black states, of finding institutions of law, commerce, education other than those associated with former subservience. For Jessie it was the notion that people could externalise an influence by making some common object of use symbolic of it, and then getting rid of the object. Ann argued with Len about what the others were saying, and Boaz and Gideon tried to analyse how far it was possible for a political movement to rule with and not become ruled by the release of irrational instincts. "Of course it's dangerous, but what can we do in Africa?—colonialism was dangerous for the whites, it couldn't last without a pay-off coming sixty years or so later, but what could they do? We can't look much further than getting what we want—" No one had noticed that the old man, Tom's father, sitting at table, had become congealed in expression and posture as if, while all around him was noise, agitation and mobility, he would never move again. Tom took him quietly out of the room and murmured to Jessie as he came back and swung a leg over his chair to sit again, "Just one gin too many, I think—he's lying down."

Len caught the domestic aside. "Passed out? Hell, he's a nice old man."

When Gideon had gone home (in Ann's car) and everyone was on the way to bed, Boaz came down again to the living-room, where Tom was making notes for a lecture he was supposed to give at a discussion club the next week. They sloshed brandy into two glasses that already had been used and began, at first deliberately, then carried away by real interest, a long discussion about a book on Chinese navigation pre-dating the Portuguese exploration of Africa. Jessie banged with a shoe on the floor overhead; they laughed, so loudly that she banged again. With the drop of their voices, the talk lost momentum. Boaz yawned until he looked quite groggy; he wandered about the room and paused, and wandered again. His face shone waxy and his eyes were hidden like a clown's in the diamond-shaped darkness made by the recess of shadow under each eyebrow and the triangle of plum-coloured skin cutting down the line of cheekbone from beneath.

"One thing I can't stand," he said, "the way he repeats a phrase or a sentence as if he gets some meaning out of it no one else does. That sort of withdrawal ... You know what I mean—he makes you wait for him to return before you can go on with what you're trying to say." The moment he allowed himself to speak of Gideon, the brandy he had been drinking without apparent effect took hold of him like an arm hooked roughly round his neck. "If you knew the insane things that've been going on ... the whole of tonight ... 'black bastard' ... Over and over again, to myself, while I was talking ... like a maniac? 'Black bastard'. All that filthy cock, man."

He stretched himself on the sofa, and when Tom finished his

167

work he saw that he was asleep. His head was flung back on a raised arm behind his head. The fingers of the hand moved like tendrils in an effort against cramp that did not break through to consciousness; on the blank face of sleep traces of bewilderment and disgust were not quite erased round the mouth. Tom looked at him for a moment with the curiosity that is always aroused by the opportunity to contemplate suffering without having to respond to the sufferer, and then decided to leave him there, and turned out the light.

THIRTEEN

GIDEON SHIBALO GOT a message one day to go and see
Sandile Makhawula at his shop. Sandile was his brother-in-law
and they had remained friendly through Gideon's long drift
apart from his wife; in fact, all that was left of an old feeling
and an old way of life was the uncomplicated ease Gideon felt
on those occasional evenings when he remembered Sandile and
dropped in on him. Sandile was light-skinned, rather an ugly
yellow-brown, with narrow, tight-skinned eyes that added to
his slightly Chinese look. He shaved his forearms and, resting
on the counter in rolled-up shirt-sleeves, their smoothness,
through which the roots of hairs showed dark like faults under
tinted glass, betrayed a secret vanity. It was the sort of thing
one could not guess at, so little did it match the rest of his
character. The shop belonged to the father of the woman he had
married; it had always sold sugar and mealie-meal and the
cheaper brands of tinned food, as well as sweets and cigarettes
and cold drinks—he had branched out into a radio repair business on the side. "Look at it," he would say, indicating the old-
fashioned wooden counter, worn away on top like a butcher's
block, the one small glass showcase filled with biscuits, cigarettes,
cards of watch-straps, cotton reels and dead flies, and the valves
and wires of dismantled radio sets lying among spiked slips of
paper and tins of snuff. "I'm trying to make a go of it . . ." He
made fun of his own ambitions to run the place like a shop in
town, yet he went on doggedly, persuading the old man to get
a modern cash register one year, taking another year to get him
to allow the fly-embossed Zam-buk advertisements to be taken
down and replaced with three dimensional displays showing hair-
straighteners and deodorants. He would have a house in Dube
one day—like all the other well-off shopkeepers, Gideon used
to tease him. "Well, maybe; what else is there for me?"

He held Gideon in the special regard that people have for

those who are free of their own ambitions; when he was with Gideon he felt that he himself was not entirely sold to and bound over by the goals set up for him and his kind. The fact that Gideon had slipped the moorings of his sister added to rather than detracted from this feeling of releaseful identification with Gideon, though Sandile had quite a strong family affection for her.

Gideon did not know when exactly Sandile had mentioned that he wanted to see him; he was very seldom in the township these days, and he merely happened to hear, from a casual encounter, that Sandile had been asking for him; at least two weeks went by before he remembered about it again, and called in at the shop. It was Saturday, and the place was crowded, and knee-deep in children; everything they had been sent to buy went up on to their heads : bags of mealie-meal, beer-bottles filled with milk. The thin little necks of the girls wobbled once as the burden was settled into place. "*Dumela 'me.*" Gideon pushed his way through gossiping women, and the fat ones smiled at him while the thin ones merely looked interrupted. Sandile was serving a sullen man in a leather cap with ear-flaps; the face was the thick, deadened face, greasy with drink-sweat, work-sweat, that you saw all over the townships. Sandile gave a little signal acknowledging Gideon, and when he was free for a moment called over, "You see how it is . . . come in." He meant into the tiny store-room, a home-made lean-to strengthened like a fortress, at the back of the shop.

Sandile scattered the children—importuning him with their demands for "Penny Elvies" (sweets named for the American rock-and-roll singer) or "Penny atcha", an Indian pickle—by an exclamation ending in a loud click of the tongue at the back of the throat. They swerved away like hens.

"The happy capitalist, the exploiter of the people," said Sandile. "Christ, man, this goes on until seven tonight."

"How's business?"

"Ach, I want to knock out the wall, re-do the whole place, make it self-service; you know—little gate you turn round to go in, plastic basket to select what you want, little gate to go out. But you'd have to frisk them first, that's the trouble. Turn them upside-down and shake them out. Specially the old ones with the big bozies; you'd be surprised what goes in in front there. Last week the wholesaler comes along with a lovely display card with razor blades. 'Why don't you put this up, it increases sales twenty-five per cent, we've proved it.' —Our people are backward, man, everything's got to be where they can't even stretch for it."

"Come out for a drink," said Gideon, consolingly.

Sandile took a cigarette from him and sat down on a packing-case, leaving a broken-backed kitchen chair for him. "How the hell can I? The old man's gone to fix up about his cousin's funeral."

"Where's Bella?" Sandile's wife was a district nurse, working for the municipal health department, but on Saturdays she was usually free to help in the shop.

"The baby kept her up all night. Have a cold drink?"

"Coffee, that'd be fine."

Sandile looked put out for just a second, then called to the shop. A very black youth with an open mouth and eyes that reflected the lean-to like convex mirrors brought an open packet of coffee-and-chicory mixture with a brand-picture of a house in the form of a steaming coffee-pot. This house was clearer to Gideon than the memory of any of the rooms he had ever lived in; how many times as a child had he been sent to buy that packet with the coffee-pot house on it. Clara (his wife) had still used it, in the house in Orlando. Callie Stow ground her own beans, and at the flat there was always instant coffee of some special bitter kind; for years now he had been drinking the coffee that white people drank. The sight of the packet with the picture gave him the sensation of looking at an old photograph.

"Half Nyasa," Sandile said, of the youth. He was pumping a primus. "At least that's my explanation. Dumb as he's black, that's all I can tell you. Don't you know somebody for me? They can't even measure out a shilling sugar without spilling. You could start operations for the recovery of waste sugar on this damned floor." He stopped pumping and pointed in exasperation to the cracks in the floor-boards where, it was true, there was a dirty glitter, like mica. Suddenly he grew ashamed of his preoccupation with what—switching to objectivity, as he could —he thought to be the petty matters of shop-keeping.

"So they're thinking seriously about taking up this rent campaign?" he said. "Bella's got an old aunt and she's fallen

171

months behind and been given eviction papers, and—yesterday it was—someone came from Congress and had a talk with her."

They talked politics for a while. The water boiled and Sandile made coffee. "As a matter of fact, I was hoping you'd come in sometime," he said, spooning sugar into Gideon's cup.

"Hi, hi—" Gideon restrained him.

"All right, I'll take it." He poured another cup and Gideon sugared it for himself. "I've been asking for you, but you haven't been around. Nobody's seen you."

"No, I know, I bumped into K. D. and he told me." Sandile often had small plans or deals that involved Gideon—he had got Gideon's record player cheaply for him, through one of the wholesalers, and he and Gideon borrowed odd sums of money from each other from time to time. This was the sort of thing they saw each other about. While Gideon put the cup of coffee to his mouth, Sandile said, "Clara was here. She was up here last week and she was talking to me a long time, and, well, she wants to come back to Jo'burg. It seems so, yes." He was watching Gideon, embarrassed, yet alertly anxious, as if he hoped to disclaim responsibility for what he might have said.

Gideon had just filled his mouth with the warm liquid and for the moment the impact of its taste, flooding his body, produced by far the stronger reaction. What is the word for nostalgia without the sentiment and the pleasure nostalgia implies? The flavour set in motion exactly that old level of consciousness where, in the house of the old aunt with whom he had been farmed out as a schoolboy, matriculation was drawn like the line of the horizon round the ball of existence; where, later, in the two neat rooms in Orlando, he had paid off a kitchen dresser and drawn "native studies" on cheap scarves for a city curio shop. Threshing, sinking, sickening—the sensation produced by the taste became comprehension of what Sandile was saying. He put down the cup. "What about her job?"

Sandile shrugged and slowly took the plastic spoon out of the sugar; the damp brown stuff moved like a live mass.

"I don't see the sense," said Gideon, with the face of a man discussing the fate of a stranger.

"Well, she wants to come."

"To you?" Gideon said.

Sandile looked at him.

172

"It's not possible. Anything else is not possible. It's absolutely out, that I can tell you."

Sandile did not answer. Gideon wanted to get him to speak because he could not bear to have the matter, even in the abstract of words, thrust upon himself.

"Bella knows that little girl—from the hospital, of course. She thought it was more or less off with you two, lately. She's seen her with another chap, and so on." Sandile took a deep breath and stopped.

Gideon felt himself drawing further away every second; the cosy store-room with its high barred window, the deal table and the primus, the smell of paraffin and strong soap, the familiar face of Sandile and the taste of the coffee—a hundred doors were closing in him against these things.

"Right out, I can tell you." He wanted to say "It's all finished with, years ago," but he felt a horror of admitting that there was anything to talk of about himself and the woman who had been his wife. He said, "I haven't even sent money for the child—not since about last January."

"I know. I've been letting her have something."

Gideon nodded. Sandile had never paid him the last hundred pounds for the car; it was fair enough.

Gideon didn't know how to go, but he could not stay, so he stood up, and looked without seeing round the lean-to. "So long, Sandile."

Sandile remained sitting, holding a stub of cigarette turned inward to his palm.

"That's all," said Gideon.

"O.K.," said Sandile in deep uncertainty.

The living presence of his wife, in another town, had never influenced Gideon; he felt neither tied to her nor free of her : she was a curiously negative factor. It did not seem at all odd that he occasionally spoke about his child, as if the boy belonged to him alone. Clara had been young and pretty, and it had been all right for a year or two, while she was a school-teacher's wife. Like most African wives, she stayed at home when he went out at night. She was proud that he could paint a bit and pleased that this sometimes brought in some extra money.

She would have been satisfied to see him go on painting scarves for the white shop in town, all his life; at least that was what he told himself when he began to find that he couldn't talk to her on Sundays, when they were at home together. She looked at his paintings, when he really was beginning to paint, as the wife of a gangster might look at the guns and knives present in the house. She cared only for prettiness, for the little sweetnesses and frills that clerks acquire to soften the rough chunk of the labourer's life. She was only concerned with covering ugliness and did not know the possibility of beauty. In three years he had outgrown her as inevitably as a child outgrows its clothes. Every time he looked back at her, she was lagging a little further behind. When he thought he was going away on the scholarship, it was natural that she should go to live in Bloemfontein with her mother and sister for the year that he would be away. Then had come the lengthy passport trouble, the postponement of the scholarship, the final refusal of the passport, and the months when he was mostly drunk and had no job. She had stayed on and on with her family, and she had quite a good job in a small factory. He and she simply lost sight of one another.

As he walked out of the shop and along the streets of Alexandra, the naked-bottomed children, the skeletal dogs, the young girls in nylon and the old women who shuffled along under the weight of great buttocks, the decaying rubbish in the streets, the patched and pocked houses, the bicycles shaking as if they would fall apart, the debased attempts at smartening up some hovels that made them look more sordid than those that were left to their rotting drabness—everything around him spoke of her. It was the ambition of her life to be clean and decent, yet this squalor thrust her existence upon him. Isolation rose higher in him every minute, a drug beginning to take effect at the extremities; it was his defence, but it was also alarming. From it he saw, fascinated, that she did not think it impossible to regard as "husband" a man she had lost touch with three years ago; she accepted what any housegirl or cook accepted—that a black woman cannot expect to live permanently with her man and children; she must shift about and live where and how poverty and powerlessness allow. He might have been an indentured labourer, away from home for long periods out of necessity. Three years' absence had no significance for her so far as the validity of marriage was concerned.

174

He tried on himself some specific moment of her existence—licking her lips before she spoke, fastening a wide shiny belt round her middle—as a tongue goes to test the sensitivity of a tooth. She could have been one of the women passing him in the street. He was approaching the row of Indian shops at the top of the township, now, and there were some pretty ones about, girls coming from or going to the bus terminus. He saw the thickness of their calves and ankles, the selfconsciousness of their plastic smartness. He had in his mind, mixed with the shapes and colours, the coming together of objects and movement that was always working towards the moment when he began to paint—the thin wrists and ankles, the careless style of Ann. Little breasts of a woman who bore no children. Flat belly with the point of each hip-bone holding a skirt taut. Soft thin hands smelling of cigarette smoke. "What'll we do today?" A woman without woman's work or woman's ambitions. The idea of her possessed his imagination entirely, so that when he went into a shop to buy cigarettes he unconsciously adopted the manner that came naturally to her, of assuming without offence that she must have what she wanted before anyone else's claims of time or precedence.

There had been days, lately, when he had left the flat, the Stilwell house—all of them in the city, and their life there—with an almost gleeful sense of escape. He left them and plunged back where they couldn't find him, couldn't follow, didn't know the internecine life of his home, the townships. All ambiguities fell away there, while he drank with Sol. *They* were never free, now, of him. The Stilwell house was grouped invisibly round him as an empty chair at a dinner table affects the seating of those present. But he could disappear where there was no trace of their existence, in the places to which they had banished his kind.

He turned back from the shops down one of the dirt streets. An orange-seller sat beside a bright pyramid, paring the hide of a horny big toe. Gideon walked past him and went to a yard he knew. He bought himself a brandy, but he spoke to no one and the usual talk of the other customers, of bribes to get houses, of how much a week went on hire purchase, of gambling, of police raids, of the man found murdered just near the bus sheds last night, did not draw him into its familiarity. He had meant to look in at his room, but he did not go there and took a bus to the city and went straight to the flat, where, taking on at once the automatic watchfulness that the city exacted from him as a presence that was perpetually clandestine, he went, hiding himself, up the back stairs and let himself in. When the door was safely locked behind him, he went into the living-room and sat smoking, in one of the big chairs. A knock came at the door but, as always when he was in the flat, officially there was nobody there to answer it. He heard the footsteps retreating down the corridor, and the sough of the lift dropping through the building. As he smoked he looked slowly round the objects in the room and, in the silence, a strange feeling came over his body : his skin contracted like the skin of water wrinkling under a shiver of wind.

The one place in which he felt in possession of himself was when he was in some small room with the men with whom he planned, argued, and several times had been in prison. They talked too much, they intrigued too much—these things he could criticise when he was away from them. But when he sat with them, again and again he was so much like them, so much one of them, that he was as guilty as they of the faults he criticised. Here he knew himself to be what Callie Stow had reminded him a black face didn't necessarily make one—an African. Listening to Zeke Zwane who was pompous, or Mdaka Mkwambi who was long-winded, or Mabaso who was too cautious, or Dr Thabeng who saw himself as another Nkrumah, he was at peace, he was secure among the members of an outlawed organisation who themselves, as individuals, many of them, were banned from attending meetings anyway. Here there was no shade of ambiguity; he was a man who had given up the futility of a life of choice (oddly enough, he did not admit to himself that he was actually painting again; like his presence in the flat, the fact had no official existence) and accepted the one thing possible—struggle. The struggle of a beetle on its back, most of the time. Bungling, slow as history, muddled, impeded by ignorance, growing by fits and starts, crushed, unkillable—he belonged to it and whatever happened to it would happen to him.

Nguni was talking, in terms picked up from the liberation

176

papers and news-sheets being printed all over the continent from Egypt to Cape Town, of "the weapon of withholding the people's labour".

They argued, as they had done since the failure of the last strike, to find out why it had failed. Everyone had a theory, something to fill the void of not knowing what to do next. Resolutions were approved to go from this, a special action committee, to the central committee of the national executive. Co-ordination, co-operation—all the big words flew about. People who had been lobbying watched those who had promised to back them up. The chap, Khoza, who thought slowly through a long discussion and then always came up with an objection just when the whole thing was threshed into agreement, began to talk. "I'd like to say one thing. We should put it to the national executive that we shouldn't have a stay-at-home except in summer."

Everyone ceased to listen the moment he opened his mouth. Someone gave a snorting laugh. Jackson Sijake, the lawyer, had professional attentiveness. "Yes? On what basis?"

"People need their pay more in winter. If a man loses a day's money there's no coal in the house, perhaps. It's bad psychology."

Thabeng flashed out at him, at everybody. "That's something our people have got to learn. Man, you don't get freedom from sitting over the fire, you can't choose the weather the day you're going to bring the country to a standstill."

Gideon didn't take Khoza seriously, but he put in, with his chuckle down in his chest, "I don't think it's a bad idea to plan a stay-at-home when it's likely to be easier for us. Let's think of *everything*, anything at all that will make the chances of success greater. But what we ought to do, man, is to concentrate on our organisation in small places. We must go all out to be active in the country, specially the Reef towns. It's all too loose and patchy ... complete stoppage here, everyone at work a few miles away. If you want to make a success you need months of preparation, getting people ready."

"The most successful things have been things that have just come up—look at Kgosana's march on Cape Town," Nathan Xaba said. He had still the eyes of a countryman, intelligent, slow-blinking, as if he were looking into flames.

Sijake put his hand, with the thick linked watch-strap covering the wrist, palm down on his varnished chair-arm.

"That's it. Enthusiasm, people get carried away, and then it's gone. And what can happen to you as a result of a protest march? The leaders get arrested. Perhaps some of the crowd, too. But the rest go home, pleased with themselves. A strike calls for less excitement, more staying power, and your job at stake. That's what we've got to concentrate on getting over to people."

"You've forgotten that a march can end up with shooting," Xaba said.

"Yes, with shooting. But when you're dead you're dead. You don't have to think what's going to happen to you next."

Sijake was young and plump with a diaphragm that bulged his shirt-front over the belt of his trousers. He liked sports coats of hairy tweed, and his initials were embroidered, in tiny letters, unobtrusively, on his shirt-pocket. He had the authoritative manner that often goes with a smooth, square face. He had been, illegally, to Accra and to Cairo, and got back undetected. In prison he was the one who represented them all and prepared memoranda concerning their rights as prisoners, headed delegations to the governor, and primed them with answers for the Special Branch interrogations. He was constantly being arrested, between political imprisonments, for not having his identity or tax papers in order, for fast driving, and for breaking the banning order against his attendance at gatherings or travelling outside the area to which he was confined. He defended himself and was acquitted on one legal technicality or another, time and again. He and Gideon had done a lot of jobs together. With complicated arrangements that sometimes involved changes of borrowed cars from town to town they drove over the borders into Swaziland or Basutoland to visit people who were in exile since the last State of Emergency. Gideon was not under a territorial ban at present; Sijake said to him that night after the meeting, "You'll be around in July, I hope?" He was referring to the school holidays.

The woman whose husband's house they were in entered, looked at them as if she expected them to be gone, ignored their greeting and went out again. She was dressed in her day-clothes but her head was tied up for the night in a doek.

"Sure."

178

"I think it would be a good thing if you went all over the Transvaal in that time—every dorp and little town. We'll arrange contacts everywhere. Draw up a report on what they're doing, how active branches are, and so on. Spend a few days wherever they need help with organising." He added in English, "We're lost in this rabbit burrow of underground, Boetie."

Gideon had an impulse to give himself time by lying : "I don't really know. I said something about doing some coaching. Indians whose kids are trying for matric."

"We need someone to go, man, we need it."

"I'll let you know. I'll find out what's going on."

There was a gleam on the bathroom floor that turned out to be a lipstick-case, and the dregs of red wine had dried sourly on glasses. "They must have had a party last night," Ann said. "Were you there?"

"Looked in," he said, without interest. "Their friends are not up to much."

Although she liked the casualness with which he accepted the run of the flat, because that was just how she herself lived, there were times when he said something cold; a part of her held back for a moment from their presence together in the room and lagged shamefacedly towards some old loyalty. The two advertising men would have no idea that he dismissed them like that. The natural corollary to this thought—that he was living on them—did not come into it (she would have lived on anybody) but the hint that he exacted from them a price of their white privilege under the cover of friendship, set up a distant conditioned opposition.

She had introduced him to the idea of making his own frames for his paintings, because she thought the sort of thing the framers turned out imprisoned his work in something mass-produced and alien to it. Like Len before him, he was amused by the confident way she tackled obstacles : "How're we going to make these corners right, they ought to be mortised or whatever it is." "Ah, rubbish. That's not necessary. There are all sorts of marvellous kinds of glue you can get. That stuff that little boys use—aeroplane glue. I'll get it. The joins'll be covered by the linen, anyway."

They worked outside on the balcony, squatting on the floor,

where the mess didn't matter. He wore a blue and white Italian cotton shirt that she had bought him. She did not bother to paint her face and her grey eyes and thick eyebrows and lashes had the furry darkness of some creature surprised by daylight. They laughed and argued and got things wrong, lapsing into silences of fierce concentration. She broke finger-nails and every so often stopped to suck a finger that had got hurt. They tired and stopped to smoke, leaning against the balcony wall and hidden by it from everything but the living-room of the flat, and the sky. "I don't see why you shouldn't be ready for a small exhibition—say, even by July. Eben Swart's gallery would be good. Or the small one at Howe's."

"Wouldn't have more than twenty pictures—counting the old ones that everyone's seen too often."

None of the seven or eight oils and numerous sketches he had done of her could be used; they smiled at each other at the thought of this. "Perhaps in another town," she said. "On another planet," he said. They continued to talk lazily of the chances of putting a worthwhile show together, and then, without any change of tone, he said, "I may not be here in July. Most likely not. Something I've got to do for Congress."

She kept smiling at him, a dent between her eyebrows, her mouth pressed together as if she were sure he would go on to say something else. He said nothing and went on smoking.

"What sort of thing?"

He gestured, and the movement put the whole thing out of her ken, took him back to a place where she did not exist. "A lot of travelling about, talking and so on."

"I'm supposed to go to Moçambique," she said.

"Going to go?" His voice sounded hoarse with the effort at naturalness.

"Yes, I think I'll go. Terrific trip."

He put his hand on the flat of her waist, where her breath rose and fell evenly beneath her dress. He felt an immense pride in her beauty and her toughness. He was filled with arrogance about her. He lifted her pale face distorted between his hands, the lips showing a gleam of teeth, the eyes giving nothing away in their many-coloured mottling, their tinsel fragments imbedded in glassy shadow. She pushed up his loose-clinging shirt and rested her head on his bare chest. To him her eyes seemed closed, but she was gazing out of lowered lids at the smooth skin, hair-less, contoured by ribs and muscle; the colour of aubergine, but there was no shine to it. She smoothed the ripple of a rib with one finger. She was ashamed to let him see something that troubled her lately when she was with him, though she forgot about it instantly they were not together : the dark positiveness of his skin, the mattness of it, the variations like markings shading one part of his body in difference from another—some nerve in her had become alive to it. She dwelt on it in secret as soon as she touched him.

She put out her tongue and passed it quick and hesitant where the skin slid over the rib. She was always afraid he would look her in the eyes and find her out. When he did see her her face was confused, open, something that had been there already breaking up, like a sky of merging and melting cloud. He saw there only what he was feeling himself, the irresolution and confusion that he felt between himself and the one thing that he had had proved to him, that he had decided on, finally, that lay at rock-bottom under all that now obliterated, now exposed it in his being : the validity of whatever he did with the group of men who met in the back rooms of shops and in other people's houses. All warmth and truth was there; didn't he know it? Away from *that*, cut off from it, when his life was over he would be a dead cat flung in the gutter. How could it become cloudy, receding? Something that didn't strike him deep, where the will is? He lost himself, his confusion in the confusion of her face.

PART THREE

FOURTEEN

THE FIRST FEW nights Jessie awoke suddenly sometime in the night and heard in the sound of the sea the voices of argument and the cries of children teasing one another. She was sure someone was there, walking through the house behind the muffle of the sea yawning away; the little girls were calling her. Things were being knocked aside and slowly falling ... She was alone and her mind went on twitching and pulsating in response to all that recoiled upon it up the stairs and in the living-room, round the table and on the landing, from behind the closed door where the strange shapes of musical instruments were and the smell of another woman, in the enclosed verandah where Morgan lay and Tom stroked papers drily one on another.

The Stilwell house was not there. She listened and there was nothing but the sea; all voices were its own, all sounds. The sound was an element, like its wetness.

The mornings were light early. Moths and other flying creatures, clinging to the curtains, fell feebly away in the sun and crawled about the cracked concrete floor as she pulled the curtains aside with the first sound of the day and her occupation of it—the runners screeching faintly along the rust of the rod. The sea moved towards her shiningly out of the night; it was immortality, it had been there all the time. She went back to bed and when she woke again the room was hot, and the water all dazzling peaked surfaces.

Between them—herself standing on the verandah in a dressing-gown, Clem, Madge and Elisabeth in their pyjamas on the coarse short grass—and the sea, were high dunes sloping down bushy green, splendid aloes standing out against the water with their green serrated leaves peeled back and the rags of last year's clinging to the bole, and groups of strelitzia palm crowded by spoon-leaved dark, short trees, bushes with torn silvery leaves, a mesh of shrubs and ground-creepers. It was not jungle; it made no darkness. It shone and shook and swayed in the sun. Along the coast where the village was, people had planted Scotch firs that were thinned by the wind and the heat and disappeared into the haze. She knew these skinny trees, growing in the dry sand and making it hurtful with stunted cones. Over above a pale red roof, a monkey-puzzle was set down where some retired mine manager or insurance agent had made things nice for himself.

The atmosphere in which she moved, from house to open doors, where the sea was, was a constant switch from a peculiar, dead, fusty stuffiness to blasts of intoxicating softness. The house was not as she had remembered it but was rather part of the memory of other beach houses as she remembered them and as they appeared to be, even when one did not live in them, but passed them, deserted, perhaps, and looked in, standing on the rough concrete supports that held them above the gap between the floors and the foundation that was left open against rot and termites. The walls of such houses were not grown thick with layer on layer of human personality, but were thin and inter-changeable as the shells that gave shelter to various sea animals, first holding some blob of animate mucous, then inhabited by one crab or another. And all the time, as the sea washes in and out of all shells, sand, wind, damp, warmth entered and flowed through these houses; ants streamed over them as if they were part of the continuing surface of sandy earth, bats lived in them as they lived in caves, and all the silent things, the unnoticed forms of life—mould, verdigris—continued to grow as they did on natural forms.

She thought she recognised the water-tank, but when she looked at it closely it was clear that it was fairly new, so that even if it was there that she had washed the sand off her feet, the tap and tank itself were certainly not the old ones she had known. In any case, the village had a proper piped water-supply now, and a health board to certify it, and, of course, the house was connected up to the mains; the tank was only for watering the grass.

The house had been four narrow dark rooms surrounded by an open verandah on all sides. But walls had been knocked out and parts of the verandah filled in with rooms and even extended for the purpose. The concrete blocks moulded to simulate stone of

186

which it was built were painted a dim green and the floors everywhere were red granolithic thickly polished and marked off—
when the concrete was wet, long ago—in yard squares that held
dust and sea sand in the grooves. The house showed signs of
some sort of upheaval, fairly recent, which already had begun
to yield to the landscape. Apparently the old couple who had
lived in it for years had left (been forced out, maybe, in one of
Fuecht's drives of concern about his possessions?) about two
years before Bruno Fuecht died, and the house had then
evidently been smartened up for a more profitable letting. There
was a big refrigerator with a deep freeze compartment, although
the stove was an old paraffin burner, converted to use electricity.
The furniture was the usual sort that comes to rest in seaside
houses : a couple of heavy stuffed chairs that were once part of
a "suite", re-covered by amateurs in material from the local store,
a standard lamp like a long pole of brown barley sugar, old
black dressing-tables with drawers that stuck. Perhaps the later,
smarter tenants had added furniture of their own that they had
taken away with them. In the lavatory they had left a printed
notice :

"To ensure the satisfactory working of this sewerage system
(septic tank) great care must be taken to see that the following
articles are not deposited in the system :
"Cold cream, vaseline, sandwiches, sawdust, moth balls,
cannon balls, golf balls, fish balls, press balls, footballs, cricket
bats, curtain rings, telephone rings, engagement rings, smoke
rings . . ." The list went on in this strain, ending up : " . . . red
tape, brassières, two-way stretches, mosquito nets, hair nets,
fishing nets—or, in fact, any article at all which may cause
the breakdown of the system.
"God save the sugar farmers.
"Given at Isendhla Beach this day, the twenty-fourth of
December, 1958, under my hand and great seal.
"BIG CHIEF SHAKA."

The house retained no impress of the life that it had contained,
first permanently, and then from time to time. Each room was
like a person who had no memory, blank, carrying the objects
of its purpose—table, bed, cupboard, as a name-tag. Jessie went
from one to the other, meeting herself in strips of wardrobe

187

mirror, pushing a fist into an unmade bed, sitting down suddenly. The windows stuck. When they were shut everything outside was seen through a dim cataract of salt. Reddish heaps of powdered wood appeared overnight from the ceilings.

After a week, she made no more claim on the house than any other creature that drifted in and out of it. It was shade she and the children came under when they trailed up from the beach; there was food there, somewhere to lie down; she was no longer contained by walls but had a being without barriers moving without much change of sensation from hot sun to cool water, from the lap and push and surge of water to the damp, blowy air. When her eyes were open they followed the sea; when they were closed the movement was in her blood.

The porpoises went by in the swell beyond the breakers, or, when the water was calm, closer in. She watched them as a child watches the game of another family of children, projecting into the pleasure of her half-smile an inkling, from her own experience, of their sensations. Where the grass was not shaved down by the mower, low mauve flowers the shape of sweet peas came out in dew or rain, and closed away invisibly when the sun shone. At night shrill bells went off everywhere in the bush and voiceless creatures flew in to the light and left transparent wings on the floor; in the morning, they were swept out. Madge cut branches of wild gardenia and put them in beer glasses that the wind blew down. Whatever was beautiful was webbed by spiders and dust and alive with the attentions of big agile black ants. They watched out for snakes on the path, and when they were in the sea occasionally remembered sharks, as though evil were impossible in that buoyant suspension on the world's watery back.

Clem was embarrassed because Jessie wore old canvas shoes that had flattened into mules under her heels, and did not put her hair up with care. Jessie stopped wearing the shoes and went barefoot "like Boaz", as Clem said in reproach. "But *you* go barefoot all the time, at home too."

"Well, we're children."

When they drove to the store Jessie put on a bare-necked dress and perfume and made up her face. Clem capered about before her, as if she expected a sensation. They drove along the path with bush making a noise like a finger-nail on the glass of the car windows, and then away from the sea on to the road that divided cane-fields. The moment the sea dropped out of sight something seemed to have been switched off and the car was hot in the silence. Indian children plodded along the road, back from school. An old black cane worker with the bearded, moustachioed "fine" face of Zulus in Victorian missionary chronicles appeared with a panga hanging from his hand. The road crossed the lines of the cane-trucks and there was a point where you could see far inland, across the curves covered with the pile of cane to flat-topped mountains holding their outline in the heat-shimmer and distance. As far as you could see, and further, it was Shaka's country; less than a hundred and forty years ago the black king had trained his prancing armies and spread his great herds of cattle here.

The road led round the golf-course and back towards the sea again, to the village. The hotel was there, in the thin firs. Cars round the bowling-green; old men in shorts and old women in schoolgirls' hats were bending and straightening on the grass. Everyone with a good position on the mine had thought of a retirement like this; the faces were familiar ones, that went early into middle-age and stayed there, helped by the uniformity of false teeth and glasses, far into old age. What had possessed Bruno to will, as if for peace, to end up along with them? An impulse that never came to anything, of course; except perhaps that he could always remind himself that his "little place on the Coast" did exist, proof of an intention.

An Indian with expanding bands holding up his shirt-sleeves was directing some piccanins who were piling up empty brandy crates outside the hotel bottle store. More children—porcupine-headed Indians with faces eager to please, dusty African brats with unself-conscious faces, one or two coloureds with yellow skins, the legginess of white boys, and hair as black as the Indians' and as curly as the Africans'—hung about the caddy master's hut. There were games with sticks, scuffles and yells. The Indians watched with tremendous eyes, jerking their younger members to order. Cooks with baskets over their arms stood talking while their masters' dogs wagged puzzled tails, waiting. The caddy master, another Indian, with thick white-streaked hair and a bad-tempered open mouth showing brown teeth, upbraided somebody, scattering dusty legs. Big cars rolled

189

slowly down from the hotel and white children, raw-faced from the beach, stood aside clutching loaves of bread or ice-creams.

The store kept stuffed olives and caviar, as well as the usual supplies, for there were some smart houses along the hotel end of the beach now, and on the sun-decks and behind the picture-windows people from Johannesburg brought the eating-habits of their way of life with them. Occasionally you saw a man dressed in the white trousers, navy scarf and espadrilles of some-one who had been to the Riviera in the Thirties; or a blonde lion-headed girl in tights who might have been walking along in Saint-Tropez in the present time; both were received with the same lack of impact by the local residents in the khaki shorts and sand shoes they had worn without change, in comfort and suitability, through both eras. Jessie's children were stimulated by the store, not only by the garlands of blown-up plastic toys, the tin pistols, the comics and the sweets, but by the link, through the atmosphere of buying and selling, the miscellaneous activity set in motion by the exchange of even petty sums of money, with the city life they came from. It always surprised her to notice how healthily children accepted *as life* the things that were to imprison them later—the arbitrary picking up and putting down of buses, the herding of traffic lights, the crowded desperateness in shops, the whole acquisitive palsy. How was it that these same children grew up to become neurotic, ulcerous, under it? She herself had been just like them; there was no excitement, for the little bourgeois girl from the mine, like buying something. When did it turn into an activity that drained without replacement; when did the faces poked across the counters for their money's worth become so clearly marked as faces possessing nothing of worth? What made you want *things* so fiercely and meaningfully as a child, and then come to a time when you bought without lust, out of need, and never out of *wanting*, which was a differ-ent thing, stemming from needs spiritual and unconditioned? One did not know when the lust died, for first it was put aside by sex and the tremendous effort gathered together by even the meanest of living creatures to blossom or feather, to put out a perfume or a fascinating way of talking, to stamp a love-dance in a forest or walk down a street with a message in the way each knee brushed past the other. And only when this was over and

190

accomplished did you have eyes for other desires again, and suddenly discover that of all that was displayed on the counters and hanging on shelves and set out under soft lights—of all that was offered to make you want, there was nothing that would not break or clutter or occupy falsely where it had been done without.

Every day, no matter what she was doing, she looked out at the sea and saw the porpoises passing. She had no idea that they were going to be passing, but when she looked out, there they went. She had this. It had survived. Neither petrol fumes nor phenobarbital, book-keeping nor all-night drinking parties had finished it. Living creatures came by out there in the wide water and she was able to know it. She never thought about it. But there they were. Some days they were going along steadily, each movement the length of their bodies through the swell. Sometimes they cut in formation through a sloping wall of glassy grey. Occasionally one shook himself terrier-free out of the water, made the arabesque dictated by his own weight, and splashed into it again. She had no means of communication with them except whatever it was that made her know when they were there; there was no reason to suppose that they did not have the same sort of knowledge about her.

Tom had assumed that she would take Morgan with her on holiday but she had protested, disintegrating into a kind of helplessness that forced Tom to plan for her, all the time with a feeling of disbelief because he knew there was always so little you could do for Jessie. He would say to her, the morning after she had argued adamantly, "Well, what have you decided?" and she would say listlessly, "I suppose he'll come."

He looked at her and away from her, dismayed, searching. He made as if to speak and then said something else. "What'd he find to do with himself here, that's the trouble. I don't mind having him—"

"No, I know. He'll have to come." And the night before she had explained how impossible it was for her to contemplate a month with Morgan sitting across the breakfast table—the little girls were companions for one another, what on earth would she do with *him* all day?

"If only Boaz would make up his mind whether he's going to

Moçambique or not." (The reasons for Boaz's indecision became suddenly irrelevant; it was annoying of him not to be able to be counted on for his offer to provide Morgan with just the right sort of camping holiday, complete with the mixture of adventure and self-reliance that would be good for him.)

"Well, even if it's off with Boaz, maybe we could get some other boy to stay here with Morgan. Then I could manage."

"No, you'll never be able to get any work done. You'll be nannying all the time and cursing me, quite rightly. They'll drive you crazy."

But the more she showed herself obstinately bowed to accept the inevitability of Morgan, the more Tom felt constrained to find some way out for her since she made it clear she couldn't help herself. He had already made a great mistake, when the whole business of Morgan accompanying her had first come up, of suggesting that it would be a good opportunity to talk to him a bit, to get a little nearer to him in the easiest manner, since they would be set apart, alone together, from the smaller children without any other grown-ups around to claim her. But apparently the pursuit of Morgan was dropped; or perhaps it was so intense that she couldn't face him alone with it. Tom didn't know. Anyway, she reacted so strongly to Tom's suggestion, jeering at a picture of herself subject to Morgan's anecdotes, in which he was not interested and to which she was not listening, that Tom didn't pursue it. In the end, without any actual decision being come to, she left for the house at the sea as soon as her month's notice at the nursing home was worked, and a few days before Morgan was due to come home from school. The Moçambique expedition was still up in the air. One day Boaz was packing and talking practically, as if preparing to go, then there were signs of highly emotional talks with his wife, a charged atmosphere of things in balance, and his departure was unlikely.

Tom always wrote to Jessie about Morgan, just as if she always remembered to ask about him in her letters. That was one of the corrupting, wonderful things about Tom : he pretended for her when the real thing was painfully lacking in herself. He pitied her in her strength of wilfulness, her difficulty in pretending to herself. She did not resent this pity, unintrusive, so delicately expressed. She wondered what she did for him, of the same secrecy and necessity. Even between Bruno and her mother there had once been signs of things like this; it was only in the worst, last few years of his life that everything they knew of one another was emptied out upon the table, as a bankrupt turns out his pockets so that you may see for yourself the worthless miscellany with which he is left.

Once she had begun to make preparations to go away that did not include provision for Morgan, the thought that she ought to be taking him left her. It was as if there had never been any question that he might come. He was in her mind, not very insistently, sometimes as the result of some sight or object in the house or on the beach. One morning she was walking along the firm shoreline near the hotel with the little girls, after a swim. The thud of her heels went through her head; drops of water flew from her thighs. They passed the slender figure of a young man fishing, making a loop behind him and his mess of bait, newspaper, and rumpled sand. As they came down to the water's edge again on the other side, she was aware that she was walking, now, as a woman does when a man is watching her. Later Elisabeth wandered over to the same young man and got talking; she was given the present of a dead sardine. When Jessie and the children went up from the beach at midday the fisherman was squatting over his equipment, and as she made some casual remark in acknowledgement of the present, he looked up. She saw that the man she had been conscious of as she walked away from him over the sand was a boy, a boy Morgan's age. "That's nothing," he was saying to the children's enthusiasm and her polite admiration of his catch. "My dad and I came down at half-term, just for the weekend, mind you, and we took back thirty-four shad and a small barracuda . . ."

When she took off her wet bathing suit at the house she noticed that the dark shine of sunburn was beginning to cover the map of tiny red veins she had on her right leg, near the knee. It could scarcely be seen at all. There was the satisfaction of some small reprieve. She looked over her shoulder at her naked back and backside and legs in the mirror. How long? Five years? Six? (What did the bodies of women in their forties look like?) A few years and she wouldn't be able to look at this any more.

About her face she had different thoughts. Clem's reproaches made her realise that at home she was constantly composing her face, not just with the re-touches of lipstick or powder at different times through the day, but also with the confrontation with her own expression which these bits of touching-up before a mirror brought. Here sometimes the whole day went by before she saw her face again, once she had brushed her hair after swimming. Her face was left to itself. She wondered how one might look if one let a whole month go by without that check on what one's face is saying that comes automatically with a glance in a mirror. What extraordinary things there might be in a face naked, open, weathered by an absolute freedom to take on the cast of feelings as rain and sun and wind move through the sky. At the end of it, a look might have come into the open that had never been allowed out before. The unguarded moment would have taken over altogether; nose, mouth, and, most of all, eyes.

Even when a man does something out of character it often turns out that what he really is has not failed to give the venture an unmistakable twist somewhere. Bruno Fuecht had bought his plot and house "on the Coast" with the apparent intention of any of the other mine officials who looked forward to life in a cosy community centred round the bowling green and the golf course, one day, past sixty. But as it turned out, the development of the township had come at the other end of the beach, and his house, after all, remained alone almost at the limit of the opposite boundary.

If Jessie walked up the beach in the direction of the hotel and the other houses there were people on the sand, fishermen, bathers and dogs. To the left of the path that led from the house to the beach there were no houses and no one came by except an occasional Indian fisherman from somewhere back in the cane. A juicy-leaved plant trailed right down on to the sands. On windy days she sat among the dunes where it grew, private and quiet. On other days she liked the firm-packed sand near the water, or the inlets among the loops of sand and rocks where the salt-greasy rocks provided a strangely comfortable kind of furniture, places to lean against, ledges to put things on, and also, at eye-level of a half-closed eye, crevices filled with the minute and dependent life of the sea, sealed until the tide opened

194

it to food and life again. Each wrinkle in the rock lined with these crumbs of being gave not the anthropomorphic pleasure of more highly-developed living things, with an existence that a human being always guesses at in simplified terms of his own, but the pleasure of pure form. Volute, convolute, spheroid, they were order, perfect order at the extreme end of a process the other end of which was the perfect disintegration of the atom bomb. They were so small and fragile that now and then Jessie would crush one with a fingernail.

The children liked to lead her up the other end of the beach, towards people. (It was there that they had met the fisherman.) And sometimes she herself, needing nobody, free of everybody after days on the deserted beach, would find an impersonal warmth in the casual presence of people, simply people, she did not know. Women sat with their legs straight out before them in a V, gazing at the sea; they were really sitting down, after a long time. Young girls and their men lay on their faces, prostrate like worshippers. When she was among these groups and knots of people, isolated from each other by the strange perspectives of the sea, whose light, suffusing the light of the sun, creates an effect of distance, so that a figure twenty yards off seems far away, just as he is already out of hearing because of the sound of the sea—when she was somewhere on the sand among them, her consciousness was a plot without a theme. The simple narrative of the beach occupied her, the link-by-link happenings. A child got into a rubber canoe, was launched into a pool, and slowly overturned at the same point every time the preparations were repeated. A man cast his line for a while from one place; then, after a certain interval, moved up somewhere else. A woman in a leghorn hat with a yellow ribbon smoked and talked to a man with a bald head who, at some pause to which she seemed to return again and again (as the child in the canoe capsized again and again), took her hand and, stretching it out the limp length of her white arm to his knee, ran his own palm in a smoothing gesture up from her wrist to shoulder. A young servant in a kitchen-boy suit came down to the beach from one of the houses with a tray of bread spread with marmite. He sauntered to the children with the canoe, pausing to gaze, almost sniff, not so much at the sea as at the whole beach; his strong bowed legs, arms and head were very black against the unbleached cotton suit with its loose shorts, red band round the neck and sleeves, and ridiculous belt sewn high up at the back of the blouse. The children gathered round him. He stood talking with them in Zulu, eating, too, as they shared out. When they had finished, he went dreamily up the sand again, looking round, lifting his head into the breeze. He was dispossessed of everything but a moment of superb idleness.

At night Jessie was lethargic after dinner and felt she could have gone to bed when the children did, but by ten o'clock she was enjoyably awake and passing, with the silence and confidence of one who is alone, between the warm darkness where the sea was breathing, on the grass, to the open living-room, where she read late. One night the telephone rang—there was a telephone, on a party line, but she knew no one to ring her up, and though she had idly noted that the house's particular code was three rings, she expected so little to hear it that, had it come at some other time, among the other combinations of rings that she had ceased to register, she probably would not have noticed it. But the telephone was only vocal at certain times of day, when the village was conducting its affairs, and in the early evening, when trunk calls were cheaper; it always fell silent after nine o'clock at night. On this night it rang quite firmly through the rooms, like a visitor who strides in calling out "Anybody home?" Jessie thought it must be a mistake and lifted her head, not putting her book aside. It was three rings, all right; she got up and went to the kitchen, where the black box hung on the wall. When she picked up the receiver there was a confusion of crackling, faint jumbled voices and distant ringing. She tried to get in touch with the exchange, by hanging up, turning the little crank at the side of the box and then shouting "Hullo? Hullo?" into the receiver again, all in the self-conscious manner of a city person unused to such contraptions. But there was no response and she quickly got impatient and went back to read. The book was Teilhard de Chardin's *Phenomenon of Man*, a book that, that year, people were reading who, without distinctions of worth, had last year read interpretations of Buddhism, and the year before Simone Weil, or Ouspensky. They were read, quite often, in the same half-secret, deprecating way in which the same people, when they were twenty, had read treatises on sex (*The Function of the Orgasm*), for people between thirty and forty

196

tend to have toward the meaning of their existence the anxious, suppressed urgency which at twenty they felt about sex. The real doubters and the mere consolation-seekers often go to the same sources; and it is the consolation-seekers who usually find something that will serve them—and if they do not, go on to another and yet another source, finding consolation in the activity of the search, if nothing else. The real doubters include those for whom politics has gone as deep as sex, but the consolation-seekers are not intelligent enough to have sought any kind of discipline outside themselves; they have never wanted to change the world : only to get their sweet lick of it. This was how Jessie defined these categories for herself. But the Chardin book was nothing for the consolation-seekers; only the title would console them, with its assurance of distinction and uniqueness. And she was reading it, here, without any of those spurious thrills of release and comfort by which a desperate flux of personality gives itself away; her mind followed the movement of the writer's mind in a spirit of enquiry that stretched, muscle by muscle, to keep up with his. She went along with the book, did not scuttle back to her own little hole with the first scrap she could use in some much unpicked and re-made rag, part-garment, part-nest, part-shroud, that she had been putting together.

On the beach in the daylight she read novels, even some poetry. Some of the books she had brought with her from home were no use at all; there is no way of telling before you live in a place, in the way it creates, what you will be able to read there. One or two things were dead right; bringing Conrad was inspired, of course. How perfectly the book and the day you looked up to from it merged when the book was *Victory*! (Tom had put it in for her, bought it in one of those students' "classics" editions, neat and small, on India paper.) A novel by a West Indian writer was fine, too; she liked to read about these negroes whose way of life had a familiarity but brought none of the pain with which she was indicted and identified when she read novels about home. There was also a paper-back Thomas Mann translation. She had never read Mann in what she thought of as her "great reading days"; halfway through *The Magic Mountain* he had been put aside as a bore, old-fashioned. Now she was making the discovery that the massive style was not a Victorian catalogue of "character" and furniture but a terrifying descent through the "safety" of middle-class trappings to the individual anarchy and ideological collapse lying at their centre. Even a comfortable description of a man's walk with a dog : "It is good to walk like this in the early morning, with senses rejuvenated and spirit cleansed by the night's long healing draught..." fell away suddenly under foot like a rotten mahogany floorboard—"You indulge in the illusion that your life is habitually steady, simple, concentrated, and contemplative, that you belong entirely to yourself... whereas the truth is that a human being is condemned to improvisation and morally lives from hand to mouth, all the time."

The business of choosing books to match a mood or atmosphere was a bit of an insult, really—whether to the writers or herself she didn't bother to decide. It was something amusing to mention to Tom in a letter—she often dreamed letters to people, on the beach, sometimes people to whom she had owed a letter for years. (She did write Tom's, of course.)

She was reading on the beach on a morning so quiet that her book actually seemed to sound aloud. It was a cloudy day with the heat of the hidden sun coming hypnotically off the blurred shine of concentrated radiance on a smooth grey sea. The grey moved oilily and broke in slow rolls, hesitantly, upon the sand. The tide was out, the rocks looked flattened. Once when she gazed up without focus she saw a woman pausing as if she had just come down "their" path, the path from the house. She kept the figure in this same dreamy gaze and then felt the pull of its attention on her. The woman was making for her, moving with the slightly ploughing gait that the heavy sand, up there where the tide did not pack it smooth, made necessary. It was Ann. Before she could make out the face, Jessie knew from the look of attention that the face had fixed upon herself that it was Ann coming.

The girl stood there holding her shoes in her left hand; seemed to begin to lift them, as if to wave, but then did not, and came on.

She saw she was recognised and came faster. "Jessie."

"How did you find me?"

There was no wind and no sound in the airless air. Their voices dropped to the beach like dead birds. Both were amazed, as if Ann had given up thought or hope of her being really there.

"I tried to phone you. It went on for hours."

"Oh, last night! That was last night?"

"Yes, I hung on and hung on, I think I actually heard you shouting hullo at one point."

"I was just about to go to bed." Jessie scrambled up and now they were both standing. "I thought the exchange was crazy—eleven o'clock—and no one ever rings me anyway. I nearly didn't answer..." They might have been two people bumping into each other in a coffee-bar after a misunderstanding about a meeting-place. Ann went into an animated, exaggerated explanation about how difficult it was to find someone who knew where the cottage *was* . She was laughing, making faces of mock despair, drawing deep breaths of exasperation, and the hand that she put up to her face now and then made the gesture tremulous. She wore one of the full skirts and dark shirts that she liked, but her hair looked limp, and the thick line of pencil behind the thick eyelashes was smudgy and unrepaired. The white skin with its few small black moles shone new and strangely exposed to the hot, open radiance. Yes, it was strange to this place; the understanding rushed in on Jessie while the girl was talking. She had a moment of violent dismay, cringing fiercely from the intrusion. They began to walk back toward the house, and Jessie knew; it was only a matter of form that Ann paused, turning on to the path, pressing on the leaf of wild ice-plant that became a juicy stain under her foot, and said, "Gid's in the car."

FIFTEEN

THE BACK OF his head and one arm, stretched along the top of the seat with the hand dangling, had the look of a person obdurately real, almost ordinary, at the centre of an upheaval. Jessie saw the sight in dissolving unbelief—he had gone out of existence, for her, into the situation he had created : he was here, alive. He didn't turn his head. He let them come up in silence.

Jessie had difficulty in bringing out a smile or the normal platitudes of greeting; and she could see, as he at last moved his head when they were facing his profile, that he knew this. He said, like a survivor, "You picked a nice quiet spot for yourself. Hullo . . ."

"Why don't you get out?" Ann chided, smiling. He gave her a glance to make sure of the signal; he continued to half-smile at Jessie, beginning remarks he didn't finish, lapsing into his selfish chuckle. "Hell, I don't know why . . . stuck here, I guess. You want to look for this place in the dark, man, the end of the earth . . . you're sure this is really where you live, eh . . .?"

". . . I had no idea anyone was really trying to get me."

"Bring the cigarettes," Ann said. She was frowning into the glare, business-like now. He was out of the car, leaning back into it to get his jacket. "And that—no, my other one, the underneath—" He hung himself with her saddle-bag, then fished for something on the floor of the car and came up with one of the satchels made of woven mealie leaves that Zulu women sell on the road. The floor was crowded with newspapers, bruised apples, the cellophane from cigarette packets, a pineapple, milk cartons, a half-drunk bottle of brandy, and on the small back seat there was a new tartan rug and one of the lumpy, grubby cushions off the verandah chairs at home.

"The trouble is that all the houses around here are known by the names of their owners, but no one would know what you were talking about if you asked for Fuecht's because my step-father never lived here and the place's always known by the couple who lived in it for years—Grimald's cottage."

"Well, of course we were spelling Fuecht to everybody, black kids, old women in the fields . . ."

"Tom should have told you."

"Gid kept saying how confusing life is in the country. All the time he was moaning about how simple it is to move around among a million people with names on the streets and numbers on houses—" Ann began to giggle as one does at something that was not funny at the time, making common cause in amusement at him with Jessie. With the ruthlessness of a woman who wants to secure something for a lover or a child, she imposed upon them the pretence that she and Jessie were leading the man into the house with a shared sense of warm attention. They moved in a dazed, ill-assorted progression between the hibiscus bushes, down the cracked concrete steps to the back of the house, that lay below the level of the track : Jessie with sun-scrubbed face and brown hands with white nails, blanched clean in the physical honesty of salt water and abrasive sand; the other two full of the creased shadiness of those who have been too long in their clothes.

It was half past eleven in the morning. Jessie led the way into the house that acknowledged no ownership. "Would you like tea? You've had breakfast?"

Ann went to the windows of the living-room like a weekend guest, hands on her hips, looking at the sea. Gideon sat down in the middle of the divan that did duty as a sofa, sending up the sound of broken piano strings. He leaned forward with his hands clasped, elbows on knees, and looked round slowly from under his brow. "Any chance of a brandy in the house?"

"Of course. Beer, too, I think. Would you like a beer, Ann? I'll look in the fridge—I bought myself a couple of cans the other day."

"Milk," said Ann. "A big glass of cold milk."

Jessie went into the kitchen. The young Zulu who was care-taker of the house when it was empty, and worked for the occu-pants when it was let, stood stirring a mug of tea. He said "Missus?" and she said "It's all right," and if he did not under-stand the words he understood the tone and the smile, and she took the milk and a jug of water out of the refrigerator and arranged the tray for herself. She emptied a packet of biscuits on to a plate and unwrapped a piece of cheese, sweating in its red rind.

When she came back to the living-room with the tray Ann was deep in a big chair and Gideon had taken one of the stiff, curled-edge magazines left in the magazine rack by previous tenants and was turning the pages without looking at them. Ann sat up and drank the milk and cut a chunk of cheese, and Jessie said, "The brandy," and took a bottle out of the sideboard. She put the iced water beside it, but he poured himself a big neat tot and drank it off. Ann pressed him : "Have some cheese. Don't you want biscuits?"

"Where are the children?" she asked Jessie. It was as if she had been particularly fond of them, like one of those adults who use children to draw attention to themselves, making a great show of their ability to get on with them and forcing their presence upon other adult company. Jessie answered as if this were so. "Down at the rocks somewhere, I suppose. I'll have to go and fetch them."

They began to talk again about the search for the house in the dark the night before. Gideon kept screwing his eyes up, shaking his head, and then forcing them open again, in punctuation. Once or twice his mouth fell slackly and he breathed aloud in a catching pant. Ann's air of normal animation had breaks in it when she seemed to lose the thread of what she was saying. Suddenly she demanded, "I've got to sleep. Can I have a bed somewhere?" Jessie, like the sane momentarily made aware of the exhausting fantasies of the mad, suddenly realised that they must have been up all night, perhaps more than one night. "Where were you coming from yesterday, anyway?" she said.

The comfortable distance between herself and them closed; at once they were drawn tight together, with a jerk. Ann's head rolled wearily to her shoulder where she stood, then, for a second, she and he looked at each other in the way of people who share some experience—something ugly, privileged, survived— that will never come out in the telling. He would not speak, he lit a cigarette as if what there was existed only when he looked at her. "Where we were coming from—?" she laughed encouragement to herself, awkwardly. "Where we were coming from. Oh well that's another thing. —Look, I've got to lie down now."

Jessie went back to the beach to fetch the children. All the way down the path and over the sand she said to herself the things she should have said, wanted to say. She had lived so calmly for the past few weeks that her sulky outrage affected her like a strong emotion. She was hotly disgusted at the namby-pamby way she had received the two of them, just as naturally as if they had been neighbours dropping in for a cup of tea. A glass of cold milk! Why hadn't she said at once, right away, at the car, what are you doing here? What have you come here for, dragging in the whole show, the witnesses and the events, the spies and the distractors?

Her solitary stake of quiet personal belongings lay on the sand abandoned. The clouds that underhung the sky had blown away in a north wind and the sea was dyed hard blue by a clear sky. She felt as if she had left the place already. She found the children and they trailed up to the house in the mesmerised glitter of midday, to a monologue kept up by Elisabeth.

Jessie knew how, when you were alone in the house and the children came up the path that gradually drew them level with the house, their voices flew in before them. She thought of the two sitting in possession there, and turned away inwardly, stubbornly set against the moment when again she would walk in with some normal, casual remark. Her feet slowed like a child's in dread; it was important to her to delay confronting them again, even by the meaningless little time so gained. But the voices must have flown in unheard. The curtains of the room she had indicated to Ann were pulled and neither of them was to be seen. Jessie felt ridiculously relieved, as if they really were not there. She ate her lunch of fruit and cheese in the midday dream, served by silent Jason in his clean red-check shirt, not answering the chatter of the children.

Afterwards she sat on the verandah. She smoked and rested her eyes on the horizon of sea. The sun was behind the house in the afternoons and the shadow that fell before it was deep, the brightness beyond it searching. The curtains bellying convex then concave on the windows that gave on to the far end of the verandah remained closed. She thought of him, going over him slowly and repeatedly, as if she were describing him. A black man sitting in the car, with the small ears they have and the tiny whorls of felted black hair. ("Wool" : but where was it like the soft, oily, or silky washed fleece of sheep?) A black man like the thousands, the kaffir and picannin and native and nig of her childhood, the "African" of her adult life and friendships; the man; the lover. He was these. And none of them. Shibalo. When she saw his back, in the car, he was for a steady moment all the black men that had been around her through her life, familiar in the way of people not known as individuals. She had known him in this way a long, long time; the other way hardly at all, by comparison. Did he pick his nose as some of the other Africans she had been friendly with did, out of nervous habit, while he argued? These were things one got to know, as well as the quality of the mind, when one began to enter into individual relationships with people. Frenchmen and Germans cleaned their teeth with slivers of wood while you were eating. What did she do, when she was alone or in the other aloneness of intimacy, that offended against that ideal of a creature living but not decaying that is kept up in public? Tom pared his toe-nails and let the cuttings from the clippers fly about the bedroom, so that she sometimes found a piece of sharp, yellowish rind in the bed or fallen into an open drawer. She felt some revulsion always but it passed because she was in love with him sexually; his flesh was alive for her : therefore he was dying continually. Perhaps you can accept the facts of renewal through decay only where there is love of the flesh.

She was waiting for the moment when the man appeared from the sleep and silence behind the curtains. She had the feeling, half-mean, half-powerful, of a person of whom something is going to be asked. What did he expect of her, Gideon Shibalo? You had always to do things for them because they were powerless to do anything for you. But did this mean that there was no limit to it, no private demarcation that anyone might be allowed to make before another? Because he has no life here among us, must I give him mine?—thinking that this was wild exaggeration, that what was in question, what she was jealously disgruntled about, was an intrusion on her holiday. If he does not know where to take his girl, is that my affair, too? Her almost superstitious withdrawal from the idea of the Davises coming to live with her nearly a year ago had come back in a sweep of confirmation since this morning, with Gideon Shibalo confused unnoticeably with Boaz. The girl, too; what had she to do with this girl she'd kept meeting about the house all year, always with the smile on her face that you get from the stranger who bumps into you on a pavement? Yes, what? She accused belligerently. "A glass of milk". Did I exist for her before the moment when she asked me that? Does my existence begin when she is forced to walk in on it, and cease when she walks out? Jessie went over the girl sharply, noticing like a jealous woman that she had carried off the arrival, but only just; there were schoolgirlish touches. She had made an idiot of herself; or very nearly. No doubt the intention was aplomb. Well, it certainly hadn't been that. She had scraped through, making this mad—no, preposterous entrance just plausible. Just plausible enough to stop my mouth, she thought; and a different version of the meeting on the beach went through her mind, wide open, breaking the liaison between them and her even before the first meaningless convention of greeting could be used to ratify it. Like all lovers whose affair presents difficulties, involves others, and attracts attention, they'd become vain—distressed, maybe, but a bit proud of themselves at the same time, feeling nevertheless that there was something attractive in the idea of being associated with them. In with them; she recoiled from the idea. To take its place, rationalisations began to occupy her seethingly. They'll have to go because of Jason, she thought. I can't even speak to Jason in his own language. How can you expect a simple chap like that to understand? He stands aside and bows "Nkosikaz'" to every white bitch who pushes him off the road with her car. A chap like Jason has nothing but his peace of mind. You can't take it away and leave him dangling; because he hasn't got politics yet, and you can't free the private man in him before the political man . . . A fat lot she cares about people like that. In a whole year, has she ever really *said* anything, except "It was marvellous fun" or "Let's do this" or "So-and-so's got a marvellous idea, we're going to . . ."

Gideon appeared in the doorway that led from the diningroom to the verandah. It was nearly six o'clock. He tugged at his ear and shuddered wearily. Without speaking (she must still be asleep inside) he came over and squatted on the steps. He did not seem to see the sea but deflected the course of the ants on the steps with his shoe and gazed with abstracted attention round the verandah roof, as if he had some professional interest in the construction or the moths and praying mantises clinging there.

"You slept five hours." Confronted with him, Jessie was relieved, now that the moment was here, of the difficulty of it.

He smiled, not at her. "Good God. I was very, very tired."

"The brandy's where you left it, in the living-room. Bring the gin—in the cupboard, there." She got up and went into the kitchen for soda and ice. The floor had been newly polished with thick red polish that smeared off like lipstick; there was a strong smell of fly-repellent. There was something of the hospital matron in Jason's merciless insistence on the cruder and more uncomfortable aspects of cleanliness. The lawn-mower was chattering between the back of the house and the track.

Gideon poured them each a drink, and, settling down in the chair where she had sat all afternoon, she said to him, "Where are you going?"

"Oh." He had his glass in his hand but he put it down again between his feet, where he squatted. "That's just it." In a moment he picked up the glass and drank it off, as if he were alone in a drinking-place. "We were not too sure. Then yesterday we found ourselves somewhere around here" (how far does that cover, Jessie wondered) "and Ann had the bright idea of looking you up."

"Harewood Road isn't exactly somewhere around here," she said. It was the address of the house in town.

He gave his chuckle. She noticed again his way of talking to himself rather than to you. "I'm well aware of that," he said. Asking for an explanation was so out of character for her; he appeared to save her the embarrassment of the attempt by ignoring it.

She said quite gently, "I don't know why you came to me, you know," and for the first time he looked through the off-hand impersonality of his manner and was about to speak when Elisabeth ran round from the garden and stopped, at the sight of a visitor, to sidle instead of tear up the steps. She knew Gideon Shibalo from home, of course, though she had forgotten that at lunch-time her mother had said that Ann was in the house, and another friend, the man who drew their pictures. He

206

said, "Hullo, it's Madge, eh?" and she gave him a routine smile for grown-ups as if he were right. She felt her mother's eyes on her in a way that she was still a bit small to interpret; Madge or Clem would have understood that their presence was in some way restrictive to the grown-ups at that moment. Her mother said in a voice specially for her, surprised, enthusiastic : "Where you been?"

"Mowering with Jason."

"And the girls?"

"Gone to find lucky-beans on the road."

"It's time for your bath, love."

"Awwwrh . . . let me wait till they come, I want to bath with them . . ." and as she saw on her mother's face softening and then capitulation, her tone of growling complaint changed swiftly, within the sentence, to cheerful sweetness.

"I'll go back and do a bit more, shall I?"

Madge and Clem came noisily through the house. "Shh, someone's sleeping," said Jessie, but they ignored her, and the visitor too, being old enough to find it very difficult to remember to greet guests, and irresistible to imitate them crudely, and giggle, once safe in bedroom or bathroom, at any real or fancied peculiarities they might have. "We've found hundreds. There's another big tree full we found, further up than yesterday. We went miles," Clem boasted ecstatically to Elisabeth. Elisabeth was impressed and greedy. "—No wait, not those, that one I want for myself." Clem held out of her reach one of the black pods that had been emptied from her skirt on to the verandah. "Here, I don't want them—" said Madge, suddenly satiated. She dumped her whole gleaning on Elisabeth and began examining the marks left in her hot palm by a handful of loose beans. The hard little red beads with their black eyes rolled all over the verandah. Gideon said to one of these unidentified pretty female children, "You should make a necklace out of them. You get a sharp needle, and you make a hole through each one . . ." "Oh yes, I know," said Madge, charmed at once by the attention. "You can buy them in the street in Johannesburg. You see African women selling them. And you can use them for eyes for things; Elisabeth's got a monkey like that."

Jessie was occupied for the next hour with seeing that the children got bathed and preparing dinner. Jason pared the

207

comforting cabochon of each potato down to many deeply-cut facets and left them soaking in cold water; he also cut green beans into shreds and steeped them. Then he waited for her to come and do what she would with these materials, being very helpful in the most unobtrusive yet not self-effacing manner. He understood the names of common objects that they worked with and the verbs for certain tasks.

She saw him through the V made by the double poles of the pawpaw tree outside the kitchen window, toe-ing up the slope at a run with the lawn mower, and she called to him. He mowed always either in blue overalls or, as now, naked to the waist, in his usual shorts; but whichever the outfit, he had the look of one of those young men in training for some athletic event who loped around the city streets at home on summer evenings— the look of listening to some smoothly-running inner mechanism. While she trimmed meat she heard him draw water from the tap outside and in a few minutes he appeared, freshly washed, and in a clean, flapping shirt. They had got on all right without words, and now she felt—part of the intrusion she saw in everything—that the fact that she now needed to be able to speak more than naming the objects she touched was the end of something, even of another kind of privacy.

"Visitors," she said to him. She held up her hand, spreading five fingers. "Visitors. Five at the table. All right?" "Five," he confirmed shyly, in English.

She went between the kitchen and the rest of the house, coming to linger outside for a few minutes now and then. The children were there, after the bath, so she and Gideon were in a truce of their chatter. The city ritual of evening drinks had fallen away for her while she was alone. (Sometimes she chilled a two-and-sixpenny bottle of white wine and drank some of it at lunch—the rest did for cooking fish.) He filled her glass when he replenished his own and she took it up again each time without remark. It was the hour of the day she never missed; half-involved, along with him, in the children's game, she saw the surface of the water gliding shining over depths which were already dark, so that the sea was not a colour but a gaze, intense, gathering, glancing. A long bluff of beige cloud turned smoky mauve, like a distant prospect of land. From the point where the coastline took a backward bend and disappeared behind the firs that marked the community, the coloured sky began to thin and blur as if she saw it through breath upon a window-pane. Vaporisation perfectly dissolved this world, eddying in always from the right. When it could no longer be seen you knew that it had reached the dune; the house; the verandah. It became palpable though not visible in a darkness without distance that made sea and sky and the arm's length of blackness all one. She liked to put her hand out into it, like water (the children had turned on the light); she said to Gideon, a little stimulated by the gin, and belligerently friendly now, "I notice you never once looked."

"What at—?" He had just triumphantly broken his inquisitor (Clem) in the game where you must not answer "Yes" or "No" to any question. "Now you, Mummy, your turn," Clem hammered. "He's the winner so he must be the one to ask. Come on, Mummy!"

The presence of a man rounded out the group into a family; other evenings she had not been expected to join in the little girls' games : they had almost forgotten about her, sitting quietly in the dark near them. Once or twice she and Shibalo got quite caught up in the nonsense, and argued animatedly about some point of fairness. The children wavered between admiration for his skill at beating them and despair at losing. Elisabeth became what was known among them as "cheeky", flinging herself at Gideon, hiding her face so that no one knew whether she was crying or laughing. "Boy, if my brother was here he would've beat you," Clemence jeered warningly. "Just see if my brother Morgan was here." Jessie looked at the little girls with a break of curiosity; she had not thought that Morgan had his place in their scheme of things.

They had dinner without Ann—"Should we call her?" Jessie deferred to Shibalo, and he said calmly, "I think the longer she sleeps . . ." They had drunk enough to meet as the two people they were, independent of the situation that presented each to the other in a particular light. They were amused by the children and linked in being adult. Jason brought in the food and for a moment seemed bewildered, not knowing where to put it down. As he served Gideon he mumbled some greeting and Gideon answered him absently. Jessie had the sensation of brushing over something with only a twinge of awareness. When the children

209

had gone to bed—or at least were out of the way in their room for the night—they continued to sit on at the table. There was the air of the confidential imposed upon them, like people lingering in a deserted café.

"Yes, you come here for a bit, you bring your children, you go back to town again—" He spoke as someone does who takes it into his head to contemplate for a moment, without interest, out of his own deadlock, a kind of life that he has not taken notice of before.

"This is the first time I've been here since I was a child," she said. "It isn't my house. I haven't got houses here and there."

"I had an idea . . ." he excused himself in careless pretence.

"You had the wrong idea," she said, matching up to him with a grin.

He gave a deprecating, culpable sniff of a laugh. "I've had a lot of ideas—" Her existence was dropped aside, he returned to reality, and paused after the first phrase, searching for accuracy. He weighed his hands in slow jerks in the air, he was looking for the right shape of gesture, and as he brought them up to either temple they became, while he talked, first blinkers, and then curved into a frame : "—You get it set, marking it off for yourself from the rest that's going on. But that's not real, there's no place where things really are contained at right angles, a tree doesn't stop at a line drawn down the middle. You land up miles—miles outside. Where you think isn't where you act. When you get going, get moving, begin to push things around, smash things up, it's not there."

"You still in with Congress?" she said.

"I'm still in Congress."

She said, "You know, all that—you forget all about it here." She laughed.

"Oh yes?"

"Yes, I mean it . . .?" She was smiling at him, fiddling with things on the table, drawing his thought harmlessly out into the open. "The only black man I can't speak to, and the whites I don't speak to either—I just look at them sometimes, like looking at a Boudin . . ." The tension of holding the intruders at arm's length produced the impulse towards a careless openness. She lazily said what she pleased whether he (and she herself) liked it or not. "I can tell you it's true that you could probably live here without thinking of it right until they came up from the cane with knives and sticks and finished it off without giving you time to give it a thought."

"You could?" he conceded, half-challengingly, half-ironically. The whites he knew never put themselves in this sort of context; it was always as if he and they were considering a third kind of person there. They looked at each other and laughed. When she said to him again now, "I don't know why you came to me," he only leaned across the table and took a banana and answered in the dry, amiable insolence between them, "Didn't think you'd mind so much." And added, almost with sympathy, "Is it because of him?" He meant Boaz.

"Has there been something final?" she said, forced to ask, slumping in her chair.

"They were talking day after day. I hadn't seen her for two days. Then she phoned. She was in a hell of a state. All of us—" He had the face suddenly of a man who sits thrown against the wall, open to blows, given up, his only defence do-what-you-like-to-me. "Then she picked me up in the car."

"When was this?" Jessie was as impersonal as a clerk filling in some form.

"Thursday—Friday. A week ago."

While he was speaking Ann had wandered in, her hands pushing up the sleeves of a dressing-gown as she clasped her elbows. She came forward and then paused, following with slightly open mouth what they were saying as if she had walked in on a scene that she knew and was listening to hear that all went as it should. She looked far more exhausted than before she had slept, and held her eyebrows high and frowning.

"A week ago," said Jessie. She looked at them both. They felt the meaning, surprise, rise in her; they ignored it, like people pretending modesty.

"Do they know where you are?"

"No . . . Well, no."

". . . we've been on the move," Ann spoke. She pushed up a crumpled table-napkin and slid on to the table, supporting herself with one leg on a chair. "I see there are some towels in the cupboard. Can I have a bath?"

Jessie got up practically, but before she went through the door, she said it: "You really can't stay here, you know." She was

looking at them both kindly, truthfully, doing away with arti-
ficial casualness.

Ann said, as if it were a matter of interest and had nothing
to do with intentions, "Why not?"

"The boy—for one thing. I don't know what someone like
that would make of it."

Ann burst out laughing. "But since when would you care
about a thing like that?" She was surprised into objective
amusement, offering it as a reassurance to Jessie about herself.

In the bedroom that had not been used until that afternoon
Jessie hauled down towels. "Only one of them's a decent size—
I didn't bring a lot." She put them on one of the rumpled beds.
"I bought these the day you came, last year; my only prepara-
tions," she said with a smile.

"I suppose we can stay the night?" said Ann.

Jessie sat down on the bed, holding her bare ankle. "You see,
I don't know you at all, Ann, it's just as if you walked in here
for the first time. Boaz says to me, you know how she is, she
wouldn't do this, she would do that, but, as I keep telling him,
I don't know at all how you are."

The girl had the open, dazed look of someone who emerges
from one of those dark journeys at a fun-fair that really only
progress through a canvas tunnel hung with ordinary objects like
feather-mops and clinging cloth, but that establish a link between
fearful fantasy and the ordinary.

She stood there unembarrassed, only a little unsure. "I suppose
I don't think about people the way you do. I mean we'd slept in
the car two nights and I thought of you being just here, on your
own, with this house."

It was fair enough. People like themselves kept open house in
a particular way; it was nothing to do with "social" life and there
was no regulation of times and days : somebody needed a place to
work or to be alone in, a place to live through a certain stage in
his life—one granted it or claimed it according to circumstances.
Yet Jessie was strongly aware that she was not "just there", and
the two could not be "just there" in this shelter with her. This
was not the old house, the Stilwell house where life was various.
This place was completely inhabited, for the present, by *her
being*; couldn't they sense it?—she thought : it must fill the
place, like a smell. If they came to her here, it must be through

some special and deeply personal connection with that being.

She fought the idea, because the instinct to protect herself made her want to prevent Ann from discovering it. She stopped herself from saying "But why me? Why to me?"—with its reminder to the girl that Boaz was the one she, Jessie, knew. She said, returning to the observer's tone, mildly curious, "A week. Where, for God's sake?"

"Oh, all over the show . . ." Ann dragged a small case on to the bed, opened it on wild disorder—suddenly the room where it must have been packed existed between them, the room where all the stringed and bulbous instruments leaned against the walls, and Boaz sat, bare feet under the table; Morgan's old room— "Gid had some friend near Messina, we went there, then we thought of Basutoland, I don't know, any old where," she took a piece of clothing out, looked confused, "—where's the top, dammit?—He's a sweetie, this chap Mapulane, but of course it was impossible, he's got a jolly nice little house and they were marvellous but it's *in* a reserve . . . Then we thought we'd go to another friend of his, that's the one in Basutoland, and I've never seen Basutoland anyway. Well, that didn't work out . . ." She laughed; her hands began to turn over the contents of the case again, slowly.

"Was there some sort of decision behind this? D'you know where you're going?" Jessie asked.

The girl picked up the bath-towel, a tin of talcum and a packet of cigarettes. "I don't know what happened. The whole thing was finished. It felt O.K., really. And then while we— Boaz—were talking about other things, about ordinary things, beginning to be ordinary again—you know, just hanging around in the room together talking and tidying up a bit and so on—I began to feel scared. I can't explain it. I began to get absolutely panicky, and I couldn't tell him, I would've felt such a fool."

"I'd better phone them and say you're all right."

"Tom wasn't there. He'd gone to spend a few days with his father."

"I know. I had a letter from him at the old boy's. But he'll be back by now."

"No bath for two days. Just bits of washes in clean, A.A.-approved rest-rooms while my driver took petrol." Her face was blank for a moment, then she laughed.

Jessie passed through the dining-room, seeing the outline of Gideon sitting smoking on the dark verandah. She went into the kitchen and, for the first time, hesitant, took up the motions of using the telephone again. The exchange told her that there would be a two-hour delay before the call came through, but Jason had only just finished washing up and closed the kitchen door behind him when the telephone rang and there was Tom's voice at the end of a tunnel. It was not the Tom to whom she wrote the letters that belonged to the mainstream of timeless life, but the Tom of their segmentary everyday existence among the bobbing crowd of demands that matter singly and momentarily. He called, tinny through the megaphone of distance, "I was just writing to you, I got back yesterday", and she said "I know", meaning that she knew his news. "They turned up here this morning. They're here." There was a second's awkward silence. "Well, that's something."

"They're here now."

"Are they all right?"

"Yes, all right. I thought I'd better let Boaz . . ."

"Yes, well, he couldn't think where they could go, that's the thing. You understand . . ."

She knew how he must be looking; she knew what his face must be indicating that he didn't need to say. Although they could not see each other, familiarity made their communication as elliptic as if they had been face to face.

"The trouble was, I wasn't here, you know, but Morgan . . ."

She said, "Morgan what?" losing his voice.

"Morgan, I said. I was at the old chap's but Morgan stayed at home. He was here. I don't know how much—anyway, apparently she just suddenly announced she was going, couldn't stay. Everything was all right before; only the night before. So I thought. Well, Boaz'll have a load off his mind, he . . ."

"But why to me?" she cupped the receiver and shouted an urgent whisper. "I said why to me?" Her whole body was clenched for an answer, as if by some miracle, or, better still, by some good sense, he would give her a simple answer that would let her out, have her rid of them.

She heard him laugh. A tiny hooter bleated and a voice said, right in her ear, "Three minutes." "Well thank Christ," he was saying. "It'll be all right. I mean they're all right there, no

214

one . . . We thought they'd be picked up any day. It's safe there, isn't it?"

"I've told them they can't stay."

"Oh. Well, I don't know. Look, darling, it's no joke. Boaz is only worried about one thing now. Understand? Jessie? If she gets picked up . . . Jessie?"

But it seemed that the police had nothing to do with it, nothing to do with what she was thinking of, nothing to do with them.

"I can't believe in it," she said, and he said, "I didn't get it—what did you say?" and she couldn't say "I can't believe that that's the danger."

"Morgan sends his love." The change in the voice told her that the child must have come up and be standing by the telephone.

"Yes. And mine. Don't put him on the phone, I want to talk to you . . ." but Morgan's presence with Tom at the other end of the line, and the presence of the others (she could hear someone moving through the dining-room on the other side of the door) at her end, made it impossible. Disjointed trivialities filled the last minute. "I'll write to you tonight," she called while he shouted goodbye, but his yielding, embarrassed "All right" was cut off, leaving her to it.

SIXTEEN

She did not write a letter, but unrest, like the excitement of an unfinished discussion, invaded deep sleep sometime toward morning. A disjointed dialogue went on, first in the eternal second where a dream unrolls and is comprehended totally and instantly, then slowed down to the more ponderous comprehension of the wakeful mind in the ordinary dimension of minutes passing. Have I been awake ten minutes, an hour? At first, though ferreting fully awake behind closed eyes in her sleeping body, she did not know, but gradually the pace that bore the night along became recognisable and measurable without the clock face, as animals feel the pace of the seasons.

Boaz is only worried about one thing.

How impossible, how unfair for Boaz that the time should come in a situation like his when the *one thing that matters*—the reality—gets flung aside by something external and irrelevant. A line in a statute book has more authority than the claims of one man's love or another's. All claims of natural feeling are over-ridden alike by a line in a statute book that takes no account of humanness, that recognises neither love nor respect nor jealousy nor rivalry nor compassion nor hate—nor any human attitude whatever where there are black and white together. What Boaz felt towards Ann; what Gideon felt towards Ann; what Ann felt about Boaz; what she felt for Gideon—all this that was real and rooted in life was void before the clumsy words that reduced the delicacy and towering complexity of living to a race theory. It was not a matter of being a man or a woman, with a mind and a sex, a body and a spirit—it was a matter of qualifying for a licence to make use of these things with which you happened to be born. It was all a routine matter, like the brass dog-tag put away in a cupboard or the third-party-risk insurance disc stuck on the car's windscreen every year.

Did Boaz worry about the routine matter ("only one thing

now") because he loved her and didn't want to see her go to jail? Because he had brought her here and felt responsible for her anyway? Like everything else personal, his reasons were of no importance. The routine matter was something they all flew instantly in their minds to prevent reaching its conclusion; the external reason that differences and even indifference were dropped for, as for war or natural disaster.

But it was still the one thing that didn't count. Not between Ann and Boaz and Gideon. Not between Ann and Boaz and Gideon and Tom and herself. Not in that house and not in this. I don't want to do anything because of a dog licence—she saw the script streaming under her hand; at the same time Tom reading it, answering. —Or because I just happened to be here in this house. Real disinterested kindness is the only sort that's any use and it comes on impulse. How often in a whole life does one really have that impulse? —She was completely awake now, inhabiting her body from the weight of the cast-off clothes on her feet to the slightly mouldy smell of the pillow under the left side of her head. —She thought with clarity and for herself alone : all other forms of kindness are only actions performed to conform with an image of oneself as a decent, generous person. Like any other image, you get confined in it . . . from the limit of clothes weighing on toes to the other limit where ear and cheek end at the pillow.

In the morning Ann was up early. Jessie found her already sitting in the sun on the grass.

"There's something out there. I've been watching. Swimming out there. Dolphins." She was all admiration at everything, as if she had just arrived.

"Porpoises."

"They leap right out of the water !"

"Yes, we see them every day."

The sea was some marvellous shining creature that had come up into the world overnight, light streaming off its back. In the radiance they both had the grimace that becomes a smile. Raucous brown birds with yellow beaks were strutting, flying and alighting; their activity seemed to stem from the figures of the two women, as if the birds had been released from their hands.

The girl's outstretched fingers held the tousled hair pushed up from her face; it was smooth, filled out in contour again; at her age exhaustion or conflict leave no mark—like visible new growth the tendrils of a warm flush of blood under the skin reached up her neck. She wore the short cotton gown she had worn so often on Sundays at home.

"Where d'you swim?"

"Oh anywhere. There are sharks everywhere." They laughed.

"Do you want to go down?"

"Oh I must have one swim. —Do you go?" she said, meaning at that time of day.

"Often."

"Ah, it's heavenly . . ." she said, as if she would fly, or melt.

Jessie lent her a bathing suit. They met again in a minute, on the verandah; Gideon was in the bathroom. They went barefoot, quietly, down through the wet undergrowth, breaking wet spider-webs, and when they were almost on the beach a small figure thudded into them from behind. "I wanted to come!", Madge was panting, her face thick with reproach. "Well, you have come," said Jessie. "I wanted you to wait for me to get my costume." "It doesn't matter, you can swim without it."

Ann was not claimed by the interruption; Jessie was reminded, this is the way she sees me, always in the context of demands she doesn't know, always in the acceptance that I myself, my single being, have quite naturally ceased to exist. But the thought fell away before the sensation of chill sand underfoot and the light-headedness induced by the cool, huge air drawn in on an empty stomach. They swam for about half an hour and came up cheerful from the cold water. Jessie said to Ann after breakfast, "Look, Gideon'll have to sleep in the living-room. This Jason may talk to his friends. He has to come into the rooms to clean up, I can't keep him out . . ." Her tone was sensible, planning, and Ann was quick to catch it. She said, biting at a thread of skin beside her thumb-nail, "But what about last night?"

"I pulled the things off your bed and dumped them on the spare in my room."

Ann laughed.

"We don't know about these old colonels around here," said Jessie. "We don't want some local Ku-Klux posse riding up —you know?"

Ann said, "Oh, all right then," thinking that she would tell Gideon about the arrangement when they were alone, but Jessie came upon him smoking in the living-room and explained at once, "That divan'll have to be your bed, I was just saying to Ann. I don't trust friend Jason, or rather the people his friends may work for."

"What sort of people?"

"I don't know them by name, but I know them well enough."

"We'll push off, Jessie," he said, almost affectionately, completely reasonable. "No, we'll push off."

She picked up *Victory* where it lay, open, page-down, on the carpet, and put it on a chair.

The radio was playing (Gideon must have fixed it; it had not worked since Jessie's arrival), smoke hung in the air, there were litchi pips in an ashtray. When she came back from the beach the first few days she always found Gideon and Ann in the living-room, the shape of their presence hollowing it out after the passing of a morning there. They greeted her ordinarily, concluding for the time being heaven knew what long, inarticulate, meaningful discussion, what private silences. They had invaded her; but she stood in the doorway and felt herself shut out by the self-sufficiency of lovers : she had forgotten it. They drew her back that much, each time, into the temporal world, took her back from the self that persisted in continuity to what could be lost. For a moment she was the one who had nowhere to go.

Soon they began to spend hours out on the grassy mound in front of the house, and even to appear on the beach. Alone or led along by the children, sometimes with Jessie, they passed loop after loop of rocks and sand and lay on one of the small deserted beaches that must have looked exactly the same when Vasco da Gama sailed past in the fifteenth century. There was the feeling —of all fecund, tropical places where plant and insect life is so profuse—not of hostility to human beings, but of the indifference that man feels as hostility. Here there was no account taken of anyone who walked upright on two legs; the close groves of strelitzia palm between the arms of two rocky promontories were impenetrable—any sailor shipwrecked here in the service of the East India Company could not have got up from the beach to the interior that way, but the slim grey monkeys, tossing themselves from fronded head to head to eat the juicy spikes of the white and flame-blue flower sticking out there, found it an ordinary thoroughfare. A dead seagull on the sand was busy as a factory with the activity of enormous flies, conveyor-belts of ants, and some sort of sand-flea that made a small storm in the air above and about the body. Butterflies fingered the rocks and drifted out to sea. Dead fish washed up among smashed shells were pulled apart and dragged away to their holes by crabs. There was not *nothing here*, but everything.

No other person came. Ann went into the village one day and brought back a pair of swimming trunks for Gideon and gradually he found himself doing what she did, lying for hours as if he, too, had been washed up on this shore, like the fish or the seagull. This abandonment to the natural world was something that seemed to come so easily to the two women; even while he succumbed to it he watched them with some kind of alienation and impatience—it belonged to a leisure and privilege long taken for granted. If he sat about doing nothing it was always a marking-time, an hiatus between two activities or desires. It was a matter of despair, exhaustion or frustration. You lay on your bed in your room and drank because you could not do what you wanted to do. Outside in the township everybody, from the beggar who dragged himself across the road with bits of motor-car tyre over his stumps to the B.A. graduate who found himself a sinecure advising white manufacturers on how to tempt the blacks to buy more, was fully occupied every hour of his life with the struggle to wrest a share of living—and that meant position, responsibility, respect and power, as well as money—from the whites. All time and breath and strength were used up to compete with their privilege.

"How long'd you been here before we came? A couple of weeks?" he said to Jessie one afternoon.

"That's right." She was reading, some little cotton rag of child's clothing keeping the sun off her head. Ann was in the water.

"What'd you do? Same as now?"

She leaned on the book and smiled. "I was alone. It isn't the same."

"What's it all about, this alone business?"

"What business?"

"I asked your kid Morgan one day why he hadn't gone away with you, and he told me, my mother likes to be alone."

"Did he say that?" She looked pleased and yet annoyed, as one does when one hears of an astute remark made about oneself by someone to whom one has given no opportunity or justification for understanding.

"I'd always thought painters liked to be alone," she said, questioning his question to her. "—Had to be alone, were alone."

"I'm not a real one, I suppose. I don't feel it. There's always a feeling of others around, even if I'm working."

"Really?" She began to have that look of pursuing the other person that comes when interest is roused. "But what about those empty landscapes of yours, with the dust?"

"Just fooling about. Seeing the sort of thing some painter had done and trying it out." He often went in for the sophistication of deprecation; he hid behind it where no one could get at him.

"Even when you're actually there with the canvas in front of you—" She returned to it, disbelieving.

"Yes, man, there's always the business of a friend who's going to turn up in half an hour, or something on your mind."

"You feel connected all the time."

"Mmm. You've got the pull."

"When you're alone, you're connected but there's no pull," she said. "Now that you are here, I feel lonely."

He gave his chuckle, looking at her with the air of not knowing what to expect.

"Because you're making love," she said. "You see?"

"Are you jealous, Jessie?" he said, bantering, flirting a bit, because he did not know what to say.

But she was not embarrassed, but quite serious and at ease. "No, not jealous. At least I don't think so. Left out. Left out of something, that's it. Perhaps a bit jealous, as well. I don't have love affairs any more."

Ann came up, beaded with water. She dried her face, blew her nose, shook out her hair from the cap, and lay down beside Gideon. She touched him with her sea-cold hand and mumbled for a cigarette. Presently there was a commotion where the little girls were playing at the edge of the water. Elisabeth came screaming over the wet sand, her lumbering shape, clumsy with pain or alarm, repeated in wriggling purples and silvers on the mirror surface. She held out her wrist, wrung in the other hand. Clem and Madge followed, regarding her distress with admiration. "The white part of a wave . . . she just put her hand in next to my foot . . ." A rough blue thread was buried in the red weal that had risen round the plump brown arm. "Oh poor old thing! They are beasts . . . all right, now, I know it's sore . . . get some of those leaves, Clem . . ."

"I saw a couple of blue-bottles when I was in," said Ann. And as Jessie broke the leaves of the ice-plant that grew nearby, and squeezed them on the sting, "Rub quite hard, that's the best way. —It really does hurt like hell."

"What is it?" Gideon said with distaste, leaning on his elbow.

"Haven't you ever been bitten by a blue-bottle?" Ann said.

"What on earth is it, anyway?"

"One of those balloon-things that get washed up. The wind brings them in," Jessie reminded him.

They showed him how the stringy appendage of the creature had attached itself to Elisabeth's flesh; Madge raced off to bring a specimen of the whole creature, gingerly lifted up on a handful of sand, to demonstrate to him.

"You mean to say you've never been bitten by one?"

"Hell, no, I should think not."

"But you've been to the sea sometimes?" said Jessie.

"Only once to Cape Town and then to Port Elizabeth. Congress conferences. We drove around the docks and on Sunday a couple of us walked for a bit on one of the coloureds' beaches somewhere near Cape Town."

Jessie had managed to get the blue thread away from the child's wrist; the pain had subsided and Elisabeth sat as if listening for its diminishing impulses. Jessie looked at him over the head of the child leaning against her, and thought again how he never seemed to see any of it—sea, sky, or green. He was like a fox, panting blindly out of breath in a hole.

They went up to the house in a peaceful little procession, the child riding on Gideon's shoulders with her sandy legs round his neck.

SEVENTEEN

NOTHING COULD BE a greater contrast with the life they lived now than the week that had preceded it. Fragmentary references to that cropped up, more or less amusing anecdotes, before Jessie, but these were lip-service to a demand neither wanted to meet in themselves, either alone together, or singly. They had lived through something that remained undealt with. Blocks of experience can lie like this for years before they are tackled; sometimes they are never taken hold of at all, cluttering up one of those lives that become like an attic, a jumble of disparate things between which no relation has been established.

Both knew that some form of desperation had made them drive away. Being lovers, both had accepted that this desperation was love; the collective term for the hundred ambiguities of their being together and apart—the wearing thin of interest between them sometimes when they were together, more than punished by the vividness of each for the other when they were apart, the calm with which the interlude of their knowing each other seemed to blend into their separate lives, when they sat chatting, and the crazy obsession with which the interlude filled the whole of living once a day was begun in which it was regarded as over. Fear of the vacuum it leaves behind is as common a reason for prolonging a love affair as continuance of passion. Ann's inexplicable feeling of "panic" that she had mentioned to Jessie probably came from this fear. Her voice on the telephone (she had taken the single, decisive, outside chance —if he had not happened to be at the Lucky Star at half past one that day she would not have tried again, perhaps, not there nor at the flat nor further away, as far as the townships that took him in and closed over him)—her voice brought him back to swift excitement from the sober, not unhappy but flat acceptance that he would be spending July working for Congress in the dorps and locations. He was saved from the reluctance of doing what he really wanted to do. Stirring a vortex in the grey coffee that Callie Stow had made it difficult for him to drink, he had been going to go and see Jackson Sijake in his own time. He had already forgotten the lie about coaching Indian students; was forgetting other evasions. But Ann's voice had it : the thing that Callie Stow lacked entirely, the element of self-destruction that found a greedy answer in himself. It was in the voice, that note that takes some of the fear out of life by suggesting that not everyone regards it as such a carefully-guarded gift, after all.

They drove away that bright winter afternoon into the actuality of the escape that everyone put into a phrase and never believes in—"I'd like to go off somewhere, just pack up and go." It was no different, in its real intention, from the times they had driven into the veld to picnic while other people sat in offices. She looked at his hands on the steering-wheel; he noticed how her head, beside him, tipped back from the chin in her particular way. But although there was the reassuring sameness of their two selves enclosed in the small car, the release and pleasure, as usual, of being together after absence, and the enjoyable consciousness, for each, that absence made minute physical detail and gesture an object of secret observation and wonder—although all these were marvellously the same, this particular impulse was to take them far out of the depth they had sounded between them. They had come together in the constriction of sheltering cracks in other people's lives—Boaz's patience, the Stilwells' tolerance, the young advertising men's indifference. These seemed irksome but in fact provided a private status for a relationship that, publicly, did not exist. Once they had left behind them, by a few miles, the recognition of a certain group of individuals that they had the free choice of being together, and the anonymity of the city, where such recognition has the chance of passing unnoticed, everything changed for them.

Ann's response to black people and the world that they were forced to inhabit was one of pleasure; she saw the warmth and vitality, the zest and freshness that existed there in spite of all the white man could do, missed by the white man. She saw the defiant fun of it, not the uncertainty, pain and brashness. She enjoyed the gawping white face staring from the passing car when she and Gideon sat eating chicken at the roadside; but then she had gone home to the Stilwell house when the day was ended. Now, as it got dark, there was the reality of the lights of a country hotel, with family cars drawn up beside rondavels and waiters in their white suits hurrying past on the other side of the windows, and she could not walk in and sign the register and lie talking in a hot bath as she had done hundreds of times, on countless journeys. She said nothing, but it was difficult to believe, in the bones of unreason, where habit is formed in the very pattern of expectation in the body.

At a petrol station she went into the tearoom attached to it and drank a cup of coffee and said, "I want one to take to the car," and the fat, laconic woman behind the counter shouted to the waiter, "Take coffee out to the madam's boy."

She ran across the wide country street to see if she could buy a thermos flask but only an Indian fruit shop was open. Gideon was smoking a cigarette, standing by while the tyres were pumped, and when she got into the car again he came up to the window and said, tersely intimate, "Want something?" She moved her head and smiled, implying that she had only meant to stretch her legs.

The place was called Louis Trichardt, and where the street-lights splashed into the darkness they washed clear of it drapings of cerise and orange bougainvillea. The humps of mountains raised the skyline all round, close to huge winter stars; down in the powdery yellow light of the town she watched some white youths wheel their bicycles up the street and a group of little Moslem girls in trousers playing round the pillars of the fruit shop. Gideon got into the car again; the road lifted up into the mountains that ran together in blackness. There were houses here and there, and a couple of garden hotels shining lights behind the thick lace of trees. Even though it was winter the sub-tropical forest filled the car with the strong, green, stirring odour that is the smell of the earth's body. The town dropped behind them like a place that was not a real habitation but a scene representing part of an actual town, in a play, and having, in fact, nothing in the darkness beyond the few props and one-dimensional façades set up in light.

In the half-hour when she had picked up Gideon on the Johannesburg street-corner and they had driven, just as if nothing had happened, through the city with the familiar checks and stops of traffic lights and street-names, he had said, "I want to show you Mapulane's place, in the Northern Transvaal." That was enough; after the suddenness and completeness of action, they did not need anything more than the simplest objective.

They came out on the other side of the mountain pass and began to follow the sand roads and tracks of a reserve, in the dark, and there were no signposts, as if the black country people who used the roads could be expected to find their way like cattle. It was late when they arrived at the hummocks of a small village, gone back into the landscape in the darkness. The car woke chickens first, then dogs. The friend was a teacher, and had the only white-style house, a brick cottage with a verandah and a wire fence. He lit a lamp, brought out food, with the dazed smiling face of one who sees, the first time for a long time, an admired friend, but he had had no warning of their coming nor any idea who Ann might be or what she was doing there. He kept saying, in English, to include her, "This is wonderful!" and starting up guiltily to refill the kettle, to poke the fire he had quickly got going in the stove, or merely to move, alertly anxious, round the room on the watch for any neglect. He seemed particularly troubled because he had no meat to offer them : "You wouldn't like a couple of eggs? We've always got good eggs from my mother's hens."

Gideon enjoyed the spectacle of this generosity and concern before Ann. "James, take it easy, man, we've had plenty."

"You're sure? Some milk? You don't have to be afraid to drink the milk—it's from our own cow."

"I couldn't manage another thing." Ann's assurance seemed to make him more and more aware of the inadequacy of what he could offer, past midnight, to people he had not expected.

"You're just dead beat, my girl, ay?"—Gideon leant across the table and gently tugged her earlobe, while her smile turned into an uninhibited yawn. James Mapulane saw at once, in this small exchange, what Gideon perhaps meant him to; he and Gideon went out to fetch the things from the car, talking again in their own language.

Ann was not often subjectively aware of places she found herself in. She was one of those people who carry a projection of

226

themselves around as a firefly moves always in its own light. Left alone, she felt the room close around her, in a strange authority. It was like the first room one becomes conscious of in one's whole life : the room in which one first opens one's eyes on the world— and sees the bulk and outline and disposition of each piece of furniture as the shape of the world. The houses she paused in, the rooms where she slept, the coffee-bars and youth hostels and hotels and borrowed flats that she used and passed on from— they flickered by, anonymous and interchangeable. In this room the objects were the continuing personality of people who had worked and planned and changed, putting into their acquisition the ardour of much else never attained, so that the pieces of furniture themselves became landmarks towards the attainment, and the difference between the teak sideboard with its bulbous carved legs and the flimsy bookcase leaning askew under the pressure of textbooks, grammars, paper-back classics and news-papers was the death of a generation and the birth and work and aims of another. It was a room that fitted no category; there was the big coal stove in it, and the sofa, squeezed in between the sideboard and the table, was somebody's bed—grey blankets were thrown back where whoever it was had been hastily pushed out when she and Gideon arrived.

It might have been Mapulane himself; anyway he insisted that he would sleep there now, and give them "the other room". "I'll make myself very cosy here, that'll be quite O.K.," he said, ignoring the rumpled bedclothes that showed that someone already had been sleeping in the living-room, and Gideon and Ann ignored this too, out of a polite convention that amused her : in the sort of life she lived, it was taken for granted that you slept wherever there was something to sleep on, and no one would have found it necessary to pretend that there were enough bedrooms to go round. Mapulane went in and out busily, and there were voices; someone must have been sleeping in "the other room" as well, and have been persuaded to quit it; the dark neat little place smelled like a nest, of sleep, when Gideon and Ann were taken into it, though the bed had been freshly made up with sheets as well as blankets.

It was the first time they slept together, in a bed, all night. She woke up in the morning with the happiness of waking in a foreign country; so it was that she had wakened in peasant houses in Italy, in fishermen's cottages in Spain. Hens were quarrelling hysterically and children's voices carried from far away. She was alone in the bed and two men were talking in a language she didn't understand in the room next door : Gideon and his friend. She got up and looped the curtain aside and tried to open the little window, but it couldn't have been opened for years, and was stuck fast. Outside in the clear sun were the mud and thatch and tin houses of the village, a blue haze of smoke from cooking fires, a dog blinking against the flow of morning warmth. She knocked on the pane with the knuckle of her first finger, and although a woman with a tin basin of mealies on her head passed unnoticing, two little children playing on the bare, stamped ground looked up and changed to swift astonishment. For a moment Ann was surprised, then remembered, and smiled at them, the foreigner's friendly smile. Everything about the dark cold small house, smelling like a fire gone out, and the activities stirring around her, filled her with the titillating sense of entering this life in a way she had never done before. Because of Gideon it was all invested with the charm of something novel and yet annexed.

The other members of the household had been out of the house since daylight. Later in the morning a strong elderly woman came in from the fields, barefoot, businesslike, her head tied up in a long spotted doek. Mapulane introduced his mother and she stood through the formalities with the face of one already primed for this. Then she plunged into a long harangue with Mapulane's half-grown sister, full of commands, as they moved about the stove and yard together.

Once the old woman, passing Ann, stopped as if she had just seen her for the first time, and crossed her arms. "All the way from Jo'burg. A long way. Oh yes . . . a long way, eh?"

"Not so bad." Ann wanted to make the most of this overture. "It was awful to disturb you like that so late at night."

But it was not an overture, nor even a conversation, but a set piece, a symbolic politeness to keep her at bay. The good-looking old woman went on with impersonal admiring concern, "Myself I don't like to journey far. All that way. And cars, cars . . . Oh yes, a very long way."

She turned abruptly back to her own affairs.

During the two days the visitors were in the house, the

228

members of the family stopped talking and often even left off whatever it was they were doing when Ann came into their presence. They were polite and courteous; she was made conscious of her clothes, her manner, as if she were seeing them from the outside.

"They're old country people," Gideon said, fond of them, of her; bringing them together in his attraction to both. He had spent most of the day talking to James and was alone with her for the first time since morning, walking out over the veld. "They don't think they have the right to 'like' you—I mean, to have personal ordinary feelings about a white "

"I got on fine with the Pedi women. They couldn't even talk English, but I used to go in and out of their huts and play with their children—"

"—Tribal people." He was stroking her hair in agreement while she was speaking. "These are mission people; the old man's a preacher, Sophie goes to mission school. They're nearer to you and so much further away—understand?"

"When I asked her if the water in that big jug was for drinking she called me 'madam'." Ann was accusing, almost annoyed with herself for confessing this.

Gideon laughed. But he was not really interested in the background members of the household, with whom he exchanged passing talk, easy in his masculinity, the naturalness of his manner towards his own people, and the aura he had about him as the clever friend from the political world that the son of the house shared with him in distinction and risk.

The village was beautiful if you put out of mind the usual associations that go with the idea of a beautiful place to live. Apart from Mapulane's house, that they could see standing out so distinctly from the rest, the houses were square mud ones with grass roofs or tin ones held down by bricks. In some there were windows and painted wooden doors; all were a mixture of the sort of habitation a man makes out of the materials provided by his surroundings and the sort that is standard when his environment becomes nothing more decisive than an interchangeable *mise-en-scène* of his work. They were a realistic expression of the lives being lived in them, lives strung between town and country, between the pastoral and the industrial; in spite of their poorness, they had the dignity of this.

The village stood on a hill faceted with rocks gleaming in the sun, among other hills like it; they exchanged flashing messages in dry heat and silence and there was no witness but the personages of baobab trees. Ann and Gideon found themselves among these trees as among statues. They did not grow gregariously, in groves, but rose, enormous and distinct, all over the stretch of empty land. Like the single leg of a mastodon, each trunk weighed hugely on the pinkish earth; the smooth bark, with the look of hairless skin, shone copper-mauve where the sun lit up each one in the late afternoon, as it does the windows of distant houses.

Ann and Gideon could not have been further from the world of ordinary appearances, earth covered with tar, space enclosed in concrete, sky framed in steel, that had made the mould of their association. They walked over the veld and already it seemed that this was as it had always been, before anyone came, before the little Bushmen fled this way up to Rhodesia and the black man spread over the country behind them, before the white man rediscovered the copper that the black men had mined and abandoned—not only as it had been, but as it would be when they were all gone again, yellow, black and white. They did not speak, as if they were walking on their own graveyard.

Mapulane said, "You're not too comfortable, I'm afraid— stay as long as you like, man," but he admitted to Gideon, in an impersonal way, when they were talking about his position in general, that things were "a bit tricky". The Native Commissioner would be bound to find out Ann was there. Gideon said lazily, "She helps with research about African music, eh—? She's been in reserves all over the show—"

Yet he was not seriously opposing Mapulane's need for caution; he knew that the good chap was already suspect enough on account of certain activities with political refugees on the run that the Commissioner suspected but hadn't yet been able to pin down. Mapulane had had mysterious visitors before now; they came and went before their presence could be investigated, and that was the best way.

He and Gideon had long talks about politics and the personalities of politics; whether Sijake was too much under the thumb of the white leftists who advised him, whether he could handle Thabeng, whether Nguni could be counted on in a mess. Listening to Mapulane's way of speaking, sitting with the tall, thin, "respectably" dressed figure near him (Mapulane kept, perhaps as a protective colouring, perhaps because, despite everything, some part of him corresponded to the image, something of the black teacher's humble assumption of a status that doesn't ask too much), Gideon felt the free running of a special, unimpeded understanding that comes with certain friends. Mapulane never said two words to him that did not go deeper than the words and touch off some recognition of an attitude or an idea that lay awaiting some such claim in himself. Yet when they left he saw in Mapulane's affectionate face what he was thinking now that he was driving away. The small head on the tall body, the glasses, neatly-parted hair and frowning smile— the smile was one of tolerance, helplessness at something that couldn't be enquired into; there went Gideon, landing up with this white girl, losing himself with a white girl on the way, the hard way that didn't provide for any detours. Here Mapulane did not follow him; only regretted him.

The baobabs passed, slowly turning forms as the car approached, then left them behind. The Rhodesian border was only a few miles away. Ann was one of those people who, because of the very casualness with which they regard formalities, are usually equipped to go anywhere. She had her passport lying somewhere in the suitcase she had hastily packed—the passport was simply kept there, anyway; in half an hour they could be over the border—no doubt someone like Mapulane could smuggle Gideon across somehow, if she and Gideon really wanted it. But she said nothing, just sang a little, as a soldier sings on a troop-ship or a transport lorry bound for some destination he does not expect to know. The border was something she and Gideon had not approached; they did not know how far or near they were from it in the real measure of their distance from the life that lay on the other side. They knew one thing : that it was irresistible to be together. Whether they wanted to make this fact responsible for the rest of their lives was not something they had troubled themselves with yet. Neither had she ever asked herself how long they could go on not troubling; not cowardice but a confidence rarely impaired by failure allowed her to come upon such things without preparation. She was bored by self-doubts and anticipations; she trusted herself to know what she wanted as she knew the moment to cross the road in traffic.

Gideon thought about James Mapulane's face, but he did not think about the border. He had not thought about the border since the time when he was supposed to be going to Italy, and had thought about it all the time, the form constantly changing like a cloud taking shape from what is in one's mind—now the actual veld and stones and baobabs, the wide brown river of this border near Mapulane's, now the sands and the kraals hedged with euphorbia that led to the one in Bechuanaland, now simply the outline and end of something, an horizon over which he was a still smaller dot within the diminishing dot of a silver aeroplane.

They slept in the car on the way to Basutoland. It was a small car and even the back seat, which Ann had, was very cramped. In the morning they were dazed and stiff-necked and she said, "We're going to buy a tent." He had slept in all sorts of places but never in a tent; that belonged again to that world of pleasure jaunts and leisure that black children did not have.

"Oh look . . ." A stretch of tall yellow grass, where the saka-bula birds flew, trailing their long tails, was passing her window. "A house there—imagine a house in the middle of that . . ." She had never had a house of her own, but all over the world she saw places where a house might be, and to which she would never go back.

"I like a place with trees. Right in the middle of trees. You know, one of those houses where the light is striped, all day long."

The sluggishness of the cold and stuffy night in the car lifted as they drove, and their responses, that had coiled away back to themselves in separateness, began to warm and open.

"But grass all round, as high as your head, as far as you can see . . . Let's go down there a bit?"

"What for?"

"Oh what for, what for."

Ann strolled over the whole earth as if it belonged to her, for she did not question, which amounted to the same thing, that there was nowhere where she wasn't wanted. He brought a blanket out of the car and when they had walked a little way

232

they sat hidden in the grass, leaning comfortably back to back, eating bananas and smoking, coming back to life.

He said, "What time is it?"

"Are you hungry?"—because this was his usual way of suggesting they ought to get a meal. She leaned over and broke off another banana, offering it to him. But he wanted somehow to attach this space of existence, which he and the woman both contained and were contained by indivisibly, to what he had all the rest of his life—to that constant bearing away upon actions and desires. He was not hungry—not in any way at all. He wanted nothing, and had in himself everything. He did not need to touch her, even without touching her he possessed her more completely than any woman he had ever had. She lay back and closed her eyes. He watched her a little while as she slept, the pulse in her neck the only moving thing in the silence about him, and then he got up and went in search of a reedy place that he had noticed, not far off, from the car; if there was water there, he wanted to wash. He smiled at the thought of the sight of himself, walking through the veld with her cake of perfumed soap and a nylon toothbrush.

Ann opened her eyes on one of the beautiful, untidy birds, swaying almost within reach of her hand on a thick dead stalk of the grass that was high as a wall round the nest the blanket had broken into it. She sat up with a cat-yawn. Her body was with lack of it. The strands of the bird's long tail tangled in panic with the grasses as it took off. She stood up to watch it and saw a man standing a few yards away.

"Hullo," she said. "Did I startle you?"

"You all right, lady?" He had the slow sober speech of the country Afrikaner speaking English, but his voice was the voice of a man of substance, sensible and sure of himself. He did not come closer but watched her smiling her big smile at him, tucking her shirt into her skirt, a beautiful girl with the long brown legs he associated with the city. There was that immediate pause, filled with the balance of sleep, where before it had been hollow quarter taken and given, between an attractive woman of class and a man old enough and just worldly enough to recognise it. He was a farmer, in a good grey suit, thick shoes and the inevitable felt hat that country Afrikaners wear—on his way to the lawyer or the bank, most probably.

"I've just had a lovely snooze, that's all. You don't mind, do you?"

He softened into a more personal manner. "It's not my land, it's my neighbour's, see? But I just thought you was in trouble. The car there, and so on."

"Thank you *very* much."

"You're not on your own here? There's a lot of drunk boys around on Sunday—"

She snatched the conversation : "No, no, my husband's here, just gone over the—"

"Oh well, that's O.K. then, sorry to disturb you—" He was eager to be affable now, specially friendly in that indiscriminate comradeship that white people feel when they meet in the open spaces of a country where they are outnumbered. Her own voice had tipped over in her some vessel filled with fear that she didn't know was there; it poured into her blood while she smiled at him, brilliantly, smiled at him to go, and was afraid to look anywhere but at him in case she should see Gideon standing there too. Just as the man left and she heard a car start up away on the road, there was the figure, the hieroglyph in the distance that she could read as the quiet, slouching walk, the narrow khaki trousers, the blue shirt that was her present.

The car must have been gone five minutes by the time he came up. As he grew nearer a run of trembling went through her several times; she had the dread of something approaching that couldn't be stopped. She wanted to run back to the little car. When he stood there, paused as he came through the grass to their little clearing, and looked round it as one does round a room where one senses immediately something has happened in one's absence, she laughed excitedly, braggingly, and half-whispered, half-wept, "A man was here! A farmer! I've had a visitor!"

He looked at her, looked all round him.

Then, "You're sure he's gone?"

"Oh he's gone, yes he's gone, I heard the car, he's gone." She was rocking herself with him, digging her fingers into his arms. He had never seen her so emotional, without a gleam of challenge in her. Suddenly it all came to her as if it had happened : "I wanted to run like mad to you when I saw you but I was terrified he might still be looking. —Any minute, any minute,

234

you might have— He thought it wasn't safe for me, can you imagine, I couldn't get rid of him. I wanted to rush to you—" She broke off and began to giggle, holding his hands and moving them in hers in emphasis of her words—"A kind farmer. He was, really. A nice man."

"Let's get off his land," said Gideon.

"Oh no, it's not his. He told me, it's his neighbour's."

He was pulling up the blanket. They fell into a pantomime of crazy haste, dropping their things, struggling and laughing, tussling.

What she had spilt was like mercury and rolled away into the corners of her being, impossible ever to recover and confine again.

The car surrounded them with the clutter of their inhabitation, enclosing and familiar as an untidy room where one day is not cleared away before another piles on top of it. Already they had a life together, in that car. Like any other life, it was manifest in biscuit crumbs, aspirins, cigarette boxes kept for the notes on the back, broken objects of use (a pair of sunglasses, a sandal without a buckle) and other objects that had become indispensable, not in the function for which they were intended, but in adaptation to a need—the fluffy red towel that was perfect for keeping the draught off Ann's knees, and the plastic cosmetic bottle that they used to hold lemon juice. Already the inanimate bore witness to and was imbued with whatever had been felt and thought in that car, the love-making, the hours when nothing was said and attention streamed along with the passing road, the talk, the fatigue, the jokes. When Ann settled in and her eyes dropped to the level of the grey dashboard with its tinny pattern of grilles and dials, the dead half-hours were marked there for her : the time when she did not know why she was here rather than anywhere else. If the exciting silent dialogue of her presence and the man beside her ceased for a moment to sound in that place in herself where she had first heard it, she grew restless, pacing the logic of slots, circles and knobs.

Gideon telephoned from a dorp post office to tell his friends in Basutoland that he was coming. The people themselves, who ran a store in the mountains, had no telephone, of course, but a friend in a Government office in Maseru would give a message to his brother, who would pass it on to someone else—Ann did not question the circumlocutory mystery by which the warning of their arrival would reach its destination. She was charmed with and proud of the tightly-interlocking life where Gideon was as free and powerful, in his way, as some white tycoon arranging his life by telex. The call took the best part of the afternoon to come through, and then Gideon came back to the car to say that the man in Maseru knew straight off, without any further enquiry, that Malefetsane was away from home, gone to Vryburg on some family business.

"He said, come to *his* place in Maseru," he said, dismissing it. Of course, the man thought he was alone.

They felt flat, cheerful with each other in the slight embarrass-ment of disappointment.

"I want to buy a tent."

"Oh Christ," he said. He ran his hand across the back of his head. "I need a hair-cut. Malefetsane would have cut my hair for me in Basutoland."

"It looks like the filling of an old mattress. I remember the mattresses at boarding-school being emptied and picked over on the grass. —Let's get a tent."

"Who's going to put it up and take it down."

"I know all about tents," she said. Hadn't she and Boaz lived in them for weeks?

"Yes, I know," he said quietly.

They decided, quite suddenly, to go on to Basutoland in any case; Gideon knew someone else there, lots of people there; someone would give them a place to sleep. They were driving in the dark again; the days had no recognisable shape, balloon-ing and extending into unmeasured stretches of time. The car broke down, but they were not far from a dorp and, flashing a torch, Ann waved a passing lorry to a stop. "I'll get a lift quicker than you will," she said. Businesslike both of them, he kept out of the way in the dark. She came back within an hour, bringing a new fan-belt and a big polony sausage and some beer. She had got a lift back easily, too; she was in the triumphant good mood which successful escapades always induced. Gideon put on the new belt and they went on. Fifty miles further, before they could cross the border, the car stopped once more, and although she worked beside him with her teeth clenched and her hands trans-

ferring their oily dirt to face and hair, neither his fair knowledge
nor her bullying, practical flair helped them to get the thing
going again. They waited for hours, but no car came by on that
lonely road at that hour of the night. Very early in the morning
there was a lorry loaded with fruit-boxes, thundering down on
them. The Indian driver was friendly, "There's room for him in
the back," he said, of Gideon, as he helped her into the cab. "Oh
it's all right, there's room here next to me," she said, and Gideon
climbed in beside her in silence.

At the garage where their benefactor left them no one had
come to work yet. She put up both hands and stroked Gideon's
cheeks with their little tufts of whorly beard and said coquet-
tishly, "Are you very, very tired," though she knew he would not
answer. They sat on an oil-drum beside the old-fashioned one-
armed pumps and waited. When the petrol attendant came, in
the baggy skin of old overalls, with a breakfast of dry mealie-
meal in a jam tin, Gideon persuaded him to go on his bicycle to
wake up the white owner-mechanic. The big black man licked
his fingers clean, wrapped the tin carefully in its newspaper, and
went off. Presently he returned; the owner said he could take
the break-down truck himself and bring the car in. Gideon
would go with him. "Go to the hotel and have breakfast," he said
to her, out of hearing of the other.

She looked at him. "Should I?"

He was getting into the truck; he nodded once, vehemently.

Alone in the dining-room of the commercial travellers' hotel
she ate porridge and eggs and bacon and drank cup after cup of
grey coffee. She asked, at the reception desk, whether she could
pay to have a bath. The receptionist was not on duty yet. The
Indian wine-steward-cum-waiter, with his professionally amiable
smooth face, said efficiently, "Is madam not resident here? I
don't think it's allowed if you're not resident."

As soon as the car came back she took the thermos flask and
ordered coffee to fill it, and sandwiches. "Picnic hamper for the
road, madam, certainly I'll do it for you." From the oil-drum
she watched Gideon biting deeply into the bread, bent with the
other man over the open engine. A rumpled-looking fair man
arrived at last. He unlocked a plywood booth within the hall of
his garage. "Come and sit down in my office." It had the wet
black smell of oily rags, there was an old varnished desk piled

with invoices and glossy pamphlets put out by the motor corporations, an office chair with a broken back, a grass chair that she sat in, three calendars showing coy girls with cloud-pink breasts popping from wisps of chiffon or leopard skin. Everything was covered with gritty dust. She wanted to go back to the workshop, but she sat out a decent interval; for the first time in her life she was instinctively following a convention of behaviour, fitting an identity imposed from outside herself. In due course the garage owner came back and said in the encouraging, confused way of doctors and mechanics, "Seems to be a leak of some kind. Battery's O.K., but the points're the trouble. Acid or something on them—but we're trying to file them down and see . . ."

She got up, released.

"Would'ja like a cup a tea?"

"No thanks—I've had breakfast at the hotel. I'll just go to the car—some things I want."

"Make yourself at home here." He reminded her of the hospitality of his office. "You travelling alone with the driver?"

"Yes," she said. "Yes, I have to get to Maseru, you see . . ."

From the car she called, "Gideon," in a soft neutral voice that came to her. He walked over obediently. She was bent from the front seat, pretending to search for something on the floor, and she signed to him to lean down toward her. Their faces were suffused as if with physical effort, hers was red and almost coarse, a vein stood out down the side of the bridge of his nose. "For Christ's sake! How long will it take? Is it bad?" "Can't say. I don't know if they know what they're doing. I suggested a new battery but they haven't got the right one for this car." "But can't they patch it up so that it'll get us to Maseru, then what's-his-name, your friend, can get it to a decent garage." "Everything should be fixed, they've done it, but the thing won't kick over. It's just dead."

She was uneasy about knowing her part so well. "I've got to sit in that office." Her eyes had, to him, the bulging look of someone who is held by the throat. He had never seen her almost ugly; he noted it with the cruelty of objectivity and then felt warm to her in a way he had not connected with his feeling for her before—the way he felt when he had a joke with the gossiping crones in their dirty dresses stretched across old breasts,

238

in a location yard, or when Sol was holding forth late at night. It was as if he met her in some part of his life where he could not have expected her to be.

The car took the whole day to repair and, when it became clear that this was going to be so, she went to the hotel and took a room. She was "resident"; she could go down the granolithic corridors to the "Ladies" now, and let the water run resoundingly into the deep enamelled iron bath with its four iron claws. She went between the room at the hotel and the tin workshop of the garage, that heated up under the winter sun as the hours went by. The garage owner came and stood beside her, hands on hips, whenever she came into the workshop; in the hotel room she lay on the cotton bedcover patterned with an Arcadian scene of shepherdesses and sun-dials and looked at the curtains on the window where the same pattern was repeated but had almost faded away; she slept and woke, and her cigarette left another burn beside those that marked the night-table with its emergency candle in a tin holder. She never got a chance to talk to Gideon again, except for the remarks he passed at her, rather than to her, about the car, as he worked with the petrol attendant, helping the garage owner. She prevailed upon the wine steward to give her a plate of cold meat and salad and a knife and fork and recklessly took it, covered by another thick hotel plate, over to the garage. The garage owner smiled at her for being a woman, and soft. "You didn't have to pay for a meal like that for the boy, mine would've given him something." She saw him eyeing the plates, plates from the hotel dining-room, the plates white people used. At once she asked some question about the car; how much longer could it take, now?

She spent the night in the hotel, alone, eating again opposite the huge black wooden chiffonier that hid the entrance to, but not the noise and smell of, the kitchen; going to bed in the room. Gideon slept in the garage on some sort of a bed provided by the petrol attendant. There were rooms for commercial travellers' boys in the hotel yard, the garage owner said; she could get one of those—but she lied in shame for the dirty outhouses, "They're full."

Everything vanished but these practical details that had constantly to be worked out in the mind; the wangling of decent food, the arrangements for somewhere to sleep, the endless concentration on the coils and nuts and boxes within the gut of the car, and the news of it, the consultations about it. She said "Good morning, Gideon", standing with the garage owner. She walked away with the man whose pink jowls were creased by his pillows. Gideon looked refreshed. He was shaved and had a clean shirt on. She wondered how and where he had managed this. All the mystery of the simplest mechanics of daily living parted them.

When they were on the road at last again, time had changed and stretched and swollen. No longer had they been a few days together; the other afternoon, the afternoon they had left Johannesburg, was far off. She said to him, "Stop for a minute somewhere." She was stretched out in the seat beside him gawkily, her head flung back, smoking, the elbow of one arm cupped in the other hand. "What's wrong?" "Just stop."

With the engine cut off there was silence for a moment until the passing sounds of the empty road came to them—a chirrup as a bird flitted by, and the crack of a dry stalk in a mealie field. She was frowning intensely, provocatively, blinded by what she wanted to say. She kissed him suddenly with the powerful in-vitation of a woman who wants to be made love to. While he was uncertain how to respond, as a man is at the wrong time and place, and stroked her arm in some soothing, trifling caress, she sat up and said, "That bloody hotel."

"What did you expect?" He made a gentle joke of it, and the reference became nothing more than a comment on the poor food and half-clean room.

She said, "Gideon, Gideon, Gideon," ruffling him, touching him, putting his hand up under the hair on her neck to reassure herself.

"Is there any sense in going to Basutoland?"

He chuckled. "I only hope so. Why not?"

"But if your friends are away?"

He said nothing.

"Let's go to Natal for a few days." She had not thought of it before, it came to her suddenly, as she relied upon things to do. "There's a house there we can go to . . . away up the coast."

"Who's there?" he said.

"Jessie's house." She was practical now.

"Stilwell's?"

"It's some cottage she inherited when her stepfather died. She's alone." Neither of them thought of Jessie as more than a name to a place that would do. It was, of course, because of her that it would do; she was one of their kind, she had a generic familiarity even though, in the blur of unimaginable family life in which they saw her, she seemed too remote from themselves to be taken account of.

EIGHTEEN

"... It was because of Boaz, I suppose, that first night when I spoke to you," (Jessie wrote to Tom) "but it isn't now. I'm not putting up with them for anybody. They live almost like anyone else, here. Of course you can't refuse them that chance—how could I? Probably this isn't as big of me as it sounds, I don't quite trust myself over the idea of a 'chance', when I see it written down . . . Test? Hurdle? Of what? They seem fonder of one another than I thought. Specially her; I mean I always thought of her as thriving on affection rather than giving out any. Playful, yes, but not tender, with B?" When she skimmed through the letter she paused in vague dissatisfaction, and to make some token effort to satisfy herself transposed "Test" and "Hurdle".

Ann and Gideon had gone for a walk on the beach at night; presently she heard their voices, intimate in the dark, and they came up the verandah steps. Ann was wearing his thick sweater. "D'you want some coffee?" she said as they went into the kitchen. Jessie said no, she didn't think so, but when they had made it, they brought a cup for her and called from the living-room that it was ready. She was drawn into their company and sat in one of the big chairs with her feet under her for comfort, because a wind had come up. "Here." Gideon handed her the sweater that Ann had taken off.

Wrapped in their warmth, she thought : they've been making love out there. Ann was talking about fishing. Where could they go, she asked, aware of the absurdity of her enthusiasm—she had found some tackle lying about the house. "Ask Jason," Jessie said to Gideon. "He must know all the local lore."

"I suppose he would," Gideon looked at her uncertainly.

"If a man asks your advice about fishing, you may feel a little friendly loyalty toward him? Don't you think?" She smiled at Gideon.

"You may start boasting about your new friend, and where he lives."

"That's true."

Gideon said, "Why were you so worried about him?"

"Oh it wasn't him ... All the other things too difficult to explain, or nobody's business."

"It was a bit of a shock," said Ann, with a smile, of their arrival.

Jessie could smell her, the smell of her hair and the perfume that clung about the room at home, in the woollen collar rolled down round her own neck. "A year ago, *then*, I didn't want Boaz and Ann to come to us. But I didn't do anything to stop it. It was the sort of thing Tom and I have always done. One must be open to one's friends. You've got to get away from the tight little bourgeois family unit. In a country like this, people like us must stick together—we live by the sanctions of our own kind. We haven't any anonymous, impersonal code because the South African 'way of life' isn't for us. But what happens to you, yourself ... I don't know. The original impulse towards decency hardens round you and you can't get out. It becomes another convention."

"What's wrong with that?" said Gideon. "If you're satisfied you're doing what you ought to do?"

"It's all a bit too snug. You can easily forget that it's only the best you can do ... for the time being."

"You want to get right into the struggle then, man." Gideon gave slightly scornful advice.

"Oh ... it's not all politics—not for whites, at least."

He laughed.

"... Yes, I suppose it is. The whole way we live becomes a political gesture above everything else. Well, that's part of what I mean—there's no room to develop as a person because any change in yourself might appear to be a defection. And yet if you can't change, can't stretch out, how can you be ready for some new demand on yourself? In time you don't even remember, really, how you arrived at the position you've taken up."

"What sort of demand are you thinking of?" Gideon said, weighing her up.

"Well, if you want to live like a human being you've got to

243

keep on proving it. It's not a state automatically conferred upon you because you walk upright on two legs, any more than because you've got a white skin."

"You might have to prove it in jail one day. You know? Your house won't be big enough any more."

"And when I come out of prison will you punish me all over again? What'm I going to do with my white face?"

They both laughed. "What's the alternative for you?" Gideon said.

Jessie drew her head back through the neck of Gideon's pullover like a tortoise, and took it off. She pushed away the strands of hair that clung to her face with the crackle of static electricity, and said, "Imagine Tom and me, along with the whites, shooting down blacks. 'Those that I fight I do not hate, those that I guard I do not love.' Christ, I'd rather you shot me. —I'm going to bed. Don't leave the door open, will you, that gorgeous lamp'll blow down again."

She came upon Gideon in the living-room next morning while Ann had gone up to the village with the little girls. He was drawing, absorbed but not prepared, the paper backed by a wad of newspapers, his head falling back negligently now and then on the plump chair. Jessie twisted her neck to see. He softened the thick charcoal line with his thumb. "She's beautiful," Jessie said.

"She is."

She watched him, amused by his attitude of repose, while his hand and eye worked on on their own.

"Gideon, you've got a wife somewhere, I suppose?"

"In Bloemfontein, to be exact."

When she had been in the living-room a certain time, she was always drawn to the curtain that sagged and the bit of carpet that had frayed away. Sometimes, as now, she even wandered up to these things as if she were going to mend them. She slid out of her sandals and stood on the divan to take a look at the top of the curtain, where it hooked to a rail. "I've got a child, too," Gideon said. "I don't know if I'd know him if I saw him somewhere."

She was trying to work loose a runner that had rusted against the rail, and her voice was tight with effort. "Oh why is it like that?"

"You change."

She could not get the runner free and stopped, with the confusion of an obstinate task in her face. "But it's like lopping off fingers. In the end your life is nothing but bits and pieces."

He did not want to be reminded of the woman who had been his wife and did not know what had made him suddenly mention the child. "What's gone is gone," he said.

"Then what's going to be left in the end?" She stood there on the bed. "In a year's time, in five years, *this*'ll be gone perhaps. You'll see yourself here as if it happened in someone else's life."

He saw that this frightened her in some way, but there was no room in him for curiosity about others, there was no part of his apprehension that was not cut off by the concentration of forces that had brought him there; by what he shared with the girl, and what he could not share with her. He could not answer the woman, either, with the rush of affirmation for the present that suddenly came to him—but *this* is my life! Yet she spoke as if he had : "You can't pick and choose," she said. "You have either to accept everything you've been and done, or nothing. If the past is going to be past, finished, this will be as lost as the things you want to lose."

"There are things that are over and done with," he said. "You must know how it is."

"I know how it is. You shed yourself every now and then, like a snake."

"Got to live," he said with a shrug.

"What's one going to be, finally? The last skin before one dies?"

He laughed. "—Ah but it's different. You have a nice settled life that goes on, a home and so on. If things get too hot here, you'll take your husband and your children and go and live the same way you've always done, only somewhere else, isn't that so, Jessie? —You've got the man you want, haven't you?" he added.

"Yes, but I lived before I loved him, and maybe I'll go on living after. I had another husband. I have another child. Sometimes I don't know him when I see him..." She seemed to expect something, and he looked up for a moment, "But I am what I was then as well as what I am now; or I'm nothing."

His attention covered the restive, furtive look in his eyes. She knew this withdrawal that came sometimes in the closest conversation, when you were made aware that you had lost yourself in the white man's preoccupations, when you were relegated to a half-world of doubts and nigglings that only whites afforded and deserved.

"I don't see much sense in digging up the past."

She smiled, looking at him from a distance. "We're not talking about the same thing. It's a question of freedom."

"Freedom?" He was astonished, derisive.

"There's more than one kind, you know."

"Well, one kind would do for me."

"Yes, perhaps it would, because you haven't got it. Perhaps you'll never have to ask yourself why you live. —A political struggle like yours makes everything very simple."

"You think so?"

"Of course it does. You're completely taken up with the practical means of changing the circumstances of your life. —Right, the ideological ones, too. The realisation—whatever you like to call it—the *sense* of your life would be the attainment of this change, or how near you'd get to it, before you die. One knock-out experience after another falls on your head, you die a dozen times, but the political struggle sticks you together again in the end. You're always whole so far as that's concerned. It's all done from outside, and from necessity."

"I don't think it's quite as passive as all that," he said ironically.

"Passive! That's the whole point. It's *all* action, agony, decision —oh my God, it's wonderful"—she made a mock blissful face, to break the mood between them.

He continued to work on his drawing after she had wandered out of the room. In each successive sketch it grew simpler, as the single line drew up the many into its power; the face disappeared the way an actual face disappears into acute awareness of it. Suddenly Ann was there, putting down a few little paper packets, momentarily still in the guise in which she had been seen in the store and the post office: the youthfully arrogant jaw and lips showing something of the beauty and desirability carelessly hidden by dark glasses and wild short hair. "Blades, cigarettes, soft rubber—this's the only sort of thing they had." He tried it, erasing one of the abandoned sketches. "They're all too hard." "I told them I'd bring it back if it wasn't any good." He smiled at her rough treatment of shopkeepers.

246

She was sitting in a chair with the blank regard of the dark glasses upon him. "I've got exactly four pounds and seventeen shillings," she said.

He gave a questioning grunt. "I've got a couple of pounds."

"No, you haven't, you've got about fivepence less than I have."

"Fivepence more."

She remembered the glasses and took them off; he saw something he had never seen before, tears in her eyes as she was looking at him. "I hate them," she said. "All around me in the shop and the post office."

He knew she was afraid of going back to Johannesburg, to decisions and questions and advice and being answerable to others. But if they were to leave the country and go away together they would still have to go back to Boaz first, back to the Stilwell house where everything that had begun remained unresolved.

He was used to attack and recklessness in her and the change that showed in her sometimes now both dismayed and roused him. So she loved him, she was really his woman, this bright creature; he felt it under his hand when he was making love to her now, he felt it when she walked towards him in a room, or passed him food at table. But at the same time safety was gone out of their relationship : each had put himself in the other's hands. Now he felt the weight of her being, strange, new, unaccustomed; and he gave over to her what was not even his own to give : he was aware of Mapulane (watching him drive off that day), away on that periphery to which passion banishes out of sight and sound the yelling, gesticulating influences that set themselves against it. He lay on the sand between the two women he could see with half-closed eyes, and among the children who ran to him with their treasures, and on this lonely beach destiny and history overlooked him; he could ignore both Shaka's defeated kingdom around him, and the white man's joke about it that he read each time he went to the lavatory . . . "vaseline, sandwiches, sawdust . . . God save the sugar farmers. Given this day . . . under my hand and great seal, Big Chief Shaka." The black warrior and the white man's derision of him; the savage ruined past and the conqueror's mockery of it; both were dead and he suffered from neither.

The passion between Gideon and Ann set the pace of days

that passed without slowness or haste or in fact any of the usual apprehensions of time. Jessie remembered that she had once thought, of Tom and herself, how you had to stop the ordinary business of living in order to love properly. As she walked down the path from the house in silence behind them, their relaxed, lightly swinging arms, backs of the hands just touching now and then, seemed to regulate the rhythm of her breathing. Wherever a group of people live together there are those from whom life emanates—anyone in whom, at that time, the force of vitality is swarming, as a particular tree among others is set electrically alive by bees. Jessie had for so long been the one at the centre; it was strange to her to feel now that this had passed from her. She had said to Gideon, "I don't have love affairs any more"—but, at the same time, she caught herself walking along the beach conscious of a man's eyes on her. The man turned out to be a boy the age of her son. She looked at the two lovers, passing a cigarette back and forth between them, lingering over what had touched each other's mouths, silent together, speechless, enfolded in themselves before her. Perhaps it would be Morgan who would have the love affairs now. She thought of his hands; tender, gaunt, strong and timid—he could be mistaken for a man, he was a man. She walked miles up the beach, away from the lovers, away from the little girls.

When she came back, Clem and Madge had buried Gideon up to the neck in sand; his head rested on the thighs of Ann's curled-up legs and her head watched over him, eyes closed to the sun, in a strange, naked, sleepy smile as if even his joking commonplaces with the children carried some code for her. Jessie took the children in to swim and then went up to the house with them. "I love Gid," Madge said, confiding, admiring.

"I don't mind him being black," Elisabeth agreed.

"Do you mind sometimes when other people are?" Jessie asked.

"I don't think it's pretty," said Elisabeth.

Clem began a long lecture about how unkind it was to talk about the colour of people and how you mustn't hurt their feelings, and how it didn't matter at all what colour you were, you were just the same—like people having blond hair or dark hair.

"Don't boss me," said Elisabeth, confidently. She was very

248

successful and flirtatious with Gideon, and insisted, with the tyranny over guests that Jessie disliked in children, on his coming to kiss her in bed before she slept each night. But Clem had already lost sight, in an attitude, of her natural response towards people; an attitude of necessity impressed early in order to counter the generally-accepted one. If you did not find blackness abhorrent and outcast, was the only alternative the fastidious suppression of all personal responses in the common denominator of shared humanity? Did it follow that, because you weren't repelled, you couldn't admit to being attracted, either? Did one have to be so afraid of emotion—*any emotion*—in this business?

Through the ordinary contacts of daily life about the house together, Jessie knew that Gideon was not unaware of her as a woman; there was no covert desire in his behaviour towards her, but she knew that, quite legitimately and quite harmless to his complete preoccupation with Ann, there existed an objective recognition that she, Jessie, was a woman to whom one could make love. This recognition exists in silence and without a sign between a man and many women, or a woman and many men, in situations where there never has been and never will be anything more to it. In bus queues, across shop counters, in the houses of friends—everyone recognises those who exist for himself and for whom he himself exists in this way; just as there are others, even the beautiful and apparently desirable, with whom one has no sexual concomitant. Gideon did not desire her, he was in love with another woman against whom she was not even in the running in the general world of sexual competition, because she was too old—sixteen years too old—but he might have desired her in another time and place. He might have; and this, combined with the sixteen years between her thirty-nine and Ann's twenty-three, meant that she herself could have been Ann —once, somewhere.

She was at once set at a remove from the love affair and at the same time curiously close to it. She was jealous no longer of the mere fact of love-making going on behind drawn curtains or in the darkness that stretched to the sea. Once when she returned to the house unexpectedly at a time when she thought the two of them were out, she opened the door into Ann's room to look for a vanished pair of scissors. She was barefoot, from the beach, and the house was silent; the two lying there did not wake up as she gazed at them. She felt neither the guilty recoil of one who sees suddenly, as a spectator, a part of life where one is never a spectator and only a protagonist, nor the shame of the voyeur. She looked with calm a moment at the ancient grouping of the two bodies, the faces flung away from each other, the arms lax where they had held; all that had been centred rolled apart in sleep. Ann's one brown-tipped breast was pressed out of shape, like her cheek, by the angle at which she lay on her side, with the whole of the lower part of her body swung across if she were lying face-down. And he lay on his belly with his head over the outstretched arm whose curved fingers, no longer within reach of her head, still conformed to the shape of it. His dark body had a shine going down the curve that followed the groove of the spine to the short, gleaming roundness of the buttocks. Their faces were sweaty. A fly rose and settled indifferently on either. Clothes dangled from the bed and lay sunk upon the floor; round the edges of the curtains, a frill of fire ran where the midday sun was held out. Jessie slowly closed the door and went away.

That afternoon they all went to a beach ten miles further up the coast that the children thought of as a place foreign and exciting. It was much like any other beach along there, but was reached by a track that went through eucalyptus forests instead of sugar-cane and had a cold and thrilling smell that was like some ritual preparation for arrival. The beach and rough green about it had been declared an Indian beach township, but this was so recent that there were only two ugly little villas, one chalky pink and the other brilliant blue, and both empty and deserted except for an African family and some chickens in a hut down among the mealies and stunted paw-paws of each plot. These people did not venture on to the beach, anyway; the picnic party was perfectly safe from prying eyes. The necessity for taking care that Gideon was not seen had become something that they considered openly and took for granted without embarrassment or pretence, as some daily medical treatment that at first seems impossible to carry out while keeping up a semblance of normal living soon adapts the norm to its own queer needs. The children, not knowing why, but always racing eager to give their report, ran down first, as usual, to see if there was anyone on the beach. Then the two women and Gideon followed. The little girls tore off their dresses and ran into the pools in the nude; there was no reason why they should not do this on the beach where they were living, but they did it only here.

Jessie had unopened letters in her canvas bag among towels and bananas; one was from Tom, and she read it without comment, but the other was from her mother: "She wonders if she should come down next week for the last few days... would it be convenient. —Well, it would be extremely inconvenient..."

"She's seen us," Ann said, weighing sand in her long hand. "Once; in your house. No; perhaps she didn't really see us together."

"But how was that?" Jessie was half-interested.

"When we were in the car, I ran back for the key and then I realised she was there... in the dining-room, by the window..."

"Did she call you or something?"

Ann smiled, surprised at how well she remembered the details. "No... well, I went in and she said something strange to me— she'd been there all the time and she knew I hadn't noticed her. Something about—there are always other people and then one day you become one of them yourself... something like that."

"Old people sit and watch like greedy cats," said Jessie cruelly.

"No, she was rather nice, in a funny way."

Jessie saw that there was some loyalty between the girl and the old woman whom she herself had never thought of as aware of each other's existence.

Gideon was amused as he often was at the customs of white people. "Fancy, she asks if she can come to her own house..."

"Oh it was my stepfather's. They were not like married people usually are—nothing cosy about them. I don't suppose she's been here since I was a child."

A few moments later Ann said, "Are you going home, then?"

Jessie said, "When?" to gain time, not for herself, but for the other two.

"Next week."

"Well, school begins."

She had never asked them what they were going to do. She had the feeling that they never talked about it, that they had hidden from it, escaped it until now when, as inevitably happens,

251

the chance remark that her mother wanted to come for the "last few days" had discovered them. "I'm going in." She was pushing her hair painfully under a rubber cap. Sand from her body sprinkled down on their heads as she got up. "Oh—sorry!" "It's all right." Ann took a paper handkerchief and began to use a corner of it, very gently, to flick the grains out of the convolutions of Gideon's small, well-made ear.

"He should bend his head to that side," said Jessie.

He shook it. "It's all *right*."

"Wait a minute." Ann persisted in her attentions to the ear. She said to Jessie, looking up at her, "Did you ever see anything so perfectly shaped?" He jerked his head as if he were being bothered by an insect. "I know," said Jessie.

When she came out of the water he was busy helping the children lug something into the pools. She walked over to them, pulling off the cap so that the deep, indrawn breath of the sea returned to her again in a gasp. He got the swollen plank afloat and came to the rock on which she had climbed to see. "Shipwreck," he said. She smiled, watching the children, watching this game, like every other, fall into the pattern of what they were : Clem taking charge, Madge at once suspecting that her chosen part was not the one she wanted after all, Elisabeth forgetting, in her roistering pleasure, what it was supposed to be about.

"Can we go back together?" he said.

"Yes, if you want to."

"She doesn't want to go back," he said.

He began to pull winkles off the rock and throw them into the incoming tide that sucked and struck against the rock where they sat. "You can't get a thing like this sorted out in five minutes." He was speaking for Ann, and Jessie answered, unconvinced, to give him the reassurance this asked, "Of course not."

"What do you make of Boaz?" he asked.

"Why?"

"So nice and polite and so on, very much the good chap. Never says, what's this all about?"

"To you? But why should he? I'm sure he's talked enough to Ann."

"It's pax when I'm around." After a pause he said, "D'you think he'd be like that with anybody?"

252

She looked at him quickly. Perhaps he wanted a lie from her, but she had done with lies, even the good lies. "Probably not."

He said, "She'd feel different about doing this if he'd just once stand up to me, you know?"

"Oh of course, if the other one can be got to behave badly at once everything's much easier. But here you have his nature, which is perhaps a bit of the natural victim's, plus the special situation. Civilised love affairs are bad enough, but this one's particularly civilised."

"If I were white," Gideon turned to her, wanting to confront her word by word, "you mean he'd tell me to go to hell."

"And her, too. Maybe."

"Good God." He was scornful, confused, and all the time the balance between trust and half-trust quivered between them, and she looked down, where the water swirled loud with foam, and she seemed to plunge—"I don't think I'd ever have to give this business another thought. I believed it was all settled, once and for all, long ago. It's the truth, the rational truth, that a love affair like yours is the same as any other. But you haven't come to the truth while it's still only the rational truth. You've got to be a bit more honest than that. Do you know what I think while I look at you and Ann? Do you? I remember what was left out when I settled the race business once and for all. I remember the black men who rubbed the floor round my feet when I was twelve and fourteen. I remember the young black man with a bare chest, mowing the lawn. The bare legs and the strong arms that carried things for us, moved furniture. The black man that I must never be left alone with in the house. No one explained why, but it didn't matter. I used to feel, at night, when I turned my back to the dark passage and bent to wash my face in the bathroom, that someone was coming up behind me. Who was it, do you think? And how many more little white girls are there for whom the very first man was a black man? The very first man, the man of the sex phantasies ... Gideon, I'd forgotten, I'd left it all out. It's only when something like you and Ann happens one suddenly needs to feel one's way back."

He was looking tightly ahead as if under an insult.

"I suppose Boaz thought it was all settled, too. Years ago. But none of us knows how much getting free of the colour bar means to us—none of us. It sounds crazy, but perhaps it's so important to him that he can't help putting it before Ann, even. It sounds crazy; but even before her."

They did not speak for a while, and the sea cut under the rock and tore away, bearing off what had been said.

"Where would you go, to England?"

"She thought Italy." He did not want to mention the scholarship that he had given up, but that Ann saw simply as something that could be arranged again.

"What about some other part of Africa?"

"It doesn't matter much." Ann was coming towards them along the shore-line, her feet pressing the shine of water from the sand as she walked. They both watched her approach, but it was his vision of her that prevailed, so that Jessie saw her as he did, a glowing face, salt-stiff, blown hair, his shirt resting like a towel across her shoulders, and a line of the flesh—the white of a freshly-broken mushroom—that was hidden by the boned top of her bathing suit showing in a soft rise against her tanned chest as she walked. In this unselfconscious sauntering stalk everything was taken for granted, everything that had ever been struggled for and won with broken bodies and bursting brains— the struggle up from superstition and pestilence, religious wars and industrial slavery, all the way from the weight of the club to the rubber truncheon : the fight of man against nature, against men, and against himself. Gideon said between clenched teeth, "The other things I've been beating my head against the wall for —I don't want them any more." He was making, in the presence of a witness, an offering, throwing down the last that he had before the demand that he could not measure. And he laughed because of the present glory of it, as the figure came on, approaching, enveloping, over the sand. He jumped off the rock, staggered a moment in the knee-high wild water, and then ran up to the dry sand. When she came he took her by the shoulders in some playful exchange, knocking the shirt off. They stood there talking, arm's-length from each other, her head impudently, affectionately bent, his thumbs pressing the hollow under each collarbone. The sun had ripened her skin like fruit, and even in the house the warm graining beneath which the blood lay near, brought to the surface by slight inflammation, gave her the look of someone seen by candlelight.

NINETEEN

Rᴀɪɴ ʟᴇᴀɴᴇᴅ ꜰʀᴏᴍ the horizon over the sea, and all, sea and rain, moved so quietly that the waves fell with the isolated sounds of doors shut far away. An *epoussé* glitter now and then broke the dream with a reminder of water.

Clem, who less than a year ago had been as unhampered by conceptions of time as her sisters were, now felt her being determined within it as the life of a character in a play is contained in sets arbitrarily put up and taken down. "Our last three days." She was dismayed, she protested against the limits that obsessed her. Madge and Elisabeth chimed in with her, but forgot, next moment, that the game of bears in caves that the darkness under the high old beds in their room provided, would not go on for ever. "Let's always play this," they said to each other.

Clem took her rebellion to her mother. "Why does it just have to go and rain on our last three days?"

"You've had a whole month when it didn't rain."

But Clem's sense of time had no dimension in the past yet, she was concerned only with the margin by which the present extended into the future.

Jessie gathered stray books and clothes wherever she happened to come upon them and put them on the spare bed in the room where she slept. She went through the contents of the magazine rack in the living-room, setting aside the children's ludo board, some crumpled dolls' clothes, and falling under the aimless fascination of reading snippets in the old magazines that had been there when she came and would be left behind when she went. Gideon and Ann stepped over the clutter that surrounded her as she sat on the floor. Their comings and goings were minor; they spent the days talking of the practical facts of rooms and rents and fares in other countries, like some ambitious young couple planning to spend their savings on a visit abroad. Ann even sat mending the unravelled sleeve of Gideon's blue Italian shirt. Sometimes Gideon was silent for long stretches as he sipped beer and drew. They went tramping out in the rain, and once drove away through the mud and came back stretching and preoccupied, focusing upon familiar things with the daze of people who have shut themselves away to talk.

Jessie picked up a drawing of Gideon's while they were out. Well, at least it wasn't Ann again—seeing that it was abstract. But why be glad of that? Malraux spoke of the artist as one who annexes a fragment of the world and makes it his own. She did not know whether Gideon needed that more than he needed to share a common possession of what there was to be shared. Perhaps he needed to be a man more than he needed to be a painter. Not just a black man, set aside on a special form, a special bench, in a special room, but a man.

As she looked at the charcoal drawing that was almost like a woodcut in its contrast of thick black lines and spidery-etched connections, she thought it moved the way the water did that day when she and Gideon were talking on the rock; but the association was probably one that existed only in her own mind.

The day before they left was clear, with a colourless sky that turned blue as the morning warmed. The sea remained calm; the sand, beaten flat as a tennis-court, dried with a rain-stippled skin and took incisively the oblique cuts of crabs' delicate feet and the three-branched seals imprinted by the claws of birds. Gideon and Ann came down to the beach soon after Jessie and the children. Like invalids, after the rain, they sat against a rock and smoked, both in long trousers, he in his sweater and she with her grey trench-coat pulled round her, only their feet bare. Jessie looked up from her book at some point and saw Gideon strolling towards the children. She and Ann chatted intermittently, and then Jessie decided to go to the village to get what was needed for a picnic lunch on the road next day. She was brisk, standing up with her hands conclusively on her thighs for a moment; she had about her the confidence of a woman who is about to return to the place where she belongs and who already takes on the attractiveness the man who is waiting there will see in her—an attractiveness made up of the freshness imparted by absence, the comfort of something well-known, the strength and weakness of her régime. For once, Ann was inert by contrast; her out-flung legs, her bent head that moved only to draw slowly on a cigarette made a figure that had come to a stop, there on the beach.

The shop in the village was not full, but service moved with a peculiar country slowness. You were supposed to help yourself from the grocery shelves but the grouping of things was haphazard—Jessie had to give up and wait her turn to be served at the counter.

The man and woman behind it conducted their business in an easy, talkative way, while a few Africans hung about on the fringe of the whites, hoping to get a turn sometime. A big pasty woman, with an identical daughter leaning on the counter beside her, was trying to decide on a tin of jam—"Ah, but how often do you get it these days that it's not all mushy, like a lot of porridge . . .?"

The assistant was a little grey-skinned woman without breasts or lips or eyebrows, but whose head of hair, distinct from the rest of her, was fresh from the hairdresser's, elaborately swirled and curled, stiff and brilliant yellow. "Not Calder's Orchard Bounty, Mrs. Packer, I can guarantee you that. Same as you, I hate jam all squashed up's if its bad fruit they put in it, but this is what I take home for myself."

The next customer ahead of Jessie was a handsome woman with the air of authority that goes with a gaze that follows the line of a splendid slope of bosom. "How are you today, Mrs. Gidley?" The assistant took her pencil out of the centre of a curl and although the whole mass moved slightly, like a pile of spun sugar stirred by a knife, not a hair was drawn out of place. The tone of voice rose a little to meet the status of this customer, not unctuous, but no longer matey. "Stanley—Mrs. Gidley's chickens, in the back there. —I put them aside first thing this morning, while I could get the pick for you. Or don't you want to take them? We can send the boy, no trouble at all, he's got to go up your way, before twelve? —Stanley, just a minute—"

"Oh could you? Oh that would be nice—but I'd forgotten about them anyway—all I wanted was to know if you'd be good enough to put this up somewhere—" The woman was leaning across the counter on one elbow, smoothing a home-made poster.

"Oh that—" The yellow head twisted to look. "I heard about that—yes, I should think I would! It's getting too much of a good thing. My daughter was saying to me, Saturday afternoon and Sunday's the only day you've got, if you're working, and then the whole beach is full of them."

The gracious voice said regretfully, painedly, "Well, we do feel that some arrangements ought to be made. Something that will be fair to all. One doesn't want to deny people their pleasures. There has been a suggestion that a part of the beach ought to be set aside for them . . . but of course, once you make it official, you'll get them coming from other places, and the Indians, too . . ."

"It's all the servants, you see, that people bring down with them. That's it, mainly. Down from Johannesburg and they've got their bathing suits and all just like white people . . ." The assistant bent her head towards the large woman and laughed indignantly, in spite of herself. "We get them in here, let me tell you, quite the grand ladies and gentlemen they think they are, talking to you as if they was white."

"Well exactly, they're not our simple souls who're content to chat in their rooms." Her kind of laugh joined pleasantly with the assistant's.

The man behind the counter plonked down two frozen chickens. "Look at this, Stanley, Mrs. Gidley's just brought in a poster—there's going to be a meeting at the hotel on Tuesday."

"Well, don't you agree—we feel that, as residents who've built up Isendhla, we want to enjoy our beautiful beach in privacy . . ."

". . . she said to me, I didn't want to go into the water with all those natives looking at me . . . in trunks they were, too, the men."

The majestic bosom had turned to the man. "Major Field suggests that we might set aside a stretch . . . Up near Grimald's cottage, then there would be no question—"

With thanks and profuse friendliness the woman left the poster and turned on her high heels and made her way out, backing into Jessie, gasping a smiling apology, as she went. Jessie caught full on for a moment, like a head on a pike, the fine grey eyes, the cheerful bright skin, the full cheeks and un-lined mouth of a tranquil, kind woman.

The woman behind the counter set the meat-cutter screech-ing back and forth across a ham, and, while she was weighing

258

out the slices for Jessie, remarked, "This always used to be such a lovely clean beach . . . I don't know if you was down on Sunday? You'd of thought they owned it, that's the truth . . . undressing all over, behind the bushes."

"No, I wasn't down."

"Where are you staying then?"

"I've got Grimald's cottage."

The woman pulled a face that was quickly suppressed. "Oooh, that's out of the way, isn't it?" she said, loading Jessie's basket with pampering tact calculated to take her mind off anything else.

Jessie was occupied for an hour or so in the house when she got back; then she got as far as the terrace and stood looking with a kind of disbelief at the wild, innocent landscape; the rain-calmed sea, the slashed heads of strelitzia above the bush almost translucent green with the rush of sap. The sun put a warm hand on her head. But nothing was innocent, not even here. There was no corner of the whole country that was without ugliness. It was no good thinking you could ever get out of the way of that.

She went down to the beach. Ann came slowly to meet her. "Is Gid up at the house?" she called.

"No, why?"

Ann was smiling, but she said, "Well, I don't know what's happened to him, but he hasn't been back . . ."

"You mean since I left?"

"Mmm," said Ann, watching her expression.

"I saw him wander up the beach."

"Yes, I know. I've walked right up beyond the third lot of rocks, but he doesn't seem to be anywhere."

Jessie looked around the beach, as if she expected to be able to say: there he is. She was conscious of Ann watching her, ready to take a cue from her. She sat down on the sand, waving to the children. "When you start walking here, you go on for miles without noticing it. He'll get hungry soon, and be reminded it's time to turn back."

Ann was still standing. "I've been miles."

She drew a half-circle, dragging her toe in a ballet step over the sand, making a deeper and deeper groove. "Some fishermen came past while I was lying down."

Jessie indicated surprise.

"The children shouted and I opened my eyes and there they were, in a jeep, of all things."

"White men?"

"Oh yes. Lots of equipment." She pointed up the beach where Jessie now noticed two long lines of ploughed-up sand.

After a minute, Jessie said, "Perhaps Gideon saw them and thought he'd keep out of the way."

"Yes, but then he'd have gone up to the house from the bush," Ann turned at once with the quick dismissal of someone who has already considered and discarded the same conclusion. "—Wouldn't he?" Jessie saw she was hoping for an alternative to be suggested.

"No, well, he might have gone a long way round." But what other way was there? If he wanted to cut back to the house, he wouldn't walk further away in order to do so. "He'll turn up." She wandered off to the children. Ann lay on her stomach on the sand, head resting on her hands. Jessie tried to round up the little girls. "It's lunch-time. Put your shirt on. Madge, isn't that your cap, there? No more water, Elisabeth—" but they dawdled and ignored her.

"What's the time now?" Ann asked.

"About half past one."

"And when you left?"

"I don't know—tennish—after ten."

At last the children began to drift up the beach towards the path. Madge hung back and shouted, "Ma, I'm waiting for you." Jessie did not answer but she felt the pull of that imploring, obstinate figure turned on her. "Go on up," she called. "I'm coming," and, sentenced, Madge dragged away over the sand, far behind the others.

Jessie tried to work out what Ann was thinking. Her eyes went over the hunched shoulders and the lovely dip of the waist, the fingers thrust into the hair. The girl wore one of his shirts again; the clothes of a lover are both a private reassurance and a public declaration : another kind of woman would wear rings and jewels, but for the same reasons.

"I must pack." Jessie's remark rolled away, unanswered. "We ought to leave fairly early tomorrow," she added.

"Oh I'll get things together tonight. There's so little."

Ann swung round and sat up suddenly. She giggled a little,

and, eyes searching Jessie, said, "What on earth can he be doing? Are we going to be here all day?"

"I think we should go to the house. He'll come to the house when he turns up, anyway."

Ann continued to look at her and look away with an attempt at casualness, childishly nervous, smiling, pressing her lips one against the other. Her eyes met Jessie's deeply, dazzling, evasive in their displayed frankness, guilty in their innocence, as if she had done something that was about to be found out.

"But what *could* happen to him?" Jessie asked.

Ann was not looking anywhere now, though her gaze was holding the other woman. Her eyes seemed trapped, swimming with the tinsel fragments that made light refract in their depths. As a confusion of thoughts conceals sometimes stops one's mouth so that one loses the power of speech, so there is an aphasia of sight, when eyes cease, for a moment, to show anything but mechanical responses to light and the trembling of objects.

"Well . . . he wouldn't just walk out into the sea . . .?"

The moment it was said she was smiling at the absurdity, the preposterousness of it.

Jessie laughed too. "But why on earth should he do such a thing?"

In Ann's deep blush she saw the unconscious desire to have the course of this love affair decided by something drastic, arbitrary, out of her own power.

When they got up to the house they found Gideon about to come down to the beach for them. Ann was almost shy to approach him. "I went for a walk," he said from the top of the steps. "I had no idea it was so far."

"That's what I said!" said Jessie.

Ann was carrying the trench-coat, hung by the loop from one finger, over her shoulder. He came down the steps and took the coat from her. She said nothing.

The children had been given some lunch by Jason, and were already playing on the track at the back of the house. Jason was in his room, as always between two and four in the afternoon. The three of them sat in the dim cool dining-room eating cold meat and cheese that had been left set out.

"And what are you going to do now?" Jessie said suddenly. They waited but she did not go on.

"Ann'll probably come back with you to the house tomorrow," he said, passing on something that had been decided as part of a plan. He looked at Ann, who was watching Jessie.

Jessie made some automatic assent. But her feeling of distaste for the contemplation of them returned to the way they were before, with Ann coming home at night to Boaz, rose uncontrollably and communicated itself to them.

"And then?" The appeal did not come from personal identification with their position, but out of something wider, urgent —the concern with human dignity as a common possession that, lost by individuals, is that much lost for all. She felt the same sort of involvement when she saw someone fly into a brutal temper : in any action callow, inadequate, not carried through to the limit of its demands of courage and sensibility.

"She's got to get it all finally straightened out with Boaz."

Ann said, "I must sell the car." Everything that ever happened to her was simply announced obliquely and casually, in the form of such practicalities. That was how she dealt with unwieldy emotions, giving her confusion an appearance of headstrong sureness.

"We won't be able to see each other for the next week or two anyway," said Gideon, alluding to her return to the Stilwell house. Now that the love affair was no longer an escapade they would have to become cautious, prudent, fearful, where they had been brazen and careless; they could not risk running into trouble before they managed to leave the country.

Jessie was thinking of his need for friends and money to smuggle him out. "It won't be too difficult."

"No. But it's got to be quick and quiet." He paused. "I know the ropes." Already passion had become discipline in him.

"I suppose you wouldn't like to buy my car?" Ann thought that Jessie had inherited money from Fuecht. "We need cash."

Jessie shrugged off the question as something that Ann must know was impossible. "You'll be all right once you get to England, won't you? Surely your people will help."

"I shouldn't think so, not this time," Ann said.

"We won't be able to get much further than Tanganyika, to

start with," said Gideon, eager to explain, almost anxious, wanting to have the worst admitted and therefore that much defeated. "If I can get out I'll wait for her there."

Jessie helped him to some more meat and turned with the plate to Ann, but she gestured it away. "I looked for you right up to the third rocks," she said presently.

Gideon was opening beer for Jessie and himself. "Yes, but I'd gone further than that, right to where there's that steep cliff, you know?—and I sat there for a bit, and when I started to come back the tide was so high I had to go through the bush."

"You didn't see the jeep?"

"I came along a path. Was there a jeep?"

Jessie remarked, "Ann says some fishermen came along the beach in a jeep."

"Well, a jeep couldn't get further than the third rocks anyway." He sat down and began to eat. "Fishermen. We've been left in peace until now."

"It lasted out our time," Jessie said. "There's something to be said for having held out for nearly three weeks."

"Oh I don't think a couple of fishermen're anything to worry about. You'll be able to make a regular hide-out for your criminal friends down here, Jessie. You say your mother's not going to use it."

"The residents of Isendhla are a vigilant lot. Just because they're retired you mustn't think they've gone soft, Gideon. I heard this morning in the village that they're having a meeting to stop the cheeky servants from Johannesburg playing around on the beach in their off-time. Wearing bikinis, too, just like the white ladies."

He began to chuckle to himself. "Is that it?"

"That's it. On our beautiful Isendhla beach where all tensions are forgotten, and the tolerance and gentleness of a non-competitive life prevail."

"What are they going to do with the stinking black brutes?"

"There's talk about setting aside a remote bit of beach for them—say, up at Grimald's cottage."

Gideon slid back in his chair, and put a hand over Ann's to share the joke with her, but she was inattentive.

"Good old awful Johannesburg, nice and vulgar and brutal, a good honest gun under the white man's pillow and a good

263

honest tsotsi in the street," Jessie said. "I think we'll get going about eight tomorrow morning, all right?"

Before the house emptied of them, it seemed fuller than it had ever been, for their possessions were piled up in the rooms, and the beds, though stripped, held hair-brushes, medicine bottles, damp bathing suits and toys—things for which there was no place in the Stilwells' suitcases or that the children did not want to be parted from during the journey. At last they were ready to go. Gideon was making Jason laugh as they loaded the cars, talking Zulu. When Jessie wanted to say goodbye to him he was back in the kitchen, and when he saw that she meant to shake hands with him he became confused, brought his palms together in a kind of silent clap, and then took her hand awkwardly, his fingers damp from the sink.

When they had gone he brought out his polishing cloths made of squares of old blanket and his two tins of polish, one red and one brown, and smeared the floors thickly, replacing the dusty footsteps and the spoor of the children's bare feet with over-lapping circles of concentric shine that came up under the progress of his hand. He took the few bananas and bruised apples that remained in the bowl on the table out to his room; the smell of fruit was gone from the house. In the bathroom, he found a used blade and put it, carefully wrapped in newspaper, in the blouse pocket of his kitchen-boy suit. He swept out one of Gideon's charcoal drawings that had fallen under the divan and been forgotten. In the lavatory, he carefully replaced the drawing-pin that had come loose with a curling corner of the declaration that he was unable to read but whose official look he had always interpreted as a sign of importance.

The lucky-bean seeds remained, month after month and year after year, where the children had spilt them that day and they had dispersed and settled, red-and-black eyes, into the cracks of the verandah.

PART FOUR

TWENTY

THE BLACK SPRING of burned veld stretched for miles beside the road. They came up out of the sappy green of the coast that knows no seasons and remembered that winter had cut down to the bone in their absence. Already the hard, bright land was cleared, cattle hoof-marks dried to stone in what had been vleis, rocks split by frost. The black territory, as if shaded in on a map, ran round pockets of resistance formed by scrubby trees, and blanked out the shallow veins that marked the beds of dry streams. It was the black not of death but of life; peach trees along the railway tracks were blooming crude pink out of it, and there was a frizz of something light, hardly green yet, over a young willow. Jessie was not aware of a change of tone and pace in her being but it took place nevertheless, just as the engines in an aeroplane settle to the number of revolutions which constitutes their cruising speed, once the height of that speed has been reached. She drove without getting tired, and managed the children capably and companionably; a temporary state that made all others seem inexplicable. When they stopped to eat or to stretch their legs, she and Ann and Gideon had the confidence and easy closeness together that people often find only when the experience they have shared is about to be summed up by their return to those who are outside it. Before, Jessie had resented being drawn into the close orbit of Gideon and Ann; now she felt that they had also been drawn into hers. Gideon made a fire, when they had lunch, to please Elisabeth—there was nothing that needed cooking. There was no wood about and he used dry grass and cow-dung and was affectionately praised by everyone. The three grown-ups sat round Gideon's fire drinking gin and tonic and laughed a lot about nothing in particular; everything that was said seemed a witty private joke between them. Elisabeth stood behind Gideon with her arms possessively round his neck and laughed when the grown-ups did.

Jessie packed the picnic things back into the boot of the Stilwell car, while Ann handed them to her. The girl stood with her arms hugged against herself, gazing round with the alertness of a last look. "When I think of what it was like driving the other way! Those two days while the car was being fixed! You know, when the man in the garage looked at Gid, and I stood next to him seeing Gid at the same time, it wasn't the same person we saw . . ."

"It won't be long."

Gideon was trampling out the fire. First he had scooped up sand in his hands to pour over it. "Anybody got a rag?" He came over dusting his palms together. "What's the matter?" he murmured intimately to Ann. "I want to go," she said fiercely, sulkily. "Yes, we are *going*." He aped her intensity.

"Oh, not to Johannesburg." She walked away and got into the car; she drew the old towel that kept the draught off over her knees, and took a cigarette.

Gideon struggled to close the faulty catch of Jessie's boot. He clicked his tongue at its recalcitrance, once it was done. "You'll help her."

"Whatever I can," Jessie said.

He clicked his tongue again. "I'll have to keep out of the way. It's bad, you see."

"Ann seems only just to have discovered what it's all about."

He laughed. "I know. She was like a kid playing hide-and-seek. Now she finds there really is something creeping up after her. I want to get her out as quick as I can. She's got nothing to do with this sort of thing, man." He was thinking of Callie Stow, who knew how to keep intact, untouched, her loves, her passions and her beliefs, even while the dirty fingers of police spies handled them. But he did not want Ann to change; like many people he confused spirit with bravery, and he saw her old thoughtlessness and recklessness as courage. He did not want to see her acquire the cunning, stubborn and patient temper of a political rebel. To him she was herself, her splendid self, a law to herself, and limited as little to the conventions of opposition as to the conventions of submission. She loved him; she did not love him *across the colour-bar*: for her the colour-bar did not exist.

"Come, my girl, let's push off," he said, putting a hand on

Jessie's shoulder. The gesture admitted her to the sort of moment she had been waiting for, not consciously, and she spoke. "Gideon, shall I keep in touch with the child—when you're gone?"

He was not annoyed at the reminder, he was not indifferent. But he said, as if he took a chance on what was expected of him, "I'll make some arrangements to send money every month or so, as soon as I can."

"No, that's not it," she said. "I could give him news of you, and I could send you photographs."

"Perhaps it would be better to let it go," he said. "There's an uncle looking after him, a good friend of mine. When I've got money I'll see that he gets it."

She was looking at him with a trapped, uncertain face. He patted her hand. "It's all right, Jessie, it'll be all right."

She drove ahead of them, parting an empty countryside where a tiny herd-boy, flapping like a scare-crow in the single garment of a man's shirt, waved to the car. Little groups of huts were made out of mud and the refuse of the towns—rusty corrugated iron, old tins beaten flat, once even the head of an iron bed-stead put to use as a gate. The women slapped at washing and men squatted talking and gesticulating in an endless and un-imaginable conversation that, as she passed, even at intervals of several miles, from one kraal to another, linked up in her mind as one. In this continuity she had no part, in this hold that lay so lightly, not with the weight of cement and tarmac and steel, but sinew of the earth's sinew, authority of a legendary past, she had no share. Gideon had it; what an extraordinary quality it imparted to people like him, so that others were drawn to them as if by some magic. It was, in fact, a new kind of magic; the old magic lay in a personality believed to have access to the supernatural, this new one belonged to those who held in them-selves for this one generation the dignity of the poor about to inherit their earth and the worldliness of those who had been the masters. Who else could stretch out within himself and put finger-tips on both touchstones at once? No wonder the girl had turned her back on them all, on Boaz with his drums and flutes, on Tom with his historical causes, on herself with her "useful" jobs, and chosen him.

But a few days later, when Jessie happened to have to drive

269

through the township where Gideon lived, the continuity of the little communities of mud and tin on the road was picked up again. Mean shops and houses lurched by as she bounced along the rutted streets; her errand (for the Agency, where she had found herself at once temporarily employed again because of some staff crisis) took her first to a decent, two-roomed box of a house between two hovels. She sat among shiny furniture behind coloured venetian blinds; then in an office converted from an old house, where a money-lender and book-keeper, with a manner of business irritability and suspicion, hovered over the scratchings of a girl clerk who went about in slippers between black exercise books and a filing cabinet like a weary woman in her own kitchen. The verandah outside the place was littered with the torn-off sheaths of mealie-cobs, and children with mouths and noses joined by snot watched from the gutter. A mule was being beaten and a huge woman, strident-voiced, oblivious of her grotesque body and dirty clothes, bared her broken teeth at a man. Gideon had someone he loved here; parents, perhaps; friends. Taking Gideon, Ann was claimed by this, too, this place where people were born and lived and died before they could come to life. They drudged and drank and murdered and stole in squalor, and never walked free in the pleasant places. When they were children they were cold and hungry, and when they were old they were cold and hungry again; and in between was a brief, violent clutch at things out of reach, or the sad brute's life of obliviousness to them. That was the reality of the day, the time being. Oh, it would take courage to choose this, to accept it, to plunge into it, to belong with it; for that was what one would do, with Gideon, even if one were to be living in another country. Even among strangers in Italy or England, Ann's lot would still be thrown in here, among these men and women and children outcast for three hundred years. Jessie found fear in herself at the idea of being allied to this life, and was uneasy, as if she might communicate it in some way, unspoken, to Ann. She fought it, denying its validity, but fear doesn't lie down at the bidding, like a dog. Not even for love, that is supposed to cast it out : she remembered how Ann had said ". . . when the man in the garage looked at Gid, and I stood next to him seeing Gid at the same time, it wasn't the same person we saw . . ."

Jessie was stopped by a policeman just past a cinema gutted in a riot some years before and never restored, and asked for her permit to be in the township. One of the easy lies that even the ruling caste has to learn to tell came readily : "My washgirl didn't turn up this week, and I had to find out what she's done with my things—" She had told the tale several times before, and it was always adequate.

"You really think she wanted him drowned? But you said one must believe she loves him?"

Jessie talked of Ann and Gideon but there was conveyed to Tom in the telling not only her experience of them but the vein that the experience had opened into herself.

"She's in love with him, there's no getting away from it, whatever we thought about her before." The familiar background to the Stilwells' intimacy, that looked the same whether they were in fact far removed from one another or drawn closely together, had been taken up again; she was cutting out a dress, at night, while he worked on some students' papers. "But I don't know what she wanted . . ."

"Wanted him drowned . . . you said so "

"Being in love with him isn't simple; I mean, the whole business isn't. We say it's just like falling in love with anyone, but it isn't, the whole affair isn't. Not for us either. You said at the beginning Boaz couldn't behave just as if this were any man running off with his wife. And Gideon knows it. Boaz wants to treat Gideon like any other man, but he can't because Gideon isn't a man, won't be, can't be, until he's free."

"About Boaz—all right." Their attitude in the business of black and white was something they shared completely without individual reservations. Yet now Tom felt the difference between them of two people, both of whom are familiar with a terrain through organised tours, one of whom has been lost there . . . Jessie went on sticking pins firmly through paper and material, privately carrying on with her task, while her voice drew him into an admittance of something that existed like a deed committed between them. "Ah, Tom, don't ask me to postulate it. We don't see black and white and so we all think we behave as decently to one colour face as another. But how can that ever be, so long as there's the possibility that you can escape back into your filthy damn whiteness? How do you know you'll always play fair? There's Boaz—he's so afraid of taking advantage of Gideon's skin that he ends up taking advantage of it anyway by refusing to treat him like any other man."

"Yes, yes, but all right—what 'harm' could you do or I do to Len or Gideon or anybody else?"

"But how can you be sure, while one set of circumstances governs their lives and another governs yours?"

Tom said shortly, "I don't see Ann thinking about this, though."

"One knows things sometimes simply by being afraid, you know that?"

Later when they had gone to bed, he returned to it, saying in the dark, "If she really loves him, as you say, what harm can she do him?"

Jessie was silent for a moment, but as Tom put his arm under her head, she said to his profile showing like a mountain range close to her eyes, "First he couldn't get out on his scholarship because he's black, now he can't stay because she's white. What's the good of us to him? What's the good of our friendship or her love?"

For the Davises there was that withdrawal of people into their own affairs that often comes about when some crisis in which others have been involved shrinks back to the orbit of the protagonists, once a decision has been made. They did not need to discuss the details of their parting with Tom and Jessie; they needed to recover, even from the most sympathetic and familiar understanding, all that they had revealed of themselves in the distress of the last few months. It was necessary for Boaz to forget, at least for the present, the demands he had made on Tom while they were alone together; it was necessary for Ann to forget how close she and Gideon had drawn to Jessie in the house at the sea. It was a relief to the whole house, though when they all met the atmosphere was the drained, numb, considerate one of the railway or airport hall, where the end of something is reduced to the choice of a magazine to take into the void, and the solicitous provision of cups of coffee to wile away the remaining half-hour. The help—that is, the continued intimacy —that Gideon had thought Ann would need from Jessie would have been an intrusion; in the end, Ann and Boaz knew each other so well that neither needed, or could be provided with, a defence against the other.

Gideon came to the house quietly once, and talked alone with Boaz and Ann; there was no dinner-party afterwards, and Gideon would not even stay for a drink. Boaz was seeing a lawyer friend of the Stilwells; Len came to consider taking over Ann's car. Jessie met him in the garden as he left. "Well, are you driving away?" He came up confidentially and said, "They want cash. I understand that. But it's out, for me, then." "The best thing is to advertise." It was the subdued small talk outside the sickroom door. Jessie walked to the gate with Len. When they were a little further from the house he said, "The husband's a nice guy. What went wrong?" They both laughed, giving up at the inadequacy of the reason why it shouldn't. "I didn't take them seriously, honestly." He was talking of Gideon and Ann. "I'd never have taken them seriously. But the whole town's talking now. Everyone knows they went off together. Everyone's asking me this and that." By the whole town he meant all the intricate subcommunications of the town-within-the-town where the traditional human exchanges replaced the decreed separations. But Jessie felt no interest; the sensation buzzed over something that had already escaped out of reach of sensation.

She had a pleasant lunch with Gideon and Ann at the house one day, when everyone else was out. She did not know if they still met at the flat, but she gathered that they were seeing each other briefly, very discreetly, and probably through the agency of some friend not previously associated with them. The three of them talked mostly about the house at the sea and their time there, almost like people who meet to renew a holiday friendship. When Gideon left he looked round the smoky living-room where they had sat till nearly three in the afternoon over their lunch-time coffee (it was a bleak day and the fire, Jessie and Ann agreed, was not nearly so good as Gideon's grass and dung one had been), and then at Ann, whose beautiful smile rose to her face as if it existed for him and would always be there when he looked to her. Now it came to him as encouragement : not to be afraid to pronounce the future, not to be afraid to count on it. He put his arms round Jessie and held her, and kissing her, said, "When are you coming up to Tanganyika? Or will it be London? But Tanganyika's a good place, eh?"

TWENTY-ONE

S HE KNEW THEN that she would not see him again.

But she could not have guessed how this would come about,
and for what reasons, that, if they were in the room that August
afternoon, she failed to be aware of. The cigarette smoke that the
three of them had breathed out of their nostrils and mouths
hung like warm indoor thunder; the fire was all red, all paper-
lantern glow, containing flame in the thinnest skin of matter, and
would collapse into nothing at the slightest shift, but the bricks
of the fireplace gave out a magnificent heat. Jessie put her back
to it. She felt a peaceful weight in her own presence, alone there,
left by the other two. I'm beginning to live vicariously, she
thought, if I can feel so involved with other people's lives and
step back and watch them go. But she knew it was something
different, something that she couldn't be too sure of yet . . .
She was beginning to slip into the mainstream, she was beginning to feel the substance was no longer something she must
dam up for herself. Passion would not leave the world grey
when it went out for her; struggle, love, the urge to grasp and
shape living went on through the agency of others, too; Gideon
and Ann held part of it; Morgan was coming up to have his
share relinquished to him, and even the small girls were not far
off. Her mind inhabited briefly the rooms of the house at the sea
that had been talked of that afternoon; wandered to Fuecht;
she thought, with the sudden summoning that brings the dead
to life, that he had dammed everything up for himself right to
the very end, right until his old claws couldn't hold anything
any more, let it all slip through, and remained clutching at
nothingness.

Three nights later the Stilwells had guests for dinner. Jessie
had left the table to help Agatha serve the main dish, and she
met Boaz at the foot of the stairs. Both he and Ann had said they
would be out, and she had not pressed them further, but now

she said, "Are you coming to eat? —Oh I like that Allen man!" The occasion of the dinner-party was the presence of a visiting Cambridge history don who Tom had told them was brilliant. He turned out to have that diffidently deprecating manner of presenting dogmatic opinions that Jessie found irresistible. "Yes, I hear he's pretty impressive." Boaz smiled, responding to her mood of animation engendered by the success of the evening. Her mind was on the sauce, that might need thickening, and she said, "Well, come in, then!"—already on her way to the kitchen. "No . . . no, I don't think so . . ." Each in their pre-occupation, they passed on. "D'you know where the key to the boxroom is?" he called after her. She was already stirring the sauce, standing well away from the stove so that her dress would not be splashed. "No key," she called. "The door's just stiff, it's never locked."

Agatha went into stony slow-motion when flustered, and there was real effort of encouragement and chivvying needed to get hot plates, hot food, and the sauce that must be served at once, all to the table at the same time. It was managed, but Jessie could not let her eye off anything while the process was going on. Tom always forgot to open the wine beforehand and, as usual, wandered about the room talking, using the bottles to emphasise his points instead of drawing the corks. He disappeared to find his favourite corkscrew, then was back again, but as he came close to her where she was serving she saw his face quite alien to the warm reflections of the room. The response to some other situation stung upon it like the outline of a slap. He was filling glasses, she was caught among plates and steaming dishes; she had no chance to speak to him, sitting down, at last, at the opposite end of the table. The don, who was young and tall, with the small head and fine skin of handsome Englishmen, took on a patchy flush as he ate and drank appreciatively, and kept his golden eyes on George Thandele, Tom's African colleague who taught law at the university. Thandele talked so steadily that he scarcely ate at all; when he paused he would take a gulp of wine like someone coming up for air. They were not arguing, but agreeing about the inconsistencies of policy in the new African states. "It's a matter of coming to terms with free-dom," Thandele said, in conclusion.

"Well precisely. There's nothing really extraordinary about a

Ghanaian cabinet minister's wife buying herself a gold bed in London while her husband's Government announces a special issue of stamps commemorating colonialist exploitation in South Africa." There was laughter down the table, and talk became diverse again. Jessie forgot about Tom for stretches of the evening, and then would catch his glance, or, in a pause of her own, watch him engaged in talk with others, and receive some parenthetic flash of undecipherable concern.

At last they met at the broad window-sill in the living-room where the drinks stood.

"They're leaving." He passed the phrase to her like a folded slip of paper. She looked uncomprehending.

"Upstairs," he said. At the word she had in her mind Boaz; then the question about the key to the boxroom, where the suitcases were . . . but these facts did not fit together, as familiar objects looked at without the sense of their relationship to each other are unrecognisable. "Who?" she said. "Boaz has just told me that they are going back to Europe," said Tom. He went off with the glass of beer he had poured for someone, and Jessie was drawn slowly into the activity of the room with the strange facility of one who has just been told something that cannot be grasped by the small, delicate apprehensions that remain independent on the oblique edge of one's being—but must be held back until it can be taken full on.

Tom went down to the gate with the last guest. She was standing in the middle of the shabby room, ready for him, when Boaz appeared. He clearly expected Tom to be there with her. "Everyone gone?" He smiled at her.

"You're going back to Europe," she said.

"It's a long story—I want to tell you one day." There was no victory in him.

Jessie was still standing in the same place, and she said, "Just —going off?"

He looked about him like a stranger, then sat down on the edge of the divan with his legs flung out before him.

"Yes, we'd better get out. We'll hop on a ship, I think we'll go to have a look at the Seychelles, and then start off at Marseilles. Wander around from there—we've been tramps before."

"And the grant?"

He made a curiously Jewish gesture with his hand, pushing the possibility away.

The girl in the grey trench-coat took to the road and whoever went with her did not expect to choose his direction. Jessie suppressed the impulse to make a sign of goodwill with some advice she didn't believe in—what he ought to do was settle her down in a little house somewhere with a couple of babies, etc. "Good luck, Boaz," she said with a dry smile, but meaning it.

He accepted it with a little ironical pull of the eyebrows; he had changed, she saw, hardened in the only way possible to someone of his still, inert nature, by holding himself off from events a little more. It was the difference between waiting to see what would come to him, and knowing what would come, even while continuing to wait. What he had got back was not exactly what he had lost, then; when he said that he and Ann had been tramps before, he was seeing the romance of their relationship as their limitation. In place of the sweeping exultant relief that he must have been almost afraid to allow himself to imagine at the possibility of taking up their old life, he showed, when Tom was back in the room again, only the energy generated by purpose that moving on provides, in the same way as the kick of a stiff drink articulates a day that is out of joint. They— he and his wife—were already removed from this house and these friends by the distance they were about to disappear into; they were together by virtue of gritty docksides, echoing halls of airports where they would be alone. Tom asked whether Ann was upstairs and Boaz said that he'd already driven her to the hotel where they would spend the night. "You won't take it the wrong way?" He turned to Jessie. "She says everyone has had enough. That's the way she feels at the moment—it doesn't mean we don't know what you and Tom have done for us . . . Only whatever we say now—it just makes us more of a damned nuisance. When we get together next time, we'll make it all right. You'll all come over, you and Clem and Madge and Elisabeth— and Morgan, Morgan too."

And Jessie smiled as if she had heard it somewhere before, while Tom, with the male gift for depersonalising an atmosphere in order to set another man at ease, said, "Pick up a cheap Greek island, man, and then give us a sign . . ."

Where was it, this island or mainland, in new old Africa or

old new Europe, where a man believed he would belong with Ann?

"No one mentioned Gideon," Jessie said to Tom. He felt her bringing guilt into the house, like someone going over the scene of a crime.

"No one was thinking of anything else. What was there to say?"

"We didn't count him in at all."

Tom said drily, "Where there are three people, one is always left out."

But it was Tom who flung the question into their hurry to get out of the house to work next morning, "What do we do about him?"

She was cold because she resented having her own background thoughts sprung among the sunlight and the breakfast dishes, as if someone carelessly touched a switch.

"Nothing for *us* to do."

Elisabeth dawdled, and Madge first complained and then began to go red and cry in case they should be late for school. Tom, who was to take them there, went upstairs and came down again, but they were still not ready, because now Elisabeth had lost her pencil. "Ask Agatha if there isn't one in the kitchen drawer, where the tin-openers are." Jessie passed on the crisis and put out her hand in the gesture she used when she wanted a cigarette from Tom. The sight of him, washed and dressed and ready for the outside world, while she still had the private pale face and unbrushed hair of the bedroom, always softened her; he dressed badly, out of lack of interest and shortage of money, in the same grey flannels, hairy jacket and brown shoes with thick rubber soles that had been the uniform when he was an undergraduate just after the war—yet this judgment was at the same time an admission of his attractiveness. "You don't think they didn't tell him—oh Christ!" She was suddenly alarmed. "Of course not. But just the same . . ."

"I'll try to get hold of him at the school."

Gideon Shibalo was not at the school where he taught, and Len could not find him, either at the room in the township or the flat in Hillbrow. Some weeks later, the Stilwells heard that he had been in Johannesburg all the time; he had thrown up his

278

job; he was drinking, people who had seen him said. None of his African friends took his drinking very seriously; he would "come out of it", or perhaps would simply become one of those who always remained one of themselves, carried along, however broken, by their unchanging recognition of what he really was aside from the brawlings and buckling legs and slurred tongue with which he was trying to destroy it.

Jessie was distressed, as women are, to hear that he was drinking. "He would have got drunk in Tanganyika or London, with her, when things didn't go right," Tom said. "You said she might do him harm, didn't you? Perhaps it would have been worse if *they* had gone off together."

"She didn't have to stick to him to harm him; it was done already."

"But what could the bloody woman do, if she didn't want him, or couldn't face wanting him?"

"Nothing," said Jessie. "Nothing. She's white, she could go, and of course she went."

They came again and again to the stony silence of facts they had set their lives against. They believed in the integrity of personal relations against the distortion of laws and society. What stronger and more proudly personal bond was there than love? Yet even between lovers they had seen blackness count, the personal return inevitably to the social, the private to the political. There was no recess of being, no emotion so private that white privilege did not single you out there; it was a silver spoon clamped between your jaws and you might choke on it for all the chance there was of dislodging it. So long as the law remained unchanged, nothing could bring integrity to personal relationships.

The Stilwells' code of behaviour towards people was definitive, like their marriage; they could not change it. But they saw that it was a failure, in danger of humbug. Tom began to think there would be more sense in blowing up a power station; but it would be Jessie who would help someone to do it, perhaps, in time.

TWENTY-TWO

GIDEON SHIBALO DID not come near the Stilwell house after the Davises had gone. Jessie was alone and unobserved again as she had wished to be before they came. Tom reminded her of this, saying, when the last of Boaz's instruments and equipment had been packed up to follow him, "It's a relief to be able to spread yourself—my filing cabinet can come back here—the desk there—"

He seemed to have forgotten his easy companionship with Boaz in an almost fussy pleasure at getting back his working room—he liked to use Morgan's room to work in. She teased him, "Only six weeks and Morgan'll be home again."

"Oh that's different. I don't mind old Morgan about."

They were a family in spite of failures and evasions. In the family either nothing is forgiven, or everything : she went over and stood against him with her cheek against his chest and her arms wrapped round behind his waist. He held her in that room in which, while they were quiet, they could notice still the scent of Ann's make-up. "You're the only woman," he said. Like all people who have been lovers for a long time, when they wanted to be loving in words they went back to the formula that had contained all that they had felt at the beginning. She was the only woman, then, for this gentle, passionate man several years younger than herself; now his image was softened at the edges, blurred a little with the tweedy pedantry of the liberal historian, frayed a little by battles for integrity in work, politics and love that he no longer always expected to win—what women were there for him to choose from, now? The thought drifted into Jessie's mind without cruelty; she said, part of the embrace, "What's happened to your shirt near the pocket? . . ."

"Oh I don't know, I haven't noticed . . ."

"Look, it's going."

He seemed to feel the relief of the Davises' departure far more than she did. She said to him, curious, several times : "You never really liked her, did you, that's the trouble."

"You always tell me that," he said, with faint emphasis. He disliked people to say things to him for the purpose of watching his reactions. Yet he could not resist what had been calculated to be irresistible : "Ann's altogether too open, too much on the surface, that girl—"

"—For you, yes I know—"

"I could never get over something unpleasant in the alert way she would turn at once to what attracted her, run her finger along it, taste it, laugh at it, point it out to someone. I don't know—she seemed to have only one reason for doing anything, one reason only, that she was alive."

"That's her charm," said Jessie.

He looked at her with familiar disbelief and doubt. "I don't understand how you could get fond of her." He thought there must be some explanation, though, that he would find out in time; he liked to follow the light and dark through which the many motivations of Jessie moved.

"You don't get fond of her, you discover that she's human, like yourself, but she's afraid to touch herself—you know, like a kid who's been told she'll go blind if she explores her own body. That's how she is about her life—she just lets it function without asking how or why."

"That would do as a definition of either a hedonist or a silly ass. And you should have left her alone like that."

Jessie was honestly astonished, though flattered, as a woman always is when someone who regards her as a force to be reckoned with demonstrates that he thinks she has again been active. "What are you talking about? She hardly knew I existed until the last few weeks in Isendhla. To her anybody over thirty, with a brood of children and a few grey hairs, is a different species."

"But she saw you took Gid seriously, didn't she? Didn't she see that you thought he was a person, somebody, that you and he talked together as she didn't talk to him?"

Her face opened up to defence. "—There you are," he said, before she could begin to speak. "You said she lived by pure reaction—she flew into this thing as a bat steers into a certain path because it instinctively feels the bulk of objects being set up where other ways were open."

"If she was influenced by what we thought of him, it was all of us—you and Boaz and all of us. We all talked to him and listened to him as if he were something special," and her voice ended in doubt. "Well, he was—he is—"

"Something special," Tom said firmly.

"Somebody special, and also a black man. For all of us there was the happiness that he was also a black man," she added, slowly, pausing before the sentence. Then she said, "—So why me?"

"Because you were a woman, and we were not. She could go ahead and sleep with him and fall in love with him, and you could not. She had to become serious about this, because you were serious about the other things."

"What rubbish," said Jessie denying with a flash of the masterfulness of which she was being accused. Defending herself, she mixed up truth and lies picked up simply as if she had reached for a stone. "She was crazy about him. She only used me as a convenience when they had nowhere else to go. I was even jealous of them."

In September Morgan came home for the holidays. There was a late cold spell so there was no question of his sleeping on the enclosed verandah, though he tramped straight up there with his things. "Oh no, we're back to normal," said Jessie, and then laughed. "—At least, Tom's using your room, but it is yours again."

"The porch is O.K. for me."

"No, it's as draughty as hell, you'll get ill."

"You should feel our dormitories. And in our showers they've got vents that can't be closed." He grinned at his own stoicism. "Anyway, I want to toughen myself a bit."

But he was accustomed to doing what Jessie decided, though he now did it more with an air of good-nature than submission. His suitcase and soccer boots moved in among Tom's paper towers. Outside a jagged cold wind drew a torn finger-nail across the iron roof and set every loose hinge and wire screeching; the untidy, mouse-nest comfort of the room attracted the three grown-up members of the family and for it they quitted the rest of the house in darkness, after dinner in the evenings. Jessie had put the little radio downstairs in the living-room before Morgan arrived; he lay on the floor beside it, to listen to certain programmes, but he did not seem to miss having it up in his room, or to want to have it playing all day long. At night, while Tom made notes or did reading for his book, and Jessie read or devised the endless adaptations of children's clothes that were required as outgrown garments were prepared to be handed down, Morgan was engaged in calculations for a model he was building. It was some kind of collapsible canoe; Jessie thought it seemed rather a simple thing, and that if he were going to make a hobby of building model boats he ought to be encouraged to do something more elaborate. She mentioned some impressive kits that she had seen in a hardware shop in town.

"Oh, those are the sort of things that old men build in their yards. With little plastic trees and things." Morgan smiled.

"Yes," his mother said, "Everything is worked out exactly to scale, authentic and so on—just as if they were real."

He put his hand down beside the bits of plywood spread on a newspaper. "This'll just be the model for a real boat—to see how the idea works out. Some other chaps and I're each working out a plan, and then we'll decide which is the best before we begin to build. Greg Kennedy's father's putting up the money, and then Greg and I want to see how far we can get down the Rooipoort River. It mustn't be too heavy, because you've got to carry it where there are rapids. But it mustn't be too small, either, because we want to have our camping stuff with us—that's why we want to try out making it collapsible."

His voice had broken completely since she had seen him at Easter, broken with childhood. She understood that the bits of wood and glue that she had seen in the category of play belonged to life. Morgan and Tom were talking about the possibility of using fibre glass for such a boat, and she remarked, "Boaz would have been your man. I'm sure he knows all about it."

Morgan said, "Oh he does. We were going to build one to take up to Moçambique with us." He still accepted with something of a child's fatalism the adult's prerogative of abandoning plans, breaking promises for reasons outside a child's ken. But a few days later, when he and Jessie were having lunch alone together, and she was going through the post, that Agatha had brought in while they ate, he said : "Any news of the Davises?"

"Mm-mm." Jessie shook her head slowly while she read. "Not a word since they left. No idea where they are."

"I had a letter—from some place in France; I can't pronounce the name. But that's last month."

Jessie was reading a long letter from her mother, and she frowned, half-lifting her hand to stay him; then, when she had come to the end of the paragraph that absorbed her, she looked up, confused, and said with great curiosity curbed by a sudden delicacy toward him : "You had a letter?"

"From Boaz. Wrote to me at school."

Jessie laughed, putting her hand over her mouth. "Well!" Then, "And what did he say?"

The boy said shyly, "They're O.K. They didn't like the Seychelles very much. He was going to give some lectures at a music festival the next week."

Jessie pushed her letter aside and weighted it down with the salt cellar. She seemed about to speak but only looked intently round the table a minute, and, catching Morgan's eyes on her, murmured, "Funny . . . I was just thinking . . ." She asked him for the jam. "No, the apricot." The exchange of ordinary objects on the table before them was like an exchange of grips; he remained calm, almost sympathetic.

"The letter I was just reading, from Granny—from my mother —there's a fuss about the Isendhla house. The agent wrote and asked her to be a bit careful whom she puts in there in future—" A quick look of amused comprehension passed over their faces, making them look alike for a moment. "Someone saw Gid on the beach *with one of the children* . . . the little girls! A black man in bathing trunks carrying a little white girl on his shoulders . . ."

"Boaz was terribly worried, all the time. I mean, he was worried about Gideon Shibalo too. You can't imagine anyone like Boaz, the way he—" The boy was suddenly able to release before her his first comprehension of grown-up ethics, of the private moral structure that each man must work out to hold himself together if he abandons or breaks down the ready-made one offered by school, church and state.

At once she was tempted to take advantage of this by confessing herself; she almost put in here, I know I shouldn't have left *you* in the middle of the whole thing. But her tremendous instinct

284

for survival held her back brutally : she had never taken up the right to the child; if there was to be anything now it must be between two adults. She picked up her mother's letter and looked at it again, reading over the agent's account of the complaint made by "certain local residents". She put the letter down and turned her face away, opening her mouth stiffly for self-control. "Why is one always having to be so ashamed for these people— why do they have to spit on everything— She needn't worry, I'll never go there again—"

Swelling along the strained line of her neck, contusing her face and distorting her mouth, he saw the tension of feeling that had made his mother's familiar and yet mysterious face what it was. It drew him more powerfully than any beauty; it was as if the flesh of life had been opened away and the heart bared, not the pretty pin-cushion of love-scenes in films, but the strong untiring muscle that pumped blood in the dark.

His discovery through Boaz found words again. "If you're really in love with someone, I mean—I always thought you must hate the other person who wants her. Boaz really liked Gideon Shibalo. I mean, I couldn't help knowing—he didn't seem to trust her not to get Gideon Shibalo into trouble."

"She's a bad little girl," Jessie said, not believing it, but because she was afraid of talking about the nature of love with Morgan. "But she's very beautiful?" she asked him in sudden curiosity.

"Oh yes," he said. "She's very beautiful." He was smiling, but he spoke surely, eagerly, from a part of life she had no part of.

She did not seem to have heard.

"You've got nice hands," she said. "I wonder where you got them from?"

Morgan laughed and, withdrawing them swiftly from the table, put them in his pockets.

"You're an unbeliever living in the midst of a fanatical cult; you still don't understand what taboo means."

"Gideon taking Elisabeth for a ride. I know what I see; I won't start thinking like a madman," said Jessie.

But Tom came home these days with his mind held ready only for his work; what travelled unavoidably under his mind's eye was dealt with at the same distance he had set between himself and the peoples and events he was writing about. Jessie was envious, as usual—her life seemed to her by comparison the ball of fur that a cat licks off itself, swallows, and gags on. Tom had been asked to prepare a shorter version of his half-completed history of black Africa for a series of special paper-backs meant to provide an historical background to present-day world politics. He was struggling to condense, into two-hundred-and-fifty pages written in two months, twenty notebooks of material intended for a book that would take perhaps three years to write. He had no time at all to go out, so Jessie and Morgan went to the cinema and to plays together while Morgan was on holiday. Morgan wasn't keen to go to a symphony concert, but Len Mafolo took him to the sessions of a serious jazz group that he kept wanting to talk about afterwards : enthusiasm was something that ripened out of sight, in Morgan, so that what occasioned it first sank away without appearing to have made much impression, then rose to the surface with some depth behind it. Jessie did not really care for parties without Tom, and Morgan was too young for the parties their friends were likely to have; she was pressed to go to several, but was persuaded only once.

It was the usual sort of party, and once there, with a thick tumbler full of warm gin in her hand, wandering from room to room in a house disarranged as if for moving, she was at home and even mildly enjoyed herself. Men she never saw except at parties came up and put their arms round her and said, as at a great and private reunion, "Come and talk to me, Jessie" or "Let's go and have a drink", and women exchanged with her greetings of exaggerated pleasure : "Oh poor Tom! Poor you! How's the book going?"

Someone brought dance-music recorded on tape while in another room little Simon Sofasonke had been pushed to the piano. Couples danced everywhere, white girls in their black sweaters leaning back and then climbing the air, pelvises thrust forward, before their relaxed, encouraging black partners, white men moving in a hushed shuffle black girls with silver finger-nails and straightened hair flattened and lacquered into a little black cap cut into ragged points round their faces. Every now and then a slender young black man with a fastidious drunken face came in and switched off the tape-recorder. "Anyone wants that stuff, he c'n tell me."

Jessie knew everyone there, and those she did not actually know by name were merely new faces in a familiar context: a bespectacled white leftist down from Rhodesia, a coloured journalist from Cape Town, an addition to the usual girl students from the university, a change in the roster of black bachelors (some of them bachelors because they never brought their wives along) who always outnumbered the women guests. A white woman who had just been charged with incitement and was out on bail was dressed as if for a diplomatic reception, in a midnight-blue velvet coat and antique gold earrings. Someone said: "How she enjoys it all!" A white man who had been in and out of prison for years on political charges, and who worked with one of the African political groups, was attacking an African leader within the same group who was opposed to his influence. The black man said, "And whoever persuaded Sijake to make that statement, he was badly advised!"

"Badly advised, was he? Shall I tell you why you think so, Mapire? Shall I tell you why? Because you're a racialist, that's why . . ."

The far-off wail of a baby—a child of the house—seemed to be heard, like a noise in the head, between the music, the talk and the movement, but was always lost before it attracted attention; it was as inconceivable, it had no more relevance, in the clamour of politics, liquor and sex, than the call of a bird in a thunderous machine-shop.

At about half past ten a fresh influx of guests arrived, mostly Africans, and one white couple who had been somewhere else first. Jessie left the room where the tape-recorder was for the room where Simon played the piano, and, slumped on a sofa with his head against the shoulder of a woman as if against a door-post, there was Gideon. He was drunk; he must have come very drunk. They had put him down there, out of the way, but apparently he wanted, every now and then, to get up and make a nuisance of himself, because the woman had the air of sitting there kindly to restrain him. She was a big black girl with a pretty face and the solid legs and strong arms of a nurse. Jessie had come into the room to get away from the noise, and although the room was not much less loud than the one she had left, she felt the blare displaced at once by a deep, uncomplicated affection for this man. It flowed in in peace, one of the simplest things she had ever felt in her whole life. The experience of the disastrous love affair, to which she was so close, lay like the memory of a battlefield between herself and this battered man—one of the greedy ones, like herself : she knew what he saw, now, when he seemed to look through walls. His face was grey and the dark of his lips was split with red, was flowering patches of bloody colour, scarlet and purple, like some strange streaked tulip. She went up to him, putting aside her old superficial feeling that he would want to avoid the Stilwell household. But he was drunk, and did not answer her. She spoke to him again, and his gaze recognised something, though perhaps it was not her. He mumbled, "White bitch—get away."

Somebody said, "Get him out before he spews over everything, for God's sake."

"Even the pigment in his lips has changed—from drinking, you know how horrible it goes. What's going to happen to him?"

Jessie stood drawn up before Tom as before a tribunal.

Tom turned away. "He'll be all right. He'll go back and fight; there's nothing else."

When Jessie saw Gideon again, he clearly had no memory of what he had said to her. They continued to meet in a friendly fashion, sometimes in the Lucky Star, occasionally at the houses of friends, but the sense of his place in the Stilwells' life and theirs in his that she felt that night never came again. So long as Gideon did not remember, Jessie could not forget.

If you would like to know more about Virago books, write to us
at 41 William IV Street, London WC2N 4DB for a full catalogue.

Please send a stamped addressed envelope

Book Tokens

**Give them
the pleasure of choosing**
Book Tokens can be bought
and exchanged at most
bookshops